Pembroke Branch Tel. 6689575

THE
WALLS

Withdrawn from Stock
Dublin City Public Libraries

D0542113

Also by Hollie Overton

Baby Doll

THE WALLS

HOLLIE OVERTON

CENTURY

1 3 5 7 9 10 8 6 4 2

Century
20 Vauxhall Bridge Road
London SW1V 2SA

Century is part of the Penguin Random House group of companies
whose addresses can be found at global.penguinrandomhouse.com.

Penguin
Random House
UK

Copyright © Hollie Overton 2017

Hollie Overton has asserted her right to be identified as the author of this
Work in accordance with the Copyright, Designs and Patents Act 1988.

First published in Great Britain by Century in 2017

www.penguin.co.uk

A CIP catalogue record for this book is available from the British Library.

ISBN 9781780895086 (Hardback)
ISBN 9781780895093 (Trade Paperback)

Printed and bound by Clays Ltd, St Ives Plc

Penguin Random House is committed to a sustainable future
for our business, our readers and our planet. This book is made
from Forest Stewardship Council® certified paper.

MIX
Paper from
responsible sources
FSC
www.fsc.org   FSC® C018179

To Mom, always and forever "in my pocket"

THE
WALLS

Love and death are the two great hinges on which all human sympathies turn.

B. R. Haydon

Dear Ms. Tucker,

I hope this message finds you and your family happy and healthy. I am following up on the request I made regarding the date and time for my interview with *48 Hours*. I have been in contact with Debbie, the lead investigative reporter, but she said she has not heard from your office. I know I've said it to you, but I will say it again to anyone who will listen. I am innocent. I did not murder my children. I cannot and will not stop fighting to prove my innocence. But the clock is ticking. The state of Texas is committed to executing me. My lawyers believe that if people actually heard the facts of my case, they'd see the truth. All I want is a new trial and I'm hoping these interviews will help secure publicity to help pressure the courts to grant one. I look forward to seeing you this week and discussing my upcoming interviews in person.

Warm regards,
Clifton Harris

PEMBROKE BRANCH TEL. 6689575

CHAPTER ONE

Mom, move your butt or we're going to be late."

Kristy Tucker heard her son's voice, annoyance dripping from each syllable. She glanced at the clock and cursed under her breath.

"I'm coming, Ry," she said, quickly pulling her brown hair into a bun. She grabbed her purse and headed toward her bedroom door, nearly tripping over the edge of the fraying gray carpet. She steadied herself and raced downstairs toward the kitchen. No matter how hard Kristy tried—setting her alarm half an hour earlier, washing her hair the night before—she could never get her act together in the morning. And on execution days, forget about it.

Ryan, on the other hand, had been up for hours. At fourteen years old, Ryan was neat, orderly, and incredibly driven, the polar opposite of Kristy. She found her son seated at the dining table finishing his bowl of oatmeal, his sandy-brown hair neatly combed, and dressed in his usual uniform: pressed jeans, a collared black button-up shirt with a red-and-black-striped tie, and his beat-up old black cowhide boots. Texas

Leabharlanna Poiblí Chathair Bhaile Átha Cliath

Dublin City Public Libraries

hipster, Kristy dubbed Ryan's standard uniform. She loved how much care he put into his appearance but it did very little to help him fit in with the rednecks and jocks at school. She'd heard the whispers and teasing from kids and their parents. "That boy acts like he's too big for his britches," they'd said on more than one occasion. Kristy shouldered some of the blame. She was only seventeen when Ryan was born, *a baby raising a baby*, Pops used to say. She encouraged his differences, wanted her son to accomplish everything she hadn't.

"Hey, Pops, you owe me five bucks," Ryan said with a grin.

"Put it on my tab," Pops said.

"I'm afraid to ask. What was the bet?" Kristy asked as she grabbed her travel mug and filled it with coffee.

"How long it would take you to get ready this morning," Ryan said.

"I actually gave you the benefit of the doubt," Pops replied, shaking his head in dismay.

Kristy's father, Frank Tucker, let out a strangled laugh as he tugged on the oxygen cannula that snaked from his nose, down his body, and into a giant oxygen tank that kept his O_2 levels consistent. Only sixty-eight, Pops appeared much older, his hair wild and gray, rarely combed. A lifetime of chain-smoking had taken its toll, ravaged his lungs, and now he was basically a prisoner trapped inside his own home. But despite Pops's health challenges, his humor was still intact.

"If you'd set your alarm a few minutes earlier—" Pops began. Kristy cut him off, well aware that her morning routine was the bane of Pops's and Ryan's existence. She simply couldn't deal with their teasing.

"Not today, you two. I don't have it in me. C'mon, Ry. Let's go."

She grabbed her keys and turned to Pops. "Remember: no drugs and no hookers."

"I'm not making any promises," he said with a chuckle.

Kristy smiled. "I'll be back late. Let me know if you need anything from the store on my way home."

"I'll be fine, Kristy girl," Pops said. "You take care of yourself."

Kristy gave Pops a quick peck on the cheek and headed toward the front of the house, Ryan shuffling behind her. She opened the door and found herself greeted by a tidal wave of hot, humid air. Not even March and the temperatures were already soaring into the nineties.

She drove east along the 105, heading toward Conroe High School. An arm of the massive Lake Conroe shimmered in the morning sun as they whizzed by. Stretches of white wooden fences and green grass ushered them toward the city. In the passenger's seat, earbuds in, Ryan sat hunched over his refurbished second-generation iPhone, simultaneously listening to music and texting. Kristy's long hours working at the prison often meant that morning drop-off was the only chance she had to catch up with Ryan, which was why she normally enforced a strict no-cell-phone policy in the car.

But today she welcomed the silence, trying to brace herself for what lay ahead—interviews with death row inmates and the execution of a brutal killer and serial rapist. *Just another day at the office.* Kristy witnessed people die year after year. Yes, they were all convicted killers but it still wasn't normal. Besides, she knew it wasn't just work that was troubling her. Her life seemed stagnant, chronicling each month by Ryan's latest accomplishment or Pops's newest ailment. Some days she woke up with the sense that something terrible was going to happen. Today that feeling seemed worse. Kristy's *sense of impending doom* occurred before every tragic event in her life. Kristy sighed. She simply couldn't handle any bad news today.

Fifteen minutes later, Kristy pulled up a block and a half from Ryan's school. Lately, he hadn't wanted her to drop him at the front entrance. Kristy wasn't stupid. She knew Ryan was embarrassed by her beat-up old pickup. Or maybe he just wanted to assert his independence. She understood it intellectually, though her heart still hurt when she thought about Ryan pulling away from her. The downside to the two of them growing up together.

"You okay?" Ryan asked, eyes widening with worry. He'd always been a sensitive kid, overly concerned with what Kristy was thinking and feeling.

"Of course. Why wouldn't I be?" she asked.

"You can do something else. Get a new job."

Her smile faded. "Ry, don't start. I make decent money and get really good benefits."

"But you hate it."

"So what? Most people hate their jobs. That's why it's called work."

"Most people aren't committing murder," Ryan said pointedly, and it took everything in Kristy's mind not to lose her temper completely.

Kristy's job as a public information officer for the Texas Department of Criminal Justice required that she serve as mediator between inmates, the press, and the prison system.

Despite the challenges and the pressures, it also required that she act as a witness during executions.

Her job had always been hard on Ryan. She'd done her best to explain to him how the justice system in Texas worked: There were rules, and the men and women on death row had broken those rules in the worst possible way and they deserved to be punished. But Ryan had a tender heart and a curious nature. The older he got, the more he hated watching his mom stand up in front of TV cameras and talk about executions as if they were commonplace, like they weren't something that the rest of the world considered barbaric. Kristy had spent years listening to her son's passionate arguments. She'd assumed that it was just a phase, until last year when, eyeing the crowd on her walk to the death house chamber before an execution, she spotted him. There was her son in a crowd of protesters. She'd gasped, staring at him as he proudly waved a sign that read EXECUTE JUSTICE. NOT PEOPLE. Kristy wanted to rush over and tell Ryan to get his butt home, but she couldn't. She still had a job to do.

Quietly seething at her son's disobedience, she sat through the execution of Mitchell Hastings, a thirty-year-old drifter convicted of murdering his sister and her best friend, while Ryan stood outside the prison gates chanting, "No justice. No peace."

Deep down, Kristy was proud of Ryan for being so strong in his convictions. But if any of the reporters had caught wind that Kristy's own son was anti–death penalty, it would have been a PR nightmare. She could have lost her job. On the drive home that evening, Kristy told Ryan he was allowed

to have an opinion, but this type of behavior wasn't accept-
able. This was her livelihood. It was what kept the roof over
their heads and food on the table. Ryan respected that but
he wanted Kristy to look for a new job. Even now, months
later, he'd e-mail her job postings, with subject headings like
New Jobs. No Killing Involved. But she simply wasn't going to
indulge him today.

"You're going to be late," Kristy said. For once, Ryan didn't
push back.

"All right, Mama Bear, I'll see ya later," he said, grabbing
his backpack.

"Love you, Ry."

He didn't respond, climbing out of the truck and slamming
the door behind him. Kristy watched Ryan hurry down the
block, waiting until he turned around the corner. God, she
missed the days when she would drop him off and he would
throw his arms around her and say, *Mama, I love you more than
the moon and the stars and all the planets in the universe.* But that
didn't happen now. Fourteen-year-olds weren't exactly open
vessels of emotion.

Kristy navigated the pickup down the long stretch of highway, the miles clicking by, a pop-country tune playing on
the radio. She switched it off, not in the mood for overpro-
duced melodies. She made a left turn, gripping the steering
wheel, and headed toward the entrance of the prison where
her day would begin. Set on 472 acres and surrounded by
forests and fields, the Polunsky Unit in Livingston, Texas, was
an expansive complex connected by walkways and encircled
by two perimeter fences of razor wire with guard towers.

The buildings that housed Texas's male death row inmates were set apart from the others: three concrete rectangles with white roofs, each with a circular recreation area at the center. In total, the prison housed 2,936 inmates, 279 of them on death row.

Kristy made this drive once a week, arriving every Wednesday morning like clockwork, but she never acclimated to the work. She never grew accustomed to the stern guards with their rifles pointed in the tower above her, or the desperate inmates she met pleading their innocence and begging for her help, or the ones admitting their guilt without an ounce of remorse.

This wasn't Kristy's dream job. Not by a long shot. Knocked up at sixteen, Kristy vowed that even though she would be a teenage mother, she wouldn't be a statistic. She would do something with her life. She earned her GED and then, with Pops's encouragement, she took night classes at Sam Houston State. Kristy studied communications and psychology, working part-time in various administrative capacities at the prison to help pay the bills. Pops had been a prison guard and so had his father before him. Despite Kristy's insistence that she could find a job on her own, Pops kept harassing the head of the public information office and before Kristy even graduated from college, she'd landed a job as an assistant to one of the public information officers, or PIOs, as they were known.

Part of Kristy had hated the idea of being surrounded by criminals—men and women who had done terrible things—but she'd told herself it was temporary. She'd planned on going to graduate school, studying psychology, and becoming a social worker. She figured her experience in the prison system would be an added bonus on her résumé. Working with and getting to know the inmates strengthened that resolve, made her want to help those in need before they ended up behind bars.

But raising a kid was a nonstop, 24/7 job. Then Pops's health began to fail, and Kristy got a promotion and a raise and then another raise. Nine years later, she was still here, the graduate program applications growing dusty in her desk drawer.

Now this was her life, week in and week out—meeting with violent inmates, trying to make friends with jaded, disheartened reporters desperate to write something that mattered. These days, Kristy found herself skirting the truth when people asked what she did for a living. *I'm in public relations*, she would say, hoping they wouldn't probe, hoping she could make it sound more glamorous than it was.

She had to shake off this doomsday feeling. She had a long day of interviews with death row inmates ahead of her, and they would require every ounce of her emotional energy.

Each week, the prison held media visitation for death row inmates. Mondays were reserved for women incarcerated at the Mountain View Unit. Wednesdays were when the male inmates at the Polunsky Unit were interviewed. For two hours, reporters were able to visit with prisoners who had received prior approval from prison officials.

Kristy parked her truck and entered the Polunsky main gate. Guards waved and called out hello, busy opening packages and sorting mail, the ordinary nature of their tasks contrasting starkly with the people who would be receiving these deliveries.

Kristy went through the metal detectors and grabbed her bag on the other side. She was greeted by Bruce, one of her

favorite guards, a thirty-something redneck with liberal lean-
ings who liked discussing Nate Silver, *The Bachelorette*, and his
favorite, *Real Housewives*. Despite the friendly nature of the
staff, everyone here understood the dangers they faced when
they walked through these doors. You had to work hard to
keep the darkness and anxiety from seeping in, an ongoing
battle Kristy wasn't sure she'd ever win.

Bruce led her toward the warden's office. Kristy rarely went
to death row itself, but the reporters had been complaining
about the quality of her stock photos and she was tired of
hearing them bitch. Today, before her interviews began, she
had arranged with the warden to take new photos of death
row cells. Warden Gina Solomon greeted her warmly.

"Warden Solomon. How are you?" Kristy said.

The warden, late forties with a severe bowl cut and bright
green eyes, shook Kristy's hand. "How's the family doing?"
she asked.

"Can't complain," Kristy said. "My son just made the
debate team. First freshman to do that in ten years," Kristy
boasted, her motherly pride on full display.

Warden Solomon nodded. "That's nice."

But Kristy heard the false cheer in her voice. The warden's son was a star quarterback at Montgomery High School.
Kristy hated that she let it bother her. Who cared if anyone
else was impressed by Ryan?

"Should we get going?" Kristy asked, changing the subject, hoping to avoid the warden's enthusiastic stories about
this week's playoff game and her son's skills on the field.

Flanked by Bruce, they headed through the labyrinthine

halls of the prison, the two women chatting about the upcoming cold front. Weather was a popular topic for prison staff,
everyone longing to be outside and away from these dark and
depressing cells. They turned down a long corridor and the
mechanized gates buzzed open. This was death row.

Kristy regarded the sign posted at the entrance to the cellblock: NOTICE. NO HOSTAGES WILL EXIT THROUGH THIS GATE.
This sign served as a reminder that these inmates were not to
be trusted, that in here, your life hung in a delicate balance.

Moving down the hallway, Kristy's senses were assaulted by
a wave of smells that no amount of training could prepare you
for: piss, shit, sweat, all of it mingling with a hopelessness and
desperation so profound it seemed to seep into your bones.

"Take your time," the warden said. Kristy nodded, but she
intended to finish this task as quickly as possible. She hastily
snapped photos of the hallways and rows and rows of cells.
Inmates' faces peered out through the tiny shatterproof windows on their cell doors. Some of them recognized her.

"Yo, Miz Tucker, my lawyer's got questions for you."

Some were heavily medicated and desperate.

"These motherfuckers are torturing me. You gotta get me
help."

Others were lost causes.

"That's one fine piece of ass. Come here. I'll show you what
a real man is like."

"I'll kill you, you motherfucking, cocksucking bitch. I'll
kill all of you."

Not much shocked Kristy. Not anymore. She was used to
hearing men talk like this. Inmates in prison weren't that different

from regular folk. Some were kind and polite. Some were mentally ill and should never have been put on death row in the first
place. Others were wretched, miserable souls with no chance of
redemption. Sometimes it was hard to tell who was who. It had
taken Kristy years to adjust, but their words no longer rattled her.
As a PIO, she had to appear in control, unmovable.

She stepped into an empty cell and snapped more photos.
Polunsky was often called "the hardest place to do time in Texas,"
and Kristy agreed. All the inmates were kept on lockdown
twenty-two hours a day in these small solitary cells. Even their
one hour a day of recreation was caged, no contact with any other
inmate. With no access to phones or televisions and no contact
visits, inmates were basically entombed in these cells. It was about
as close to hell on earth as you could get. Kristy couldn't imagine
being trapped behind these walls, day in and day out.

She scanned through the images on the digital camera she
had borrowed from Ryan, checking to make sure they would
suffice. Good enough. She couldn't wait to get the hell out of
here. She craved sunlight and fresh air. Kristy stepped back
into the hall where Warden Solomon and Bruce were waiting,
and followed them back down the hall.

For some reason, right before they reached the exit, Kristy
glanced over at one of the cells, inexplicably drawn to it.
Through the tiny sliver of glass, she spotted an inmate, his
body splayed out on the floor beside his state-issued cot. *Baby
Killer Harris.* That's what the press and some of the guards
called him. Kristy knew him as Clifton Harris. He had been
sentenced eight years ago for killing his two young children.

"Jesus Christ, he's bleeding," Kristy said, turning toward

the warden. She hated how shrill and high-pitched her voice sounded, like this man had a paper cut and not wrists that were flayed open. The warden stepped forward, looking through the window to confirm that what Kristy was saying was true.

"Get some more officers down here. Now!" Warden Solomon shouted to Bruce, who pressed a button on his radio, the squawking sound echoing down the halls.

"Get back," the warden yelled at Kristy. The buzzer sounded and the cell door's lock opened. Unable to wrench her gaze from Clifton's pale face, his blue lips, his eyes rolling back in his head, Kristy rushed past the warden and pushed the door open, kneeling beside Clifton, touching his neck and searching for a pulse.

"Hold on, Clifton. Just hold on."

Clifton's eyes fluttered open, haunted, life slipping from them. A bloodstained hand reached out, grasping Kristy's wrist.

"Ms. Tucker, I can't do this no more. I can't," he said desperately, that same hand now reaching up to grab Kristy's collarbone. "Just let me go," Clifton begged, his hand starting to squeeze.

Kristy's breath caught in her throat. She remembered that sign at the entrance. NO HOSTAGES WILL EXIT THROUGH THIS GATE. She had rushed in here without thinking, worried that Clifton might die, desiring to help someone for a change, to do something instead of just being a bystander in her life. But Kristy realized in this moment that her unease, that sense of impending doom, had been an actual warning. With this convicted killer's hand around her throat, Kristy wondered if Ryan had been right all along, that by staying in this job, by accepting what they did here, Kristy had made a fatal mistake.

CHAPTER TWO

There was so much blood, thick and sticky, a deep maroon that stained Kristy's hands and her khaki pants. She wasn't sure how long she knelt beside Clifton, his expression desperate and pleading. Seconds. Minutes. An eternity and yet no time at all. For someone who witnessed death behind a glass wall, who saw executions occur on a monthly basis, nothing had prepared her for being this close to it.

"Let go, Clifton. Please," she whispered, and he released her and closed his eyes. Maybe he thought she was giving him permission to give up. Tears pricked at Kristy's eyes. Never before had she been so close to such despair. Masculine hands grabbed Kristy and yanked her to her feet, and shoved her into the hall as guards streamed into Clifton's cell.

"Goddamn it, Kristy, are you trying to get yourself killed?" Mac Gonzalez said, glaring down at her. Mac was one of her closest friends, a longtime guard working on death row. At six foot four and two hundred and thirty pounds, Mac towered over Kristy. He liked to joke about his size. *Mexican people are never this tall. I keep asking Mama Gonzalez if she was getting a little on the side.* He wasn't joking now; his face contorted in disapproval.

Kristy's trance was broken. She could hear blaring alarms, the frenzied shouts of the inmates reacting to one of their own in peril, a cacophony of rage, anger, and sorrow playing out in slow motion before her.

"You know better than that. Stand back and don't move," Mac barked.

Kristy flattened herself against the wall, obeying like a scolded child. Her eyes darted back to Clifton, still sprawled out on the cell floor. Guards surrounded him, trying to locate the weapon he'd used to slit his wrists. Kristy had broken protocol and put herself in danger. If Clifton were desperate enough, he could have faked his suicide attempt and taken her hostage. She had failed to follow the rules. She was trembling uncontrollably now, staring down at her pants, now crimson colored.

Generally, suicides, even unsuccessful ones on death row, inspired anger and annoyance from the staff. Reporters often painted the guards as incompetent, criticized them for being unable to monitor someone that was under constant super-vision. Human rights groups would jump on the bandwagon, creating an uproar about the morality of the death penalty and the suffering of the inmates that were kept in confine-ment while awaiting their death sentences. Kristy generally found attempted suicides just as bothersome as her colleagues. They created a mountain of work, falling on Kristy to inform the media and public at large about what had occurred. The questions were endless.

"Are you denying that the prisoner was murdered by a guard?"

"Or a cell mate?"

"Or a white supremacist?"

"Or the Mexican Mafia?"

"Is this some kind of cover-up?"

But today her concern was only for Clifton, his blood pooling onto the gray concrete in puddles. Clifton's highly publicized crime and subsequent refusal to confess made him a pseudo-celebrity. Reporters flocked to listen to him; movie stars and music icons set up money for his defense. Kristy had been visiting Clifton every Wednesday for over eight years now. He loudly and vocally proclaimed his innocence, but others would say this was just another ploy to solicit sympathy. In the criminal justice system, especially in Texas, there was no sympathy. There are more people on death row and more executions in Texas than in any other state in the United States. If a jury voted to send you to death, it was almost guaranteed that you were going to die.

Kristy watched as a gurney was procured and the guards rushed Clifton down the hall toward the exit. Every inmate on the row had some kind of reaction to Clifton's last-ditch attempt at escaping his execution, howling, screaming, and banging on the glass. Some called out their condolences.

"Cliff, my man, hang in there."

"Don't let those fuckers break you."

Others couldn't care less.

"Burn in hell, baby killer. You fucking piece of shit."

As Clifton hovered somewhere between life and death,

a fleet of armed guards would transport him to a waiting ambulance, and then on to Saint Luke's, the nearest trauma center, where medical personnel would work desperately to save his life. If he didn't make it, Kristy's job would require her to release a statement to reporters that Clifton Harris was deceased. If Clifton lived, he'd be treated by doctors and returned to his cell to resume his life, or what was left of it.

Kristy's innate intuition that today was going to be a nightmare was spot-on. She turned and headed down the long gray halls, Mac falling into step with her.

"You know the rules. You've had all the training," Mac began.

"He was bleeding out. I wasn't thinking."

"You have to think, Kristy. These animals could fucking kill you. God, you scared the shit out of me."

He stopped short and pulled Kristy in for a hug. She let him hold her for a second and then she pulled away. Last year she'd made the mistake of getting involved with Mac. She'd been vulnerable after a particularly brutal execution, a man who begged the entire time for his mother. Kristy watched as the woman, in her seventies, bent and broken, wailed for them to stop. "Please don't kill my boy. He's all I have."

All Kristy could think about that night was how this woman had kissed her son good night and read him bedtime stories and now she had to watch him die. After that execution, all Kristy wanted was companionship, and Mac, who had harbored a crush on her for years, filled the void. He took her dancing, bought her Cuervo shots, held her tightly, and when Kristy had kissed him and asked if she could stay the

night, he'd said yes. They'd fallen into bed, sweet and a little clumsy. A nice evening, she told herself, but nothing life
altering. And yet despite her hesitation that night turned into
dinners out at TGI Fridays, trips to the batting cages, some
make-out sessions in Kristys pickup, but there was no passion,
no fireworks. She tried to pretend. Tried to tell herself that
nice was okay. That with all the evil she saw day in and day
out, nice was good enough. But Kristy realized after a few
months that she was never going to love Mac. Not the way he
deserved to be loved. When she gave him the *we're better off as
friends* speech, Mac effortlessly accepted her rejection, as if it
were inevitable.

"No worries, Tucker. You're not my type anyway. A bit too
much of a know-it-all," he said with a cheerful smile.

Despite his agreeable nature, Kristy sensed his disappointment. He'd moved on, started dating Vera, an adorable RN.
Sometimes though, especially late at night, when Kristy's
entire being ached, when she was desperate for someone to
hold her, on the nights she had to witness a victim on their
knees, wailing over the loss of a family member, or the nights
her worries about Pops's medical bills or Ryan's impending
college tuition seeped in, Kristy wished she'd settled for *nice*.

"Kristy, that wasn't like you. You have to be careful," Mac
said again.

"I couldn't agree more," Warden Solomon chimed in as
they reached the exit of death row. "I'd like to speak with you
in my office." Mac gave Kristy a *hang in there* pat on the back,
and she followed the warden to her office.

If Kristy thought the low point of the morning was finding

Clifton on the brink of death, she was wrong. Kristy sat in the
warden's office and endured a thirty-minute lecture in which
Warden Solomon reminded her in painstaking detail about
the rules and regulations that she was expected to follow as an
employee of the Texas Department of Criminal Justice. Kristy
nodded and clucked in all the right places, promising the next
time she saw an inmate bleeding out she would do absolutely
nothing. Fortunately, the warden missed her sarcasm or at
least pretended to. Once her dressing-down was complete,
Kristy's next order of business was canceling today's inmate
interviews. Some of them would be spoiling for a fight; others would be demanding to see their lawyers, using Clifton's
suicide as another example of the mental anguish they experienced. The guards also had to do a thorough search of the
cellblock to make sure there were no other weapons and that
each cell was secure.

This meant Kristy had to face her own firing squad—half a
dozen reporters who had driven or flown in from all over the
country. Needless to say they were pissed, all of them rushing
off to tell their editors about missed deadlines or to pitch new
stories. One reporter, a portly, balding man, seethed with
rage, spittle flying all over Kristy as he spoke.

"You people don't give a shit about our deadlines."

Kristy had to bite back her response. No. She didn't give
a shit about these reporters and their deadlines. Not today.
Not when she had witnessed such suffering. Not when the
inmates were riled up and itching for a fight. She didn't care
about them at all.

As the reporter walked away grumbling, Kristy wondered

how long it would take before she lost her own humanity. For her to see these men as just another story, to care so little about someone else's suffering. Sometimes she worried that it was already happening.

At long last, she was free of Polunsky, at least until next week. Kristy dreaded the shit storm that awaited her when her boss, Gus, found out about Kristy's "infraction."

Navigating the old Chevy back into town, Kristy turned on the air conditioner to find nothing but humid air blowing from the vents. She tried to adjust it, seething silently. She had just spent six hundred dollars to fix it. How typical, she thought. Something's always broken.

Kristy looked out the spotty windshield as she coasted along the 45. To the east and the south, she could see the coastal plains, Bahia grass swaying gently in the breeze. To the west were the rolling hills stretching down through Hill Country.

She passed Lake Livingston, the tranquil blue water sparkling in the sun. The traffic eased up as Kristy neared Huntsville, and the trees turned immediately into the tall stoic pines of the pine curtain that ran through the Deep South. Driving along those roads, after what she had witnessed today, knowing that she still had to sit through an execution, Kristy forced herself to focus on beauty where she could find it, cataloging it for later when the ugliness of the job threatened to consume her.

Each time she drove past the picturesque Courthouse Square, Kristy always thought Huntsville seemed like a town with secrets hidden beneath the quaint, tranquil exterior. The main street was inviting, with well-preserved historic

buildings. But people died all the time in this town. She imagined their ghosts roaming about side by side with the locals
in their Lucchese boots and rhinestone-studded jeans, many
of whom were also employed by the Texas Department of
Criminal Justice.

Kristy's destination was the Huntsville Unit. "The Walls,"
as it was more commonly known, was a colossal, foreboding
structure crowned by razor wire and encompassed by a
two-block-long redbrick fortress. Death row inmates lived
at Polunsky, but the Walls was where they'd take their last
breath. The Walls was home to the most active death chamber in the country. Kristy pulled up to the prison and headed
to her office in an administrative building across from the
death chamber. Today they would add another name to the
list of the executed—Tyler Watkins, a serial rapist and murderer, was set to die.

Kristy entered the office to find a group of reporters
camped out, the "early birds," she dubbed them. The vibe
in the room was jovial, some reporters texting, some surfing
the Internet, others making crude jokes about Watkins's last
words. "I bet he begs like a pussy for his mother," she heard
one reporter say. Another reporter was passing around a jar,
collecting money and placing bets on how long it would take
for the man to die. Kristy was used to all of this, a familiar
routine for the public information officer. Her job required
that she remain calm and unemotional, but after what she had
endured at the prison, Kristy wanted to shout at them, *Stop it.
Give me some goddamn peace.*

"You ready to watch this motherfucker die?" Gus Fisher, Kristy's boss, asked. Kristy sighed. No such luck.

She turned to find Gus, the director of the public information office, hovering behind her, a gleeful smile on his ruddy face. A tiny bulldog of a man—five foot three and bald except for an embarrassing fluff of black hair on top of his head—Gus had been Kristy's boss for a little over a year, and yet she still couldn't get over the zealousness with which he approached this part of the job. She often thought that if it were up to him, they'd bring back public hangings and charge a fee. Not that Gus was some kind of advocate for victims' rights. He didn't know anything about the victims and rarely gave their families the time of day unless he thought it might ingratiate him with the higher-ups or the press. No. Gus was a petty man with a god complex who had landed a job that made him feel godlike. She'd heard through the grapevine when he got hired that he'd failed to qualify for the police academy three times. His cousin was married to the deputy governor, which was how he wound up here.

Kristy was actually next in line for Gus's job. When her former boss, Jack Woefel, announced his retirement, everyone was convinced that Kristy would get the promotion. She'd been working in the press office for over seven years, had a good rapport with the inmates, and could handle all the varied, often difficult personalities one encountered when working with reporters. After word about Jack's retirement spread, Kristy walked down the halls, accepting congratulations from coworkers. The celebration was short-lived and ultimately quite embarrassing. Kristy still remembered the sting of rejection when she'd heard from the Powers That Be about Gus taking over. But it wasn't surprising. Texas good ole boys wanted good ole boys in positions of power, "not some damn woman telling them what to do."

She would have been less annoyed if Gus weren't so damn incompetent. There had to be two public information officers present at an execution because the press was split between two witness rooms, victims in one, and inmates' families in another. Cold, detached, and aloof, Gus never spoke to the warden, the chaplains, victim services staff, or family members. God forbid he'd go near an inmate before an execution. It was so beneath him. The only part Gus loved was the aftermath of the executions, as he was desperate to get in front of the cameras and soak up the attention.

Gus wasn't a fan of Kristy's. She could tell he found her uppity, didn't like that she was smarter than him, and resented the easygoing manner in which she interacted with reporters. He relished putting her in her place, calling out any and every minor mistake, real or perceived. That's why Kristy had to play nice. But today she was short on self-restraint.

"Gus, do you mind showing just a little less blood thirst?"

Gus narrowed his brown eyes in disapproval at Kristy, somehow misinterpreting her angry furrowed brow for empathy.

"Don't tell me you have a soft spot for Watkins. You *do* know why he's here, don't you? The man killed three women, raped 'em before and *after* they were dead," he said.

"I know what Watkins did. I was working here when he

was sentenced. I just think it's our responsibility to show some restraint," Kristy said.

As death row inmates went, Watkins was one of the more despicable, discussing his multiple murders as casually as one discussed one's brunch plans. Gus shook his head dismissively. He may as well have patted Kristy on the head.

"That guy gave up his right for restraint when he murdered those women."

Kristy knew Gus was trying to pick a fight and she refused to indulge him.

"I wanted to explain about what happened this afternoon. About Clifton."

"Yeah, Gina called and gave me an earful. It was fucking stupid on your part."

Kristy nodded, used to Gus's lack of restraint. She braced herself.

"Kristy, why the hell haven't you answered your phone?"

Startled, Kristy looked up to see her assistant, Carmen, hurrying over. Shit. Phones weren't allowed in the prison, and having forgotten it at the security check-in too many times to count, she always left it in the glove box. She was so shaken by what had happened with Clifton, she had forgotten to grab it.

Carmen generally possessed an innate sense of calm and order that Kristy envied. Her hair always fell in dark, glossy waves just below her shoulders; her teeth were so white she belonged in a Colgate commercial. But she wasn't calm today. Her eyes were wide, an uneasy expression on her face. Kristy knew that something must be very, very wrong.

"Is this about Polunsky? It's all sorted out," Kristy said.

Gus snorted. "We'll see about that."

Carmen didn't bother masking her intense dislike for Gus. She glared at him and turned her attention back to Kristy.

"It's Ryan. There's been an incident at the high school. You need to get over there. Right away."

CHAPTER THREE

Kristy told herself that Ryan was safe, but these days there was no such thing as a safe place. Schools, hospitals, churches, they were all potential targets. Kids brought guns, set up bombs, enacted their own revenge agendas. Or worse...what if Ryan had done something? A teenage boy's brain wasn't fully formed. They lacked impulse control. She'd seen hundreds of male inmates, boys who committed terrible crimes as teenagers and were now serving out life sentences. Her mind was spinning from zero to one hundred about all of the terrible possibilities. Carmen reached out to Kristy, taking her hand, trying to reassure her.

"The principal called and said the police were dispatched but she would make sure nothing official happened until you got there."

Kristy exhaled deeply. She'd thought her sense of foreboding had to do with Clifton, but this was so much worse. Maybe it was because of her daily proximity to the worst of humanity, but she'd always been terrified that something might happen to Ryan, that she might not be able to protect him.

She glanced at Gus, who looked panicked; probably worried that if Kristy left, he might have to do actual work.

"I have to go," Kristy said, almost to herself.

"We've got an execution today," Gus said, as if Kristy were personally injecting the drugs. "And people are already calling asking about the baby killer. What am I supposed to do?"

"Didn't you hear what Carmen just said? Ryan needs me."

Gus was silent, gaping back at her as if she were speaking a foreign language.

"I'll handle it," Carmen said. "I can take care of all of it."

"Carmen's ready. She can oversee tonight's execution if I'm not back," Kristy replied, annoyed that this was even a discussion. Gus grunted.

"If she screws up, it's on you," he said and stormed off.

Gus was not a fan of Carmen's. When he first arrived, he'd made a not-so-subtle pass at her and she'd promptly set him straight. *I've got a serious girlfriend, and if you so much as even glance in my direction, I'll sue your ass and the entire TDCJ for sexual harassment.* From that day forward, he declared Carmen persona non grata. Kristy, on the other hand, adored the young woman. She was ambitious and working in the press office to save money for law school.

"I've got it handled here," Carmen said. "Go take care of your boy."

Kristy squeezed Carmen's hand in gratitude.

"Thanks."

She bolted out of the office. Her chest constricted and her hands trembled so badly she almost couldn't get the key in the ignition. Ryan had to be okay. He had to. Kristy grabbed her cell phone from the glove box, started up the truck, and headed to Conroe. She had half a dozen missed calls and texts. She put on her Bluetooth and quickly dialed. Pops answered on the first ring.

"Pops, what the hell is going on?"

"Hell if I know. Those goddamn fools wouldn't tell me anything. Said they had to speak to Ryan's legal guardian, like those sons of bitches don't know who I am. I mean, how many times did they see me up at that school, picking you up from cheerleading practice? I swear to God, Kristy Ann, all these rules and regulations in this world and there's nothing but anarchy. If I still had a goddamn car, I'd have driven down there and taken care of all this myself."

Pops couldn't even walk outside to the mailbox these days, shuffling around his tiny wing of the house at a pace that made a tortoise look superhuman. The idea that he'd even be able to walk down the long gravel driveway and climb into his truck was ridiculous. But she didn't have time or the emotional energy to let this devolve into another fight about a matter that had been settled months ago.

"I'm sure Ryan is fine," Kristy said, trying to convince herself as well as Pops.

"You've got to discipline that boy, Kristy. Coddling won't do him any good."

"Pops, I'm pulling into the school," Kristy lied, refusing to endure Pops's lecture on her parenting skills.

"Fine. Don't listen to me. All I'm trying to do is pass along a little knowledge before I die," he said, wheezing heavily.

"I appreciate your help, Pops, but I don't think..."

Kristy heard Pops hang up. She didn't have time to worry about his hurt feelings. She tossed her Bluetooth onto the passenger's seat and focused on the road ahead, speeding down the interstate, switching in and out of lanes to avoid other cars, never letting her speed drop below seventy-five. In record time, she pulled into the sprawling parking lot of Conroe High School.

On the football field the blazing southern sun glistened off the marching band's instruments as the Tigers' fight song played over and over again. On the sidelines, shiny-haired cheerleaders were tossed up into the air, soaring so high they almost disappeared into the sky. *I used to be one of them*, Kristy thought. A lifetime ago.

Her stomach lurched when she spotted two Montgomery County sheriff's cars parked in front of the administrative building. She practically hurled the truck into a space and sprinted inside.

As she hurried down the hallway, the smell of chalk and athletic sneakers overpowered her. God, she hated this place. It reminded her of all her failures and missed opportunities. Kristy arrived at the administrative office, searching for Ryan. Instead she came face-to-face with Alice Valdez, the school secretary. She perched at the front desk, her ombré hair teased to cartoonish heights, her too-dark makeup creating a clownish appearance. She eyed Kristy with the mixture of pity and disdain that appeared permanently etched on her smug face. Alice was two years younger than Kristy and had been a legendary high school gossip, spreading all sorts of rumors about who had knocked up Kristy Tucker. Four kids later, Alice had only gotten worse. The minute Kristy left, Alice would be detailing Kristy's failures as a mother across the PTA phone chain.

"I'd like to speak to Principal Barnhardt," Kristy said to Alice.

"She's in the gym with Ryan. The police are there too," she said, her tone dripping with judgment as she gawked at Kristy. Some days she thought it might actually be easier handling convicted killers than people like Alice. At least with the inmates she understood exactly what she was dealing with.

Kristy rushed toward the gym, which was located on the other side of the school, and bumped right into Principal Liza Barnhardt. Her silver hair was short and expertly coiffed. Her turquoise blouse and matching Southwestern-inspired jewelry were the perfect complement. Liza was gazing down at Kristy's pants. Kristy looked and saw the bloodstains. Shit. That's why Alice had been staring.

"There was an incident at Polunsky. With an inmate," Kristy said. Liza nodded, concern etched across her face.

"I'm fine. But Ryan? How is he?" Kristy asked.

"He's okay. I'm just trying to talk some sense into everyone. Follow me."

In high school, Kristy spent two years as Liza's pupil, coasting by in Honors English with minimal effort. Liza endlessly praised Kristy's writing, even pulling her aside one day after school.

"Kristy Tucker," she'd drawled, "you're a smart girl, smarter than most of your peers. But you're letting yourself get distracted. Don't waste all of this potential."

Still reeling from her mother's death and more focused on maintaining her popularity than studying, Kristy had politely told Liza to mind her own business. Of course she regretted not listening to her teacher, but that's what being young is all about—thinking you know everything before you actually do. Kristy could still remember telling Liza the news.

"I'm pregnant," she whispered, clutching the sonogram in her hand as if Liza needed factual proof in order to accept what Kristy was saying. She didn't tell Liza about Ben, the sweet-faced musician she'd met at a frat party, the guy who got her so drunk she couldn't even remember his name the next morning. She didn't say anything, even when she experienced slut shaming (they didn't call it that back then) so extreme, in Kristy's mind, there was no other choice but to drop out of school. Pops and Liza tried to convince her she was making a mistake, but Kristy wasn't brave enough to endure the girls snickering at the lunch table or the boys asking if they could bang a pregnant chick. Now here she was, standing across from her former teacher, now principal, reliving her teenage failure all over again. They hurried down the empty halls, moving at a fast clip.

"What's going on, Liza?" Kristy asked.

"Did you know Ryan has been taking martial arts courses?" Kristy stared at her incredulously.

"You're kidding." She shook her head in disbelief. Ryan was the ultimate bookworm. He hated PE and often asked Kristy to write a note so he could skip it.

"So you didn't know?"

"Ryan isn't exactly the martial arts type," Kristy said.

"He broke Scotty Welch's nose in gym class today."

"Not possible. Ryan...he's...he always calls himself a pac-ifist. He won't even kill a cockroach."

"Well, apparently he's had a change of heart. Ryan told me he's been taking martial arts classes at the YMCA."

Kristy's cheeks flushed with humiliation. How was it possi-ble she didn't know what her own kid was up to? Yes, Kristy's job was relentless. Anytime an inmate managed to access social media accounts, or a prisoner filed a lawsuit asserting human rights violations, or a new appeal or stay of execution on a death row case was granted, it fell to Kristy to handle the fallout. She had to reassure the public that they were safe while she babysat the press corps. Despite all those demands, Kristy had done everything she could to make Ryan under-stand that he came first. Her efforts were there in the car rides to school, the notes she wrote on the napkins in his lunch box, or the times she would make the thirty-minute drive home, just so she could cook Ryan dinner and read him a bedtime story, and return to work once he was asleep.

But Ryan wasn't a little boy anymore. Kristy was an idiot for thinking he didn't still need her supervision. This was her wake-up call. She'd take Ryan on a tour of the prison, get him a visit with some of the biggest, baddest lifers she could find. She'd orchestrate her own personal *Scared Straight*. There was no way in hell she was letting this spiral out of control. Poor decisions ruined lives. Right now Kristy had to keep the police out of this. If this ended up on Ryan's record, it could ruin everything.

They were almost at the gym. Liza leaned into Kristy, her voice barely a whisper.

"Just between the two of us, Scotty Welch is an asshole. He comes from a long line of entitled assholes. But Tim Welch is a good ole boy. Maybe if you appeal to those sensibilities, you can get him to drop the charges."

Kristy rushed into the gym to find two sheriff's deputies talking with Tim Welch. His son, Scott, sat nearby on the bleachers holding a blood-soaked towel to his nose. Ryan was seated on an adjacent bleacher, as though he and Scotty were boxers who had been sent to their respective corners. Ryan sat with his entire body folded into himself. Wasn't it seconds ago that her son was a pale, shy five-year-old waiting for Kristy to register him for pre-K? She went into Mom mode, scanning Ryan's body to make sure he wasn't hurt. She spotted the ice pack he was clutching, his knuckles bruised and bloody.

She made eye contact with Ryan and he stood up.

"Mom, are you okay? What happened?"

Kristy looked down at her clothes, at Clifton's caked, dried blood. She wished she had changed but there was nothing to be done about it now. She hugged Ryan.

"It's nothing, Ry. Just work...What the hell happened here?"

"Scott called me a faggot, Mom. I'm sick and tired of it. I'm not gay. They know I'm not gay and even if I was, would it matter? I don't care what you do to me. But I'm not going to apologize for defending myself."

Ryan wasn't gay. She found out when she made the mistake of borrowing his laptop once and he hadn't cleared his browser history. No, the trouble wasn't Ryan's sexual orientation. The trouble was in this school, in this town, Ryan was too well-read, too curious, too outspoken and different to fit in with the jock and redneck culture that admired sameness. Ryan liked books about the fall of Rome and Watergate. He liked meditation and art history, and didn't give a rat's ass about the Cowboys' starting lineup.

"I'm going to take care of this. Don't move! Don't say a word."

Ryan slumped back onto the bench. Kristy hurried over to where Liza was standing with Tim Welch and the deputies, all of them waiting to see what Kristy would say.

"Officers, I'm Kristy Tucker, Ryan's mom. I understand there's been an altercation with my son and I'm hoping to get a little clarity."

One of the officers started to speak, but was cut off by Tim's harsh drawl.

"Well now, Ms. Tucker," he began. Kristy noticed he emphasized the *Ms.* "Looks like your boy's taking out his frustrations on my poor Scotty. Violence like that just can't be tolerated." She wanted to laugh. Jocks like Scotty Welch used violence and intimidation on a daily basis. How ridiculous all of this was. Just looking at the two boys' vast difference in size, it seemed impossible Ryan was the perpetrator. Scotty had at least three inches and twenty-five pounds on Ryan. But bringing that up wouldn't do Ryan any good.

"Mr. Welch, could we have a moment alone?" Kristy asked. He hesitated. He wanted her to beg. "Please," she said. He nodded at the deputies, who stepped away. Kristy would put into use all the skills she'd gained in working with macho misogynists who expected special treatment just because they were men in positions of power. If she could handle them, she could handle Tim Welch.

"Tim, hate seeing you under these circumstances," she began.

Of course he interrupted her. "I sure do too. But your boy was out of line." Kristy wanted to tell him to fuck off, but she nodded.

"Looks that way. I'm sure you can understand the challenges of being a single mother raising a son. I know Ryan is sorry for what he did."

"I'm sure he is. But there are rules. We have to send a message to these kids that this type of behavior is unacceptable."

"Listen, I work over at the Walls and I see what happens when the laws are broken. But I'm sure if you look back at what we both did as kids, you'll think twice about pressing charges." Kristy wondered if Tim was calculating his own misdeeds or if he even remembered the band geeks he beat up back in their day. Too bad they didn't have social media back then, Kristy thought.

"I'm just not sure I can overlook this, Kristy," he said.

She sighed, knowing she'd have to swallow her pride yet again.

"Not every kid is lucky enough to have a father figure in his life," Kristy said. "Scotty is lucky. And I'm doing my best, but maybe what Ryan needs instead of punishment is a bit of understanding. What would you say if Ryan helped out at the dealership? Anything you need, car washes, working in the office. Hell, you might be able to offer him some guidance, make sure he's doing the right thing."

The last thing Kristy wanted was for Tim Welch to offer her son advice, but if this kept him out of legal trouble, she'd do anything.

"Please, Tim, I'm begging you," Kristy said. "Please, let's just work this out." Kristy could almost see Tim puffing up, like a blowfish, loving how much power he wielded over her. He glanced over at the officers and Liza.

"Y'all know what? I think we can all agree that Ryan made a mistake and a two-week suspension will do the trick."

Kristy wanted to argue the suspension, to say hell no, but she saw Liza, her eyes pleading with her to give in. As pissed off as Kristy was, at least this way Ryan wouldn't get caught in the system.

Tim and the officers stood, waiting for Kristy's response. She gritted her teeth, wishing she could punch this smug asshole in the face.

"That sounds fair," Kristy said.

"You're lucky Mr. Welch is so agreeable," one of the officers replied, motioning for his partner to follow him out.

Tim snapped his fingers and Scotty stood, shooting daggers at Ryan as he followed his father out of the gym.

Kristy wanted to scream. She wanted to break things. These people were messing with her kid's future. This suspension meant Ryan would miss a big debate tournament, an important step on his road to claiming the state title. Winning at state, especially as a freshman, would put Ryan on the fast track for college scholarships. Without scholarships, there was no way Kristy could afford the school of his choice, and that's what she wanted—for Ryan to have choices. But she had to look at the positives. Ryan wasn't going to jail. That's what mattered.

She returned to Ryan. He stared at her with those big brown eyes, wide and pleading the way they always were when he was in trouble. His Puss in Boots eyes. They were an effective tool in his *don't be mad at me* arsenal. She'd always found it impossible to punish him when he brought those out.

"What did they say? What's happening?" Ryan asked.

"You stood up for yourself. That counts for something in my book. But not another word until we're in the car," Kristy said.

"I need to talk to Ella."

Ella was Ryan's best friend. The two of them had been attached at the hip since Ella's family moved to town when Ryan was in the sixth grade.

"You can talk to her later. Go on. I'll meet you in the car."

Ryan slumped out of the gym. Kristy turned to Liza, who was waiting patiently.

"Thank you for calling me. For making sure he was looked after," she said.

"Of course. But if Ryan's going to continue martial arts training, he should understand there are consequences. Next time, he could face expulsion and criminal charges," Liza said.

"There won't be a next time," Kristy promised. She'd make damn sure of it.

"Ryan is remarkable, one of the best kids I've met. He's going to make us all proud," Liza said confidently. Tears pricked at Kristy's eyes. She had to get out of this gym before she lost it completely.

"Thank you again," she said as she rushed out of the school.

Kristy found Ryan sitting in the truck, staring down at his phone in disbelief. Ryan's hair was too long and she had to fight the urge to brush it out of his eyes. She still couldn't believe her son had lied to her about taking martial arts classes.

Lying was a deal breaker. It had been ever since Ryan was in the first grade and he stole a Butterfinger from his teacher's desk. He denied doing it, even though the teacher caught him red-handed. After the parent-teacher conference in which Kristy and the teacher discussed the incident, Kristy decided to use the knowledge she had gained at work—use guilt to gain a confession. She would use Ryan's innate goodness against him.

"I don't care what people think about Mrs. Richardson. She's a liar. I mean, I know you. I know you would never steal anything," Kristy said.

She kept at it for an entire evening, even taking Ryan to Pizza Hut as a treat, ordering extra cheesy bread, apologizing over and over to him, explaining that adults weren't always right. Before the check arrived, Ryan broke down, begging her for forgiveness as tears streamed down his tiny cheeks.

"I stole the Butterfinger. I knew it was wrong but Adam Kennedy called me a chicken and I just wanted to prove them wrong. Mama, I'm so sorry I lied."

They made a pact. "No matter what happens, promise you'll always tell the truth. I promise too. Honesty always," Kristy said.

Ryan reached out to shake her hand. "Honesty always." They shook on it and as far as Kristy knew, he had never broken that promise. Until today. Nine years later, Kristy's disappointment was just as profound as it had been sitting in that tiny desk chair, listening to Ryan's teacher.

"What do we always say?" she asked Ryan.

Ryan didn't answer.

"You lied, Ry. We said we'd never lie."

"All right, so I lied. And I'm sorry. But Scott had it coming."

"I'm sure he did," Kristy said. "It doesn't change the fact that what you did was wrong."

"It's bad, isn't it?" Ryan asked. "What are they gonna do to me?" he asked.

It wasn't fair to delay the news. *Rip off the damn Band-Aid,* she told herself.

"Two weeks' suspension."

He turned away, staring out at the football field as he processed the news. Ryan pounded his fists against the dashboard.

"Fuck. Fuck. Fuck! These assholes...they always win. They always..."

He was right to be upset. In Kristy's experience, the assholes always won.

"I'm going to miss the tournament. They gave me a shot and now I'm going to let the whole team down," he said, swiping at his falling tears.

"Who said you couldn't still help the team?"

"I'm not grounded?" Ryan asked, eyes wide with surprise.

"Oh, without a doubt. But there's no reason the team has to suffer because of your deceit. They can come over and prep at the house after school. But that's it. You're grounded for two weeks. Not for defending yourself. For lying to me about your martial arts classes."

"I'm sorry. I just...I couldn't keep letting them pick on me."

"So you decided to become Jackie Chan?"

He shook his head. "Jackie Chan? Really, Mom? So lame."

"You know what's lame? Lying to your mom. Beating up your classmates. When did you start taking martial arts?"

"About three months ago. Ella had dance class at the Y and I started talking to the martial arts teacher about Scott and the other guys hassling me. He suggested I sign up for his class. He said he'd been picked on as a kid and that's why he began training. I swear, Mom, you should've seen Scotty's face. He couldn't believe what I did."

Kristy wanted to smile. She wanted to hear the play-by-play of how it went down because those kids weren't any different from the ones who'd bullied her into dropping out. But violence, acting out without thinking about the consequences, was not the answer.

"What's this man's name? This martial arts teacher," she asked Ryan.

He shook his head.

"No way. I tell you and you'll go all vigilante on his ass."

"I'm not going to go anything on his ass, and watch your tone. Do you know how serious this is? They could have pressed charges if they wanted. It's important I have a conversation with this man so he understands the skills he's teaching teenagers have real-world consequences."

Ryan slumped into his seat.

"I'm still waiting," Kristy said. Ryan sighed, the fight gone out of him.

"It's Lance. Lance Dobson."

Kristy started up the car and pulled out of the parking lot.

"I'm dropping you off at home. There's a frozen pizza in the freezer and salad in the fridge. Make sure Pops takes his meds and doesn't drink more than one beer."

"Where are you going?" Ryan asked, a slight whine in his voice. God, Kristy hated when he whined.

"I'm going to have a chat with Mr. Dobson."

CHAPTER FOUR

Kristy lit a cigarette and inhaled deeply as she drove down the long stretch of back roads. The sweet smoke filled her lungs, her crushing anxiety slowly dissipating with each inhale. She had quit smoking a few years back. After Pops's diagnosis, she understood she'd be a hypocrite asking him to quit if she couldn't. But Kristy always kept a pack in her glove box, allowing herself one cigarette after an execution, a way to decompress. At this very moment, Carmen and Gus would be waiting for a phone call from the warden to announce that Tyler Watkins's execution would begin. Tyler Watkins would be in his cell, less than twenty-five feet from the death chamber, waiting for the inevitable.

What made everything with Ryan even more upsetting was Kristy's understanding of violence and the havoc it wreaks. Ryan was too young to know that one hasty decision, one bad move, could cost you everything. Kristy pulled into the parking lot of the YMCA, which sat in an oversized lot off Interstate 10. It was one of those ridiculously large rectangular buildings, similar to Walmart and the other big-box stores that dominated the landscape. Ryan always called the buildings here in Texas soulless and unimaginative. He was obsessed with European architecture, educating Kristy on how those structures were erected with the idea that long after the builders were dead and gone, they would be remembered. Here in Conroe, their epithets would read, *Cheap and quick.*

Kristy took one last drag off her cigarette and stamped it out before entering the YMCA. The front desk clerk, a perky blonde in lavender spandex, gave Kristy a dismissive once-over and returned to her cell phone, texting with an unparalleled intensity and focus.

"Excuse me," Kristy said.

The blonde didn't even look up, fingers flying over the keypad.

"Memberships are fifty dollars a month. Thirty-five if you pay three months in advance."

"Actually, I'm looking for Lance Dobson."

The blonde's head sprang up, zeroing in on Kristy with renewed interest, her tweezed eyebrows raised as she waited for Kristy to offer more information.

"Lance Dobson? Is he still here?" Kristy said.

"Are you a friend?"

Kristy leaned against the counter and plastered on a smile.

"Lance and I are like family."

The girl's relief was obvious. She returned her attention to her phone, waving Kristy away. "Down the hall, last door on the left."

Kristy followed her directions and reached the training

room. The grunts, the thud of impact as bodies hit pads, and the smell of sweat transported her back to the prison. The threat of violence always lingered there. These sounds put her on her guard, and she had to remind herself there was no threat here. Not for Kristy anyway. Lance was a different story.

Gym bags and water bottles littered the walls and corners. In the center of the room on a giant foldable mat were two men of similar weight. One appeared to be early forties, his tribal-patterned yoga pants snugly hugging his muscled physique.

The other man looked late twenties, wearing loose black pants, his build slightly denser. Kristy didn't know why, but she was certain the man in the tribal pants was Lance. He possessed a masculine confidence so ingrained he'd probably never been self-conscious a day in his life.

She stood silently, watching the two men spar. Kristy had seen her share of fights break out in the prison yard. Most men who were incarcerated had grown up with violence at home, at school. Many were boxers, amateur and above.

In this match, the fighters were at an expert level. Their punches went back and forth as each man gained and lost the advantage. Within a few seconds, the man in the black pants made a miscalculation and his opponent seized him, trapping him on the mat, his arm locked around the younger man's throat. Jaw clenched, anxious for a victory that appeared moments away, he muscled the hold until the younger man tapped out.

Just like that, the intensity of the match dissipated. The two men slowly untangled from one another and stood up, shaking hands.

"Carlos, you dropped your gaze and lost sight of your surroundings," the older man said, running his hands through his slick black hair. "You know how I took you down? It's simple. It's all about focus. You have to focus on your opponent and forget everything else. It's not easy. For example, you might have noticed that sexy-as-hell woman standing in the doorway watching us. I sensed her the second she walked in the door. I smelled her perfume, heard her footsteps, and I can tell by her expression she's not pleased with me, though I'm not real sure why. But even with all those distractions, I stayed focused, which is why I was able to kick your ass."

He then turned to look at Kristy, a lazy grin illuminating his face. God, she hated men like him, the type that thought their good looks gave them a free pass in life.

"Are you Lance Dobson?" Kristy asked.

"Guilty as charged. And this beast of a man I just humiliated is Carlos."

Carlos smiled shyly at Kristy.

"Nice to meet you, ma'am."

Kristy nodded politely, but this wasn't cocktail hour. Lance Dobson was screwing with her son's future, and she wasn't going to let him charm his way out of this.

"I'm here to speak with you about my son, Ryan Tucker."

"Oh yeah. Ryan's one of the good ones. Give me a sec." Lance gave Carlos a fist bump.

"Work on your focus, C-Town, and don't be late next week or I'll make you regret it!"

Carlos headed out and Lance swiveled back around, his attention solely focused on Kristy.

"It's great to finally meet you. Ryan is a helluva kid. Athletic, quick, smart as hell."

"Ryan assaulted a student today."

Lance did a double take, eyes widening with shock.

"Shit," he said, his Southern drawl stretching the word out so that it was nearly three syllables.

"'Shit' is right. My son was suspended from school for two weeks. He broke a kid's nose. He was almost arrested."

"Jesus. That's a damn shame."

"A *damn shame*? You're teaching my kid potentially life-threatening skills and all you can say is 'that's a damn shame.'" Kristy's anger was apparent, her voice rising.

"I drill into all of my students that this is a serious practice with serious consequences. I'm sorry that Ryan didn't understand that, but you had to know the risk when he started coming here."

"I didn't…" She stopped herself.

Lance exhaled in frustration and ran a hand through his sweaty hair.

"Ryan turned in a signed consent form. All minors are required to submit one for insurance purposes. He said you were on board. I even asked Ryan if we would be seeing you at our practice matches, but he said you worked a lot and might have a hard time getting away."

Jesus. Could this day get any worse? Of course she worked a lot. She had a family to support. But if she'd known this was something Ryan cared about, she'd have shown up. All he had to do was name the time and place and she would be there.

"When Ryan comes back next week, I'll have a talk with him. We'll get this straightened out," Lance said.

Kristy shook her head emphatically.

"He won't be coming back." Kristy turned to go.

"Wait!" Lance's hand gently touched her arm and she shook him off, the frustrations of the day bubbling over, her powerlessness nearly overwhelming her.

"My son is not some thug. Did he tell you that he's on the debate team? They've got a real chance at winning state. Did you know he also helps coach an Urban Debate league in Houston? He gets up every Saturday at five a.m. and takes the bus two hours each way to help coach kids whose schools don't have our resources."

"Ms. Tucker, I know," Lance said.

"Then you should know Ryan is not some townie loser who is going to be stuck here forever. He's going places."

"I can see that. If you would just listen . . ."

But Kristy was done listening. She wasn't going to let some man tell her what Ryan needed.

"No, you listen. I don't bust my ass working a shitty job, dealing with sociopaths and murderers every day, to have my son wind up like one of them. I'm going to say this once and only once—stay the hell away from him."

Kristy hurried away. She wasn't going to fail Ryan. No matter what she had to do, Kristy was going to do right by him.

CHAPTER FIVE

It was pitch black by the time Kristy pulled into her driveway, exhaustion consuming her. She parked and heard her phone buzz. Reaching into her purse, she unearthed her cell phone and saw the text from Carmen.

Tyler Watkins. Dead at 6:27pm. Not much to report. Closing the office at 9:27pm. Hope Ryan is okay. Hugs, Carmen

A wave of relief crashed through Kristy. At least she'd gotten a reprieve from today's execution. It wasn't much to be grateful for, but it was something.

Pops was at the kitchen table, wearing pajama bottoms and his worn Dallas Cowboys jersey, hunched over the refurbished laptop she'd gotten him for Christmas, playing solitaire. He glanced up and shook his head in dismay.

"Jesus, you look like you were rode hard and put up wet," Pops said.

Kristy laughed.

"Thanks, Pops. That's real helpful. How's Ryan?" Kristy asked as she threw her purse on the kitchen counter.

"Boy has a burr so far up his butt, I don't know how he's

able to sit down. Tried asking him what was wrong but all I got was a grunt before he stomped downstairs."

"I told him to heat up dinner for you. Did he—"

"I can feed myself, Kristy Ann."

Kristy wouldn't take the bait. Pops never prepared his own food. He wouldn't even reheat leftovers.

"I'm gonna heat up a pizza. You want some?"

He wouldn't turn her down. He never did.

"I guess if you're making some for you, I'll have a slice. Wouldn't want you to eat alone."

Kristy moved over to the freezer and grabbed a frozen pepperoni pizza, peeling off the plastic and placing it on the tray and into the oven. She cracked open a bottle of cabernet, hoping Pops wouldn't give her shit about drinking on a weeknight. Sometimes he was so damn judgmental.

"So, you want to tell me what Ryan did, or is it some kind of state secret?" he asked.

"He beat up a kid. Broke his nose."

"Which kid?"

"Scotty Welch."

"Good for him. All those Welch kids are total shitheads."

"Well, Tim's dad disagreed and so did the cops. I had to eat some serious crow to make sure he wasn't arrested. So rather than jail, Ryan's been suspended for two weeks."

"You've got to be fucking kidding me," Pops said. He began railing against the system and promising he was going to sue those fuckers. Kristy let him vent while she bustled around the kitchen. Sometimes she liked it when Pops went on one of his rants. It made him seem like the strong, powerful man he used to be. After several minutes, he ran out of steam and Kristy managed to change the subject, chatting about work and Gus and the various reasons they hated him. Pops liked hearing about her job, said it made him feel like he was still part of the crew.

The oven alarm beeped and Kristy dished up the pizza. They ate in comfortable silence, her father's heavy breathing accentuated by his chewing as he devoured half the pie. Kristy was savoring her last few sips of wine when she heard a loud knock at the door.

"You expecting someone?" Pops asked.

"No, I wasn't."

Pops stood up.

"It's fine, Pops. I'll get it," Kristy said, knowing that he would take ages to even reach the door. He settled back into his seat and Kristy hurried down the hall. Through the peephole, she saw Lance Dobson standing there, his handsome face etched with concern. Kristy swung open the door.

"Mr. Dobson, I thought I made my feelings clear back there..."

"You did. I acted like an asshole and I had to make it right. I know what happened today was serious and needs to be treated that way. But I'm here because I want to urge you to reconsider letting Ryan train. I'll speak to him. I'll do everything I can to ensure this doesn't happen again, but I just... I *was* Ryan. I was that outsider kid. Super smart but I didn't have the proper outlet for my anger. I know what happens when you're lost or missing something. And even if you say no, that he can't train with me, I just couldn't go home until I saw Ryan and made sure he was okay."

Kristy stared back at Lance, his expression so contrite, his handsome features shadowed with worry. Was Ryan lost? Was there something missing? She didn't want to think she'd failed him, but he was a boy without a father. As much as she hated admitting it, maybe he had been affected. Kristy didn't know what to do. Lance tried again.

"Please. If I could just speak to him, I think we could work this out."

There was no sense of the jokester or lackadaisical man she'd seen back at the Y.

"Can you wait here for a few minutes?" she asked him.

"I'll wait as long as I need to."

Kristy headed back inside.

"Who is it, Kristy girl?" Pops asked.

"It's just one of Ryan's teachers. I can handle it."

"You sure?" Pops asked.

"Go on to bed. I'll fill you in on everything in the morning."

After a brief hesitation, Pops stood up.

"All right, I'll see you tomorrow." Over the years there had been a back-and-forth, Pops wanting to make decisions on how Ryan was raised. Kristy always pushed back. Ryan was her son. She needed to parent him her way.

Pops shuffled to his wing of the sprawling ranch home and Kristy made her way downstairs to the basement, or Ryan's "studio," as he liked to call it. She knocked, then let herself in. Ryan lay sprawled out in bed, watching a movie on his laptop. He saw Kristy, slammed the laptop shut, and bolted upright.

"What did Lance say? Did you freak out on him? Did you tell him I'm sorry?"

Kristy held up her hand to stop the onslaught of questions.

"Calm down. Before we discuss Lance, I need to know why you didn't tell me you were taking these classes."

He avoided eye contact, focusing on a space directly above her head.

"Ryan?"

"I don't know. You always make such a big deal out of everything. The classes were fun. I liked hanging out with other people besides Ella and the guys on the team. Even though I'm not very good, all the fighters respect how hard I try. I liked having something all my own. It wasn't some big conspiracy against you. I promise."

Maybe Ryan was right. Maybe it wasn't a conspiracy. It just felt like one.

"Mr. Dobson is here to see you."

Ryan almost leapt out of bed.

"Is he upset?"

"Well, he's not thrilled."

Ryan didn't even wait for Kristy to respond. He bounded up the stairs and she rushed to follow. Kristy reached the front porch a few seconds after Ryan.

"I'm sorry, Lance. I really am."

"You shouldn't be apologizing to me. It's your mama you were deceiving."

"I know." Ryan's eyes darted over to Kristy.

"I spent my whole life wishing I had a mother who gave two shits about me. You're not just gonna throw away what you've got. Are you?" Lance said sternly.

"No, sir." Ryan was deferential to Lance, an unwavering respect in his eyes. "Can I still train? I mean, I'm grounded now, but once that's over can I go back to the Y?"

"Not my call. Can't say I'd blame your mama for saying no. But if she agreed to let us keep training, I'd do whatever it took to earn her trust. We both would, wouldn't we?"

Kristy had remained silent until then, but she was impressed with Lance. It took a lot of courage for him to come here, especially after the tirade she unleashed on him. But it was Ryan and those damn Puss in Boots eyes that turned the tide.

"Don't make me regret this," she said, looking to Lance and then to Ryan. Lance smiled his biggest, most charming smile.

"You have my word."

Dear Ms. Tucker,

I'm writing to apologize for the events that occurred last week. If I'm being truthful, I still wish you hadn't found me but I know you were just doing your job. I know what you saw must have been troubling and I am deeply sorry for putting you in that situation. I am making a full recovery and will continue fighting the good fight. I hope you'll accept this written apology and I look forward to speaking with you in the future.

Warm regards,
Clifton Harris

CHAPTER SIX

Kristy wasn't sure what to think when Lance promised to help with Ryan, but she was pleasantly surprised. She had been worried about returning to work and leaving Ryan at home with Pops, the two of them moping around the place, like a modern-day *Odd Couple*, watching TV and eating junk food. But Ryan wasn't moping. He was pushing himself to the limits with his schoolwork and his training with Lance.

In the mornings before work, Kristy would find Ryan camped out at the kitchen table, doing his homework. In the late afternoons, Ryan's entire debate team descended on her home, piles of research covering the table while Ryan led strategy sessions. By the time Kristy returned home from work, she'd find Lance and Ryan in the front yard, dripping with sweat, the two of them grappling on the giant training mats Lance brought from his gym.

She was grateful that things at home had stabilized, but she couldn't say the same about work. Her sadness over Clifton's suicide attempt lingered, clinging to her as she went about her days. Kristy wanted to visit Clifton in the hospital, but the warden denied Kristy's request. Gus wasn't happy about it either.

"Why the hell would you want to visit the baby killer?" Gus asked with a roll of his eyes. "Don't you have enough work to do?"

Kristy told Gus it was in order to give the reporters a proper assessment of Clifton's condition. It was true that she'd been inundated with questions, but Kristy had also seen Clifton's suffering up close and personal. Was it so wrong that she wanted to make sure he was all right?

A week after Clifton's suicide attempt, he was back in his cell at Polunsky under twenty-four-hour suicide watch. Kristy received word from Warden Solomon that Clifton wanted to resume all of his scheduled interviews. Before that happened, she needed to have a strategy in place if Clifton wasn't comfortable discussing his hospitalization and the events that led to it. Kristy didn't know why she was so anxious meeting with him. She'd read his letter. He didn't hold any grudges against her or ill will toward her.

Surrounded by peeling white and green paint, Kristy sat in the small drab cubicle where inmate interviews were conducted, her feet nervously tapping on the ground. There was never any direct face-to-face contact. Thick panes of bulletproof glass separated inmates and visitors, with only an oldschool rotary phone connecting them.

She sat in the plastic chair and watched as guards ushered Clifton toward her. Leg, arm, and waist restraints were fastened tightly, white gauze covering both his arms. Head lowered, he shuffled along, compliant, the fight completely drained from him. Kristy had first met Clifton eight years ago. At that point, he had served three years and his death row appeals were winding through the judicial system. He was a quiet man, always respectful, something you couldn't say about other inmates. Child killers are the lowest of the low in prison. Inmates and guards have it out for you, and Clifton endured his share of abuse. She'd seen him with black eyes and broken bones, but the guards said he never ratted out the perpetrators and he never fought back. He'd once told Kristy that the things that happened to him each day were simply distractions. He had to stay focused if he ever wanted to get out of this place. But maybe that fighting spirit had been worn away by all these years locked up and his approaching execution date. Watching as Clifton settled into the chair across from her, Kristy couldn't believe how much he'd aged since she'd seen him last.

When news first broke of his arrest, Clifton's face was plastered on every news broadcast and magazine in the country. Tall and broad-shouldered, he'd once possessed a confidence that made him hard to ignore. But incarceration had changed all that. At forty-three, Clifton's mocha skin was pale and splotchy, a by-product of the lack of sunlight. He'd lost most of his hair. His prison jumpsuit was falling off his once powerful frame. His skin appeared sallow and sunken, his eyes flat and listless. The lines around his mouth were deep and pronounced. Broken blood vessels were visible on his nose and around his eyes. Clifton settled into his chair and reached for the phone that allowed him to communicate with her. Kristy did the same.

"You hanging in there, Clifton?" she asked gently. The guards posted nearby couldn't hear the conversations. This was one of the few safe spaces for the inmates to share their stories. He attempted a polite smile, but it came off like a wince.

"Doing my best, ma'am."

She wanted to say something comforting, but everything running through her head seemed empty and meaningless.

"I spoke with the producer at *48 Hours* and we're still scheduled for two weeks from today. They're insisting on discussing your suicide attempt or they won't do the interview. It's your call. You don't have to do it."

"No," Clifton said, looking down at his wrists. "I don't mind talking about it." He hesitated, then looked back up at Kristy. "I still wish you just let me die," he said.

"You know we couldn't do that." Kristy paused. There were likely lots of other guards who would have laughed as they watched Clifton bleed out. It had happened before. Kristy corrected herself. "*I* couldn't do that."

"If I just had another two minutes..." He trailed off.

Kristy was silent, searching for what to say. Clifton filled the gap.

"I guess you want to know why I did it," he said.

"You received your execution date. Three months from today, isn't that right?" One of the rules Kristy learned early on when discussing death row details was not to sugarcoat them when the inmates were discussing their fates. It made you seem like you weren't on board with what happened behind these walls. Working here, you either agreed wholeheartedly or you learned to fake it.

Clifton shifted in his seat. "No. It wasn't that."

He paused, considering. "Last Tuesday was my Mikey's

birthday. He would have been fifteen. I woke up thinking about what we'd do. He loved pancakes. We'd always go to McDonald's and I thought about buying him a puppy. How stupid. What fifteen-year-old boy wants pancakes and a puppy? But in my mind he's forever four. And I keep hearing his voice: 'Daddy, it's my birthday. I'm gonna be a big boy now.' I wasn't even thinking about this place or the execution date...all I wanted was to see my kids again."

It was irrational but Kristy wanted to apologize for saving his life. She couldn't seem to find the words. Clifton continued.

"Watching my children burn...watching that fire...it was hell. Then they gave me death...I heard the jury forewoman say, 'We sentence this man to death,' and I thought someone would step forward, that Janice would come to her senses and say, 'Hell no, my husband couldn't do this.' Or one of the firefighters on duty would tell them how hard I fought, that I tried to go back into the burning house, that I tried to save my babies. I kept telling myself that Mikey's preschool teacher would show up and tell everyone how devoted I was, or one of my coworkers might remember how much I talked about the kids or how much overtime I put in so we could have a nice life. But no... they created this story, this grotesque story. One person said it and it spread like that goddamn fire. It spread and it burned and before the trial was over, I was Clifton Harris, baby killer. They made sure of it. And you know, my mama always said, 'You're a strong black man. You have to be better than everyone else. Get an education. Show them you're not the product of your environment.' But those bastards couldn't've cared less. They used our poverty and my father's temper against me. They didn't understand everything I witnessed, all the damage my father inflicted, made me different. I swore I wouldn't be like him. I swore up and down I'd be different and none of it mattered."

Kristy sat across from Clifton, staring into his eyes, and she wondered if what he was saying was true. Was this the face of a killer? Or was he really innocent? It was too terrible to imagine. How could she come here week after week and do this if Clifton was innocent, if any of these men were innocent? She couldn't go down that road, and yet she wasn't heartless. She wanted him to know he wasn't alone.

"Clifton, you know there's nothing I can do about your case. But I'm here to listen and answer any questions. Whatever is going on, even if you just need someone to vent to, I'm here for you. You're not alone. You can write to me and we can speak anytime I'm visiting Polunsky."

Clifton's eyes darted to his bandaged wrists. He gently rubbed them. When he looked up, his eyes were wet. He blinked away the tears. "You don't know how much that means to me, Ms. Tucker. You just don't know."

She chatted with Clifton about his family and his court dates until the first reporter arrived to speak with him. She forced herself to forget about Clifton's pleas of innocence. She had to try to compartmentalize her job. She'd never survive if she didn't.

The fact that things were going well at home made it easier to leave her doubts at work. Lance's larger-than-life presence made things a bit easier. He would be cracking jokes with Ryan and Pops and charming Kristy. Ryan and Lance's training continued despite the fact that his suspension was coming to an end. Lance must have sensed that she was still uneasy about Ryan practicing martial arts. She didn't like to watch, hurrying past them with a quick hello. Seeing her son inflicting violence was bad enough. Watching Lance overpower him, taking him down to the mat in one single strike, was almost unbearable. She'd rushed past them one evening and into the house to start dinner. A few minutes later, Ryan, dripping with sweat, bounded into the house.

"I'm taking a shower. I told Lance he could stay for dinner." And then he disappeared downstairs. Kristy turned and saw Lance leaning against the doorframe.

"I said I'd stay if that was okay with you," Lance said with a smile.

"Of course. I just put the chicken in the oven so it'll be about twenty minutes." She gestured to her glass of cabernet. "Care for some wine?" she asked. "We could sit out on the porch for a few minutes," Kristy said.

"I'd love that."

Kristy poured him a glass and they headed outside, settling onto the porch swing, Lance on one end, Kristy on the other.

"I've noticed you haven't watched a lot of our practice sessions. Ma'am, I just want to assure you that I'd never hurt Ryan," he said.

"You don't have to call me ma'am," she said. "Kristy is fine. And I know it's a safe space and you're just training, it's just…"

She paused, trying to find the right words.

"It's just… what?"

"It looks so painful."

"Well, in the wrong hands it can be, but the reason I teach judo and not other forms of martial arts to kids is because of its history. 'Judo' actually translates to 'gentle way' and was created in Japan in 1882 by Kanō Jigorō. It's derived from jujitsu and it's the art of either attacking others or defending oneself with nothing but your own body weight. Rather than using brute strength, to succeed in judo you have to be smart, use your intelligence, and learn how to give way rather than use force to overcome an opponent. A form of judo was used in the 1800s by Japanese samurai with the theory being armor protected the enemy to the extent where punches and kicks would be ineffective. A throw, however, would shock the system enough to where it provided time to disarm your opponent."

"So what you're telling me is that judo is a kinder, gentler type of fighting?" Kristy asked with a smile.

Lance shook his head. "I'm telling you when you respect the rules of the art form, it's a powerful way to hone both your mind and body."

Kristy appreciated Lance's educational lessons even if she was still uncertain about Ryan's training. She'd missed the signs that Ryan needed more, needed an outlet Kristy and Pops couldn't provide. So if this was it, she wasn't going to stand in his way.

"Well, it's been a bit tight around here financially but we can do a payment plan, maybe in installments."

Lance waved off the offer. "I just want to make things right with you," Lance said. His gaze lingered for a moment with an intensity Kristy found slightly disarming, unable to deny how good he looked in his white T-shirt and black workout pants. She chalked it up to her lack of any male interaction and glanced away, staring out as the sun sank into the horizon.

"I appreciate the offer, but I'm sure you've got bills to pay, and all this time you're spending…"

"Actually, I'm my own boss. My buddy Roy and I run a real estate business in Huntsville. And trust me, this is the least I can do." Kristy glanced over at Lance, and he smiled. She nodded in agreement.

"As long as my boy doesn't get hurt," Kristy said. "Because then I'd have to kill you."

Lance chuckled. "I'll have to remember that."

Something shifted between them after that talk. Kristy still didn't love watching Ryan and Lance practice, but after that night, Kristy found herself looking forward to seeing Lance. One night she came home from work to find Ryan and Lance gone. Her disappointment was palpable. Pops was sitting at the kitchen table, keeping Kristy company while they caught up on the day. She was just about to start dinner when she heard knocking.

"Who's ready to stuff their faces?" Lance joked when Kristy opened the door. She glanced over to see Ryan holding two giant grocery bags.

"What's all this?" she asked.

"Where's Pops?" Ryan asked. "Hey, Pops, get out here," Ryan called out.

They waited for Pops to make his way to the front door.

"What's all this ruckus?" he asked, looking at Ryan and Lance with curiosity.

"I don't have a clue, Pops," Kristy said.

"Well, y'all have been so generous, having me over for all these delicious meals, I figured it's my turn. I thought I'd grill up some steaks and baked potatoes. Y'all may not know this, but I'm a world-famous griller."

Kristy laughed. "Too bad we don't have a grill."

Lance gave her an impish smile. "You do now."

Kristy glanced at Lance's pickup and saw the brand-new gleaming silver grill in the back of the truck. It was top-of-the-line and had to cost at least a thousand bucks.

"No way. It's too much."

"Come on, Kristy. Are you gonna deny your family some of the best steaks they've ever eaten?"

Lance grinned, waiting for a response. She glanced at Ryan and saw those damn Puss in Boots eyes. Pops was eagerly nodding. Kristy sighed, almost relieved that she was outnumbered.

"All right, but I'm going to pay you back when I get my next check," Kristy said to Lance. He pretended not to hear her, ordering Ryan to put down the groceries and get the charcoal out of his truck while he set up the grill. An hour and a half later, they all sat down together, dining on the best filet mignon Kristy had ever eaten. Lance wasn't lying. The man had a gift with the grill.

Somehow this became a ritual, even after Ryan's suspension ended. One or two nights a week, Lance would drop by with groceries. Kristy would open a bottle of cabernet, keeping Lance company outside while he whipped up a feast. Ryan and Pops would join them, everyone eating dinner and laughing, Kristy's anxiety slowly slipping away.

Occasionally, she thought she saw Lance watching her, studying her, and she'd look away, cursing herself for her growing attraction to him. A man like Lance probably had an active dating life. The last thing he'd want was to be tied down with a teenage kid and her aging father. Every now and then she wondered what it might be like to kiss him, but she'd stop herself. *You're being ridiculous. He's just a friend.*

Most nights, after supper Pops would shuffle off to his bedroom to watch his programs, and Ryan would retreat to his room to do homework. Some people hated dishes but Kristy found it relaxing. Standing side by side, Kristy would wash and Lance would dry. He'd stand so close to her, Kristy could feel the heat emanating off him. Every now and then, when he'd hand her a plate, his hand would graze hers and she'd wonder if Lance experienced the same shiver of attraction. She wanted to reach out and hold his hand in hers but she had never been that courageous. Instead, she'd fill the silences, trying to get him to open up to her, wanting to know more about him.

"Not many men know their way around the kitchen," Kristy teased.

Lance chuckled but she caught the glimmer of sadness in his eyes.

"My mama took off when I was young and my father was shit in the kitchen. If I didn't learn to cook, I'd have spent my childhood surviving on beans and franks."

"I lost my mom too. Bone cancer when I was ten. I understand."

She recognized that expression in his gaze, the sadness only someone who experienced being motherless could understand. Lance quickly changed the subject back to less serious topics. The more time they spent together, the more Kristy craved his company. They'd head outside to the porch swing, talking about their childhoods under a star-filled sky. Lance was raised by his father on the outskirts of New Orleans while

Kristy and Pops had gritted it out here together in Conroe. Kristy wasn't used to talking about her mother's death—Pops wasn't exactly a fan of reminiscing—but Lance had plenty of questions. She told him all about her mom, Sarah Tucker. How she was a simple country woman, a schoolteacher who wanted Kristy to have a different life.

"There's a big life outside these city limits," her mother used to say before the mind-numbing pain in her hip made walking unbearable, before the doctors and the drugs turned Kristy into a stranger. Lance listened, asking questions, shushing Kristy when she apologized for rambling. "I like hearing your stories."

Kristy couldn't deny her attraction to him, noticing the musky smell of his cologne lingering around the house for days. Sometimes she'd find herself recounting moments they shared—the smile while they all ate dinner, the hug Lance had given her before he headed home. It was probably all in her imagination, her own loneliness magnified by Lance's kindness and devotion to Ryan. She told herself to enjoy his company while she could. He'd eventually move on, get bored by their simple family life.

Kristy was sitting at her desk, trying to write a press release for an upcoming execution when her cell phone rang. The caller ID read *Ryan*. It had been almost a month since his suspension and she still dreaded every phone call, terrified by the thought of hearing something terrible had happened to Ryan.

"Hey, bud, what's up?" she asked, leaning back in her seat.

"Hey, Mama Bear, Lance and I were thinking about heading over and grabbing dinner at Chili's. Wanna join?"

Kristy glanced at the clock. It was almost six and she was

exhausted. The idea of dinner out with Ryan and Lance sounded better than laboring over these press releases.

"I can swing by the house and pick you guys up around seven?"

"Sounds good," Ryan said. Kristy applied a bit of powder and lip gloss, telling herself she just wanted to look decent in case she ran into anyone she knew, even though the truth of the matter was she wanted Lance to compliment her in his soft, effortless drawl.

"Darlin', you look lovely," he said when Kristy arrived at the house forty-five minutes later, and she felt a rush of excitement. She promised Pops they'd bring him takeout and they climbed into Kristy's truck and headed to Chili's, the restaurant filled with families and teenagers, forcing them to nab a spot near the back. The three of them sat in a corner booth, devouring sizzling plates of fajitas, chips, and salsa. Lance and Ryan vied for the title of most salsa demolished in a single sitting, forcing Kristy to call it a tie. While they ate, Ryan filled Lance in on the intricacies of Lincoln-Douglas debates, telling Lance about his tournament.

"I guess intelligence runs in the family," Lance said. Kristy smiled.

"He surpassed me ages ago."

There was nothing extraordinary about the evening, but something was shifting. The ease with which they all interacted felt effortless. She was so grateful for all he'd done for Ryan. He was transforming physically, the lanky, spindly kid replaced by a solid, muscled young man. What was even more astonishing was the newfound confidence he'd gained. Ryan didn't slump or slouch anymore, instead standing tall and proud, now towering over Kristy at five eleven. She watched as Ryan made eye contact with the waitress and bantered effortlessly with her. Miracle of all miracles, Ryan hadn't once taken his cell phone out, because Lance had made it clear he found it disrespectful. Kristy even commented on it when Ryan went to the bathroom.

"I don't think I've seen him go this long without checking his phone," she said.

"Well, I reminded him that he won't always have his mama around, so he should take advantage while he can."

"I appreciate that," Kristy said. Lance reached out and squeezed her hand, releasing it just as Ryan returned.

The evening flew by and Kristy's disappointment was palpable when Pops's takeout arrived. They made their way to the back of the parking lot, Lance joking about the crazy woman at his open house.

"She wanted to turn the guesthouse into a home for her dogs. An entire house. It's bigger than my first apartment," Lance said with a chuckle.

Kristy's laughter echoed in the crisp clear evening air.

"Son of a bitch," Kristy heard Lance say.

"Mom!" She heard Ryan's warning, and Kristy stopped short. Across the empty parking lot, Kristy first saw her pickup's broken and slashed tires, but that wasn't what sent her reeling. Lance reached out and pulled Kristy close, trying to steady her. She gasped at the sight in front of her—her front windshield had been shattered, and spray-painted in bright red letters was the word *murderer.*

CHAPTER SEVEN

The squad car arrived, its red and blue lights spinning, bouncing off the trees. Kristy wished they'd turn them off, embarrassed by the crowd of prying eyes: Restaurant patrons, waitresses, even the kitchen staff were gawking at them. She wanted to go to each one of them and personally explain that just because someone wrote *murderer* on her car didn't mean that she was one. Even though it wasn't true, even though Kristy knew she was a good person, she couldn't shake the guilty feeling that engulfed her every time she glanced back at her vandalized truck. They'd notified the manager after phoning the police. There were no cameras installed that might have captured the vandal, he'd said apologetically before returning to work.

"Mom, are you okay? Mom? Mom!" The panic in Ryan's voice jolted Kristy from her reverie. She looked back to find Ryan, Lance, and the Huntsville Sheriff's Department officer staring back at her. Ryan was still waiting for an answer. Kristy forced a smile, eager to erase the worried expression from Ryan's face.

"I'm fine, Ry. Officer, what were you saying?" Kristy glanced back at the young patrolman, baby-faced, one of those real eager beaver types she saw at the prison, a kid who hadn't been beaten down by life just yet. He'd written the report and snapped some pictures of the car. He reminded her of an untrained German shepherd, anxious to do his job well. Martin something, she thought he said.

"The officer was asking if there was anyone who might have any reason to want to scare you," Lance repeated. He was standing inches from Kristy, his arm draped around her protectively. Kristy hadn't noticed that until now. She should pull away, she told herself, but she liked having Lance nearby, liked knowing she wasn't alone in this. Kristy had heard about guards or even wardens at various prisons getting death threats, but Kristy herself had never been on the receiving end.

"I'm a public information officer for the prison system. I interact with inmates at prisons throughout the state. But I also . . . I oversee all the press for executions at the Walls. There are a lot of people who hate what I do." *I hate it too*, she wanted to say, but she didn't.

"Any threat that stands out in your mind?"

The most recent incident was after Barry Reyes's execution. Chaplain Gohlke summed up Reyes when he said, "I'm afraid that man is lost to the devil." Anytime she'd been in a room with Reyes, even separated by thick layers of glass, Kristy could feel something sinister emanating from him. At one time, he'd been a high-powered player in the Mexican Mafia. There were rumors he'd killed at least a dozen people, but there was never enough evidence to convict him. Then one evening, thirteen years ago, two days before Thanksgiving, Reyes was speeding down the I-10 west outside of San Marcos when State Trooper Colt Reeves pulled him over. Reyes leapt out of his car and brutally stabbed the young man. Once he was done, Reyes stomped Colt's head, grinning at the dashboard camera before driving away.

Just before his execution, Kristy watched Reyes rant for three minutes and thirty-two seconds about his lifelong devotion to his *familia*. Those were his last words, his final words on earth, and he never once acknowledged the victim's family. The fact that this man, this animal, would never hurt another soul was gratifying—one of the few times Kristy wasn't conflicted by the work that she did. But then she walked out of the death chamber and came face-to-face with Miguel, Barry Reyes's brother, glaring at her, hatred in his eyes. He'd yelled *pinche puta* ("fucking bitch" in Spanish) over and over again until guards dragged him away.

But it didn't make sense to threaten her now. Reyes was dead. Not to mention the fact that the Mexican Mafia preferred bolder acts of retaliation, like beheading people or firebombing their cars. They didn't bother with run-of-the-mill vandalism.

Still, it could be relevant so Kristy told the officer about Barry Reyes and his brother. Kristy had also received threats in the past from anti–death penalty protesters, people who claimed to believe in God as the sole authority over life and death, yet didn't mind threatening Kristy's life and her family.

The officer nodded solemnly. "Ma'am, I'll file a report, but I've got to be honest with you. We could have the FBI, the CSI, and Benedict Cumberbatch himself investigating this crime and there's still a one in sixty chance this will ever be solved."

Amused by the cop's knowledge of *Sherlock*, Kristy was also deeply disappointed. He was just as jaded as she was.

"I understand," she said.

"Wait, that's all you're going to do?" Ryan asked the officer.

"I'm afraid that's all we can do," he said matter-of-factly.

"That's bullshit," Ryan said.

"Ry, please."

"I'm sorry, Mom. But what if this is some kind of sicko who might hurt you or Pops?"

"Then we'll do what needs to be done," Lance said knowingly. "Isn't that right?" Ryan nodded, a shared moment between them.

Something about Lance's tone left her unsettled. Lance liked guns. He often talked about hunting, always encouraging Ryan to join him on weekend trips. He even had a license to carry a concealed weapon. It made her uncomfortable, thinking about having to hurt someone, but she could see that terrible word painted on her car. She was well versed in what people were capable of doing to one another. She'd seen small crimes spiral out of control. Maybe she'd ask Lance to teach her self-defense moves. If someone tried to harm her, or Pops or Ryan, Kristy wanted to be ready.

"I'd never endorse violence, but stay aware and stay safe," the officer added. "I'd also recommend that you report this incident to your superiors at the prison, ma'am. It may be an isolated event but in our line of work, you can't be too careful."

She was grateful that he considered her one of them. She shook the officer's hand and Lance did as well.

"Here's my card," he said to Kristy. "If you ever need anything, please call."

"Thank you," she said, watching as he climbed back into his cruiser and headed off. Disappointment flooded her, her bravado now gone. She wanted to yell at him to come back. They hadn't caught the bad guys yet. Lance placed a reassuring hand on Kristy's shoulder.

"It's gonna be okay, darlin'," he said softly. She nodded, not quite believing it.

"Lance is right. Probably just some assholes playing a prank," Ryan said, as if reading Kristy's mind.

"Kristy, I'm gonna call you guys a cab. Y'all can head home and I'll wait for the tow truck," Lance said.

"That's not necessary. I can handle it."

"I know you're perfectly capable, but it's been a hard night and you and Ryan should get some rest. My buddy owns a body shop. I just texted him. He said we can tow the car over there and he'll give you a good deal on repairs."

Tears welled up. Kristy didn't want this to bother her as much as it did. It was just some broken glass and paint, but she couldn't shake that feeling of violation.

"Thank you," she whispered to Lance, and he nodded, his eyes never leaving hers. Ryan seemed unaware of the moment passing between the two of them.

"Hey, Mom, nothing's gonna happen to you. They'd have to get through me." God, Kristy loved this kid.

They returned home and Kristy heated up Pops's takeout while Ryan recounted the evening's events for him. Pops seemed to take the vandalism personally.

"Why do these assholes have to go around messing with my girl? You're just doing your job."

"I don't know, Pops. But don't worry. We'll be fine."

"Damn straight. They come into my house and I'll blow them all to bits."

Pops was a gun lover too. He kept a loaded pistol in his nightstand. She hated having a gun in the house, especially once Ryan came along. But Pops was proud of his right to bear arms. "Ain't no one taking that away from me," he liked to rail anytime gun rights activists suggested creating new legislation. But no matter how scared Kristy was, she wasn't going to let her fear override common sense.

"It's not gonna come to that. It's probably just some college kids playing around, trying their hands at being activists."

Kristy wasn't sure she believed that, but it sounded reasonable and she didn't want Pops or Ryan to worry unnecessarily. Pops finished eating and went back to his room to watch TV. An exhausted Ryan mumbled good night and headed downstairs to his room. Kristy had to wait for Lance to come get his pickup. She dreaded it but Kristy knew she had to call Gus. If he got wind of this incident from one of his buddies on the force, she'd never hear the end of it...

"What the hell is so important you're calling me at this hour?" Gus barked into the phone.

"My car was vandalized tonight. They spray-painted the word 'murderer' on it," she said.

"Did you report it to the police?" Gus asked.

"Of course I did."

"Then why are you calling me?"

Kristy gritted her teeth. "That's an excellent question. Good night, Gus." She hung up the phone, went inside, and poured a glass of wine. She settled herself back on the porch swing, sipping her wine and trying to keep terrible thoughts from creeping in.

It was after midnight when Lance arrived, pulling into the driveway in a Ford Focus rental car. He greeted Kristy on the porch.

"It's all taken care of. My buddy at the body shop said it'll take about ten days to make the repairs. But I brought a rental for you to use. And don't worry—he hooked me up with a good deal. It'll cost me practically nothing." Kristy almost burst into tears. Her insurance was expensive enough and it certainly didn't include rental coverage.

"I don't know how to thank you. You went above and beyond tonight," she said.

"I'd do anything for you guys," Lance replied. *You guys.* This wasn't about her at all. It was about all of them. She felt foolish about all her thoughts that there might be more between them. Lance hovered near the door. Kristy didn't want him to leave. Not yet. She glanced over at her half-empty glass of wine.

"Want one?" she asked.

"Got anything stronger?" Lance replied. Kristy smiled and

went inside and grabbed a bottle of Wild Turkey from Pops's private stash. She poured Lance a double and joined him back outside on the porch swing. She sat down, keeping that same respectful distance they always observed. Lance surveyed the sprawling property.

"This place sure is beautiful."

"It is, isn't it?"

"You can tell a lot of love has gone into making it a home," Lance said.

Kristy appreciated that. This was the only home she had ever known. There were memories lingering in every corner and crevice: helping her mother can peaches, running through the fields after their collie Joshua, feeding livestock with Pops back when he was healthy enough to tend to the cows and horses. Money was tight, the animals long gone, and the place desperately needed updating, but no amount of disrepair could erase all the good that remained.

"It's okay to be shaken up. You don't have to keep up a front for me," Lance said softly.

Tears prickled at the corners of her eyes.

"My entire life is about keeping up a front."

"It doesn't have to be. Not here. Not with me."

Kristy's heart jumped. Her stomach did cartwheels as Lance inched closer to her on the swing, his leg touching hers.

"I don't mean to pry, but Ryan never mentioned his father," Lance said.

"Haven't heard from him since the day I called and told him that he had a newborn son."

"What'd he say?" Lance asked.

" 'Can't talk now. I've got a gig.' "

"A musician?"

Kristy winced, remembering that night she met Ben at Sam Houston State, how she went back to his dorm room, how he kept playing that same damn Goo Goo Dolls song over and over again. God, she despised that song.

"Never trust a musician, right? But I was young. Went to a frat party and got a little too drunk on trash-can punch. Two months later, I'm vomiting my guts out in chemistry lab. The rest is history. I've kept tabs on him. He makes a living touring, playing backup guitar for bands you've never heard of. I keep waiting for Ryan to ask me about him, to want to meet him, but he hasn't shown any interest."

"He's got you. He doesn't need that piece of shit," Lance said harshly. He sighed. "Excuse my language, but my mama walked out on us. I just never understood how anyone could do that to their child."

Kristy wasn't sure why—maybe it was something in Lance's tone, or the closeness or the wine or the stress of the evening—but a sob exploded from her. Lance wrapped his arms around Kristy, gently rocking them both back and forth on the swing.

"Shhh...it's okay, darlin'."

She sat there for what felt like ages, content in his arms, until her sobs finally subsided.

"You've got a real hard job, plus all the responsibility of looking after Pops and Ryan. I can't imagine it being easy."

His voice was soft and soothing. Kristy told herself she should pull away, that she didn't want to get hurt or upset Ryan, but instead she leaned into Lance.

"I know whoever did this has their reasons, but I can't help think they might be right," Kristy said.

"You're not a murderer. You're just doing your job," Lance replied.

Kristy shrugged. "Ryan thinks what I do is wrong."

"Wait 'til he's older and life's bumped and bruised him a bit. He'll feel different about a lot of things."

"So you believe in capital punishment?"

Lance shook his head.

"Not on principle. It's not even about the inmates. It's about us as a society judging and condemning them. We should be better than they are. But, darlin', you're just doing a job. You're putting food on your table, supporting your family. You've got nothing to be sorry for."

Kristy thought about that, thought about why she even took this job all these years ago, and why she was still there when she hated it so damn much.

"I just don't know what to do, Lance. I'm just...I'm stuck."

"You've got a great kid, and kids don't turn out great without proper guidance. You're a smart, driven, beautiful woman with loads of talent. Darlin', you're only stuck if you think you are," Lance said softly.

She glanced over, his green eyes boring into her. Without thinking, Kristy leaned in and kissed him. His breath was warm and inviting. He tasted of whiskey and peppermint. He kissed her softly at first, and then it gradually intensified, his hands roaming over her body, searching. Kristy allowed herself to get lost for a moment, her stomach lurching like she was at the top of the highest roller coaster and plummeting downward. She hadn't experienced a kiss like this in...maybe ever. But this wasn't about her. Lance was Ryan's friend and mentor. He was also Kristy's friend; someone she had grown to count on. She'd already gone down this path with Mac. Kristy pulled away, trying to regain her composure. She smoothed her hair and stood up.

"I'm sorry, Lance. I shouldn't have done that. I shouldn't..."

Kristy stared down at the ground, her face flushed from the wine and that damn kiss. Damn it, why had she kissed him? He wasn't saying anything. She'd embarrassed herself by being too forward and now she had to fix things.

"We're friends, Lance. I don't want to ruin that and I'm sure you don't either," Kristy said.

Lance stood up, his expression unreadable in the shadows.

"Right. Of course," he said. "I'd better get going. Be sure and lock up. I'll check on y'all tomorrow."

Kristy watched as Lance climbed into his pickup and drove away. She had done the right thing, but Lance still seemed upset. Was it possible that he wanted their relationship to go deeper than friendship? If so, why hadn't he said something? Lance didn't seem like the type to hold things back. Maybe he was just disappointed that now she had put him in that position, but she was simply too overwhelmed and flustered to think clearly. She collapsed into bed, her dreams haunted by masked men chasing her, carrying pistols, chanting "murderer" over and over again. After a sleepless night, Kristy dragged herself out of bed. At breakfast, Ryan's eyes had giant dark circles as well. He wasn't happy to hear that Kristy still planned on going to work.

"What if someone tries to hurt you?" Ryan asked.

"I'm surrounded by guards with rifles. Work is the safest place for me."

Whenever Ryan didn't get his way, he shut down completely, wouldn't say a word. It was a trait he'd picked up from Pops and it drove Kristy crazy. They drove to school, both of them tense and silent, Ryan not even bothering to say goodbye when they arrived, just slamming the car door instead.

At work, somehow, someone had gotten a tip about the incident at Chili's and reporters were calling, demanding answers.

"What the hell is going on?" she asked Carmen when she slipped into her office.

"Hey, you okay? I was so worried."

"I'm fine. A little rattled, but I'll live."

"Well, then I'm sure you'll love hearing that Gus is on the warpath. Says this is bad for the office to be dealing with this kind of thing."

"Oh, isn't that nice. I'm glad to hear he's concerned for my well-being," Kristy said.

Carmen snorted. "Yeah right."

Kristy raced over to Gus's office. She understood why he would be upset. As public information officers, they were in control, spinning the story to their advantage. Once Kristy became the story, the reporters could ask anything they wanted.

"Gus, you wanted to see me?" she said.

"Yeah, make this go away. I've got my bosses calling and asking me what happened. They're so worked up they're insisting on providing you with police protection."

"I don't need—" Kristy said, but Gus interrupted.

"That's what I said. The warden disagreed. He's asked that you have officers stationed outside your residence and anywhere you go for the next few days until we can assess any potential threats. I'll be calling a press conference to get ahead of the story."

She waited for him to offer his apologies or express concern, but Gus was done and Kristy was dismissed. Later that afternoon, she stood behind Gus like the wronged woman in a police drama, head held high, face frozen in a concerned expression.

"All of us in the public information office take our jobs seriously. We will not be cowed by acts of vandalism or threats to our lives and liberty. We will do everything in our power to track down these cowards. I'd like to ask the public, if you have any knowledge about the individual that committed this act, I hope you will report it," Gus said.

The reporters shouted out questions about the possible motives, if it was because of the growing anger over the death penalty, but Kristy was under orders not to speak. She had no choice but to follow Gus out of the pressroom. She was certain she'd be dodging questions for the next week. Still on edge, Kristy found Carmen waiting in her office.

"So that went well."

They didn't even have time to gossip about what had happened before Gus stormed in. She expected him to bitch about the press conference, but he was on a different tangent now.

"We'll talk to every single asshole on death row until we find out who they put up to this," he said.

Kristy looked at Carmen, who was rolling her eyes.

"Gus, there's zero evidence that a death row inmate was responsible for this. You have no reason to accuse them of anything. We'd be violating their civil rights."

"Fuck their rights," Gus snorted, before storming out.

"Think Gus is going to look up civil rights on Google?" Kristy joked.

Carmen laughed. "Once he learns how to actually use Google, I'm sure he will."

Though she'd initially been reluctant about the idea of police parked outside her house, Kristy found herself comforted by their presence. All that mattered was that her home and family were protected. She tried to put aside her worries, tried go about her week, but a dark cloud remained. She was in the middle of a visit with Clifton when he stopped midsentence.

"They find the person responsible for harassing you yet?" he asked, his brow furrowing.

Kristy was startled, surprised that he'd heard about the incident.

"Wow. News travels fast."

"Well, we're all pretty bored and the guards like to gossip. Must have been a real shock seeing something like that."

It wasn't standard to converse with inmates about personal issues, but Kristy couldn't help herself.

"It's been bothering me all week, Clifton. I've always believed I was a good person..."

He held up his hand, waving away her comment.

"You still are. Don't let someone like that change the way you see yourself. It's the same way with me. I don't care how many people call me baby killer, I know the truth. And so do you. You're just doing your job," he said.

"I guess not everyone sees it like that."

"Well, I'll be putting you at the top of my prayer list, Ms. Tucker. You stay safe out there."

Kristy put on a brave face. That's what she had to do. At home, the patrol cars remained parked out front, the officers offering friendly waves and thank-yous when she brought them leftover supper. Lance hadn't been by the house since their kiss. She'd asked Ryan and he'd shrugged. "Lance said work's been crazy. He's not sure when he'll have time to come over." Kristy struggled to hide her disappointment. She thought about calling him but his silence spoke volumes. He regretted the kiss as well. As the days and then a week passed, there were still no leads on the vandals. The police offered their apologies but they had limited resources, and the officers moved on to more pressing matters.

Life returned to normal or as close to normal as Kristy's life ever was, except there was a giant, gaping Lance-sized hole in it. Ryan said Lance was in Austin for a real estate conference. She wanted to ask how long the conference would last, when Lance was planning on coming by again, but she refrained. The last thing she wanted was for Ryan to know that she'd screwed up things with Lance.

She'd almost convinced herself that it was okay, that she didn't care if he never came back. But the following week when she came home late from work, she found Pops, Ryan, and Lance finishing dinner. Her heart nearly stopped. She grabbed a plate and joined them, listening to the chatter around her, but Lance seemed uneasy, never once making eye contact with her. When the meal was over, Lance stood up.

"I think I'll get going," Lance said. "Kristy, you want to walk me out?"

"Sure," Kristy said, a nervous tremor in her voice. She shot a look over at Ryan and Pops, worried they had noticed, but they were already saying good-bye as they headed off to their respective rooms. Kristy and Lance stood on the porch, the single light bulb casting a shadow on Lance's stoic features.

"I'm afraid I can't come around anymore," Lance said.

"What? Please don't say that. We love having you here. I'm sorry about the kiss. I tried to tell you that before. I don't want to ruin our friendship."

"That's the problem. I've got a lot of friends, Kristy. I've been coming around here for months. At first, it was just about Ryan, but then all I wanted was to be near you. I figured after enough time had passed, I'd figure you out, but you're a real closed book. I was just about to throw in the towel and then you kissed me and I thought, maybe she feels the same way I do. But then you started going on about us just being friends and, darlin', that just isn't enough. And that's what you want, right?"

Kristy wanted to scream, *No! That's not what I want*. But she was afraid . . . of losing control, of getting her heart broken, or breaking Ryan's heart. At least that's what she'd always told herself. It made it easier not to take risks, to keep herself distanced from people. Lance anxiously shifted from one leg to the other. He always seemed so confident and in control, but not tonight. She saw he was on edge, eyes heavy, laugh lines and frown lines appearing even more prominent, as if he hadn't been sleeping well either. Lance sighed.

"I've done my share of screwing around. That's not what I'm looking for. I want you. You're beautiful and smart and kind and a wonderful mother. But you've got a full life and you're clearly not looking for anything right now. Nothing wrong with that. I'm not looking to mess anything up for you. I'll still be there for Ryan. He's a good kid and I won't give up on him. I'll stop in and visit with Pops from time to time. But what we're doing now, playing pretend, I can't do that anymore."

He reached down and gently kissed Kristy on the lips.

"You're a good woman, Kristy Tucker, and you deserve good things."

Lance ambled down the driveway toward his pickup. Kristy watched him go, a heavy pit in her stomach. Frozen, paralyzed by uncertainty, she stood in the driveway as Lance fished in his pocket for his keys. Kristy had spent so many years focused on Ryan and Pops, focused on doing the best she could at a job she hated. She was always so goddamn worried. But now that worry was going to ruin something before it even started. She wouldn't see him sitting in her kitchen, making terrible knock-knock jokes or arm-wrestling Ryan or trading barbs with Pops about the best offensive lineman in the NFL. But that was her choice. She was only stuck if she decided she was.

"Wait! Lance! Wait!"

Startled, Lance looked up. Barefoot, Kristy raced across the driveway and ran toward him, throwing herself into his arms. She kissed him again, but this time she didn't pull away. She wasn't going to let him go. It was Lance who broke their kiss, his eyes twinkling.

"I'm sorry," she whispered.

"What for?" Lance asked, wiping away the tears that were streaming down Kristy's face.

"Because I almost let you go."

Lance grinned, a smile that nearly sent her to her knees.

"Good thing for both of us that you came to your senses," Lance said, picking Kristy up and kissing her until she was breathless. As Lance held Kristy in his arms, that familiar sense of impending doom bubbled up in her, and then, just like that, it was gone.

EIGHTEEN MONTHS LATER

Dear Ms. Tucker,

Hope you had a great holiday and married life is treating you well. I've been in a bit of a funk. I'm sure you know that my children died a few weeks before Thanksgiving so this is an especially hard time for me. On top of that, we just received the court ruling and they've denied my most recent appeal. According to the courts, the judge's impropriety in my case, including his vocal statements against African Americans, did not merit further review. So it looks as if I will finally be receiving my new execution date. I could be angry about this but I'm grateful I had these past eighteen months to keep fighting the good fight. So let's continue on with the interviews we have scheduled. Until they put that needle in my arm, I won't ever give up.

Warm regards,
Clifton Harris

CHAPTER EIGHT

Kristy sat at her kitchen table, staring down at her laptop, researching judo techniques. She'd become obsessed with learning the names that went along with the movements. *Kansetsu-waza* was a joint-locking technique. *Osaekomi-waza* was a pinning technique. There were choking techniques as well. She'd memorized these moves and the names, remembering when she'd joked with Lance that judo was a gentler form of martial arts. That wasn't true. Not even close.

Kristy's laptop dinged, signaling a new message. She clicked over to her e-mail and saw in the subject line: *Featured Wedding Photo.*

Kristy,

I'm so excited to share the news that your photo has been selected as one of the *Houston Chronicle*'s top wedding photos of the year. Hope you and Lance are still blissfully happy. Thanks again for letting me be part of your special day! Xoxo Rebecca

Kristy stared at the photo in question, her favorite out of hundreds. She'd even framed a copy and hung it in the bedroom, wanting that photo to be the first thing she saw each morning. It was taken at the end of their wedding night, just Kristy and Lance alone on the dance floor, Kristy's simple and elegant ivory gown hugging her curves, her dark wavy hair cascading around her face. Lance had taken off his suit jacket and loosened his tie, his hands draped around Kristy's waist. Her head rested on his shoulder, a shared look of bliss on their faces. A digital image that fairy tales were made of. That's what she'd believed. That's what she wanted to believe.

"Reliving the magic?" Lance asked, and Kristy nearly jumped out of her seat, hoping Lance didn't notice the judo web page link and question her about it. He leaned down, wrapping his arms around her, as he studied the photos, gently kissing Kristy's neck, his hand reaching into her robe and caressing her breast. Less than a year ago, Lance's chiseled body had inspired awe and desire. But now, she feared his strength and power, wondering what kind of damage he might inflict if she spoke too loudly, if dinner wasn't ready on time, if her clothing was just a bit too tight for his liking. He was a well-trained fighter. With a well-timed flick of the wrist or a chokehold, he could paralyze Kristy or even worse. She spent a great deal of time trying to hide how afraid she was. This morning, she plastered on her best smile.

"Our wedding photo is going to be in the *Chronicle*," Kristy said. Lance pulled away, his smile disappearing, replaced by a scowl, his grip tightening ever so slightly around her neck.

"Were you planning on asking me first?" Lance asked.

"Yeah, I just got the e-mail. Of course I was going to ask you. It's not a done deal. We'd have to sign a waiver."

"I don't want everyone knowing my business. Tell her thanks but no thanks. Our wedding day was for us and our family. Understood?"

Kristy nodded, quickly shooting the photographer a courteous reply declining the opportunity and thanking her yet again for capturing such a perfect day. She wasn't lying when she said it was perfect. A year and a half ago, it appeared that Kristy had met a man not only worthy of being part of her family, but a man she loved in every way. She'd been convinced that Ryan would freak when she told him that she and Lance wanted to start dating.

"Ryan loves me. It's not gonna be an issue," Lance said confidently. Kristy seized her opportunity to broach the subject that next morning while driving Ryan to school.

"Lance is really nice," she began awkwardly.

"Yeah, I know."

"We've been spending a lot of time together."

"Yeah. Wait, do you want me to ask him to stop coming around?"

"No. Actually...I mean, I was just...I mean, Lance and I..."

Ryan looked over at Kristy and sighed dramatically, in typical teenage melodramatic fashion.

"Oh God, you like him...I mean, you *like* him?"

"He likes me too," Kristy said, her voice a bit defensive, like a lovesick schoolgirl.

"Really?" Ryan asked. Kristy found it amusing, watching

him assess her, as if he was seeing a real person for the first time and not just his mother.

"I don't want to make you uncomfortable, but we'd like to go out. See where it goes."

Ryan shook his head and Kristy could tell he was still trying to process this.

"I just didn't think you were his type."

"And what type is that?"

"I don't know. Younger."

"He's ten years *older* than me," she said as she smacked him on the leg. Kristy launched into her best Quasimodo impression.

"Your mother deserves love, Ryan."

In spite of himself, Ryan snorted.

"God, Mom, you are such a freak. You know once Lance figures that out he'll hightail it outta here?"

Kristy had considered that possibility as well. She had expected Lance to get bored by the ordinary sameness of her domestic life, but he had embraced it. Six months after they met, they agreed that it didn't make sense for Lance to keep his condo in Huntsville. He moved into her house and settled in effortlessly. Ryan and Pops loved having him around, and Kristy couldn't remember the last time she was this at ease. She didn't ask a lot of questions about the future, content to take things day by day. Lance had other ideas.

Eight months after their first meeting, Lance organized a birthday dinner in town for Kristy. She wasn't exactly excited about turning thirty-three, but Lance insisted they celebrate. She arrived home from work to find the entire place engulfed in darkness.

"Pops? Lance? Ryan?" Kristy called out, feeling nervous, reaching into her purse for Mace. Call it a hazard of the job or the vandalism that occurred earlier in the year, but Kristy often feared the worst. She gasped when she entered the living room and found the entire place decked out in candles.

Pops was sitting in his recliner, wearing his favorite denim collared shirt and a pair of slacks, face clean-shaven, with his hair slicked back. Leaning against the wall in the corner, Lance was dressed in a starched white long-sleeved shirt and gray blazer. Kristy spun around and saw Ryan in his own white button-up T-shirt, his hair neatly combed. No, wait, he'd actually gotten it cut without her having to ask.

"What is this? Pops? Lance? What's happening?"

"Kristy Ann, take a breath," Pops said. She saw a twinkle in his eye that she hadn't seen in ages. Lance cleared his throat, wiping his hands on his jeans as he moved closer to Kristy. He stopped, inches from her, the two of them face-to-face.

"I've been planning something real special. Go big or go home, right? But all that fuss and hoopla doesn't seem right. What matters is all of us in this room. You know my family never gave two shits about me. I used to dream about what it would be like to have a family, to have people that I rely on. Meeting you and Ryan and Frank has made me excited to plan for the future, so I'm just gonna say it. Kristy Ann Tucker, will you marry me?"

She couldn't believe it. Lance was on one knee, holding out an emerald engagement ring. She'd fallen hard for Lance. He made her laugh, challenged her intellect, and blended into her family effortlessly, but she wasn't expecting marriage. Things like that never happened to Kristy Tucker. They happened to women with thinner waists and less baggage. Women with shiny hair and capped teeth. Lance was still holding out the ring, a smile from ear to ear as he waited for her to speak.

Kristy looked at her father and Ryan for approval.

"Damn, Kristy, don't keep the man waiting."

"C'mon, Mom. What's your answer?"

Kristy's tears were flowing as she nodded and smiled at the same time.

There were shouts of excitement from her father, whoops of joy from Lance and Ryan. Lance lifted Kristy off her feet and kissed her again and again.

"I'll always be yours, Kris. And you'll always be mine. No matter what. I want to hear you say it. Say you'll be my wife."

Overwhelmed with joy, holding on to Lance, Kristy leaned in and whispered her answer over and over again so he would know how much she wanted this.

"Yes, I'll be your wife. Yes. Yes. Yes."

Kristy's wedding day had dawned, cool, crisp, and not a cloud in sight. The small chapel was covered in pale yellow roses. Kristy had asked Carmen to be her bridesmaid. Ryan served as Lance's best man. Pops, dapper in a gray suit and lavender tie, proudly led Kristy down the aisle without his oxygen or his walker. They kept the guest list small. Kristy's old boss, Jack, and his wife were there, Gus and his wife, Meg. Lance had tried to convince Kristy not to invite him, but work politics required it. There was a smattering of other work friends, Bruce and his wife, Mac and his girlfriend, Vera. On Lance's side, he invited his business partner, Roy, and his wife, Yolanda, as well as a few coworkers from the real estate office and the guys he coached at the YMCA. As far as family, Lance didn't have any, at least none he cared to invite. His mother had run off and his father died when he was in his thirties. "You're my family now," Lance said. They exchanged handwritten vows, each of them revealing their own hopes and dreams and how they would support one another. Then the preacher pronounced them man and wife, and Lance kissed Kristy passionately, tears streaming down his face as he whispered, "I'll never let you go." At the time, Kristy found it endearing. Now it seemed like a warning.

They were ushered to the reception in the stretch limo, a surprise Lance had booked. When Kristy stepped inside the barn, owned by Roy, she'd gasped as she surveyed the hundreds of pink and yellow roses. Endless strands of twinkle lights and candles cast a romantic glow over the long farm tables.

Lance and Kristy were greeted by a mariachi band, another gift from Roy. Kristy didn't think it was possible to cry any more until Ryan stood to make his best man toast.

"Growing up, I didn't care about my dad. He bailed on my mom and me and I didn't want to waste my time thinking about him. And I didn't miss having a dad. Mom and Pops gave me plenty of love and attention...sometimes too much." The crowd laughed and Ryan grew more confident, standing taller, so handsome in his gray pinstripe suit.

"I didn't know what it meant to have a father until Lance came along. He listened to my worries about school, taught me how to do a perfect leg sweep, gave me advice on how to get a girl to notice me as more than just a friend," Ryan said, his gaze landing on Ella. "And it worked."

There were more chuckles. Kristy's son was blossoming into manhood right in front of her and she couldn't have been prouder.

"I won't lie—when my mom asked me if she could go out with Lance, I wasn't crazy about the idea. I was actually kind of grossed out. But I know how hard she works and how she deserves good things in her life. So today, in front of all of our family and friends, I'd like to raise a glass to my mom and her badass new husband, Lance, and wish them a lifetime of love."

The crowd toasted and cheered. Lance gently wiped away Kristy's tears. As the night wore on, the photographer captured a moment in time before everything went to hell. Now here she was, staring at this photo, their happy faces, her optimism mocking her.

"Morning, Mama Bear. Morning, Lance," Ryan said. "What's shaking?"

"Your mama is getting all sentimental," Lance responded, and Kristy smiled on cue. That's what Lance expected, for Kristy to follow his cues.

"Just looking at the wedding photos."

"If we're not careful, she'll make us watch the wedding video again!" Ryan teased.

Lance grinned. "I wouldn't mind that."

Kristy hated that video now. It was a distorted reality that only captured pre-wedding Lance. Post-wedding Lance was someone different entirely.

"You ready? I need ten minutes and I can drop you off on

my way," she said to Ryan, desperate to escape the confines of her home. The tables had turned. Her home was now a prison, her work a refuge.

"Actually, I told Ry I'd give him a ride to school," Lance said.

Kristy wanted to challenge him. *Hell no. This is my kid. Taking him to school is my thing.* He monopolized Ryan's time, making sure Kristy was never alone with him. She thought about arguing, but Ryan would side with Lance now and Kristy would pay the price later.

"Sounds good, fellas. I'll see you later."

"I'd say have a good day, but you're gonna watch someone die so I guess that wouldn't make sense," Ryan said. He was less sensitive these days, something else he had picked up from Lance.

Kristy stood up, knowing she had to get moving or she'd be late.

"Kristy," Lance called out. She froze, the low treble in his voice signaling that she'd done something wrong. Ryan didn't seem to notice, busily texting on his phone.

"What's wrong, Lance?" she asked.

"Nothing. Just wanted to give my wife a good-bye kiss."

He smiled but it didn't quite reach his eyes. Kristy hurried over and Lance wrapped his arms around her. Kristy winced, his hands digging into her bruised rib. Lance didn't seem to notice. Either that or he simply didn't care. Kristy didn't know what was worse.

"Be safe out there, babe, and I'll see you tonight."

Kristy headed upstairs, glancing back at Lance and Ryan, the two of them chuckling as Lance poured them both giant bowls of cereal. Later, Kristy drove down the interstate, her mind spinning, wondering what the hell she had gotten herself into.

The first time she saw a glimmer of Lance's temper was a few weeks after the wedding. She'd organized a night out with Lance's friends, Roy and Yolanda, as well as Mac and his girlfriend, Vera. Dinner in the Woodlands, then dancing at Mickey's, a country-and-western bar that Lance loved. After a few songs Kristy, sweaty and thirsty, whispered to Lance, "Babe, I need a break." He'd nodded agreeably, wrapped his arms around her, and led Kristy back to the table while the others continued dancing.

Kristy rarely smoked but she was a little tipsy and craving a cigarette. She grabbed Roy's pack off the table and went to light one, cradling it between two fingers, when the back of Lance's hand slammed into her mouth. The cigarette went flying, and Kristy stumbled backward. She reached for the table to steady herself. Lance stood there, shaking his head. Embarrassed, Kristy scanned the room to make sure no one was watching, as if she herself had somehow done something wrong.

"Jesus Christ, Lance. What the hell was that?" Kristy asked, keeping her voice low.

"Darlin', you know how I feel about smoking. Those things practically killed your father. No wife of mine is going to poison herself with that crap." He pulled her close, gently kissing her mouth.

Kristy thought about making a scene, but the others were returning to the table. Lance started cracking jokes, and Roy ordered a round of Cuervo shots, and the night continued on.

Wasn't it easier to just let it go? Lance clearly hadn't meant to hurt her. He was looking out for her. As the days passed, still a blissful newlywed, Kristy convinced herself that Lance's outburst was an isolated incident. It was simpler to tuck it away in the deep recesses of her mind.

It's where she often stored things she didn't want to think about, all the unpleasant moments in her life. This was the place in the deepest part of her mind where she stored all the executions she had witnessed over the years. Some of the condemned men walked to the death chamber with dignity, stoic, their heads held high with pride. But most didn't. Most men hollered and screamed and begged for their lives, cursed God and the government and the justice system and everyone else they could think of. They dragged their feet and some even had to be carried, limp, heavy, wet with sweat and urine. Eventually they lost the will to fight, but before that moment they created heartbreaking spectacles impossible to forget.

The memories didn't always remain there; sometimes they came roaring back with such crisp clarity, particularly late at night, that what little sleep she got was restless and haunted. But Kristy fought to bury that incident with Lance. She loved being married to him, loved introducing Lance to her coworkers. "This is my husband," she'd say with pride. She loved the warmth of his body in bed, the nights curled up on the sofa watching Netflix with Ryan and Pops. She loved doing projects around the house, helping Lance paint and garden, watching their home come to life. She'd wake each morning, Lance's arms holding her tightly, his muscled chest rising up and down as he peacefully slept. Sometimes he'd wake and catch her watching him. He'd smile and ask, "Darlin', why didn't you wake me sooner?" and then he'd kiss her and they'd make love. Kristy was experiencing a kind of love she had never believed in, the kind of love Pops shared with her mother. Despite that one flicker of uncertainty at the bar, Kristy's black-and-gray world was now vibrant, almost Technicolor. Kristy even found it easier to shake the workday off knowing she had Lance waiting at home.

She wanted to believe that Lance's fuse had been triggered by her ill-timed nicotine craving and nothing more. But deep down she couldn't silence that nagging voice that said something wasn't right.

A few months passed. Sure, there were little things, the time he punched the car window when he felt she was driving recklessly, or smashed the jar of peanut butter because she bought the wrong brand and he had decided they should cut back on their sugar intake. But these were all things he was doing to protect her. They weren't malicious.

Every time she worried about Lance, he would do something to make her fall in love with him all over again. They were lying in bed one night when Lance looked over at Kristy.

"Ryan mentioned that parents' night was next Tuesday. I've got a private lesson at the Y, but I could always get Carlos to cover."

Kristy didn't answer, blinking back her tears.

"Darlin', are you crying?" Lance asked in surprise.

"I've just been doing all of this alone for so long."

"We're a family. That's what families do, or so I've heard," Lance said with a wry grin. At parents' night, Lance held Kristy's hand, leading her from one classroom to another, charming all of Ryan's teachers, eagerly inquiring about Ryan's progress and how he was doing. Liza pulled Kristy aside as Ryan showed Lance his latest project for his 3-D modeling class.

"I don't think I've ever seen you this happy," Liza said. Kristy smiled. She was happy. At least until they were leaving the auditorium. Lance gripped her arm, his voice low.

"What the hell was that?" he asked.

Kristy didn't know what he was talking about, his fingers digging deeper. She looked around to make sure no one was watching, glad that Ryan had opted to get a ride with Ella.

"What are you talking about, Lance?"

"Telling everyone I'm not Ryan's dad. You said 'stepfather' fifty goddamn times."

"I didn't mean to...I mean, I wasn't thinking."

"Well, next time you will. If you want me to act like a father to him, then treat me like one," Lance said as they reached the exit. Almost as if he knew people would be watching, he released Kristy and kept moving toward the parking lot. Kristy stepped out into the humid night air, rubbing her arm, blaming herself for making Lance feel disrespected. She tried to apologize on the drive home, but Lance had already forgotten it, insisting that they grab dinner and drinks at Kristy's favorite Mexican restaurant.

The weeks passed without incident and she began to breathe easy. She should have known better. One evening Kristy ended up stuck at the office, trying to fix the mess Gus's new intern made when she sent out a press release announcing the execution of an inmate who *wasn't* actually being executed. Kristy spent hours fielding angry calls. The victim's family was pissed, convinced they'd been denied the chance to watch their family member's murderer pay. The inmate's family thought they'd been denied a final farewell.

Exhausted, she rushed out of work at seven thirty and made the long drive home. When she arrived, Lance didn't even bother to look up from his laptop. When she asked if he was all right, he just shrugged and said, "It was a long day."

She didn't think much about Lance's mood, still fuming over her own work drama while she made dinner, simmering the pasta sauce and vegetables. Ryan came bounding into the kitchen, chattering nonstop about his sixteenth birthday. It was less than two weeks away and Kristy had mentioned to Lance that she wanted to take Ryan to their spot at the Sam Houston National Forest. They hadn't been there together in years, but when Ryan was in second grade, the first Saturday of every month, no matter how tired or overworked Kristy was, she would pack a lunch— bologna sandwiches, potato chips, and fruit salad—and they'd head off, hiking along the Lone Star trail until their feet ached, stopping midday and sharing a picnic under the shade of the pine trees. Ryan would entertain Kristy with fun facts about the US presidents, and she would tell him stories about Pops and her mother and how they used to hike these trails. As time passed, the tradition faded, but she thought it would be fun to have a picnic, just the two of them. Then they could meet Lance and host a surprise party for Ryan at his favorite Mexican restaurant. Kristy should have known better than to try to get some one-on-one time with Ryan. These days Lance called all the shots.

"Still can't wait for my brand-new Jeep," Ryan joked.

"Aren't you funny?" she said. Ryan laughed.

"Jeez, Mom, a kid can dream," Ryan joked. She'd looked over at Lance but he was silently sipping his beer. Pops interrupted, asking Kristy if she remembered to order the refill for his inhaler, and she spent the next twenty minutes on the phone with the pharmacy trying to get them to deliver it. It was close to nine before they all sat down for dinner. Lance remained muted. Kristy noticed but was too exhausted to comment, letting Ryan and Pops fill in the silences. The minute Lance finished eating, he mumbled good night and went straight to bed, leaving Kristy to wash up. She didn't mind, still decompressing from her shitty day.

When she came up to bed, she closed the door. Lance stood by the window, shirt off, clad only in jeans.

"Hey, babe, are you sure you're okay?"

He didn't say a word, but took three giant strides until he reached Kristy. He grabbed her arm, his fingers digging deeper and deeper, until she yelped. Something flickered in Lance's eyes; was it excitement or regret? She thought he was going to let go but instead, he reached over and placed his right hand over Kristy's mouth. With his other hand, he punched her right under her solar plexus. Kristy gasped, the force of the blow activating her entire nervous system, triggering her brain and body simultaneously as she toppled onto the gray carpeting.

No, Kristy thought. *No. No. No.* She sat motionless on the floor, sprawled out, sucking in air, trying to reconstruct the events that had occurred. Lance stood above her, his expression unreadable.

"I don't understand. What the hell...? I mean...Jesus..." Kristy gasped, her breath coming out in spurts. She could barely speak, not sure if it was because of the force of the blow, the surprise of it, or both. Lance knelt down beside Kristy, pulling her close so that they were face-to-face. She tried to resist, to pull away, but he held tight, his mouth inches from hers, as if he were trying to breathe the life back into her.

"Darlin', I was so goddamn worried when you didn't call or text tonight. No one heard from you. Not Pops or Ryan."

"My phone battery died. I told you that," Kristy said. She was constantly forgetting to charge her phone. Lance wasn't interested in her excuses.

"You work in a prison, Kristy. It's a dangerous place. I started thinking about all the bad things that could happen. I just got so worried. We're a team now. You have to remember that."

"You hurt me, Lance," she said.

He was silent for a moment and then he shook his head, kissing her tenderly.

"Fear makes you do crazy things, darlin'. Next time you'll let me know if you're going to be late."

It didn't even register to Kristy that Lance hadn't apologized. That there was no remorse. No contrition. She was too busy trying to understand how it was possible that Lance had just assaulted her. That's what the police would have called it. That's what it was. She had worked in law enforcement long enough to know that. If this were anyone else, if anyone but her husband had done this to her, she would have called the police. She would have watched as the cops hauled him off to jail. But she didn't call anyone. She didn't tell Ryan or Pops. She never said a word to Carmen or Mac. Yes, Lance had hit her, but he wasn't some stranger off the street. How could she? This was her husband. Her *brand-new* husband.

Dear Ms. Tucker,

I hope you're feeling better. I saw Miss Carmen and she said you'd been out sick. Drink lots of fluids and get plenty of rest. That's what my mama always said and my mama was never wrong. Anyway, I sure do hate to pester you but with my execution fast approaching, my lawyer Bev has been in contact with several high-profile reporters. We would love to schedule as many interviews as possible to get more public support regarding my case. I realize you are a very busy woman but Carmen said you were the person who made all the decisions so I've enclosed names and phone numbers of various media outlets. At the top of the list is some hotshot rapper who wants to meet in two weeks to discuss a documentary he's doing about wrongful convictions. I've never heard of him but some of the fellas in here said he's big-time so hopefully you can reach out ASAP. In my limited experience, them Hollywood types tend to have short attention spans. As always, I greatly appreciate your continued assistance.

Warmly,
Clifton Harris

CHAPTER NINE

On any given day, when an execution was scheduled, Kristy spent the entire morning bracing herself for what lay ahead. Once she was inside, standing shoulder to shoulder with all the other witnesses, the entire room collectively holding their breath, she'd count down the seconds, watching from outside her body as another criminal was dispatched, wanting it all to be over. But today, Kristy was grateful to be here, understanding there was something wrong with preferring a front row seat on death row to being in her own home. Yet here she was, waiting for Marcus Masters's final moments to unfold, grateful she had a place to escape Lance and his mood swings.

The small room was made up of some unplastered brick walls, all of them painted a confused kind of green. Kristy always wondered if this color was an attempt to render a small amount of calm for the inmate, or the witnesses. Or was it just the color the maintenance crew happened to have lying around? She found these random thoughts filling her head, trying to block out the realities of her own life. She didn't know Marcus at all. During his time on death row, Marcus had denied hundreds of interview requests. He didn't write to anyone, didn't hire new lawyers to appeal his execution. Marcus and the state were in agreement—it was time for him to die.

Marcus was only eighteen years old when his parents were shot and killed in a home invasion, when an errant bullet ricocheted off the wall and lodged in Marcus's spine. He wound up paralyzed from the waist down. While Marcus lay in the ICU, fighting for his life, police organized a statewide manhunt for the perpetrator. In the end, they discovered Marcus was the mastermind. He stood to inherit his parents' vast wealth, a total of four million dollars. The buddies he hired were supposed to shoot him in the leg. They missed. Once the police pieced together the crime, his two accomplices ratted Marcus out in exchange for a lesser sentence, sealing Marcus's fate. Kristy used to wonder how the family had missed the signs that Marcus was unstable, the things he said, the things he did; but then she thought of Lance. She had taken his protectiveness in those early months as considerate. She had believed the stories he told her about his fight training, thinking he wanted to use it to empower people, when really it was about dominating. *Love blinds us all*, she thought. No matter how much she loved Lance, she couldn't seem to live up to his expectations.

The toothpaste tube wasn't properly folded. *"It goes upside down or it gets messy."*

She'd forgotten to flush the toilet. *"So disgusting, Kristy. What are you, a goddamn animal?"*

"The toilet paper points down like the patent. You know it drives me crazy the other way."

Sometimes it wasn't even about what she did that morning. Sometimes it was something she'd done days or even weeks before.

"You think I don't speak right? Is that why you corrected me in front of your friends? Because Mac and Vera are so goddamn special? You think I'm a retard because I don't read books all the time like you and Ryan? Do you?" Sometimes these verbal assaults were almost more exhausting than the physical ones. Those were over in an instant, Lance moving on like nothing happened. But the onslaught of negative comments left Kristy constantly second-guessing everything she did and said.

Kristy did her best, learning to read Lance's moods, to anticipate his needs. They had gone almost a week without an incident, life humming along. But this morning Lance reminded Kristy that she needed to work harder. Kristy's mistake crystalized the second Lance shoved her through the bathroom door and she glimpsed her hot pink curling iron, the light still flashing bright green.

"How many times have I told you to unplug that thing when you're done? Look at this. Just look! I burned my goddamn hand," Lance said. He took the hot iron and Kristy held up her hands, trying to mount what would be a pointless defense. She'd come to realize that in the court of Lance Dobson, there was no judge or jury. Only executioner.

"Lance, I promise I won't forget again."

"Promises are meaningless, Kristy. Actions are what matter. One of these days you'll learn that." Lance shoved Kristy against the wall. Her face smashed into the peeling ivory paint as the sting of the iron sizzled on the back of her legs.

"A real man wouldn't do this to his wife," Kristy said. In response, he dug the hot iron deeper into her flesh. Recently, she'd begun pushing back, calling Lance out, hating how cowardly not saying anything made her feel. But fighting made no difference. If anything, it only made the assaults more brutal.

Kristy strained against Lance but she knew it was useless. She could never overpower him, his body finely honed for violence. She softly sobbed as he held the hot wand to her flesh, counting to ten like she was a naughty child. The pain worked its way up from Kristy's thigh, settling in her throat. When he released the iron, Kristy was moaning in agony, clutching the porcelain sink to steady herself.

"Darlin', let this be the last time I have to remind you that your carelessness affects us both." And then just like all those other times before, he was gone, hurrying off to work, to the real estate office where he wowed potential homeowners with his charming tales of family life.

She stood there, waiting for the searing pain to subside. The physical violence was sporadic and unexpected, a smack here, a hair tug there, a raised eyebrow or punishing stare that signified more punishments were imminent if she didn't satisfy whatever mood Lance was in. Lance didn't appear troubled by these events. The only time he acknowledged anything was wrong was one night when they were lying in bed. Lance was gently caressing Kristy's back. She hated that her body still responded to him, hated that she still wanted him. But she loved Lance and he relied on that to control her.

"We're lucky, Kris. We've got a good thing here, and I should know. My parents were never on the same page. My mother didn't listen to my father; in fact she outright disrespected him. And my dad was too goddamn passive. He wouldn't make her listen, and then she left us. She ruined everything. But you and me, we get to do things over. We get to do them the right way."

The right way? Kristy didn't know what the hell that meant. How could she know what was right when he kept changing the rules?

"Any last words?" Kristy heard the warden ask, and she was transported back to the death chamber. Usually, Kristy spoke to the condemned before they were taken to the execution chamber, assisting them if they wanted to issue a statement to the press. Marcus had refused to speak with anyone, even Chaplain Gohlke. He was one of the few death row inmates Kristy encountered who hadn't embraced God while in prison.

Marcus hadn't put up a fight when the guards came, allowing them to lift him into his wheelchair and wheel him toward the death chamber. That's what got to Kristy: imagining how powerless you had to be to be physically carried to your own death. Or maybe she understood it more now, feeling like a captive, trapped inside the walls of her own home, no different from these men. As the injection was administered, a flurry of questions ran through Kristy's mind: Did he miss his parents? Did he regret what he'd done? Was he a good person who'd made a terrible decision? Or was he just born evil? She couldn't stop thinking about Lance's lack of remorse, his eyes cold and lifeless each time he hurt her.

Tonight Marcus stared through the glass partition where his sister Elizabeth sat, the same sister who testified against him, actively seeking the death penalty. Elizabeth was attending Baylor University when the murder occurred. She came to the execution as a guest of the prosecution. Elizabeth was vocal in her outrage at her brother's crime. She insisted that the courts show him no mercy, just like he had shown their parents none. In his final moments, Marcus said nothing. Nothing at all. His last act of defiance was a cold, blank stare, a giant fuck-you to his sister, the recipient of their parents' millions.

Kristy watched as Marcus's eyes fluttered closed, and that impending sense of doom returned, so powerful Kristy worried it might consume her. She returned home after the press conference, Elizabeth Masters's tearful words ringing in her ears: "We just didn't know what he was capable of. We had no idea."

CHAPTER TEN

Happy birthday, dear Ryan. Happy birthday to you." Pops, Lance, Ryan's girlfriend, Ella, and twenty-five other teenagers gathered around the picnic table, singing loudly and faces aglow from the candlelight, as Ryan leaned down to blow out his candles. In the past year, Ryan had suddenly blossomed, his newfound physical prowess giving him more confidence. Kristy couldn't quite wrap her head around the fact that her baby boy was sixteen. That early dawn when her water broke seemed like just yesterday. Pops was working the day shift, so their neighbor Mrs. Roberts drove Kristy to the hospital. She was grateful Pops wasn't there. Having her father in the delivery room would have been way too awkward.

Betty, a kind, elderly, gray-haired nurse, coached Kristy through her arduous labor, clutching her hand, wiping the sweat and tears that streamed down Kristy's face, feeding her ice chips and urging her on.

"You've got this, sugar. You can do it. You're so strong," Betty chanted over and over for seventeen straight hours. Kristy had pushed so hard she thought she might come undone. Then she saw her baby boy, all eight pounds, two ounces of him. Even covered in goo, his tuft of sandy brown hair matted to his tiny head, his tiny legs and arms flailing, her baby was the most incredible sight she'd ever seen. At her touch, Ryan's cries instantly faded. "It's you and me forever," Kristy had whispered through her tears. It didn't seem possible that he was almost an adult. But here he was extinguishing all sixteen candles (and one for luck).

Ryan turned to Ella, the young redhead practically glowing in her pink party dress. Ryan pulled her in for a kiss, his smile infectious. A hollowness formed in Kristy's stomach, a profound sense that she was running out of time with him. Or maybe that's what being a parent was all about. Raising someone you loved with all your being and then having the courage to let them go. She was doing her best trying to keep it together.

Today was about Ryan. Kristy had been surprised by how many kids had shown up, including that shithead Scotty Welch.

"You're inviting him?" Kristy had asked when she saw the guest list.

Ryan shrugged. "His friends thought the move I used to kick Scotty's ass was dope. He had no choice but to be nice to me. I like the other guys, so I have to invite Scotty." Kristy was this close to saying hell no, there was no way that kid was stepping foot on her property, but Lance made the final call.

"The more the merrier, babe. Besides, we shouldn't hold grudges. Isn't that right, Ry?" Kristy lost that argument before it even began. The party had been a good distraction for Lance. He'd been so busy organizing he didn't have time to take out his frustrations on her. He'd agreed to host it, then threw himself into making arrangements.

"We'll need to do some work around the place. Get it in working order."

Lance knew how much pride Kristy took in her home. They'd already done a bunch of repairs when he moved in. "What needs to be fixed?" she asked.

"The yard needs some serious landscaping and the fence needs repainting. Ryan, are you up for the challenge?"

Ryan eagerly agreed, and each night and on the weekends they would disappear outside, painting the peeling fences, mowing the lawn, the two of them thick as thieves. Lance would come to bed exhausted, pulling Kristy into his arms, telling her how much he loved her, and how lucky they were to be a family. Though she wished this reprieve would last, Kristy knew it was temporary. She had to do something. Maybe counseling, but first she had to get Lance to agree that anything was wrong. She had been asking around about lawyers, talking to Carmen. "It's for a friend," she said. "Someone I've known a long time who's in a bad place." Carmen had given her several names. But the last thing Kristy wanted was to ruin Ryan's birthday. That's what she had to focus on.

"Who wants cake?" Kristy asked.

"I do," Pops said enthusiastically, and everyone laughed, including Ryan. Kristy started to cut the cake, but Lance grabbed the knife from her and set it on the table.

"Darlin', hold on one second. Listen up, everyone. Can I have your attention?"

Scotty Welch and the jocks inched closer to the table. Ella

and Ryan and the debate kids made their way over, along-side another group of grade school friends. Lance clapped his hands.

Everyone crowded around Lance, eagerly awaiting his announcement.

"Pops, give me two minutes and then you can have your cake. I have a little surprise for our boy," Lance said. Kristy gritted her teeth, irritated that Lance had claimed ownership of her son. *You had nothing to do with him*, she thought. *He's not yours.*

"What surprise?" she asked Lance.

"You'll see." Lance reached for his phone and sent a text, then zeroed in on Ryan.

"What's going on, Lance?" Ryan said.

"Yeah, what's happening?" Pops asked quizzically.

Lance slapped Ryan on the shoulder, a playful display of macho affection. "Your mama and I are getting a little tired of playing chauffeur. Isn't that right?" Lance asked.

Kristy hesitated. Some days driving Ryan to school was the only time she saw him. It was often her favorite time of the day. Kristy could tell from Lance's probing gaze that she was meant to respond. *Play along*, he seemed to be saying.

"You heard what Lance said," Kristy replied, wondering if anyone could spot the false enthusiasm or her strained smile. She doubted it. They were all too engrossed in the Lance Dobson show.

"Ryan, I thought about buying you a yearly bus pass, but you only turn sixteen once," Lance said.

He pressed another button on his phone. Seconds later,

Kristy watched as a brand-new black Jeep came roaring toward them, stopping just a few feet from the party. With its sparkling silver rims and a sunroof, it was, quite simply, a teenager's dream car. Hell, it was Kristy's dream car. The door opened and Mac emerged, an *aw shucks* grin on his wide, open face. Kristy stared at Mac in disbelief, her best friend, handing over the car keys to Lance, the two of them smug and satisfied with themselves.

"I recruited some help," Lance said. "Scotty's dad hooked me up." Scotty beamed, the other guys high-fiving him, a shit-eating grin on the young man's face at being in on the secret. "And Mac volunteered to be part of the surprise."

Mac grinned at Lance. "I don't think I've ever seen Kristy this surprised."

"I'm surprised all right," Kristy said, fighting to keep her rage from bubbling over. Lance and Mac had gone out for beers once or twice, but this was too much. Lance went behind Kristy's back and used her best friend to organize a birthday present for *her* son.

Ryan's expression was a mixture of disbelief and pure, unadulterated joy. An expression Kristy had never seen until right this moment, and it was all Lance's doing. She should have been happy, but Kristy had never been more devastated. She'd bought Ryan a navy-blue sports coat, for God's sake, and given it to him before the party.

"It'll be great for your tournaments," she told Ryan. Lance was turning her into a fool, someone pathetic and unimportant. Lance didn't notice her fury, his hero moment still unfolding. He turned to Ryan and held out the car keys.

"It's a big responsibility but you've proven you're ready for it," Lance said.

"Holy shit!" Ryan said. "Is this for real?" That's what Kristy wanted to ask. Her mouth hung open in disbelief, listening to the jealous murmurs of the other teens.

"Wow! How cool is that? Isn't Mr. Dobson awesome?" Ella said to Kristy, as if Lance were some kind of deity who had just walked on water.

"He certainly is," Kristy responded, resenting how Lance had turned Ryan's sixteenth birthday into his own one-man show. But that was the real Lance. In every situation, he took center stage, hating when anyone, especially Kristy, dared to usurp his spotlight.

"Go on, check it out," Lance urged, motioning Ella and Ryan forward.

Kristy normally weighed every word, calculated her phrasing and intonation so she wouldn't upset Lance, but this time she forgot herself.

"You got him a car without consulting me? What the hell were you thinking?" she said under her breath so that Ryan and Ella couldn't hear. Lance's head swiveled away from the celebration, eyes narrowing, a movement almost imperceptible to anyone but Kristy. She thought about challenging him. *What are you going to do, Lance? Punch me in the abdomen? Twist my arm? Pull my hair until I cry out? Go on. Do it. Do it here in front of everyone.*

But the thought of Ryan's smile fading as he tried to reconcile what Kristy was saying with the man he'd grown to love, or of Pops gasping for breath, his airway constricted by his anger and disbelief, terrified her.

"I think Kristy's had too much to drink," Lance would say, and they'd see her eyes were shiny from two glasses of wine. Ryan would tell her to go to bed. "Mom, you're embarrassing us."

There was always the chance that Lance would explode, reaching out to strike Kristy, sending her crashing onto the table, sending the cake flying. Ella would scream, hands covering her mouth. The other girls would rush off. Scotty Welch would hurry home, gleefully recounting the Tucker family's latest drama. No. Kristy couldn't do that to Ryan. She couldn't ruin his party. She pasted on the dutiful smile she'd patented, a smile so unflappable no one would see the cracks beneath the surface.

"Lance, all I meant to say was that it's just so generous. I don't know how I'll ever repay you," Kristy said, too afraid to take her chances that things might spiral out of control. She stood on her tiptoes for a kiss, hoping physical affection might defuse things. Lance's smile returned, his face flushed from the onslaught of accolades.

"We're a family, Kristy. One day you'll see that," Lance said softly, and Kristy heard the tinge of warning in his voice. He gave her a quick kiss.

"Now let's get this cake served," Lance said, handing the knife back to Kristy so she could resume her cake-serving duties.

It wasn't really a cake knife; it was a long, sharp kitchen knife. Its weight was heavy in her hand; it would cut through the cake without much pressure. An image of the knife cutting through human flesh flashed through her mind, right through the carotid, the artery that joins the heart to the brain. The thought startled her as the knife sliced effortlessly through the cake. She tried to shake it off, dutifully slicing and placing thick layers of chocolate on small paper plates while everyone ignored her, more interested in Ryan's new car than her sad store-bought cake. Kristy didn't know exactly what Lance was doing. Was this something he'd planned, some way to isolate her from her family, or even replace her? If so, it was working beautifully. Kristy wanted to scream at Lance, *They're my family. They're mine.*

Kristy wasn't some schoolgirl or novice in the ways of the world. She spent most of her working life surrounded by violent men, impulsive men, unrepentant men. And yet she'd been duped. Lance's true nature was beginning to surface, and not just in private. A few weeks ago, Lance announced that he'd been let go from the YMCA after a disagreement with the owner. When she pressed for more details, Lance slammed down his glass of water on the bedside table.

"Gave over two years of my time to that place, training dozens of fighters, and that pencil dick has the nerve to say he can't pay me an extra five dollars."

Lance had also fallen out of favor with his business partner, Roy, though Kristy didn't hear that from Lance. When Roy's wife, Yoli, stopped returning her calls, she asked him if something was wrong. Lance grew quiet, the kind of quiet that made Kristy uneasy.

"We're not seeing them anymore," Lance said.

"What about work?" she asked.

"I'm going out on my own. I've been doing all Roy's work

anyway, the advertising, getting new clients, while he shares in the profits. Darlin', it's better for us in the long run." She wanted details but she couldn't push. Not anymore.

She'd discovered the truth a few weeks ago while she was grocery shopping at H-E-B. Kristy spotted Yoli ahead of her in the checkout line. She waved but Yoli turned away, like she hadn't even seen her. Kristy hurried over.

"Yoli, hey!" Kristy said, relieved to see that she was okay.

Yoli's eyes darted around the store nervously.

"Where's Lance?"

"He's at home," Kristy said. Yoli looked uncertain, her eyes scanning the store as if any second Lance might leap out from an aisle. "Yolanda, what's wrong?"

"Kristy, I don't want to get into it."

She tried to leave but Kristy reached out.

"Please. I've left messages. I wanted to make sure you were okay."

"I'm fine. Lance told us to stay away from y'all and that's what we're going to do."

Kristy's stomach lurched.

"I don't understand. I thought we were friends," Kristy said.

"Friends don't swindle friends, Kristy," Yolanda said, her temper flaring.

"Swindle? What are you talking about?"

"Lance still owes us for the wedding reception."

Kristy's mouth hung open. "He said you were covering the cost."

"Of the venue. Those were the terms. We normally charge

at least six thousand to rent out the barn for parties and events. We gave it to y'all for free. But the food and the waitstaff cost money and so did the rentals and decorations," Yoli said, her voice thick with frustration.

"How much do we owe you?" Kristy asked.

"Four grand."

Kristy's mouth dropped open. That's the exact amount she'd given Lance to cover a portion of the wedding expenses. He didn't want to take it but she insisted. "We're a partnership," she'd told Lance, the irony of that statement laughable now.

"I'm so sorry, Yoli. I'll pay you back. It may take a few months but..."

Yoli shook her head.

"No. We're done. Lance has already been spreading lies about us all over town. When Roy called Lance out, he got real nasty. Lance isn't...he's not the same person we met."

"But you guys have been friends for so long."

Yoli scoffed.

"Roy and I met Lance two years ago when he moved to town. Roy was going through chemo and the business was in trouble. Lance seemed like a godsend. Looks like we were wrong about that."

"I'm sorry...," Kristy began.

Yoli cut her off. "None of this is your fault, but it's best if we don't speak again."

Kristy watched Yoli rush off, leaving her all alone in the aisle. Her intuitions were correct—there were things about Lance she didn't know.

Ryan was still marveling over the car. Mac ambled over to Kristy, beer in hand, a goofy grin on his wide face.

"Sorry to keep this from you, but Lance said he'd end me if I spilled the beans," Mac said.

"Well, a promise is a promise, isn't it?" Kristy replied, trying to keep the sarcasm out of her voice.

"Did you hear you and Pops are gonna have the place all to yourself next week?"

Kristy's confusion showed.

"Lance invited me and Ryan to go hunting," Mac said.

Of course he did, Kristy thought. He had to take everything and *everyone* that was hers and kill innocent animals in the process.

"Unless you don't want me to go?" Lance said, his booming voice startling Kristy.

"Don't be silly, Lance. I know you've been looking forward to it." Kristy smiled at Mac. "Lance has been after me to go with him for months but..."

"I know. I know. We're heathens for going out and killing helpless animals," Mac said with a wry grin.

"I didn't say that," Kristy said, feeling off balance. Lance threw a protective arm around her waist, pulling her in closer to him.

"But we know that Kristy was thinking it, don't we? My wife witnesses grown men put to death but she's squeamish about hunting," Lance said, and Mac chuckled. Kristy hated how holier-than-thou he was about her job, a stark difference from when they first met. She was worried Lance might ask her to quit, want to keep her close to home, but so far he hadn't said a word about her job.

"You're cool with us going, aren't you?" Lance asked. This time Kristy didn't have to lie. She had never wanted anything more than a weekend without Lance. His campground had limited cell phone access. She needed that time to figure out what the hell she was going to do.

"Of course. I'm sure you guys will have a great time," Kristy said.

"Good. Mac, I'm gonna get another beer. You want to join me?"

"Sure. I'll see you around, Kris." She nodded, watching the two of them walk away, wishing Mac would look at her, that he could see her spiraling slowly into despair or that she had the courage to say the words out loud to him.

The party stretched on into the night, the sun setting, a golden haze illuminating Ryan and his friends, so shiny and hopeful, still unaware of the crushing disappointments life had in store for them. Kristy watched from the periphery, sipping a glass of white wine as Lance assumed the role of surrogate dad, holding a martial arts demonstration and allowing Ryan to take him down as the entire yard, including Pops, erupted in cheers.

It was almost eleven when everyone began to head out. Lance had made his way through a case of Budweiser and some Jack Daniel's shots, and Kristy assumed he'd stumbled upstairs to pass out. Standing at the kitchen sink, she remembered how much she'd enjoyed washing dishes with Lance. He didn't do the dishes anymore. Not since the wedding. This was Kristy's domain now.

"Jesus Christ, Ryan, what's gotten into you? You're acting like . . . like a total asshole!"

Ella's shouting startled Kristy from her reverie. She glanced out the kitchen window, and through the shadows she spotted Ryan and Ella hunkered down at the picnic table. Kristy couldn't hear what they were saying, but Ryan's brow was furrowed, annoyance clouding his face. *That look*, the same one Lance got when Kristy misspoke. Ryan shrugged and looked back down at his phone. Ella stared at Ryan, like a wounded bird seeking comfort. When he continued ignoring her, Ella burst into tears and ran into the house.

"Ugh. Calm down. You're acting like a total spaz," Ryan called after her, but she didn't come back and Ryan didn't follow. Instead, he aimed his phone at the brand-new car and began snapping photos.

Ella raced past Kristy, the waterworks flowing, and ran downstairs to Ryan's bedroom. It was as if Kristy were watching a teenage version of herself, with Ryan cast in Lance's role. Witnessing Ryan's indifference at Ella's distress put her over the edge. This was not the boy she'd raised. She wouldn't allow it. She couldn't. Kristy flung open the window even wider.

"Ryan, get your butt in the house. Right now," she called out. He jumped, knowing after a lifetime with Kristy her tone meant serious business. He walked into the house, brushing his hair out of his eyes.

"What the hell was that?" Kristy asked.

Ryan shifted uncomfortably. "What are you talking about?"

"Your girlfriend just ran past me in tears. You clearly said or did something that upset her."

"She's literally driving me crazy. Nagging me all day about me talking to Kelly. We were discussing colleges. She's looking into East Coast and so am I. That's all we were talking about but Ella wouldn't listen, and I'm...I'm just over it."

"Ryan, do you care about Ella?"

"Yeah, of course...But—"

"Jesus, Ryan, there are no buts. You upset Ella. Now you have to make things right. That's what decent people do. Understand?"

At last Kristy saw a flicker of embarrassment, Ryan's cheeks flushing a deep red.

"Yeah, sure. I'm sorry, Mom. I'll go check on her."

He turned toward the stairs and then stopped, spinning around and throwing his arms around Kristy. He was all muscle, almost a man, but she prayed he would always be her baby.

"Today was amazing. The ribs, that cake, and I'm still freaking about the car. I hope you and Lance know how much I appreciate it. Thanks, Mom."

Those few minutes with Ryan were almost enough to make Kristy forget that Lance had upstaged her. All Kristy wanted to do was crawl into bed and drift off to sleep and forget. She told herself later that she should have known better. If she had continued her judo studies, if she had stopped drinking earlier, Kristy might have been more aware of what Lance was capable of. She would never forget that day. It was Ryan's sixteenth birthday. It was also the first time her husband raped her.

CHAPTER ELEVEN

Exhausted, full from too much cake and white wine, and frustrated over Lance's surprise and Ryan's uncharacteristic behavior toward Ella, Kristy had collapsed into bed. Lance murmured sleepily, his hands reaching out to caress her back and moving down her stomach, his standard move to signal that he was in the mood.

"Lance, it's been a long day."

He sighed, his hands more insistent, inching up Kristy's nightgown.

"You think I didn't have a long day?"

"That's not what I'm saying." Kristy tried to pull away. Lance's grip tightened.

"You're my wife, Kristy," Lance whispered, but it may as well have been a scream. His hands were no longer gently probing her body. He pinned her wrists against her body. The weight of his words and then the stillness came after, the silence lingering, endless and unbearable.

Kristy closed her eyes, gathering all her strength. Lance had stolen enough from her. She wouldn't let him take *this*. She tried to shove him away, her hands striking his muscled chest. Kristy's resistance infuriated Lance, adding kindling to the fire. Lance didn't even need two arms to pin her down. This was why he hadn't taught her self-defense. He wanted her powerless.

Flickers of death row flooded her brain, all those terrible moments spilling out: standing in the witness room, cold and dark, staring as one doomed man after another was led kicking and screaming to the death chamber; Clifton's bloody hand reaching out; Chaplain Gohlke's soft whisper, delivering the Litany of the Saints: "Lord, have mercy on us. Christ, have mercy on us. Lord, have mercy on us. Christ, hear us."

Kristy wasn't a believer. Not these days. Before her mother died, the family dutifully attended Presbyterian services every Sunday. Pops hadn't set foot in a church since, making an exception for Kristy's wedding. He always said, "I ain't got no business with the Lord no more."

Tonight Kristy longed for faith, for some sign that she hadn't been forgotten. She didn't scream. The idea that Ryan and Pops might see her like this, her nightgown pushed up to her chest, was too much to bear. She simply endured.

A grunt and a moan punctuated the evening. Lance collapsed back onto the bed, loosening his grip on Kristy. He sank back onto the plush pillows, his body thick with sweat and satisfaction.

"I won't be in a sexless marriage, Kristy Ann. Remember that," Lance said breathlessly. "The minute we're no longer connecting, then this relationship falls apart, and neither of us wants that," he said. Lance turned over and drifted off to sleep. Kristy lay awake, unable to move or even speak, afraid that if she opened her mouth, she might never stop screaming.

Dear Ms. Tucker,

Hope you enjoy the article I've enclosed about prison reha-
bilitation programs. Seemed like something that might be
beneficial. While I don't think there's anything the suits up
in the capitol could do to make my own situation more bearable, I think these programs would help offenders in other
units serving shorter sentences better themselves. Would
love to discuss when I see you next and hear your thoughts.

Do you ever wake up and think, despite all signs otherwise, that today might be your lucky day? I woke up this
morning feeling a bit more optimistic. I had a visit with
Bev and she brought good news. Apparently, the courts
are reconsidering evidence and there is a chance they
could grant me a new hearing based on flawed investigative procedures. I'm trying not to get my hopes up but you
know, Ms. Tucker, some days hope is all we've got.

I hope I'm not overstepping but you seemed a bit out of
sorts the last few times I saw you. It's something in your eyes
I can't quite place my finger on. Whenever I was in the dumps,
my mama used to say, "Cliff, who stole your sparkle?"

I could just be projecting (that's not my word either, I stole
that one from Oprah). Projecting means putting your own
stuff on someone else, so maybe I'm reading into something
that isn't there. Maybe I should mind my own damn business. But I do hope you get your sparkle back soon.

Warm regards,
Clifton Harris

CHAPTER TWELVE

After Ryan's birthday, Kristy tried to talk to Lance about what happened. He had crossed a line, done something unspeakable. Kristy almost couldn't wrap her head around it. But Lance wouldn't even acknowledge that there was an issue. That's what made all of this so maddening. From what she'd read, in most domestic abuse cases, the perpetrator would apologize. But not Lance. Never Lance. He wasn't sorry. He'd never once uttered those words. It was as if all of his punishments were part of some secret marriage clause Kristy had unknowingly signed.

She still had Officer Martin's business card, the sweet kid from that night in the Chili's parking lot. Lance's assault, and his refusal to even discuss what was happening were devastating. But before she pressed charges, she wanted to find out what her options were. She had to protect herself and her family.

Kristy woke up, feeling more determined and focused than ever. She'd called the Conroe Police Department to inquire if Officer Martin was working today, and the woman on the phone told her he'd be in after ten. Now all Kristy had to do was get through the workday and then she'd take the first step toward getting back her life.

Kristy's first order of business was a visit to the Mountain View Unit in Gatesville, which housed death row's few female inmates. It was a three-and-a-half-hour drive, which gave Kristy plenty of time to think. Women on death row generally avoided media attention. Like their male counterparts, they were guilty of unspeakable crimes but the state rarely sentenced them to death. Currently there were only four female inmates on Texas death row. One killed her boyfriend and his mother in a meth-fueled rage, stabbing each of them seventy times. Another helped stalk, rape, and murder two young college girls. The third murdered her husband and his male lover in a fit of jealous rage. Today Kristy was meeting with the fourth woman, Pamela Whitaker, convicted of kidnapping and murdering her own husband and now scheduled to die in two weeks, the first woman executed in Texas in almost twenty-five years.

Pamela hadn't granted a single interview, despite immense public interest surrounding her case. She made headlines in the early eighties when her husband, Roger Whitaker, a respected pediatrician in San Antonio, went missing. A few weeks later, Roger's dismembered remains were found in Dumpsters across the state. Authorities learned that Pamela and Roger's happy marriage was a fraud. Pamela had beaten her husband to death with a baseball bat, cutting his body into pieces in her own garage and scattering those pieces near the Mexican border. Video surveillance captured Pamela disposing of the body and sealing her fate. Still, she refused to take a plea deal. She never even gave a reason, forcing her attorneys to claim temporary insanity. The jury didn't buy it. After all these years, Pamela's execution was imminent.

"I'll do one final interview. That's it," Pamela said from across the glass partition. She was in her late sixties now. Once a beautiful woman who received weekly spa treatments and had a private trainer five days a week, she was now dumpy, her hair gray and stringy, her complexion yellow with splotches of red resulting from chronic rosacea and eczema infections that had gone untreated.

"I can arrange that," Kristy said. "There's a long list of interested parties."

"Whoever gets the most eyeballs, that's who I want," Pamela replied.

"Sure. I'll go through all the requests and you can decide who you prefer."

"I want to do it the day before the execution, and it has to be a prime-time interview."

"I'll do my best to make that happen."

Pamela nodded, glancing over at the guard stationed nearby.

"I killed Richard and I'd do it again," Pamela said flatly.

Kristy shifted in her seat, suddenly very uncomfortable with Pamela's matter-of-fact confession. "I should go," Kristy said, reaching out to place the phone on the cradle.

"Wait! Please don't go. I want to explain. I've never spoken about the murder before but I want to go to my grave with a clear conscience. You know Roger beat on me for so many years, called me all kinds of names that a man shouldn't call his wife. I tried to leave him, but Dr. Roger Whitaker would never let that happen. 'Wouldn't look good,' he'd say, 'for a man of my stature to get divorced. Neighbors might gossip.'

"One day after a particularly bad 'discussion,' I told Roger I was going to go to the police and I was going to tell them everything. I'd show them what he'd done. He just laughed.

" 'I've saved their kids' lives, Pammy. Their flesh and blood. You think they'll care about some pathetic housewife?' "

"But you could have told *someone*," Kristy said, thinking about Officer Martin's card in her pocket. Pamela smiled and shook her head, almost amused by Kristy's naïveté.

"Right. That's what I thought too. So the next time he lost his cool and slammed my head into our countertop, I went to the cops. I made sure to go to an officer I was sure Roger didn't know, but someone must have seen me there, made a phone call. San Antonio is still a small city; everyone knows everyone. In strides Allen Sabrio, one of Roger's oldest friends, the best man at our wedding and a captain in the department. He sat right across from me, patting me on the leg like I was some kind of German shepherd he could pat into submission. 'Pam, you're being dramatic. All couples fight.' I even tried to show him the bruises, but he wouldn't have it. 'Roger is a good man. Whatever happened, you two can work through it. Go home and talk it out.' "

Pamela scoffed. Kristy wanted to tell her to stop talking, but she'd never heard any of this. Pamela was portrayed as a liar, a black widow. Her all-American good looks had helped her nab a successful doctor, and then the media and the prosecution used that against her.

"Let me tell you, Roger was never the talking type. He made me suffer that night. So I woke up the next morning and said to hell with it. I had a few grand in cash saved up and the name and phone number of an old sorority sister in Arizona I planned to call when we got there. The boys were little. I was sure we could start over. I'd left them at a friend's house while I packed, taking only what was needed. In five years of marriage, Roger never came home early until that day. His goddamn spidey sense telling him I might actually escape. That afternoon, he came into the bedroom, going at me with the name-calling and the pushing and the threats. He grabbed the brass candleholder we'd gotten for our wedding and came at me with it. He would've killed me. I just beat him to it."

She laughed bitterly. "If I'd actually planned it, you think I'd have been so sloppy? But in the court's eyes, Roger mattered more because he was a doctor and a man. And me? What the hell did I do? I was too attractive, too opinionated. But I don't regret it, killing him. I never have. Roger was a fucking lunatic. In the end, it was the only choice."

Kristy couldn't meet Pamela's gaze, worried she might see a piece of herself reflected back. Instead, she thanked Pamela for her time and promised to follow up on the interviews, and then she hurried outside of the prison. Kristy sat in her truck in the parking lot, clutching the steering wheel, willing herself to start the car and drive to the police station. No evidence. No proof. Kristy's word against Lance's. He was so charming, so good at lying, no one would believe her, and his retaliation for her speaking out would be merciless. Despite this morning's bravado, Kristy's courage failed her. She crumpled up Officer Martin's business card and tossed it out the window, the wind carrying it as she drove away.

Two weeks later, Pamela's one-on-one sit-down with Barbara Walters aired. Barbara came out of retirement to do this interview, a ratings extravaganza in which Pamela told the exact same story she'd recounted to Kristy. The following day, Pamela was escorted to the death chamber and strapped to the gurney. Her sons, Harrison and Micah, stood beside Kristy. Two giant men in their late thirties, they began weeping the minute they saw their mother. They'd never wavered in their support, never condemned what she did. On the Barbara Walters interview, Pamela's oldest son said he'd told the police about their father's abuse but they wouldn't listen. "They just didn't care," Micah kept saying. He said his mother refused to tell the police about it. "She spent her entire marriage as a victim. She didn't want to be one in the eyes of the world."

As the minutes ticked down, Pamela looked up at the glass windows and said, "I love you boys more than you will ever know." The warden gave the signal and the poison was injected into Pamela's IV. She closed her eyes, and there was nothing but silence. Four minutes and eleven seconds later, she was gone.

Pamela's death haunted Kristy for days. She understood what it was like to be with someone everyone else revered. It wasn't just Pops and Ryan, worshiping at the altar of Lance. It was the newlyweds he helped buy a home, the city official who thanked Lance for charming an inspector to grease the wheels on a housing permit. It was Mac's constant texts, asking how Lance was doing and when they could all go out.

Before long, Kristy's only bright spot was her letters from Clifton and their subsequent visits. It was strange and she recognized that, but when she was with Clifton, there was some semblance of normalcy even though both their circumstances were far from normal. He'd taken her up on her offer, writing her letters each week. He'd share a look inside his daily life and routine, discussing the food, how it was never hot and always gray. Fresh fruits and vegetables were expensive in mass quantities so inmates rarely, if ever, received those. Clifton's dreams were haunted by endless fields of fresh apples that he could pick straight from the trees.

She'd ask Clifton questions about where he grew up—an old family farm in Bastrop—and he'd share stories. He'd inquired several times about Kristy's well-being.

"Tell me, ma'am, are you sure you're okay?"

She'd smile and deflect. "My sparkle is still here, just needs to be shined up a bit," she'd say before changing the subject. Those visits were some of her favorite minutes of the week, a time when she escaped from Lance and the overwhelming uncertainty she experienced when she was with him.

But today, as she was seated across from Clifton, the truth came tumbling out.

"Ms. Tucker, can I ask you a personal question?"

Kristy's response should have been no. It was inappropriate. Prison guidelines strictly forbade it, but she'd already been skirting the rules, scheduling all of Clifton's interviews first or last so she'd have more time to speak with him. She wasn't going to stop now.

"Okay," she said hesitantly.

"It's none of my business, but how long has it been happening?" Clifton asked softly. He motioned toward her forehead. Stunned, Kristy reached up, touching the spot on her skull, the spot she'd meticulously covered with concealer. Lance's abuse had, from the start, been calculated and carefully orchestrated and *never* visible to the public. Kristy's upper body was a popular target, her legs, her back. But this morning, Kristy was careless and so was Lance.

"What's crawled up your butt?" Lance had asked this morning while she was getting dressed.

"Nothing," Kristy said. That wasn't true. She hadn't slept in months; she couldn't eat. Lance's constant aggression was weighing her down.

"Well, whatever's wrong, get that damn hangdog look off your face."

"Lance, I'm—" she said, but his hand flew at her. He grabbed at her hair, pulling it to him to make his point, and his wedding ring snagged her right above the left eyebrow.

"I don't want my wife sulking around here all the time. It's not attractive," he said, before he headed downstairs.

Kristy spent the morning practicing half a dozen excuses while she applied her makeup. She waited for Pops and Ryan to ask what happened, but they barely acknowledged her, too busy caught up in Lance's stories. Some days Kristy worried that she might just disappear, vanish into thin air, and no one would ever notice.

Once Kristy arrived at Polunsky, she held her breath, wondering if Bruce or the warden might comment, but no one said a word. How was it possible that Clifton had figured it out?

"It's nothing. Had a bit of an accident getting out of the shower this morning," Kristy covered, her voice high-pitched and shaky. Even she didn't believe the lie coming out of her mouth.

"It was jewelry of some kind, wasn't it? A ring, I'm guessing. It just came to me today when you were touching your forehead. I saw you wincing too. Your ribs are bruised, aren't they? That's why you lost your sparkle. Someone's been beating on you. Probably for a while now."

Kristy looked around to make sure no one was listening. Some of the cubicles had recording capabilities, but the one in this booth hadn't worked in years.

"I don't know what you're talking about," she said again. Clifton's gaze seemed to bore right into her.

"Listen, I'm no one in this place. Less than no one, some might say. But I know what it's like to get beat on by someone you love. I watched my daddy whale on my mama for years. When I got older, I took the brunt of it, Daddy's fists pummeling me for looking at him funny or chewing too loudly or sometimes for existing. You were there for me when I was at my lowest, and I swear to you, Ms. Tucker, I'm here for you. Whatever is going on, you're not alone."

She'd said those same words to Clifton all those months ago. Kristy thought about ignoring Clifton, hanging up the phone and walking away. But she was drowning under the weight of this secret, the silence slowly killing her. It's the only reason,

Kristy rationalized, why she would tell this convicted killer her deepest, darkest secret.

"It's . . . It's my husband, Lance. He hurts me. The things he does . . . most of them no one can see. But the bruises and bumps are all there. It's not just the pain; it's that I don't know when he's going to do it again. I don't know why he's doing it in the first place. I never know . . ."

Kristy's expression remained passive. She'd mastered that art, but she could hear the desperation, the pleading in her own voice. She continued on, never speaking above a strained whisper.

"My son . . . he's my entire world. And my father . . . he's sick. And they can't see who Lance is. They don't know. He's convinced them, he's convinced everyone, that he's kind and decent and good but he's not . . . I'm not sure what he is. I'm trying to keep it together, I'm trying to tell myself that it's all going to be okay, but I'm . . . God, I'm so . . ."

"You're afraid."

Kristy nodded. "I just . . . I've always had all the answers. I've always been smart and done things right. And I loved . . . I mean I love him, but now . . . I just . . . I don't know what to do."

Clifton shifted in his seat, weighing his words carefully.

"I don't either," he said. "But if you run out of options, there are people in here who might."

CHAPTER THIRTEEN

It took a moment for Clifton's words to register. She stared back at him in disbelief, trying to rationalize what he had just said. He saw her stricken expression, his entire demeanor shifting, eyes widening. He leaned forward, shaking his head emphatically.

"Ms. Tucker, I'm sorry. I don't know how to do anything like that. I swear to God, I don't, but there are guys in here who could. Or they know people."

"You mean hiring someone? Is that what you're saying?" Kristy whispered, even though the voice inside her head was shouting, *Stop it, Kristy. Stop asking questions you don't want the answers to!* She thought about that knife when she was cutting Ryan's birthday cake, remembered the weight of it in her hand. But that was just a flicker in her brain, one of those terrible thoughts you have, like laughing at a funeral or wondering what might happen if you took your foot off the brake at a stoplight when a passerby was crossing. A glitch in the brain, the devil on your shoulder telling you to do something terrible.

"I'm just saying that if I could go back in time, I'd do anything to protect my family. No matter what the consequences," Clifton explained.

"It'll get better. He'll get better," Kristy said, trying to convince herself as well as Clifton.

"In my experience, that's not true. My daddy whaled on my mama for years, beat on all us kids. And I know it's gonna sound like a load of shit, but if you looked at her situation, she wasn't any better off than I am in here. Always looking over her shoulder, anticipating every move, anticipating every word, never knowing what he was gonna say or do. It eats away at you. It destroys you. When a man does that to a woman, he steals her freedom. She can never be free."

Every day Kristy heard people discussing freedom. Inmates boasting about getting their release dates and how they were gonna make it count. Reporters quizzing her about an inmate's parole date, and whether they were still a potential threat. Day in and day out, people behind these walls were fighting for freedom, fighting for their dignity, fighting to be heard. Kristy, though, had stopped fighting. She had to take control, but not the way Clifton was suggesting. Kristy couldn't do that.

"I appreciate your concern, but I can handle this," she said.

"Sure thing, Ms. Tucker. I'm so sorry. I don't know what came over me. You just seemed so lost..." Clifton trailed off. "If you have to report me, I understand."

That wasn't going to happen. What would she possibly tell the warden? "So...I was discussing my personal life with Clifton Harris and we were talking about my abusive husband and he suggested that I have him killed"? No. Kristy wouldn't be mentioning this to anyone.

"It's okay, Clifton. I won't say anything, but I have to go now."

"Wait, Ms. Tucker, please!"

Kristy hung up the phone and didn't look back. She kept it together and said her good-byes to the guards and the warden, all the while trying to silence the ticker tape in her brain, the one that kept repeating Clifton's question, or telling her the recording device in that room had been fixed and someone would soon find out her deepest, darkest secret. Kristy got into her truck and drove down the highway, speeding past the prison and the guards, trying to erase the low drumbeat of Clifton's idea. Tears began to fall. Her hands were trembling so badly she had to pull over. She grabbed a pack of matches from the console and carefully lit the Marlboro Light she'd bummed off the gate guard. Since she'd learned about Lance's strict views on smoking, Kristy had thrown away her spare pack of cigarettes. God forbid Lance found them and confronted her. She would have to stop at 7-Eleven on the way home to buy gum and douse herself with perfume to cover the scent, but the nicotine hit eased her frayed nerves. She replayed her conversation with Clifton over and over. Her mind went back to that night in the parking lot, the word "murderer" scrawled across her pickup as if it was some kind of future warning. She didn't know what to think now. Someone had called Kristy a murderer, and now Clifton was putting all these things into her head. All this time she'd convinced herself he might actually be innocent, and then he had to go and say something like that. What if he had killed his children and this was some kind of twisted manipulation? Kristy heard plenty of stories about inmates and guards starting relationships. Just last year a guard in the Lockhart Facility impregnated a female inmate and orchestrated an elaborate plan to bust her out of prison. Unfortunately for them, the woman's bunkmate ratted them out. The guard got five years, lost his home, his wife, his kids. Kristy had already fallen for one con artist. No way was she falling for another. She took one final drag of her cigarette and stubbed it out, knowing she had to return home and face Lance. She couldn't comprehend hurting anyone, but Clifton's words gnawed at her, the idea that she would have to continue living as Lance's prisoner. *You can never be free. You can never be free. You can never be free.*

Dear Ms. Tucker,

There's a good chance you're not even reading this letter. Or maybe you are reading it and thinking the DA was right. Clifton Harris is a blight on humanity, a man beyond redemption. But you're wrong. They are wrong. I keep running over our conversation, and thinking how awful I must have sounded. I'm not a perfect man but I am not a murderer. Looking back, it's easy to see why they were able to paint me as one. Everything came so easily: school, sports, girls. I had plenty of charm to go around and I relied on that. It made me lazy, entitled. I wanted to be a football player but I didn't train hard enough. Wound up working in an office selling insurance. God, I hated that job. It was soul sucking on its best day. I phoned it in, barely tolerant of my coworkers. I scammed when I could and took credit for my coworkers' success. My failures as a husband are well-known. I lied to Janice. I cheated on her. I broke all our vows. Anyone who's followed my case already knows all of that. I was a shitty employee and a shitty husband, but I loved my children. Jesus, how anyone could think I'd do something so terrible is, well, it's just not possible. But then I go and say something stupid, and now I've got you thinking everyone is right about me. But they're not. I swear to you, Ms. Tucker. Now all I can do is ask for your forgiveness. I can't begin to tell you how much I look forward to your visits. Some weeks they're all I have to look forward to.

Sincerely,

Clifton

Leabharlanna Poiblí Chathair Bhaile Átha Cliath

Dublin City Public Libraries

CHAPTER FOURTEEN

The battle in Kristy's head continued for an entire week.

He's playing you.

He's just trying to help.

You're falling for another con artist. Don't buy into it.

She considered assigning Carmen to oversee media day until Clifton's execution came up in a few months, even drafted the e-mail asking Carmen if that was a responsibility she wanted to assume. In the end she couldn't do it. Clifton wasn't the only one who relied on those visits. As sad as it was, Clifton was her only friend, the one person she could talk to about Lance and the trouble she was in. When she returned to Polunsky the following Wednesday, she picked up the phone. Clifton's tired eyes stared back at her, his body rigid, waiting to see what she might say.

"We're good, Clifton. I need you to know that we're good."

His shoulders sagged with relief; his eyes brightened.

"I'm glad to hear that, ma'am. I spent a lot of sleepless nights worrying about you."

"I wasn't going to tell anyone," Kristy said softly, knowing that she had already violated half a dozen rules by keeping Clifton's offer a secret.

"Hell, I didn't care about that. I mean, what else could they do to me? They can't kill me twice. I just didn't want you getting yourself into any trouble."

Kristy let out a bitter laugh.

"I'm not sure things can get any worse," Kristy said.

Clifton sighed, shifted the phone in his hand.

"Can I be real with you, Ms. Tucker?" he asked.

"Please," she said.

"Things could get a whole lot worse. You think I thought I'd end up behind these bars when I met Janice? Hell no. When I saw her on the quad freshman year, I nearly lost it. Damn, she was the prettiest girl at Texas Tech. Even better, she had a wicked sense of humor and didn't give a shit about that racial garbage people were spewing. She'd hold my hand, walk into any bar and restaurant, didn't care about the staring and the gossip. Falling in love with her was the easiest thing I ever did."

Kristy thought about those first few months with Lance. Clifton continued on.

"Truth is, we didn't ever fit together, not the way we should. We were always fighting and fussing over something. I ignored all of that because I wanted to be part of her world and the life she represented. She was so different from me. The way she carried herself, always in these cute colorful sundresses, her hair styled just right, not a hair out of place.

"I'd grown up poor as shit, but Janice had everything. Parents who still liked each other after twenty-five years of marriage. Two-story house with a pool. She got a Mustang for her sixteenth birthday, a trip to Rome for her eighteenth. She was the lead in every high school play, won awards in the state play competition. Janice used to joke about going to Hollywood. I'd say, 'Tell me when we leave. I'd look hella good on the big screen.' We'd laugh, the two of us reciting lines from *Titanic* or *Dirty Dancing*. 'Don't let go,' or 'Nobody puts Baby in a corner.' It was just talk. She was a small-town girl at heart and I was a country boy. We started hooking up our freshman year, seriously dating sophomore, and by senior year, I'd proposed. She wanted a simple life and I was prepared to give that to her."

Clifton paused. "I don't want to bore you," Clifton said. "But you need to understand something."

"Go on," Kristy replied, hanging on Clifton's every word.

"We tried to get pregnant, and let me tell you that shit is hard work. Took us six years. We lost the first baby after ten weeks. They called it a silent abortion. Pretty awful, isn't it? Like it's something you wanted instead of something that happened. I went to bed thinking I was gonna be a dad and I woke up to a crashing sound. Found Janice passed out on the bathroom floor, hemorrhaging so bad I thought I was gonna lose her. It scared the living shit out of me. I called an ambulance and they rushed her into surgery. Less than twenty-four hours later and our baby was gone. It wasn't actually a baby yet, the doctor said. Died too early to be real. Janice didn't agree. All those changes in her body were so damn real. She became obsessed with having a kid. There were four more miscarriages. No one talked about those at my trial. Those were my kids too, and I mourned every one of them. Janice pretended like they hadn't happened.

"We didn't have Rosie until we were thirty. Michael came along three years later. Things weren't good, but you know that from the trial. The other women didn't matter. They didn't. Sometimes I just wanted to escape all the pressure, the thermometers and ovulation kits and 'Should we do it standing up or on our back or on our side or in the shower?' I just wanted to have sex for fun once in a while.

"And you know, you've got a kid, those first few years are tough. Babies take as much as they give. We'd fall into bed, two exhausted strangers, but even when Janice and I were struggling to get along, we never stopped marveling at our babies. And then they were gone." Clifton coughed, tried to stifle his emotions. "And so was Janice. I don't know who that woman is now, the one glaring at me in the courtroom, the one on TV with all of her stories about my temper. Sometimes at night I wonder about our life together. Was any of it real? Did I imagine the good times? I don't know. But you know what I realize now?" Clifton asked, coming up for air.

"No. What is it?"

"If I'd known what she was capable of doing to Rosie and Mikey, to me, if I had known the truth, I would've killed the bitch myself."

Kristy's stomach churned. She leaned back in her seat, rocked by what he was saying.

"Janice did it? Your wife? She wouldn't. It's not possible. No mother would ever—" Clifton interrupted her, his voice rising.

"Would they? I don't know. I ignored all the signs, Janice's threats, her resentment over how much I doted on them. Did you know she was hospitalized in high school for threatening to slit a classmate's throat? Her parents had those records sealed, but I got them. One of her docs even wrote that she had an unhealthy obsession with fire."

"But she had an alibi, right? Wasn't she out of town when it happened?" Kristy asked.

"She was at a teachers' conference in Austin. Less than thirty minutes each way. No one checked video cameras or confirmed that she didn't leave her room. They didn't even check," Clifton said. "And why would they? They already had their killer."

"She killed her own kids," Kristy said softly. Before she met Lance, this would have been unspeakable. Kristy thought differently now. Evil was lurking everywhere. Kristy held her hand up over her mouth, willing herself not to get sick. The thought of anyone intentionally killing Ryan, of tossing gasoline and a match and letting him burn, was simply unspeakable.

"I've had over ten years to do research and go through the files. Numerous attorneys have tried to disprove the forensic science, to discredit the experts, all of them trying to prove that I was not the person who set that fire and burned my children alive. And yet no one ever looked into Janice. Why would they? But I'm telling you now there are certain kinds of people out there that will do whatever they want, people that don't give a shit about the consequences. Maybe your husband isn't like that. My ex-wife is and she's out there, living the life, in her million-dollar home, with her new baby girls. So when you say to yourself that it can't get worse, that everything is gonna be okay, I want you to think about me. I'm not saying you have to do nothing crazy, Ms. Tucker. I'm just saying be careful."

By the time Kristy finished talking with Clifton, three reporters were waiting to speak to him and two other inmates on her list. She finished overseeing everything and returned to the Walls and spent the day reworking press releases for an upcoming execution.

As soon as Kristy had a free moment, she fell down the Google rabbit hole. Dozens and dozens of articles about the fire, Clifton's subsequent arrest. In a *USA Today* piece, she stumbled upon Clifton's wedding photo, Janice in her tulle princess-cut wedding dress, eyes twinkling, a pure moment of joy. She remembered that same look on her face in those damn photos. How did love wind up so perverted? She wanted to understand. It wasn't difficult to obtain Janice's information. Victim services had her address and phone number. Kristy couldn't stop looking at articles about Janice. She seemed to love the camera, granting interviews to anyone who asked, taking photos, sharing her painful story "to show others there is life after loss," she always said.

Janice had married a Houston oil tycoon a year after Clifton's sentencing. They'd settled down in the Woodlands and had three children, all girls, through a surrogate. Bearing her own children was simply too painful, she'd told a *People* magazine reporter.

Kristy had spent hours reading everything on Clifton's

case. She didn't know what came over her but she had to get out of this drab fluorescent room.

"Hey, Carmen, can you cover for me if Gus comes looking?"

"Sure, lady. Is everything okay?" Carmen asked.

"Think I've got a migraine coming on," Kristy lied.

That first time Kristy drove to Grogan's Point, the tony neighborhood where Janice and her new husband lived, she just wanted to see what it looked like, thought she might catch a glimpse of Janice. She didn't see her that first day, but on nights when she could leave early without Lance knowing or when Carmen agreed to cover an execution, Kristy would drive through the neighborhood, looking through the windows of the million-dollar homes, wondering how many other people were living secret lives. Who were the abusers and who were the abused? How many magazine-worthy wedding photos had been framed and then removed, packed away in boxes?

Kristy would park at the end of the cul-de-sac and wait. On a few occasions, she caught a glimpse of Janice. Now in her late forties, Janice kept herself lean and toned. Her honey-blond highlights were expertly done, hair perfectly blown out, clothing tailored to her in muted soft pastels, effortless and restrained. She was every inch a rich man's wife. Janice's daughters were eleven months, three, and five. She had a new life, appeared to be a devoted mother, smiling and making jokes as she wrangled her daughters from their car seat constraints. From what Kristy read, and the Internet told all, Janice's new husband, William Conard, was pushing sixty, a jovial man with a hard-earned beer gut. By all appearances, they were loving parents, making a terrible tragedy into something beautiful. But no matter how much Kristy learned about Janice, the question remained—what sort of woman would kill her children, frame the husband, *then* go off and start a new life, a new family? And stay in the same town where the tragedy took place! If you believed Clifton, Janice was a sociopath who would do whatever it took to get revenge.

Kristy couldn't explain her obsession with Clifton and Janice. Sometimes thinking about their troubles made Kristy feel less alone, offered a distraction from her own life. After two weeks, Kristy had memorized Janice's schedule. Perhaps if she looked closer, the truth would become clear.

At home, Lance continued his domination. A knee to the stomach after Lance asked Kristy why she was late paying Ryan's car insurance bill, a slam against the wall because she had insulted him by adding salt to his "perfectly seasoned steak." When she thought about it, she had nothing to show the authorities but a few bruises and bumps, no injuries that would ensure Lance would be locked up for more than a night or two.

She thought about recording Lance, but he constantly monitored her phone. "Darlin', just wanted to make sure you have enough battery," he would say, then spend five minutes reading all her texts and e-mails.

She had no idea what to do about Lance, but her obsession with Janice continued. Every day now, she found herself making a detour, driving by Janice's house. It was ridiculous. What was Janice going to do? Walk out and say, "I did it!

Clifton is innocent"? But Kristy couldn't stop herself. Sometimes she'd leave work early and just stare into the windows
of the mansions, wondering how you could ever know the
truth about anyone.

One evening, Kristy lingered a little too long, expecting Janice and her daughters to return from gymnastics. She
didn't even realize how late it was until her phone beeped—a
text from Lance.

I just got home. No food. Where are you?

Shit. Kristy hadn't planned to stay this long. Now traffic
was going to be bumper-to-bumper and if she stopped to
pick up groceries, she would be even later. She headed back
home, the dread growing with each passing mile. Kristy tried
to think of an appropriate excuse to tell Lance, an excuse that
might engender sympathy instead of outrage.

An inmate tried to escape. That's what she would tell him,
hoping his anger would dissipate. Though there was always
the risk that he might call Gus and demand to know all the
details. He might even threaten to sue the state for putting
his wife in danger. Kristy's mind was still spinning when she
pulled into the driveway and hurried inside.

Seated at the kitchen table, his laptop propped open, a beer
in his hand, Lance glared over at Kristy, a charged atmosphere
in the air.

"Where's Ryan?" Kristy asked, hoping he would come
bounding up the stairs, that he might serve as a buffer to
defuse Lance's temper.

"He's studying at Ella's," Lance said flatly.

"And Pops?" she asked, a slight tremor in her voice.

"He had a headache, so I gave him a sleeping tablet," Lance said.

Shit. Shit. Shit.

"Where have you been?" Lance asked. Kristy calmly set her purse down on the counter, keeping her voice casual and light, hurrying over to give him a kiss, adjusting her excuse on the fly.

"There was an issue with one of the inmates in the mental health ward. He filed a complaint against some guards and a bunch of reporters were calling," Kristy said, thinking on her feet.

"That goddamn job," he said. Lance only complained about Kristy's job when he was upset. When he wasn't, he told her she should keep climbing the ladder. "Lots of good benefits working for the state," he'd say. But tonight her job had taken too much of Kristy's attention and Lance couldn't stand that.

"So you didn't think about me or Pops, or the fact that there's no goddamn food in this house?"

"I did. I planned to go to the store and then I got stuck at work, but I'll whip you up something. Just give me five minutes," Kristy pleaded, turning toward the fridge. If she could appease him, just for tonight, tomorrow she'd pull back the curtain and reveal the monster behind it. She had gone too far and was losing herself. It wasn't just her obsession with Janice. It was hearing herself and not recognizing her own voice. She'd wait until Lance left for work and then she would sit Pops and Ryan down and tell them everything. They'd come up with a plan together. But she was done. Kristy couldn't live like this. Not anymore. All she had to do was get through tonight.

Lance held on to Kristy's hands. He began to squeeze, harder and harder. Kristy cried out, her knees buckling from the pressure point.

"You think I'm a joke? Is that what this is?"

"No, Lance. Of course not."

"You do. You think I'm a fucking joke. I see how you're looking at me."

Even though Ryan was gone and Pops was likely fast asleep, Kristy looked toward the back of the house. "Never drop your gaze," Lance once said. What an amateur move.

She turned just in time to see Lance's fist coming toward her, a pummeling blow that landed on the side of her skull and sent her staggering backward.

Ears ringing, vision blurred, Kristy began to run but Lance stopped her, tugging on Kristy's ponytail and dragging her through the kitchen. Panic set in. Lance was dragging her to the front door. She'd read enough about assaults and murders to know that once a perpetrator moved locations, especially if they were isolated, your chances of survival diminished.

"Lance, please, don't do this. Let's talk…"

"Don't tell me what to fucking do."

He shoved her out the front door. Kristy fell, then scrambled to her feet, still woozy, adrenaline pumping, blood roaring in her head. There were no homes, no neighbors for miles, no one to see their ugly domestic melodrama unfolding. Lance dragged Kristy toward her pickup and shoved her into the cab. He climbed inside, slamming the door closed, and reached across the passenger's side to lock it.

"You move a muscle and you're dead," he growled.

He fired up the truck and made his way down the long, winding back roads. Those same roads that once seemed romantic were now terrifying, their isolation ensuring no one would ever hear her screams.

Should she grab the door handle and take her chances? What if she threw herself from the speeding truck? How badly would she be injured? Would she survive the fall only to have Lance run her down? God, the last thing she wanted was Pops and Ryan identifying her body. No. She had to keep fighting.

"Lance, you're not thinking. If you'd just stop and we can talk," she said, but he wasn't listening, his mouth set in an angry, unrepentant scowl. Kristy's ears were ringing, making it impossible to focus on where they were going. She lost track of where they were, the truck making endless turns down pitch-black back roads, gravel spinning and crunching under the wheels. She lost consciousness for a while, jolting awake when she heard Lance throw the truck into park.

She couldn't see the road, her view obscured by a dense cluster of sinister-looking pine trees. Lance opened the truck door and wrenched her arm, practically slinging her out of the truck, his fingers digging into her collarbone. Kristy tried to kick, scratch, and claw at him, but Lance deftly avoided each of her attempted attacks.

Hyperventilating, she tried to think of the instructions she'd heard in the safety courses she'd been required to take, ways to disarm your opponent, words to reach him. She opened her mouth to speak just as Lance kicked her, his steel-toed Tony Lama cowboy boot pummeling her abdomen. Kristy groaned, two more kicks coming in quick succession.

"If you really love me, you'll stop," Kristy said, her body covered in pine needles and dirt, the blood and tears mingling. Lance knelt down, stroking her hair.

"This isn't what I wanted, Kristy. This isn't the way it should be. I just want us to be happy. Why do you make that so impossible? Ryan is a good kid. Pops doesn't cause trouble. But you...you're always making things hard for us."

"I'm not, Lance. What have I ever done but try to make you happy?" she asked, every word an effort.

Lance never answered, blinking over and over again, that blank stare signaling their conversation was over. Her mind raced through all the judo moves she'd studied. *Ate waza* or *atemi waza*, all aimed at targeting vital points on an opponent. These techniques were generally forbidden, deemed potentially fatal by those who practiced this type of martial arts. She couldn't say which move exactly Lance used. All she saw was his hand coming toward her with lightning-fast speed. Kristy's scream caught in her throat and then there was nothing but blackness.

CHAPTER FIFTEEN

Blood. That's the first thing Kristy smelled when she came to, the same metallic, bitter smell that she couldn't escape for days after she discovered Clifton lying on the prison floor. She swallowed hard. Gagging, Kristy coughed, the thick red liquid staining her shirt. That was good, she told herself. She wasn't dead. Not yet anyway. Kristy blinked furiously, trying to orient herself, searching in the pitch black for Lance, her entire body aching. Was he still here, lurking in the shadows? Had he left or had he stuck around, thinking up more ways to humiliate and punish her before he killed her?

"Shh, darlin', you're okay. I've got you. You're gonna be all right."

Kristy heard Lance's slow, soothing drawl and froze. Her eyes focused in the dark. She wasn't on the ground anymore. She was back in the passenger's seat of her pickup, except now the front end was crumpled, smoke pouring from the radiator. He'd driven it to a different location, that much she could decipher, but Kristy had no clue where they were. She shifted her body to get a better look at her injuries, trying to assess what was going on. Lance pulled her in close, arms gently caressing her.

"I'm sorry I had to do this, darlin'. But I need you to listen," Lance said.

"I'm listening, Lance," Kristy whispered. "I've *been* listening."

Kristy tried to sit up but her entire body spasmed, white-hot pain shooting through her abdomen. Lance rocked her, as if she were a baby, the same way she'd once rocked Ryan.

"Shh...this is your time to listen. I want things to be good with us, Kris. Like they were those first few months."

"I wanted that, Lance. I did."

"You're talking like it's past tense."

"I can't do this anymore," she said. "I can't live like this. I won't do this anymore," she said, almost to herself. Lance had to know there was no future for them. Not after this.

His entire body went rigid, his contrite expression turned blank. He nodded his head over and over again, like a businessman listening to the details of a hostile takeover. With lightning-quick reflexes, Lance gripped Kristy's neck, squeezing her trachea. A chokehold. Kristy knew she would lose consciousness again if Lance pressed just a little harder.

"It would be interesting, wouldn't it, if Ryan just disappeared one day. Happens all the time. They'd say he was a troubled kid. Got suspended for fighting. Nearly arrested. And poor Frank, with his failing health, God knows that losing his grandson might be enough to send him over the edge. Maybe one day he just stops breathing."

Kristy's hands clawed at Lance's face. He loosened his grip

ever so slightly and she sucked in air; then he tightened it again.

"Darlin', you need to listen very carefully and rethink your previous statement. We're together now. We said vows. We made promises, and those are promises I don't intend on ever breaking. Not ever. What happens next is simple. I need to know you're paying attention. Are you paying attention? I need to hear you say it."

He released his grasp.

"I'm paying attention," Kristy croaked.

"Good. I'm going to leave here. It should take me twenty minutes to walk back to the house. Wait another ten and call 911. Tell them you were in an accident. I'll do my best to make sure Ryan and Pops are taken care of. If I don't get a call, I can't guarantee what will happen to either of them. Understand?"

She nodded. "Here," Lance said, "I'll set the alarm on your phone. When it goes off, you call."

Tears and snot poured down Kristy's face. Ryan and Pops. He'd threatened the people closest to her in the world. She needed to get to them, to warn them, but Kristy couldn't move, and Lance...he was serious. She had no doubt about that. Lance opened the truck door and scooted out.

"I love you, darlin', and I'll see you soon."

Lance's gaze lingered on Kristy. She could see it in his eyes. In Lance's mind, all of this was her own fault and he...pitied her. Lance placed her cell phone in her hands and slammed the truck door. Her head was aching; even keeping her eyes open was a struggle.

Kristy wanted to defy Lance, but what if she didn't follow orders and it cost Ryan and Pops their lives? Knowing that Lance was waiting for her to call, Kristy pulled herself over to the driver's side, wincing the entire time. Lance had definitely broken her ribs. She looked down at her bloodstained blouse. Her pickup was wrecked beyond repair. Before tonight, she had been scared of Lance. Not anymore. Now she was fucking pissed. No one threatened her family. No one.

If Lance thought this would break her, he was wrong. She wasn't going to sit by and let him destroy everything she cared about. She would go head-to-head with Lance, and let the best man win.

Right now she had to cooperate. She needed medical treatment, needed to make sure that Ryan and Pops were okay. She must have dozed off because the alarm on her cell phone brought her back. She tentatively gripped the phone, and dialed. She would follow Lance's instructions to the letter.

"Nine-one-one. What's your emergency?"

"Hello...hello, can you hear me? I need help."

"Ma'am, it's okay. Take a deep breath and tell me what's wrong."

"I've...I've been in an accident."

"Okay, ma'am. Are you injured?"

"Yes. It's my ribs and my head...my airbag exploded. I'm...I...I need help."

"Okay, do you know where you are?"

Kristy hadn't asked. She had no idea.

"No. I don't."

"Okay, sit tight. We're going to triangulate your cell phone location and we'll be sending out an ambulance. What's your name?"

"It's Kristy. Kristy Dobson."

"Okay, Kristy, hang in there. We're gonna get you some help."

Kristy closed her eyes, listening to the operator offer up standard platitudes.

"Stay on the line . . . You're just fine . . . We're coming."

The operator repeated Kristy's name over and over again. "We have to keep you awake. That's important, Kristy. Okay?"

"Okay. Okay," Kristy repeated back, fighting the wave of exhaustion.

She ran through her options. What might happen if she told the police what Lance had done to her?

My husband is a highly trained martial artist who batters me constantly. He threatened the lives of my son and my father in order to control me. He did this to me. He made it look like an accident.

She tried to imagine the face of the bored redneck cop. He might believe Kristy's story. It was so outlandish, who could possibly make it up? Maybe she'd get a restraining order, a flimsy piece of paper that would do nothing to stop Lance. Or maybe the cop would agree that a firm approach was the only way to keep the "little lady" in line. Kristy wanted to believe in the system but it failed people all the time. Pamela Whitaker. Clifton Harris. Who knew how many others Kristy didn't even know about. Even if Lance were arrested and charged, he'd make bail. Then what? She couldn't keep Pops and Ryan safe 24/7.

No. Kristy had to keep Lance's secret for now. She closed her eyes, thinking about Clifton and his offer. "There are people in here who can help." *There are people in here who can help.* Maybe he'd been right after all. Maybe she needed a monster to fight a monster.

Kristy drifted in and out of consciousness, waking up when she heard the EMT's gentle voice. Only a few years older than Ryan, his face was covered with acne scars, his soft-spoken voice kind and reassuring.

"Ma'am, help is here. You're going to be okay. We'll be transporting you to the hospital, but is there anyone you want us to call?"

Kristy didn't miss a beat.

"My husband. Please call my husband."

CHAPTER SIXTEEN

Lance couldn't have scripted Kristy's trip to the ER any better. After the medics arrived, lights flashing, the young EMT patted Kristy on the shoulder.

Kristy bit back a moan as the EMTs gently lifted her out of the wrecked truck and eased her onto a stretcher, securing her neck on a backboard.

"I know this isn't the most comfortable, ma'am, but we want to make sure you don't have any spinal injuries," the medic said.

"You're a very lucky lady."

She might have laughed if she weren't in such agony.

When Kristy arrived at the Conroe Emergency Room, she recognized the ER physician. Dr. Haunschild had treated Pops during his last COPD episode. Thirty-five with bright green eyes, she greeted Kristy, her manner calm and reassuring despite the frenzy of the packed hospital.

"Looks like you got yourself into a bit of trouble," she said gently.

"Looks that way," Kristy managed to whisper.

"Well, don't worry, Mrs. Tucker," she said. Kristy corrected her.

"It's Dobson. I got married," Kristy said. She didn't even know why she said this, hated that Lance had her so trained, it was her first thought to correct the doctor.

"Congratulations, Mrs. Dobson. Your husband should be here soon. Just rest. We're gonna get you all fixed up."

Dr. Haunschild ordered a CT scan and morphine to help with the pain. Kristy prayed that someone might recognize that her wounds weren't consistent with a car accident. A punch to the face had to look different from injuries inflicted by an exploding airbag, didn't it? And yet no one said a word or seemed to think anything was unusual. They had no reason to doubt Kristy. Why would they?

One of the nurses gently took Kristy's arm and began to hook up an IV, the needle slowly piercing her skin, a trickle of blood forming. Kristy thought about grabbing the woman's arm and whispering the truth—*My husband did this. Please help me.* But all she could hear was Lance's threat ringing in her ears. What if Ryan disappeared? What if Pops stopped breathing? He hadn't actually said the words *I'm going to kill your father and son*, but it was close enough to ensure Kristy's complete and total obedience.

The morphine kicked in, easing the searing pain in Kristy's swollen face and abdomen. Her terror subsided ever so slightly as the cloudy haze of the drug coursed through her body.

"We're going to keep you for a few days, make sure you don't have a concussion or any internal injuries. We'll get you moved to a room shortly," Dr. Haunschild said.

"Thank you," Kristy replied. The doctor gently patted her arm and then hurried out. The nursing staff moved in and out, working to stabilize Kristy's condition. She fought a losing battle to stay awake.

"Where's my wife? I need to see my wife." Lance's booming voice startled her awake, and Kristy's eyes snapped open. Ryan rushed in first, his eyes red as if he'd been crying.

Motherfucker, Kristy thought, hating Lance even more. Lance trailed behind Ryan. He reached Kristy's bedside and leaned down to tenderly kiss her forehead as he brushed her hair from her eyes.

"You had us so worried," Lance said.

Kristy smiled weakly but directed her response to Ryan.

"It's not as bad as it looks," she said.

Ryan wasn't buying it.

"Mom, you look like shit," he said, sniffling.

"Thanks a lot," she said, patting the bed. Ryan gently settled down next to her, his entire body trembling. She took his hands in hers.

"Hey, I'm not going anywhere. I'm right here," Kristy said, hugging Ryan.

"You drive too fast. I've always said that. You've got to be more careful," Ryan said in frustration. He'd picked up that trait from Lance, always blaming others for their own misfortunes. Lance interjected.

"It's terrible that they don't have proper signage or more lights. I'm gonna have to file a complaint with the city," he said. He was so convincing; Kristy could almost believe that she'd simply driven off the road. But she endured every second of his charade, trying in spite of her pain to analyze her options. She could tell Ryan right now what Lance had said to her. *Ryan, you have to stop him. And make sure Pops is okay. You have to*, she'd say, screaming at the staff to call 911. The dirty secret would be out in the open in front of hospital staff.

But even if they believed her, there were so many other things she'd have to tell them. Kristy wasn't even sure where to begin. The first time Lance hit her? The first time he raped her? She wanted to speak but the words weren't coming. Was it the morphine? The injuries? Maybe she did have a concussion. She just needed to breathe and organize her thoughts.

"Sorry, y'all, but we'll be moving Mrs. Dobson to her room and she really needs her rest," the nurse said, adjusting Kristy's IV before bustling out.

Ryan hugged Kristy again. Searing pain coursed through Kristy's body, but she didn't care. She gritted her teeth, wanting to hold on to Ryan forever.

"Don't go, Ry. Please," she begged. She could barely think, but she had to tell him.

Lance cleared his throat. "Ryan, why don't you wait outside and let your mama and I have a minute."

Ryan hesitated.

"She's in good hands, son. Go on," Lance said.

"I love you, Mom," Ryan mumbled.

She tried to form words but nothing came out. Ryan wiped at his eyes and shuffled out of the room, leaving Lance and Kristy alone.

He moved over to Kristy's bedside and caressed her battered

face. Bruises had formed on his hands but no one seemed to notice. It wouldn't matter anyway. He taught martial arts. Of course he had bruises.

"Darlin', we're gonna be right as rain from here on out. I love you more than you can even imagine. That's what you need to remember. And you love me too, isn't that right?"

Kristy nodded, forcing herself to whisper, "Yes, Lance, I love you." He sat there, sizing her up, and then, as if deciding she could be trusted, he gave her one last tender kiss and slipped away. She held her breath, waiting to see if he might return. When he didn't, Kristy finally allowed herself to drift away. When she woke hours later, she was all alone in a new cold, sterile hospital room. She tried to think about what happened next, tried to anticipate her next move, but everything seemed so unclear. The phone rang and Kristy's entire body tensed. She answered, bracing herself for more threats or intimidation from Lance.

"Hello?" Kristy said sleepily.

"Kristy...Kristy girl, is that you?"

She heard Pops's voice, shaky and uneasy.

"It's me, Pops."

"You gave me such a scare. But you're okay? My baby girl is all right?" he asked.

He was crying. Pops was crying. The last time she saw Pops cry was at her mother's funeral, and now she was the cause. She wanted to tell him the truth. *No, Pops, I'm not okay. I haven't been okay for a long time.* But Pops was no longer the fearless man who came running into her bedroom, chasing away imaginary monsters with his Louisville Slugger. Now he was a sick old man who got winded walking to the bathroom. This wasn't Pops's fight. Kristy was on her own.

"It's just a few bumps and bruises. I'll be home soon," Kristy said.

"Good. I'm so glad, Kristy girl. Lance said it wasn't that bad. I wanted to come see you but I'm just really out of breath today. But I had to call. I needed to hear your voice, just to make sure for myself that you were fine. You're fine, right?"

She was so far from fine. Kristy knew if she stayed on the phone any longer, she would come undone.

"I will be, Pops. But these damn medicines are making me pretty sleepy."

"Go on. Get some rest and I'll see you soon."

"I love you."

"I love you too," he said, and she could hear him sobbing as he hung up the phone.

Kristy hung up. She had so many things she had to do, plans she needed to make, but the drugs were simply too powerful, and mercilessly, she drifted off to sleep.

The next morning, Kristy jolted awake, the sun streaming in through the mini-blinds. Every part of her body ached, from her eyelids to her molars to the tips of her toes, but there was a part of Kristy that was grateful Lance had gone so far. All this time she kept expecting him to change, to revert back to the man she fell in love with. But she wasn't sure that man ever existed. As far as Kristy was concerned, Lance had officially declared war.

CHAPTER SEVENTEEN

Kristy's hospital stay gave her plenty of time to think. Whatever she did next, Kristy had to be smart. She had to stay one step ahead of Lance. No more careless trips to Janice's house—she couldn't be distracted, no matter how much she wanted to help Clifton. Kristy wasn't sure exactly what to do, but she needed a plan, which meant she had to stay sharp. In the same way that Lance studied judo, Kristy had to study him. The most difficult part of all this was acting as if everything was normal. While Lance assumed the role of doting husband, Kristy played the part of devoted wife. She complimented the tulips he hand delivered and sang Lance's praises to Dr. Haunschild, who agreed to release Kristy as long as she promised to rest.

"She's in good hands, Doc," Lance assured her.

While they waited for the discharge papers, Kristy motioned for him to join her on the bed. "What I said... about a divorce."

"Kristy." Lance's voice was harsh.

"Let me finish. Please. I'll do whatever it takes to make us work. You tell me what you want me to do and I'll do it," Kristy said. Sometimes she wondered if she missed her calling as an actor. She could have won all the awards for today's performance.

Relief flooded Lance, a boyish smile illuminating his face. He leaned down to kiss her.

"Let's go, darlin'," Lance said. "Pops and Ryan have pulled out the welcome wagon for your homecoming."

The nurse wheeled Kristy out of the hospital, Lance trailing behind, carrying the flowers and balloons that Carmen had sent.

"This is it right here," Lance said, gesturing for the nurse to stop in front of a gleaming cherry-red Ford SUV.

"Do you like it?" Lance asked.

Kristy stared back at him, confused.

"What is this?" she asked.

"Can't exactly drive your old truck. And it was time for new wheels, don't you think?"

Kristy surveyed the glistening new car, the nurse patting her on the arm.

"You've got yourself a keeper. Can't remember the last time my husband bought me anything, much less a new car."

Kristy had dreamt of buying herself a brand-new car. She didn't want this gift, didn't want the reminder every time she got behind the wheel that Lance owned her.

"He spoils me," Kristy said to the nurse. She turned her attention to Lance. "It's amazing," Kristy said. "Thank you." He gently lifted her from the chair and placed her in the passenger's seat.

"I'll drive home today, but after that, this beauty is all yours, darlin'."

They arrived at home and Lance was right. Pops and Ryan had pulled out all the stops. The house was gleaming from top to bottom and they'd cooked up a feast—chicken noodle soup and roast beef sandwiches. For the next five days, Kristy's every need was taken care of, until she felt like she was actually being suffocated. She didn't have a single second to herself with everyone asking her if she was feeling okay. Lance forced her to take the pain pills the doctor had prescribed, keeping her drowsy and unfocused. By the end of the week, Kristy knew she had to get out of this house. Her body was aching but the pain she'd experience walking around the office had to be better than being stuck here under Lance's microscope. But she had to broach the subject of returning to work carefully, or Lance might shut it down altogether. She waited until they were going to bed, Lance stretched out, reading some self-help book.

"Hey, babe, I'm feeling like I'm ready to get back to normal. I'm thinking of going back to work but only if it's okay with you."

Lance cocked his head, considering her question. "Darlin', are you sure? If you need more time, take it. I want you to be well."

Kristy couldn't quite wrap her head around how Lance compartmentalized the things he had done to her. How he was able to convince himself that Kristy's injuries were accidental and not a result of his own making. Only one explanation—she had married a madman.

"I'm ready to get back. But only if you're okay with it," Kristy said.

"As long as you're up for it," Lance responded.

Kristy couldn't wait to escape.

She woke up the following morning bright and early and spackled her face with makeup. It was kind of useless. No amount of concealer and powder could cover the massive swelling and various shades of black, blue, and yellow bruises, but Kristy did her best. The moment she started up her new SUV and drove out of the driveway, she heaved a huge sigh of relief.

Going back to work on a Wednesday meant double the work, since she'd have to coordinate media day and catch up on all the e-mails and phone calls, but Kristy was grateful for the distraction. She arrived at the Walls prepared for Carmen's doting, but it was Gus who surprised her, by showing actual concern for Kristy's well-being.

"Jesus Christ, Tucker, go home. You shouldn't be here," he said, eyeing her bruised face.

"Gus, here's the deal. This is my job. I'm not going home because I have work to do," she said.

Gus blinked in surprise. "Fine. Fine. Do whatever you want," he said, and then stomped off to his office.

"Haven't seen you stand up to Gus before," Carmen said.

Kristy shrugged. "Maybe I should do it more often," she replied. She had to put up with Lance's bullshit. She sure as hell wasn't dealing with Gus's.

She spent the morning going through her e-mails, requests from inmates asking for interviews, reporters wanting quotes for an upcoming story. She made the drive to Polunsky at noon, bracing herself for the onslaught of comments about her battered face.

"Dear God, what happened to you?" they inevitably asked. Kristy's ability to lie came in handy, and she smiled bravely, casually dismissing her brush with death. She was on her way to the media room when she bumped into Mac. He took one look at her battered face and whistled.

"Holy shit, Tucker, when Lance texted me about the accident, he said it wasn't that big of a deal. But he was being polite. You must have done a number on that tree."

"Damn thing had it coming," Kristy joked.

"Seriously, are you okay?"

Kristy nodded, hating that Lance had hijacked Mac as well. He reached out for a hug. Kristy held up a hand.

"Ribs," she said as a warning, and he awkwardly wrapped his arms around her. She wanted to sink into his embrace, allow him to comfort her, but it wasn't fair. She'd already made her job, chosen the flashier model instead of safe and secure. Kristy pulled away first.

"Stupid woman drivers," Mac teased. "You've got to take care of yourself."

"I will. And I hate to hug and run but I'm running late. I'll see you soon," she said.

"I'm gonna hold you to it," Mac called after her.

Kristy arrived at the visitation room at the same time as Mem, a documentary filmmaker from New York. Twenty-something with a youthful appearance and art house sense of style, Mem was eager to meet Clifton but kept darting glances at Kristy's swollen features. She braced herself for the young woman's questions but Mem didn't say a word. Maybe she thought that's just how they did things in Texas: Murder and abuse go hand in hand.

Two guards led Clifton in, the same routine every week. Through the pane of glass, they locked eyes, Clifton scanning Kristy's face, cataloging her bruises. Distraught, he sank down into his seat, no choice but to begin his interview. Kristy moved away and waited. An hour later, she shook hands with Mem, who thanked her for her time.

"I have to ask, did an inmate do that to you?"

Kristy shook her head. "No. It was a car accident," Kristy said.

Mem sighed with relief. "God, I'm just glad to know it was an accident. I can't imagine coming to work and being worried for my safety."

It was almost as terrible as being afraid for your safety in your own home, Kristy wanted to say. Instead she led Mem to the exit, fighting to keep the tears at bay. She said her goodbyes and returned to Clifton, taking a seat across from him.

"Hey, Clifton," she said. "How are you?"

"The more important question, Ms. Tucker, is how are you?"

"I've been better," she said truthfully.

"What the hell happened?"

Out of the corner of her eye, Kristy could see Bruce gazing up at the ceiling, bored out of his mind. She lowered her voice.

"I came home late and he wasn't happy," Kristy said softly. "I was at Janice's. I mean, I've been watching her," Kristy said. God, it sounded so stupid.

Clifton's eyes widened. "I don't...I'm not sure I understand. Why?"

"I don't know. To see...I wanted to know..."

"If I was telling the truth?" he asked.

Kristy looked away, embarrassed by her admission that she wasn't sure of his innocence.

"Were you thinking you might see horns? Maybe a tail?" Clifton asked, an edge to his voice.

"I don't know what I was thinking." She gently rubbed her temples, a low-grade throbbing that never seemed to go away. Clifton softened.

"I appreciate what you're trying to do, Ms. Tucker. But stay away from Janice. It's too dangerous. You've got to look after yourself now."

Kristy lowered her voice again.

"I am. You said there are men in here..."

"No. Forget about all of that. That was a mistake. I told you..."

"I have to do something. My family is all I have. He can't take that away," Kristy said.

"If I could do it all over again, I'd make sure to check all those nagging suspicions I had about Janice. When she said things that didn't add up, about the time missing when she was hospitalized in her teens for threatening a classmate, I'd have pushed harder to find out why. How much do you know about Lance? His friends, business dealings, any family who may come around if something were to happen to him?"

Kristy grimaced. She didn't know anything about Lance's past besides the things he'd told her and Ryan. Things she believed. If she had met him on a blind date or a hookup at a bar, she would have Googled him. That was Dating 101. But Lance was different. Ryan vouched for him. Pops adored him. He had a respectable business, money, good looks. Kristy trusted him at his word. None of those reasons made her feel any less stupid.

"It's okay, Ms. Tucker. Some folks are just too trusting. Even after the fire, I never asked questions, never even suspected that Janice was pointing fingers. Dig deep, Ms. Tucker. Build a case just like them lawyers, and then once you have all your evidence, decide if you're ready to cross that line."

Kristy swallowed hard. There was no way she could kill her husband, no way she could cross that line. There had to be another way. Maybe she could find dirt on Lance, blackmail him to go away. That was a possibility. Exhaust all options. That was the plan. Then she could decide. She saw Bruce eyeing her. She'd stayed too long. She offered up a smile, signaling she was almost done.

"I have to go, Clifton. Thank you."

"Be careful, Ms. Tucker. You're playing a dangerous game with someone who doesn't care about the rules."

"I guess that makes two of us," Kristy said. She would build her case and then she would decide. But if the choice was between Lance and Ryan and Pops, then it was no choice at all.

Ms. Tucker,

I am unsettled and worried, so many thoughts spinning in my head. Words are hard to come by so I'm gonna keep this letter brief. Be safe. Be smart and please know that you're in my prayers.

Your friend,
Clifton

CHAPTER EIGHTEEN

After Kristy's "accident," Lance's daily punishments eased up. He had the upper hand. He didn't need to beat Kristy to control her; he had something even better than blunt force—emotional dominance. If Kristy didn't feel like having sex, if she was too tired to cook dinner, if Lance disliked the intonation in her voice, he'd ask an innocuous question: "Think Ryan's had his brakes inspected?" or "Is it just me, or is Pops wheezing more than usual?"

Kristy heard the subtext in each of those questions. Obey or put the people you love in jeopardy. This was Lance's way of keeping her under his thumb, ensuring her complete and total obedience.

Clifton's advice regarding Lance, about knowing what she was up against, was important. Her first order of business was to do what she should have done in the first place—unravel Lance's past. It wasn't as simple as doing a Google search. Kristy was certain that Lance was monitoring her Internet history. He also checked her phone log, reading every single incoming and outgoing message, quizzing Kristy if he didn't recognize the number.

"No secrets, darlin'," he liked to say, though he kept his phone locked with a passcode. Kristy's work computer was also off-limits. The Texas Department of Criminal Justice monitored all Internet usage. If Kristy had to do something to Lance, if it came to that, she didn't want her search history to reveal any trouble or cast suspicion on her. Libraries were the perfect place to do research. Under intellectual freedom laws, most libraries destroy their search histories daily so they can't be subpoenaed later. They also offered daily guest passes and didn't record their users. The public libraries in Huntsville and Conroe adhered to these laws. Kristy chose the Huntsville Library because it was closer to work and she could slip away at lunch.

She located a computer in a small dusty corner in the back alcove. Kristy's first few searches were common knowledge. Lance's Realtor website and upcoming open house schedule, an article in the *Houston Chronicle* about a multimillion-dollar sale, an ad for Lance's judo classes. Kristy scrolled through a half dozen other listings but there was no smoking gun. Lance appeared exactly as he presented himself.

She leaned back in her seat, thinking. People started over all the time. But it wasn't easy to change your name. She knew Lance was his middle name, but he hated his first name. His mother always called him Wayne, and when she left, he said he stopped using it. Kristy cleared the browser and typed *Wayne Lance Dobson*, and just like that, an entirely different picture appeared. His spotty financial history, a bankruptcy, several bad reviews from a disgruntled business partner in Shreveport. She scrolled through, page after page, until she came across page eight of her Google search. She gasped. There in the *San Antonio Express-News* was a full-page spread, proudly announcing the wedding of one Wayne Lance Dobson.

"I just haven't found the right woman," Lance had whispered five months into their courtship, caressing Kristy's naked back. The two of them had lain intertwined in his bed in the condo overlooking the city, the promise lingering that Kristy might be the one.

She couldn't take her eyes off the full-length color photo of Lance Dobson and his first wife, Hannah Mendoza. She was tan and fit, with jet-black hair, dark eyes, and the well-honed physique of a tennis player; "beautiful" was an understatement. Thirty-seven, the former Miss Louisiana had earned a name for herself in the Lafayette real estate market.

Perhaps that's how Lance and Hannah met. Two single colleagues, rivals, competing to see who could make the next big sale. In every picture Kristy found of Hannah—the tennis tournament where Hannah's women's group took first place, Hannah on the River Walk with who she assumed was her daughter, a young girl about twelve, with the same striking hair and eyes, the two of them volunteering at an animal rescue—Hannah's smile leapt off the page.

With trembling hands, Kristy continued clicking, trying to find out how to contact Hannah. She couldn't imagine what Lance might do if he found out, but she needed to know what had happened to their marriage, why their marriage had ended. Kristy clicked on another page of search results, and that's when she saw Hannah's happy, smiling face. Above it, in bold black letters, was the word *obituary*. Lance's first wife was dead.

CHAPTER NINETEEN

Hannah Mendoza was called home to Jesus on June 16, 2012. Born and raised in Lafayette, Louisiana, Hannah is survived by her husband, Wayne Dobson, her mother, Eloisa Mendoza, her father, Hector Mendoza, her brother, Benji Mendoza, and her daughter, Lisette Mendoza. A natural-born entertainer, Hannah was an actress and a dancer who earned a BFA from Tulane University. She was crowned Miss Lafayette and went on to win the Miss Louisiana Pageant. Most recently Hannah ran a successful real estate business and was active in the Saint Francis church choir. Funeral services will be at Stetson's Mortuary in Lafayette, on Sunday, June 24, 2012.

The walls seemed to close in on her. Kristy's hands were sweating, her heart racing. Hannah Mendoza died four years before Kristy married Lance, but how? Kristy scoured the Internet, desperately searching for a cause of death, but there was nothing. Her lunch hour had come and gone, and she had to get back to the office. The uncertainty consumed her. Did Lance kill Hannah? She raced out of the library and returned to work, her thoughts consumed with all the ways Lance could have ended Hannah's life. Car accident, drowning, poison, a crack to the skull—the terrible possibilities raced through her mind, each one worse than the last.

Over the course of the next few days, Kristy went through the motions—meeting with inmates, briefing reporters on upcoming executions. She cooked dinner, pushed food around her plate, nodded and laughed in all the right places as Pops, Ryan, and Lance chatted. Kristy drank cocktails on the porch swing with Lance, gave in to his sexual advances, all the while desperate to find out what happened to Hannah Mendoza.

She considered phoning the medical examiner, but she wasn't a family member, and using fake press credentials seemed risky. She needed to speak to someone in Hannah's family. They might have answers. One evening, she asked Carmen to cover for her and Kristy ducked out early. This time she drove to the Conroe Library, wanting to keep the library staff from asking too many questions. She selected a computer in the library's alcove and began typing in names listed in Hannah's obituary. On her second try, she got a hit on Hannah's daughter, Lisette Mendoza—a Facebook page. It had limited access, only one profile photo of Lisette, now in her early twenties, with wide green eyes, short dark hair, a carbon copy of her mother.

Kristy's search turned up a small blurb in the *Austin American-Statesman* newspaper listing local arrests.

Scholarship student Lisette Mendoza was arrested for public intoxication. Police picked up Mendoza outside a local bar after patrons complained of harassment.

Lisette Mendoza, a San Antonio native, was booked on charges of driving while intoxicated and resisting arrest.

Kristy understood that losing your mother left an indelible scar on your heart, created a ripple, sent you spinning. Kristy didn't blame Lisette for acting out. That's exactly what she'd done, getting wasted with her friends, hooking up with strangers at a party, getting pregnant at sixteen.

She became obsessed with speaking to Lisette. She couldn't use her cell phone or the office phone, so the next day she took her lunch, drove to Circle K, and bought a pay-as-you-go phone. She drove back to the Conroe Library, created a fake Facebook page, and sent a message to Lisette.

Hi. My name is Ellen Stevens. I've been trying to locate the daughter of Hannah Mendoza. It's regarding a financial settlement. Please contact me at the following number: 361-422-8625.

This was an asshole thing to do, but there was no quicker way to get a response from someone than referencing money. Kristy returned to work, anxiously waiting for the phone to ring.

By the end of the afternoon she still hadn't heard back. She couldn't risk Lance finding the phone, so she hid it in the back of her desk drawer. Kristy spent a sleepless night at

home and when she arrived at the office the following morning, she saw the flashing red light and a message from Lisette
waiting for her.

"Hi, Ellen, I got your message. I'll be available until four
p.m. today. Give me a call on my cell. The number is 361-
822-3749," Lisette said, her voice flat and unemotional.

Kristy waited until Carmen went to lunch. She closed her
office door and dialed Lisette's number. Lisette answered on
the second ring.

"Hello? Is this Ellen?" Lisette said. "You said you wanted
to discuss something regarding my mom?"

Kristy felt like a monster, but she continued on. "I'm actually calling about Wayne Lance Dobson."

The voice on the other end went silent.

"Lisette? Are you still there?"

"Does Wayne know you're calling?"

Kristy could hear the panic in the young woman's voice.

"No. No, he doesn't. He doesn't know anything. I'm...I'm
Lance's wife and I didn't know that he'd been married before.
I just found out and I wanted to ask you a few questions about
your mother...about what happened to your mother."

Kristy imagined Lisette's pained expression, that familiar
ache that never goes away.

"Is this about Wayne's truck?"

"What? What about his truck?"

"Look, if I'd known I'd have the entire damn state looking
for me, I wouldn't have done it."

Kristy was trying to keep up.

"Wait...You vandalized *my* truck," Kristy said.

"I told Wayne I didn't know it was yours and he promised he wouldn't report me. I'm doing well. I'm in this halfway house. I'm sober and trying to get my kid back. I told Wayne that. I promised him I'd stay away from y'all. I'm just trying to get on with my life, okay? So whatever this is about, I don't want any part of it. You hear me? Don't call me again."

"Lisette, wait... Please."

The dial tone hummed in Kristy's ear. She thought about calling back but there was no point. She had to see Lisette. She had to find out why she'd called Lance a murderer. Did she have solid proof that Lance killed Hannah? What if that was what she could use to stop Lance, a smoking gun to show the police? She needed to talk to Lisette in person, needed to get the full story.

Now she had to track down Lisette's address. She made it easy, mentioning that she was living at a halfway house. It took Kristy two hours calling every one in Austin, but she finally located Lisette. It was easy to gain information from the homes; all you had to do was say you were a potential employer and wanted to confirm that the resident, Lisette Mendoza, resided at that address. Kristy found Lisette living at the Lonestar Recovery Center, located in North Austin.

The timing couldn't have been better. Ryan was competing in the state debate tournament in two weeks at the University of Texas. Normally, it would have been impossible to go to Austin without Lance joining her, but he already had plans.

"Darlin', it's deer season and I just got my license. But you should go. Have a good time."

With everyone gone, Kristy needed someone to look after

Pops for the night. She reached out to Mac and asked him if he minded spending the night with Pops. Mac agreed, eager to help.

Saturday dawned, the sky moody and gray. Lance slept silently beside her. Kristy studied his handsome, weathered face, the crow's-feet and laugh lines he wore so well, and her stomach churned. Almost as if he sensed her watching him, Lance stirred. She could feel his arousal pressing into her, and though she dreaded sex with him, she didn't resist. Instead, she kissed him tenderly, her voice low and sexy.

"Babe, we'll have to be quick. I've got to drop Ryan at the bus before I get on the road."

Lance stilled, his arms around her. Kristy braced herself for Lance's retaliation, but he simply smiled, offering Kristy a chaste peck on the lips.

"Go on, darlin'. I'm gonna get a few more minutes of shut-eye. Tell Ryan to kick some ass and I'll call you later."

Kristy murmured the required "I love you," and Lance turned over, effortlessly slipping back to sleep. What went on in Lance's mind when he slept? Maybe his dreams were a celebratory bacchanal in which he toasted the fact that he'd broken another woman completely, or maybe they were the peaceful dreams of a man with no conscience whatsoever.

Kristy showered and dressed in her nicest pair of jeans and a navy silk blouse. Heavy bags hung under her eyes, dark circles that seemed to have appeared overnight. Those women's magazines didn't lie when they said stress ages a person. She looked years older, her face and body ravaged by fear and indecision.

By the time she made it downstairs, Kristy was already

running fifteen minutes late. Ryan sat at the dining table, dressed in his neatly pressed white shirt, his gold tie loosely slung around his neck, his sports coat hanging nearby. She braced herself for a sarcastic comment but he was busily poring over his debate notes. He'd be seventeen in less than seven months, and before long he'd be heading off to college. All she wanted was to see him off to school, to make certain that everything he worked for, everything they dreamt about, came true.

"Sorry I'm late," she said. He looked up from his notes and smiled.

"No worries," he said. "I made you some coffee." He pointed to Kristy's thermos, filled up and ready to go. "This case is a bitch but I think we've got it."

"I don't doubt that. You're going to knock 'em dead today," Kristy said. "You ready?"

"Mama Bear, I was born ready. Got the eye of the tiger right here," Ryan joked. He was hyped up and focused, "tournament mode," he dubbed it. He picked up Kristy's duffel bag without even asking as he headed for the door.

"We're prepared. East Tyler and Houston Prep are tough competitors, but our case is solid. If we don't let nerves get in the way, I think we've got this."

Kristy loved how modest Ryan was, that he didn't feel the need to brag and boast, letting his abilities speak for themselves. Ryan's *aw shucks* nature drove Lance crazy. Over the past two years, she'd heard Lance challenging Ryan to "man up."

"You gotta own your success, Ry. Let people know you're not a punk. That you're someone they should take seriously."

Kristy never chimed in during those conversations—that wasn't allowed—but except for those brief moments at his birthday party, Ryan's humble nature hadn't changed. She prayed it never would.

They headed outside, clouds darkening, air thick with moisture, booming thunder rolling through the sleepy hills. Kristy drove, Ryan in the passenger's seat. For once, his phone was put away.

"You sure you're okay driving to Austin all alone?" Ryan asked.

"In case you've forgotten, I am capable of looking after myself. I did it for years."

Kristy didn't bother putting on her *life is good* smile. She simply didn't have it in her.

"I know that, Mom. I'm just checking. Since the accident you've seemed a little..."

"A little what?"

"I don't know, off, I guess."

Kristy covered.

"Ry, I got a clean bill of health. I'm right as rain."

"You sure?" he asked, his eyes boring into her. Kristy kept her gaze on the road ahead, determined that the cracks wouldn't show.

"You bet," she lied, because that's what she did now.

"I was thinking, instead of riding back on the bus, I could ride home with you. We could grab lunch. It'll be just like the old days, when it was just the two of us."

"I'd love that," Kristy said.

She pulled into the deserted high school parking lot, the

school bus idling at the entrance. Ryan gave her a quick wave. Kristy watched him amble onto the bus, fist-bumping his friends and sinking down into a seat beside Ella. Ryan glanced out the window and caught Kristy's eye. He held up his hand and waved. Kristy swallowed hard, trying to remind herself that he would be all right, but the sense of impending doom had returned, and she didn't think it would ever go away.

Kristy headed out of town, driving past the prison, eyeing the walls and barbed wire, the sharpshooters in the towers with their rifles. For years Kristy drove by this place and only thought about the guilty, locked away where they belonged. But now she wondered how many of the inmates were at one point just like her. Out of options? Desperate? Searching for another solution? Kristy wondered how she'd survive in prison, locked away from everyone and everything she loved. She shook away the thought. She hadn't broken any laws. Not yet anyway.

The car cruised along the highway, Kristy streaking past farmhouses and an endless stretch of gas stations, fast-food restaurants, and big-box stores. According to the woman at the halfway house, visiting hours were from nine a.m. to two p.m.

Kristy made record time and arrived at eight forty-five. She parked outside the split-level home that served as transitional housing for addicts and recently released inmates. Kristy watched the clock, waiting until nine on the dot before climbing out of her car. She was walking up the sidewalk when she saw Lisette open the front door and head down the steps.

Tiny, maybe five foot two, her short dark hair now long,

a fringe of bangs hiding her dark green eyes, her olive complexion flawless, offering the kind of perfection only youth provided. She wore jeans that were a few sizes too big and a T-shirt and cardigan, and she flipped through her phone as she made her way down the driveway. She looked delicate and fragile, like if a heavy wind blew through, she'd be swept away.

"Lisette?" Kristy asked. "Lisette Mendoza?"

Lisette startled, glancing up from her phone, clutching her purse to her. Lisette clearly recognized Kristy. She wondered how long Lisette had watched them. Was it just that night in the parking lot of the restaurant? Or did she see Kristy, Ryan, and Lance driving around, creating some kind of imaginary life, the life she once had with her mother?

"I thought I told you to stay away," Lisette hissed, eyes darting around, that same trapped animal expression that Yoli wore.

"Lance isn't here," Kristy said, refusing to back down. "My son's debate tournament is at UT and Lance is on a hunting trip in Conroe. He doesn't know I'm here. I swear."

"I don't care. Go away," Lisette said, and continued walking.

Kristy had enough of people telling her what to do. She reached out and grabbed Lisette, clutching her arm the same way Lance clutched hers.

"You know who Lance is. Or at least I think you do. I mean, you spray-painted 'murderer' on my goddamn truck. Now you're going to tell me what you know. Do you hear me? I deserve to know who I married." Kristy's voice broke, thick with desperation.

Lisette stared at Kristy, her words triggering something.

"I have a meeting," Lisette said. "AA. It's court ordered," she said, gesturing to her ankle bracelet, which would monitor Lisette's comings and goings. "I can meet you in an hour. There's a coffee shop called Dialog. It's right around the corner."

Kristy didn't argue. There was a chance Lisette could bail, but that was a risk she'd have to take.

Kristy left her car and walked to the coffee shop, all bright white interior decor with splashes of red. A bit assaulting to the senses, like hanging out in a giant Warhol painting, but the place was packed. Kristy ordered a chocolate crème donut and a chai latte and tucked herself into a corner, hoping to remain as discreet as possible. She surveyed the bustling place, longing to be one of these fresh-faced things, devouring the classics while plotting their futures.

Kristy couldn't take her eyes off a purple-haired girl in a crop top and nose ring, laughing sexily as she clung to her tattoo-covered boyfriend, his hands caressing her bare waist. What must it be like to be that carefree? Kristy had never been that girl, but right now that's all she wanted. No. That wasn't true. She wanted so much more than this life had given her. Kristy had brought work to read over but instead she sat staring into space, thinking about how different things might have been if she'd never met Lance. She didn't even realize an hour had passed until she heard Lisette's voice.

"I'm here. What do you want?"

"I want to know about your mom and Lance...Wayne. That's all."

Lisette did a quick scan of the room, and then she sank into the chair across from Kristy. Lisette had a hollowed-out expression, grief clinging to every part of her. Lisette assessed Kristy, clocking the faint but ever-present bruises on her forehead and cheeks.

"Car accident," Kristy said reflexively.

A thin sliver of a smile appeared on Lisette's face.

"Yeah. Sure it is," she said.

There was a harshness to Lisette that Kristy found unsettling. Was she always like that, or was that a by-product of growing up with Lance? Would she see that same shift in Ryan one day? God, she couldn't bear that.

"I'm sorry about your mom," Kristy said, knowing those words were meaningless. She'd heard them over and over again after her own mother died. *I'm sorry. You have my condolences. It's such a loss. At least she's in a better place.* You had to say them. It was required. But Lisette didn't bother acknowledging Kristy's trite words.

"Wayne didn't kill my mom. I mean he didn't *physically* murder her. She killed herself."

"Are you sure?" Kristy said.

"Yeah. Wayne was on a hunting trip with my grandpa when Mom died."

Kristy tried to conceal her relief. She hated that she'd become someone who was grateful that another woman had taken her own life.

"But he drove her to it. He's the reason she's gone. Day by day, he made her think there was no way out." Lisette's every word was matter-of-fact.

"But no one knew he was...?"

"Evil incarnate? No. That surprised us all. I guess we just didn't expect something like that to happen. My parents divorced when I was nine. Totally agreeable too. They sat me down and said, 'Honey, this isn't working out. But we love you. We're committed to you. Blah. Blah. Blah.' My dad remarried but Mom had a real knack for picking losers. Or guys who didn't want to deal with a kid. Mom and Wayne met at a real estate conference in New Orleans, bonding over prime mortgages. Wayne was always doing things for us, fixing our plumbing or buying a new entertainment center. He got me into judo and I got really good. Like, I almost made the Junior Olympics. By then, Dad had moved to Florida for work and Wayne stepped into Dad's role."

Kristy didn't want to listen to any more of this. She didn't want to know that she was just another number in Lance's screwed-up lineup.

"But things changed? With your mom? I mean, Lance did things to her?" Kristy asked, wanting to know that she wasn't the only one Lance had duped.

"And I didn't notice. I didn't see a thing," Lisette said.

A flicker of guilt lingered on Lisette's face. She shook it away.

"Mom died my sophomore year in high school. I had spent homecoming night at my best friend Cara's. Our neighbor went over to let Mom know that the sprinklers were on and she heard the car running in the garage. Two hours later, a cop showed up at Cara's. He said, 'Your mom's gone,' and I couldn't understand. Gone where? Where would she go? There was no note. Nothing. I was so pissed. I couldn't understand why she would do this to me. To us. That's what I kept saying over and over again those first few days. I wasn't alone. It was me and Wayne. United in grief.'"

Lisette's voice wavered.

"But he hurt her?"

"You know that he did," Lisette said, that edge stronger now. "Or you wouldn't be here."

Lisette picked at her nails, the pale pink polish peeling off, but she lowered her voice.

"It was three days after Mom died. Wayne was downstairs making funeral arrangements, calling the funeral home, the florists. 'Don't worry, Lizzy. I've got it handled,' he'd said. I saw an e-mail come in, from a different account, saw her name in the subject heading, and for a minute it was like she was reaching out from the grave. Guess she created a new e-mail address and used one of those apps to schedule it to arrive after we found her. I sat on my bed reading all the despicable things Wayne did to her. Every move he taught me, he'd already tried out on her, like she was his own personal training dummy. But I'm sure you know..."

Kristy nodded. She knew better than anyone. "He used me against her, used to threaten to do things to me in order to keep her in line. She couldn't handle it anymore. She became convinced that once she was gone, Wayne would leave too. All she wanted to do was protect me. I printed Mom's e-mail and left it on the dining table with a note that said, 'I know what you did. Get the fuck out.' When I came home the next day, Wayne was gone, along with all of Mom's jewelry."

Lisette looked down at the emerald band on Kristy's ring finger. Kristy gasped, feeling bile rising in her throat.

"Oh my God. No...no...he said this was his grandmother's."

"Not his. *Mine.*"

Kristy went to pull the ring off, but Lisette stopped her.

"Don't. I don't want it. Besides, who knows what would happen if he saw you without it."

Kristy flinched. She couldn't begin to imagine.

"You didn't tell the police?" Kristy asked.

"Mom was dead. What did it matter? And I bet you haven't gone to the police either. Because you just don't know what Wayne is capable of."

Kristy nodded, Lisette verbalizing her fears for the first time.

"So...you were the one that vandalized my truck?" Kristy asked.

"I thought it was Lance's. My boyfriend's uncle lives in Conroe and he invited us down for spring break. I'd been doing so good. Found a church I liked, was going to meetings. Hadn't gotten into any trouble. Thought I finally had a handle on things. Then I see you and Wayne and your kid and all of you are laughing and enjoying yourselves. And it was like my mom didn't even exist. Like he'd just replaced all of us with a new family. Your family. What I did was stupid but I was so pissed. I get back to Austin and all of a sudden I'm seeing news reports, people talking about how whoever did that could face prison time for threatening a state official, and I was so scared. Then Wayne showed up, and I was like, 'God,

Lisette, you're like the dumbest person on the planet.' Like, I forgot how insane he was."

"He came to your house?"

"No. That's not Wayne's style. No, he showed up at my job. I was waiting tables and there he was, sitting in my section. Said he just wanted to talk. He understood I was still grieving but he'd moved on and I needed to as well. It wasn't just for my sake, but for my daughter's. He had our pictures. The two of us playing in a park. He smiled. 'Don't look so surprised, Lizzy. We both have a lot to lose. Remember that from here on out.' I promised him I'd stay away and I did."

"We weren't together. Not then. After that night... that night brought us closer."

"He would've found another way to get you. If Wayne wanted you, he was gonna get you," Lisette said without apology.

"So your troubles," Kristy asked, gesturing to the bracelet.

"I'd been doing so well before that day. Like I could almost convince myself life was normal again. But seeing Wayne brought it all back. You ever used meth?"

"No. I never got past pot."

"Meth is like the greatest high you will ever experience," Lisette said, her voice reverential, eyes twinkling as if she were describing a trip to Mecca or meeting Jesus Christ himself. "It just erases the edge, softens and brightens everything all at the same time. Made things good for a while and then real bad."

"So... Lance never beat you or got physical with you?" Kristy asked.

"No. I think he just wanted my mom and I was part of the

package. I wished he had tried something. I'm a pretty good fighter. Wayne knows that. He trained me himself."

Kristy wanted to understand what sick, demented brain worm living inside Lance could make him do those things.

"Do you know anything else about Lance's past? Friends? Family?" Kristy asked.

"He was always having some kind of falling-out with someone. Never Wayne's fault. Far as family goes, the way he told it, his mother abandoned them, but I have a feeling Daddy dearest liked to smack his mom around and she had enough. Maybe Wayne was too young to know that part. Whatever happened, he's one seriously twisted motherfucker."

Lisette absentmindedly flicked the small pile of pink nail polish onto the floor and reached for her phone, checking the time.

"Gotta go or I'll miss my curfew," Lisette said.

"Thanks for talking to me," Kristy said, though she almost wished she hadn't. Lisette had just confirmed Kristy's worst fears about Lance. "There's just one more thing I'd like you to do."

"What is it?"

"As far as anyone is concerned, we've never met."

"You've got it," Lisette said, reaching up to touch the small gold cross she was wearing. "Do you know Scripture? God's word, I mean?" she asked.

"No. I'm afraid I'm not very religious," Kristy said.

"The Lord got me through a lot of hard times. Got me sober. Gave me a second chance with my baby girl and my boyfriend. Because of God's guidance, my dad is speaking to me again. But even the Lord knows there are some souls that can't be saved. Peter chapter five, verse eight, says, 'Be sober. Be vigilant. Because your adversary the devil, as a roaring lion, walketh about, seeking whom he may devour.' Be careful, Kristy, or Wayne will devour you and your entire family whole."

Lisette hurried out, leaving Kristy behind. The bustle of the café moved around her but all the noise seemed to vanish. She remembered Pamela's matter-of-fact story. She'd done everything right. Gone to the cops, tried to tell the truth, and no one would listen to her. Even if Kristy wanted to do that now, she had proof that Lance was unhinged. He'd already tormented one woman to death. He'd threatened not only Kristy's life but the lives of her father and son. All those burns and bruises, all the assaults and the forced sexual encounters that Kristy had to silently endure. Pamela's words kept echoing in Kristy's head. *Roger was a fucking lunatic. In the end, it was the only choice.* The same could be said about Lance. If Kristy had any doubts about Lance before today, Lisette eviscerated them.

She'd hoped that by doing her research on Lance she would find another way out. Now she knew there wasn't one. Lance was still screwing up Lisette's life, even after her mother was gone. Kristy wanted Ryan to have a future, go to college, move on, live a happy life. None of that would ever happen with the shadow of Lance hanging over him for the rest of his life. After all these months of suffering and being afraid, things were finally coming into focus. Kristy had made up her mind. She was going to kill her husband.

CHAPTER TWENTY

Not once in Kristy's entire life had murder ever crossed her mind. That day she sat across from Clifton and he'd told her there were options, even then she wasn't sure. And now, even though she'd made her decision, Kristy still couldn't shake the nagging voice inside her head screaming over and over, *You're not a murderer. You're not a murderer.* But maybe that's what everyone who'd been pushed to the brink once thought.

Kristy hurried across the sprawling University of Texas campus, eager to see Ryan, forcing herself to shut out any thought about the future and Lance, at least for right now. This was a huge day for Ryan and she owed him that.

Debate tournaments weren't like sporting events. Spectators weren't allowed, but some of the clingier parents, Kristy included, often gathered in the lobby, waiting to hear the results and see how their kids had done. She was late though. When she arrived to find Ryan and the team in the lobby, they were already celebrating. Ryan was ecstatic, eyes shining, tie loosened like a political candidate beaming after having accepted his party's nomination. When he saw Kristy, Ryan lost all form of teenage self-consciousness and bounded over and threw his arms around her.

"Mama Bear, we won! Can you believe it? We destroyed everyone. It was a total slaughter. We're state champions," Ryan said, his eyes lit up.

Kristy hugged him tightly, tears welling.

"I'm so damn proud of you, Ry," Kristy whispered.

"Ella, come here. Tell Mom how much we destroyed the other teams. Their cases literally fell apart."

"Ryan was amazing, Ms. Tucker. Everyone was talking about him," she said, leaning into Ryan.

"No way. Ella's cross-examination slayed them. She's the reason we made it to the final round. Can you believe it, Mom? State champs in our junior year!" Ryan said.

"I never doubted it for a second," Kristy said, watching as Ryan and his friends snapped more photos and hugged one another. Parents and other teammates shook Kristy's hand, congratulating her for a job well done. It was a buoyant celebration, and at the center of it all was Ryan, relaxed and confident. Whatever happened next, whatever Kristy had to do, she'd raised a good man. Lance could never take that away.

"Hey, Mom, we're gonna grab a bite on Sixth Street and then go back to the hotel and go swimming. You're coming to dinner later?" he asked.

"Actually, I was thinking about skipping dinner."

"Really?"

"Yeah, you should celebrate with your friends."

"Are you sure?" he asked.

"Yeah, I'm kind of looking forward to takeout and the *Housewives*. A little me time, you know? But I'll pick you up in the morning and we'll grab lunch, okay?"

"Sounds good," Ryan said.

"You're such a good kid. Have I told you that before?" Kristy asked.

"Maybe once or like a million times," Ryan replied. "Oh, and if you talk to Lance before I do, let him know that we kicked ass. Okay?"

"It'll be the first thing I tell him."

On the drive to the Homestead Suites, where they were all staying, Kristy's phone rang. Lance didn't get great cell service at his hunting site, so some evenings he'd drive to the nearest gas station a few miles away just to call her. In a different world, Kristy would have found it sweet, but now she knew it was just part of Lance's desperate need to control her.

"Hey, darlin'," Lance said. "Is it good news? Or bad news?"

"Great news. They won state. Ryan and the team won first place."

Lance hollered excitedly, "Damn straight they did."

"Ryan was so excited, Lance. He wanted you to know," Kristy said, realizing how ordinary their conversation was, two parents proudly chatting about their kid.

"He had nothing to worry about. Didn't I say that?"

"Yes, you did, Lance," Kristy said. *Yes, Lance, you're always right. You're the smartest person that ever lived.*

"I'll shoot him a text and tell him how proud I am," Lance said. "And tomorrow when I'm back, I'll whip him up a celebration dinner."

"He'll love that," she replied. There was a pause on the line. Kristy wanted to ask Lance about Hannah. Why did he torment her? Why had he pushed Hannah to the breaking point? Was he going to do the same thing to Kristy?

"How's the hunting going?" she said instead.

"Took down a buck this morning. This thing is huge. We'll be eating venison for weeks."

"That's great," Kristy said, feeling a rush of sympathy for the defenseless animal Lance had mercilessly stalked and killed.

"I love you, Kris, and I miss you."

"Love you too," Kristy replied automatically. Pulling into the parking lot, Kristy hung up, dreaming of a night away from all the uncertainty.

A troop of weary flight attendants beat Kristy to the reception desk. Kristy listened to their excited chatter discussing their next flights. Kristy could count on one hand how many times she'd left the state. What must it be like to travel day after day to new cities, soaking up different cultures and languages with nothing tying you down? She imagined driving to the airport right now.

"Surprise me," she'd tell the desk agent. "I'll go anywhere in the world." But wasn't that a version of what Hannah had done, leaving behind the people she loved most? Kristy would never judge Hannah, but that wasn't an option for Kristy. She'd never willingly walk away from Ryan and Pops.

She checked in and grabbed her room key and hurried down the hall. She unlocked the door and closed the curtains. Without even bothering to kick off her shoes, Kristy collapsed onto the king-sized bed. As she sank into the mattress, she reveled in the solitude. But soon the silence became unbearable, thoughts of Lance and Hannah and Lisette and Ryan and Pops crowding her brain. She switched on the TV, flicking through channels, until she landed on a rerun of *Friends*, its laugh track familiar and comforting.

At some point, Kristy dozed off. She woke four hours later, the room pitch-black, the TV blaring. She gulped down a bottle of water, ordered a large Domino's pizza and garlic bread, and opened the cheap bottle of merlot she'd bought at the H-E-B the night before.

Kristy flipped through the channels, sipping the wine, knowing that she'd finish this bottle and wishing she had bought a second. She'd given up drinking since the accident. Alcohol made her less sharp, unable to read Lance's moods. It was easier to avoid it altogether, but tonight she craved the escape, the heavy warmth working its way through her body. She hadn't relaxed in months and she needed this. *To hell with it*, she thought as she finished the bottle. She was going to walk to the store on the corner and buy another. She sifted through her purse for her keys, and that's when she saw Clifton's most recent letter. She always destroyed them once she was done reading, not wanting Lance to find them. She must have forgotten to burn this one. She couldn't be this careless in the future, but Kristy eagerly opened the envelope and began to read.

Ms. Tucker, you might be wondering how I knew about your troubles. I used to wonder how other folks didn't see it. It's always there, always in the eyes. When a man

batters a woman, her eyes change. For years, I kept thinking someone would see Mama's eyes, see the distance in
them, like she was away from her body. Away from this
world. I thought that they'd have to see what he was doing
'cause it was so clear to me.

On the nights after the bars closed, Daddy would stumble
in, reeking of cheap whiskey and cheaper perfume and she'd
keep on Daddy about his vows and his family and how he
embarrassed her, and he'd lose it, whaling on her. I can still
hear her screaming for him to stop, begging and pleading
and telling him that we were listening. Of course no one ever
called the cops. 'Let them Folks handle their own,' because
that was the neighborhood motto. Mama would wake up the
next morning, cover her bruises with makeup, and we'd all
show up at church. Sometimes she would have a sprained
wrist or a bruised cheek and an excuse to match, but most
folks wouldn't even ask what happened. Even as a little kid,
I kept thinking, why the hell won't anyone pay attention? But
I am paying attention, Ms. Tucker. I see you. I see your pain.

When we first met, you had a spark, a light that filled
you. I haven't seen that spark in quite some time. I can't
imagine doing what you do. I bet you could do this job
without ever showing kindness or consideration to all of us
on the row. Some of the staff despises us and they show it
in ways I can't even begin to say. Yet even with everything
you have to endure, you still put on a smile and show up.
That says a helluva lot about your character. So please
know that I am aware of what you're going through. You
gotta keep fighting, just like I keep fighting.

I like to imagine what might happen one day when the state admits I'm innocent. They'll owe me $100k for every year I spent locked up. I'd have a nice bit of change to start over. I'd buy a house in the middle of nowhere. I'd have a big ole yard and a picnic table. I'd eat all my meals under the stars. Hell, maybe I'd even get a sleeping bag and sleep under them. Every now and then I'd dial your number and say, "We need to catch up."

We'd go to this great hole-in-the-wall Creole place in Houston and sit on the patio. You'd tell me about your life. I'd see your sparkle was back and I'd know that you were happy and safe. You'd have left this place, gotten a fresh start. Maybe you'd be writing stories for magazines or doing nonprofit work for people like me. We'd order cold beers and heaping bowls of gumbo and the biggest po'boys you've ever seen. Maybe I'd have a new lady friend. Maybe I'd even be thinking about kids again. I know I'd have a job. I think I'd like to teach, make use of all the things I've learned in here. You'd sit across from me and you'd say, "Clifton, how can you be so happy? I mean, they stole so many years from you. I just don't understand why. Don't you have hate in your heart?" And I'd say, "Kristy"—I'd call you Kristy, not Ms. Tucker because we'd be good friends by then—"Kristy, I lost everything: my kids, my wife, my home, but every morning when the sun peeks through my curtains or when I see the stars shine down on me at night, I know that I have a fresh start. I've got my freedom and that is a beautiful thing. I realize it's a pipe dream for me but I want that for you. You should want it too.

Kristy finished the letter and read it again, wanting Clifton's hopes for the future to be true. But it was impossible to imagine how either of them could escape their situations.

She dozed off, more than a little drunk. Her sleep was fitful, full of images of a figure slumped over in a garage, the fumes pouring in. In her dreams, Kristy could hear a car running, but she couldn't get the garage door open. When she finally busted down the door, she saw Ryan's body slumped in the front seat. Her baby boy was gone. She'd done all of this for Ryan and now she'd failed him.

Kristy jolted awake at nine, that terrible nightmare still clouding her thoughts. Head pounding, mouth dry, the back of her skull aching, her stomach uneasy from the grease and cheese, she downed a terrible cup of hotel coffee and showered. No amount of hot water or caffeine could wash away the dread.

A little after ten o'clock, Kristy met Ryan in the lobby, his hair tousled, eyes bleary and bloodshot. He'd stayed up all night playing video games and hanging at the pool, but he was still on a high from his win, happily chattering to Kristy about his evening.

Kristy rarely had one-on-one time with Ryan anymore and she soaked it up. She would not allow herself to think about the future. She would focus on the here and now. She drove to Lydia's, a restaurant on the outskirts of Austin. A family-run business for almost fifty years, it was famous for its homemade chicken-fried steak and the best cream gravy Kristy had ever tasted. After a twenty-minute wait, Kristy and Ryan placed their orders. Ryan leaned forward.

"Mom, I've got big news."

"Oh really, what is it?"

"I didn't want to tell you until I was sure, but I got the e-mail today."

He handed his phone over to Kristy.

Dear Ryan Tucker,

We received over three thousand applications for this year's precollege programs. After careful consideration, we would love to invite you to participate in the Notre Dame Leadership Seminar. We are impressed with your academic standing as well as your dedication to your community at large. Our courses will challenge you and provide you with the opportunity to hone your leadership skills and to improve your communication techniques. We look forward to seeing you at the University of Notre Dame this summer.

Kristy looked up from the letter. Ryan was biting his straw in excitement.

"This is incredible," Kristy said, trying to wrap her head around what it meant. "Can we afford this?" she asked.

"All expenses are paid. Everything. And, Mom, I spoke to the admissions woman, who said that most students who do this program and apply to the college are accepted. I mean, it's one of the top schools in the country and I might actually have a chance."

"You act so surprised. I still remember when you were five and we went to the Capitol," Kristy began. Ryan groaned.

"Mom, you're not actually going to tell this story again." But he was smiling.

"You walked right up to one of the congressmen and you said, 'I'm gonna run for office one day.' I swear, the look on his face. He was shocked. He said, 'Son, you're gonna have to work hard if you want to get here.' And now this is it. Everything you've done is finally paying off."

Kristy beamed. Ryan was going to get out of Texas. He was going to escape all of the bullshit and the bullies. He was going to do everything that Kristy hadn't.

"That's the best news ever. God, I'm so proud of you," she said.

"I just…I wanted to thank you. For that trip to DC when we didn't really have the money. For everything. I mean, I know a lot has changed now—I know I gave you a lot of shit about your job—but I see all the sacrifices you made."

Don't break down, Kristy told herself. *Just keep it together. You have to keep it together.*

Kristy reached for Ryan's hand.

"You're worth it, kiddo."

The food arrived and the conversation shifted to planning Ryan's summer travels and the Urban Debate summer camps he helped organize. Kristy wanted to stay here forever in this cozy restaurant, talking to Ryan, but before long, they were heading back to Conroe. Ryan dozed, his body curled up in the passenger's seat, his expression one of pure contentment.

They arrived home to find Lance on cloud nine. His

hunting trip had been a rousing success and he'd prepared heaping piles of barbecued ribs and deer meat to celebrate. Pops and Lance were dining at the picnic table in the backyard, sipping on Budweisers. Lance and Pops gave Ryan a rousing standing ovation. Once they were done, Lance grabbed Ryan and pulled him into a bear hug.

"You're a goddamn champion, that's what you are."

Ryan laughed, soaking up the praise. Lance did praise like nobody's business.

"We destroyed them, Lance. Just like you said we would."

"Because you're a warrior and that's what warriors do."

Lance turned his attention to Kristy, reaching for her. "And here's the warrior's mama, looking so darn pretty." Lance pulled Kristy onto his lap as he sank down onto the bench, nuzzling her neck.

"I missed my girl."

"I missed you too," Kristy said, the words like marbles in her mouth.

"Kristy girl, did you have a good time?" Pops asked, his breath labored, but a grin on his face.

"It was amazing, Pops," Ryan interjected.

"How was your weekend?" she asked Pops. His complexion was good, his eyes sparkling. He looked like he'd just showered and was wearing clean clothes.

"Had myself a real good time. Last night, Mac and Vera cooked me dinner and challenged me to a game of poker. I swear, that girl is a ringer. She took me to the cleaners."

Kristy laughed but it was unbearable, being this close to Lance, his hands gently rubbing her back. She waited a moment and then delicately extracted herself from his embrace.

"I'm gonna wash up before I eat," Kristy said.

"Sounds good, darlin'. Ryan can give us the replay of the weekend's events and share his good news."

Kristy left the three of them at the picnic table and went upstairs to shower, thinking about Clifton, wanting to tell him what she had uncovered. Sometimes she hated that she couldn't just see him or call him up. She hated that he was alone in his cell, trapped just like she was. She wanted to curl up in bed but Lance was in party mode and Kristy was expected to put in an appearance.

She joined them outside, picking at her plate of ribs and potato salad, fading into the background while they chatted happily. Later that night, Kristy lay in bed, her mind spinning, when Lance reached out for her.

"Darlin', where'd you go?" Lance asked. "You've been somewhere else ever since you got back today." Annoyed that she had let herself get careless around Lance, she placed a hand on his chest.

"I'm right here, Lance." He took her hand in his.

"I closed that deal on the outlet mall. Darlin', my commission is gonna be huge. I'm thinking it's time for you to quit that job. Devote more time to us and starting a family. We haven't talked about kids, but it might be nice to have one of our own."

Kristy stiffened. The thought of having Lance's child was unbearable. She couldn't imagine being trapped with him in this house, day in and day out, Ryan heading off to school,

Pops shuttled off to a nursing home, and Kristy and a baby at Lance's mercy.

Kristy wouldn't let that happen. No way in hell. She demurred.

"Sounds like a plan. We'll discuss when I should put in my notice."

She returned to work the next day still reeling from Lance's baby bombshell. Once he got an idea in his head, he didn't let go. Kristy had to do the same. She was sitting in her office, trying to figure out her next step when Carmen knocked on the door.

"Hey, Kristy, I think you made a mistake on the calendar. You've got Clifton Harris scheduled for an interview with a reporter from the Associated Press in six weeks."

Kristy glanced up.

"Wait, what's wrong with that?"

Carmen pointed to Kristy's giant wall calendar, which listed all the upcoming executions. She swiveled in her chair to get a better look.

Kristy's heart dropped. In less than six weeks, barring any last-minute appeals, Clifton Harris was scheduled to die.

Dear Ms. Tucker,

I suppose this will be one of the last few letters I'll write to you. Makes me feel like a bit of a failure since I promised to help you with your situation, but there's not much I can do about it. Whatever happens next, you're stronger than you realize. Trust me, I know there are times when the darkness seems too much to bear. After the sentencing, I remember every second of the drive from Bastrop to Polunsky. Two hours, and I never once took my eyes off the road. I'd been well versed in how death row worked. The guards at the county jail liked to tell me all kinds of stories about what I could expect. With my limited rec time, I would see very little daylight. God, what I'd give to see dark clouds rolling in or the rainbow that follows after a July thunderstorm. I'd be the happiest man on earth. I'm hoping heaven has plenty of wide-open spaces. Not sure how I feel about doing more interviews. Doesn't seem like much point now. But I guess you could change my mind. I do want to see you again and I hope I get the chance to say good-bye.

Yours truly,
Clifton Harris

CHAPTER TWENTY-ONE

Child Killer's Execution Set," boasted the front page of the *Huntsville Item*, accompanied by Clifton's mug shot, a skulking image glowering up at Kristy. She had seen other photos of Clifton, dressed neatly in a starched gray button-down shirt and navy tie, his hair neatly combed, glasses softening his stoic expression. But those photos didn't sell papers. Clifton needed to appear monstrous, otherwise it made folks uncomfortable. The image they used of him—clad in an orange jumpsuit, hair sticking straight up, eyes wide with what Kristy recognized as disbelief but the world interpreted to be madness—was designed to make you hate him and what he did. But perception was often skewed. People never looked beneath the surface. To the world a photograph of Lance would conjure up a movie idol: clean-cut, handsome. Hannah and Lisette Mendoza had seen the other Lance Dobson just like Kristy.

She arrived at Polunsky, her stomach churning at the thought of walking into the visitation room, staring ahead at the death chamber and seeing Clifton's restrained body. How would she ever survive Gus and the reporters' callous jokes about Clifton's final hours? Would she be able to sit silently listening to the gallows humor all the reporters relied on?

No matter how difficult Kristy's job became, she'd forced herself not to get emotionally invested. This time she had failed. Kristy had no choice but to do her job, standing front and center at Clifton's execution, assisting the press in their efforts to monetize Clifton's suffering. Sell enough ads, get enough clicks, and move on to the next story. Kristy hated to see her friend turned into some kind of celebrity monster, like Ted Bundy or Charles Manson. She'd already reached out to a few journalists on Clifton's behalf, hoping they might be interested in telling a fair and balanced story, and had at least come with some good news.

"How are you holding up?" she asked Clifton the following week. She'd asked this question on hundreds of visits, but her words had never sounded more hollow. There was an energy shift from the knowledge that after next week one of them would no longer be part of this world, but Clifton appeared unfazed. He'd offered Kristy his trademark grin and a friendly nod before she picked up the phone. It almost made it worse, to watch him willingly accept his death orders. Kristy wanted to shatter the glass that separated them, take his hands in hers, and say, "I believe you." Instead, she sat there, tightly clutching the phone, hoping Clifton could read everything in her gaze.

"Honestly, Ms. Tucker," he whispered. "I'm ready."

"Don't give up the fight just yet," Kristy whispered back. "I've got one more interview next week. It's CNN and I can vouch for the reporter. She'll listen to both sides. It's a good way to be heard."

"Sure thing. I got one more interview left in me. And listen, there are so many folks fighting out there for me. No way Fiona and Bev are ever gonna quit 'til they clear my name. I may not be here for it, but I'll be up in heaven holding my baby girl and baby boy and shouting into the clouds, 'I told y'all I'm innocent. I told you I didn't do it!'"

"I'm sorry I couldn't do more for you."

"That's where you're wrong, Ms. Tucker. You did plenty. I just want to make sure you're okay. And I know I said I'd try to help you out but, Ms. Tucker, I started talking to some of the guys in here and the things they were saying...I don't trust them and I don't think you should either."

"I'm going to figure it out, Clifton. I'll be just fine."

"I hope so, ma'am. And I hope you know that you deserve nothing but the best life has to offer."

She assigned Carmen to oversee some of the details for Clifton's execution, asking her to take the lead and manage the onslaught of reporters, all calling in to ask for exclusives and quotes. Kristy hoped that once Carmen took over, she could focus on Lance, but she couldn't seem to move forward. Sometimes she'd sit in her office, trying to understand how someone like Lance would go on living his life, punishing Kristy, and Clifton would be dead and buried. Paralyzed by indecision, Kristy didn't even know where to begin. How did one set out to plan a murder? She tried to think about it from a reporting standpoint. Reporters were trained to ask the four W's. Kristy already knew the why—Lance was a violent sociopath, but the what, when, and where parts of killing her husband remained elusive. Whatever she was going to do, she couldn't stay in limbo forever, or she'd end up just like Hannah.

To Kristy's surprise, it wasn't Clifton or Lance that forced Kristy's hand and set everything into motion. It was Pops.

After months of trying, Kristy managed to land Pops an appointment at MD Anderson in Houston. She was hoping Pops might qualify for a clinical trial in their pulmonology clinic, a trial that was testing out new inhalers. If this medical Hail Mary worked, it could alleviate Pops's breathing issues and improve his quality of life. She told Lance about their day trip, convinced that he would insist on coming along. For once, luck was on Kristy's side and he had an open house scheduled, so Kristy and Pops headed off to Houston together.

Pops's doctors' appointments always tested her patience. Every time she asked Pops how he was feeling, he'd answer, "Right as rain." Then the doctor would arrive and ask him the same question and Pops would shake his head mournfully and launch into a litany of his growing ailments. Today was no different.

"Doc, my back hurts, my neck is killing me, my sides ache, and I've been coughing up gunk. Green gunk."

Kristy sat openmouthed, forcing herself not to interject, trying not to remind Pops that five minutes ago in the car, he said he was good. Despite Kristy's annoyance, the doctor was optimistic and deemed Pops an excellent candidate for the trial.

"You'll need to come back once a month for treatments.

We'll cover the cost of all your medications and parking and offer a small stipend." This news, the prospect of feeling better, transformed Pops's mood. Kristy thought about reminding him that this wasn't a cure, but she restrained herself. Let the man have his moment.

For the first time in ages, they left the hospital upbeat. It was still early and they were both starving so they headed to Red Oak Steakhouse, one of Pops's favorite restaurants, and the two of them wolfed down giant steaks and baked potatoes topped with warm butter. Pops was in high spirits. He ordered a beer and shamelessly flirted with the cute red-haired waitress. They finished their entrées and then dug into their desserts, apple pie for Pops and a brownie à la mode for Kristy. Pops was sopping up the last of the ice cream when he brushed aside his mop of gray hair and stared at Kristy with concern.

"You doing okay, Kristy girl? You seem a bit outta sorts these days."

Just when she thought Pops had lost all awareness of what was going on around him, he surprised her.

"Why do you ask?" Kristy said.

"Just a feeling. I know marriage isn't easy. Much as I loved your mama, our lives weren't perfect."

"Lance and I are good, Pops," Kristy lied, wanting to move on to other topics of conversation before she gave herself away.

"Is it work? Is that prick Gus giving you problems? I can still whip that man's ass today and twice on Sunday."

Kristy burst out laughing, downing the last sip of her chardonnay.

"C'mon, Pops, even I could whip Gus's ass."

He snorted. "Ain't that the truth. Now I'm serious, Kristy—what is it? I know something's troubling you."

She couldn't talk about Lance, but there was something else on her mind.

"You ever think anyone you met on death row was innocent?"

Pops hesitated, which surprised Kristy.

"Odds are one or two. I mean, those are just the odds, right? There was one guy, real nice fella. He'd been accused of raping and killing this college girl, and I just couldn't believe he did it. The ones that do things like that, you see it in their eyes. You feel it deep in your bones. They've got the devil's mark. This guy was so friendly and 'aw shucks,' insisting the witnesses were wrong and the medical experts were wrong. Some days I kind of felt sorry for the guy. But I believe in our system. This guy had a trial with a jury of his peers and he was convicted. I mean, that's the law. What were we supposed to do?"

Kristy wanted to say, *Don't kill them. If the evidence isn't totally irrefutable, just don't do it.*

"So you think this guy was innocent?"

Pops shook his head. "I did. Years later DNA tests revealed that he raped a whole bunch of other women. Guy was guilty as sin. The law is the law, Kristy Ann, and I did my part to uphold it."

She thought about that. If Pops, tough as nails, as savvy as they came, could be fooled by this man, was it possible that she'd been duped, not just by Lance, but also by Clifton?

"You're not getting soft on me, are you?" Pops teased, sensing her distraction.

Kristy smiled brightly.

"No. Not at all."

But Kristy had gotten soft. That's how she'd ended up in this goddamn mess in the first place, letting down her guard, allowing Lance to worm his way in. Kristy checked the time on her cell phone. If they didn't get a move on it, they'd be stuck in the hellish snarl that was Houston's rush hour and she'd have to hear Lance bitch.

"You all set?" she asked Pops.

"Let's rock and roll."

He pulled his portable oxygen tank onto his lap and Kristy wheeled him outside, toward the parking lot.

"Think we could stop by Walmart on the way home?" he asked.

"Sure, Pops. What do you need?"

"Lance asked me to print out some forms and sign 'em, and my damn ink cartridge is out."

Kristy didn't know anything about the forms. What could Lance possibly need from Pops? The sense of impending doom hit so suddenly and furiously, she almost lost her balance, nearly tipping Pops out of his wheelchair. He grabbed the armrests, frantically trying to steady himself.

"Jeez, Kristy girl, watch what you're doing."

"Sorry, Pops. Sorry," she said, trying to breathe in and out.

She opened the truck door, trying to keep her composure, grabbing Pops's oxygen tank and lifting him into the SUV.

"What forms does Lance need you to sign?"

"Something about the health insurance. He said you'd talked it over."

Pops was studying her, brow wrinkling with concern. Kristy quickly covered. "Yeah, I remember now. I just totally blanked."

"Wait 'til you get my age. Then you won't be able to remember a thing."

Kristy chuckled, her mind racing, but she had to cover. She had to keep it together until she knew what Lance was planning now.

"Let's get this show on the road," she said with a faux cheerfulness that Pops missed.

They stopped at the Super Walmart on the way out of town. Kristy purchased printer ink and paper towels, along with a cheap bottle of chardonnay. Tonight she was having another drink.

The beer at lunch had made Pops chatty, and he recounted the plot of the latest Stephen King novel, chapter by chapter. All Kristy could think about was getting home and looking at those papers. When they arrived at the house, Lance was outside manning the grill. Ryan sat at the picnic table, hunched over his calculus book. Lance handed Pops a beer. Grinning, Pops cracked it open, drinking with childlike abandon.

"Pops, the doctor said too much alcohol could interfere with your meds," Kristy reminded him.

"Jesus, Kristy Ann. I'm just letting loose for one night. Two beers ain't gonna kill me."

"You heard the man, Kristy. Just relax." Lance chuckled and pulled Kristy onto his lap again, his favorite position of dominance. Lance hated how she talked to Pops. *Stop emasculating him*, Lance would say. *The man is suffering. Let him have a little fun.* Tonight was no different.

"Lighten up, babe."

She smiled and gave Lance a kiss.

"You're right. I'm so sorry, Papa," Kristy teased, putting on her most affected British accent. "Sirs, do I have a moment to freshen up?" she asked Lance, smiling sweetly at him.

"Go do your thing. The boys and I are gonna finish tonight's feast," Lance said agreeably. Kristy slipped into the house, her smile fading instantly. She hurried into Pops's room, which was bursting at the seams with books: crime thrillers, non-fiction, romance. She once teased Pops about his fascination with "bodice rippers." Pops wasn't at all embarrassed, joking that he was getting in touch with his feminine side.

Kristy rushed over to Pops's desk, the one place that was organized, years and years of files neatly stored in plastic containers, ordered by date and event. She sank into his desk chair and opened Pops's old laptop, searching the desktop files. She scanned the letterhead and saw *Gulf Coast Insurance* saved on the desktop. Kristy's heart pounded faster and faster.

Calm down, Kristy. Calm down. She scanned the pages, a pit forming in her stomach. They weren't health insurance forms. This was a life insurance policy. One made out in Pops's name. The other in Ryan's. Three hundred thousand dollars each, a total of six hundred thousand together.

Kristy remembered Lance's not-so-thinly veiled threats about Ryan. But those threats were meant to stop her from leaving. Is that why he had these policies taken out? Did he know about Kristy's visit to Lisette? Was this his way of punishing her for being disloyal? Or maybe as time passed, Lance realized he wanted Kristy all to himself? So many goddamn maybes.

Kristy could withstand a lifetime of beatings and insults if she had to, but she couldn't survive losing the two people she loved most in this world. Ryan's laughter filtered through Pops's bedroom and Kristy heard Lance shouting out her name. She quickly shut off the computer and hurried back downstairs. She plastered on a smile and joined them all for dinner.

Afterward, she cleaned up while Lance stayed downstairs to watch TV. He still hadn't come to bed when Kristy got out of the shower. She slipped on her favorite peach silk nightgown and sat in front of the mirror at her makeup table. She brushed her hair a hundred times, something her mama always did, but a ritual Kristy never made time for. Gently brushing, each stroke long and steady, she surveyed her reflection. She usually hated looking at herself, hated seeing the woman that had allowed herself to become Lance's hostage. But not tonight. Tonight she felt stronger than she had before. No more hesitating or waiting for things to get better. That wasn't going to happen.

"What's up, darlin'?" Lance asked.

Kristy wondered how long he'd been watching her. She wanted to ask him about what she'd seen on Pops's computer. That inner voice said that it wouldn't go well, but she couldn't stop herself. Not after what she'd learned from Lisette.

"Were you gonna tell me about the life insurance policies

for Pops and Ryan?" Kristy asked. "Was there a reason you didn't? I'm starting to think you're keeping things from me. Things that I should know." She saw a flicker of anger from Lance. Then he shrugged, offering her one of his trademark grins.

"It's just smart business, darlin'. You've got to be prepared for every situation that might arise," he said, and then he went to the bathroom and urinated loudly. He didn't return to the bedroom, his nightly beauty ritual a time-consuming process. She'd once teased him about it but it was just another part of his life he had to control. Kristy drifted off to sleep, determined not to lose her courage when a new day dawned.

She felt the cold metal first, the pressure against her forehead. Kristy opened her eyes and saw Lance straddling her, his legs pinning her in place. She recognized the gun. It was Pops's. *Jesus Christ, Pops! Ryan!* She tried to sit up, but Lance pressed the tip of the gun into her skull.

"There's some confusion happening that we need to address. I love you, Kristy. I don't know how many times I have to say it or what else I have to do to show you. I take care of you. I shower you with love and affection. And I know that you struggle to do right by me and I'm okay with that. I forgive you time and again for your failures. I also tolerate Ryan and Pops. I'm good to them. But you're what matters most to me. When I saw you that first day in the YMCA, I had to have you. And as long as you and I are good, so are they. Do you understand?"

She didn't cry. Not this time. She was too furious at herself for waiting, for underestimating Lance again.

"Are they...you didn't...do anything to Pops? Or Ryan?"

Lance laid the gun down on the nightstand.

"God, no. That would ruin everything. No, they're fine. For now."

Kristy thought about reaching for the gun, a fight to the death, but she'd never won a physical battle with Lance.

"We'll do things your way, Lance. I won't question you again. Whatever you want, I'll do it," Kristy pleaded, hoping her defeated tone sounded convincing.

Kristy had already lost too much, suffered too much. She was done waiting around, done waiting for someone to save her or her family. As he wrapped his arms around her and drifted off to sleep, Kristy shook away any remaining doubts.

I'm coming for you, Lance.

CHAPTER TWENTY-TWO

Kristy understood the definition of murder better than anyone: unlawful killing that is both willful and premeditated, meaning that it was committed after planning or lying in wait for the victim. Over the years, she'd sat across from dozens of killers who admitted their guilt, all of them with excuses, justifications for their actions. "It was him or me."

She understood them better now, the tattooed men from the barrio, forced to protect themselves from a rival gang. The mild-mannered accountant who murdered his daughter's rapist, the checkout clerk who could no longer stand her boss's torment. The women like Pamela whom the system failed. They weren't any different from Kristy. They had no other choice. But that didn't make her decision any easier.

Dread owned Kristy, clawed at her insides. She was going to take a life. Not just any life. Her husband's life, a man she loved more than anything. Kristy was actually going to commit murder. Sometimes she tried to spin it in her mind, find some way to make it sound less terrible.

Take care of business.

Handle matters.

Get rid of the problem.

But it didn't matter what she called it. Murder was murder. The ultimate sin. Lance had left her with no other choice. Now the tasks that lay before her were practical matters: not just how she was going to kill Lance, but how to get away with it. Kristy had eleven years of experience hearing inmates' stories, reading their case files, and learning what they'd done wrong. What better way to plan a murder than to study these inmates and the mistakes they made? There were always patterns, the same foolish errors made over and over again that led to a criminal's arrest and prosecution. Kristy had unlimited access to the minute details of hundreds of crimes. She had media accounts and the evidence that ultimately led to these convictions. She was always a quick study, and this test would be life or death. Pamela's words rang in her ears: "If I'd actually planned it, you think I'd have been so sloppy?" But that's what happened to most criminals. Nerves got the best of them, made them careless. They got caught up in the heat of the moment and didn't plan accordingly. Kristy had to be exceptionally careful. She knew her scattered nature could be her undoing. That's why she was going to plan everything down to the second. She had heard all the stories and gleaned the essentials from them. In each of the cases she researched, Kristy could pinpoint the moment when the killer went wrong, where they turned left instead of right, the fatal flaw that landed them on death row.

While Lance continued on as if nothing was wrong, Kristy pored over her files, in the mornings, during lunch hours, and late at night in her office, making excuses that Gus was forcing her to work late. *From liar to murderer in ten easy steps*, Kristy thought.

Case by case, Kristy broke down cause of death, the alibis, the location of victims' bodies, the killer's subsequent arrest and prosecution. She studied a total of two hundred and twelve murders. The majority were crimes of passion. They weren't planned or calculated. Some were cases like Pamela's, with too much physical evidence—blood spatter on the floors of her home that she'd missed in her cleanup, traffic cams showing her near the burial site. There were other cases in which the killer used a cell phone in the same area where the victim was murdered or purchased items related to the killing at a Walmart and was identified by staff or store surveillance. Other crimes were drug related, arguments that spun out of control over stolen bags of weed or a few grams of heroin. There were the mentally ill off their meds, snapping in the heat of the moment. All of them were messy murders with loads of evidence in which the perpetrator never had any chance of escaping prosecution. Kristy had to do her best to make certain that Lance simply disappeared and no one ever suspected that she was involved.

One of the most important factors in getting away with a crime was creating an irrefutable alibi. In essence, Kristy had to be in two places at once, and they had to be quite distant from each other. In order to do that, she had to find a situation in which Lance would actually leave her alone, which had become increasingly rare. Unless he was showing a house or at martial arts class, he never let Kristy out of his sight. The only exception was his hunting trips, and those were infrequent. Even if Lance left Kristy behind, there was always the possibility that Mac or Ryan would join Lance. Fortunately for Kristy, on Lance's next scheduled hunting trip, Ryan was coaching his Urban Debate team, and Mac and Vera had a wedding in Waco. Lance didn't mind going alone. He enjoyed sitting in the middle of the woods with a couple of six-packs of Bud, staking out his prey, waiting for the opportunity to strike. It made sense, his love of hunting: It required patience, finding your target's weakness, and then destroying. That was Lance's specialty.

The next two weeks flew by. Kristy had to juggle her work responsibilities with ensuring all the details of her plan were in order. Day by day she continued going over and over her plan, trying to ensure that she had all the details covered. Lance had at least five inches on her and about a hundred and twenty pounds. She had been worried about what to do if Lance fought back, and she needed to make sure she was prepared. She'd done her best to prepare herself for any possibility. At the library, tucked away during her lunch hour, she'd studied numerous self-defense weapons. In the end, the Vipertek stun gun was one of the best on the market.

But the biggest challenge was securing a weapon. She hated guns, but that was the quickest and most efficient method. Kristy briefly considered using one of Lance's hunting rifles, but they were too heavy and unwieldy. She needed something small and error-proof. Of course there were numerous risks involved when it came to purchasing a firearm. She was a prominent figure in town. The idea of going to a gun show or buying from a private seller was way too risky. But Kristy had heard about the dark web from inmates, and Ryan had researched it in a debate topic and given Kristy the complete download.

"Pay attention, Mama Bear. The dark web is a collection of thousands of websites that conceal IP addresses, allowing anonymity for a variety of unsavory tasks, including buying drugs, guns, and all sorts of other illegal merchandise."

Purchasing the gun required many steps. When Gus was in Austin on official business (aka the good ole boy golf tournament) Kristy headed off to a "dentist appointment" and asked Carmen to cover for her. She drove to the library in Montgomery, another nearby town, logged on to the dark web, and set up a sale from someone who called himself Mad-Dogg12. For five hundred dollars, he sold her the stun gun and a Smith & Wesson .38 Special. MadDogg12 instructed Kristy to buy three Amex gift cards, two in the amount of two hundred dollars and one in the amount of one hundred dollars. She paid cash, making withdrawals on various days so nothing would appear out of the ordinary. Then she sent the cash in installments to different Mail Boxes Etc. locations in Houston.

Kristy's biggest challenge was figuring out what to do with Lance's body. She thought about dumping it in one of the many lakes surrounding the area, but she didn't own a boat, and renting one would require paperwork, not to mention Kristy wasn't a great swimmer. If Lance got the upper hand, just for one second, she could wind up overboard.

Burning the body was an option because it removed any forensic material. But the fire had to burn very hot, which meant you needed large amounts of accelerant. That was readily available at any Walmart or hardware store, but then there were records, credit card statements, security footage, potential eyewitnesses, not to mention a burn pit that could draw attention. It also wasn't easy if you wanted to burn a body completely. A crematorium furnace, she'd once read, must generate temperatures of 1,600–1,800 degrees Fahrenheit to ensure disintegration of the corpse, and even then some bone fragments might be left behind. Sometimes Kristy's research left her physically ill, but she couldn't stop now. Not when Lance was busy with plans of his own.

Burying became the most realistic option. Her research warned that it was necessary to dig a grave at least six feet deep in order to prevent scavenger animals, bears, and wolves from digging up the body. It was important as well that clandestine graves were within fifty feet of a vehicle access point. Adrenaline surged for only so long, so getting as close to the grave as possible meant the body wouldn't have to be dragged far, an important factor when thinking about size discrepancies. Kristy had checked hundreds of public land record surveys to find the right spot, until she finally located a piece of land that had been undeveloped since the 1930s. It was miles away from any campsite or hiking trails, but only fifteen miles from Lance's favorite hunting site. A true Texas wasteland. She'd spent the past two weeks leaving work early and heading out to the site, digging the grave in preparation. By the time Thursday arrived, her anxiety was off the charts, the realization that she had only one more day before she took Lance's life.

"I'm onto you, Tucker."

Kristy nearly jumped out of her chair. Mac stood at the entrance of Kristy's office, eyeing her carefully. She resisted the urge to push aside her notebook. Mac had no idea anything was wrong. All she needed to do was keep up the facade that everything was fine.

"You've lost that loving feeling, haven't you?" Mac asked, his lips curled in a mischievous smile. Kristy forced a laugh. "What's it been, weeks since we've hung out?"

"I'm sorry I haven't called. We've been so busy."

"Yeah, yeah, save your meaningless excuses for someone who cares and buy me lunch."

Kristy had planned to spend her lunch hour going over her timeline again, looking for holes in her alibi, working on her contingency plan if Lance canceled his trip. But the more people that saw Kristy going about her day, the more people that could place her if she became a suspect later on down the line, the better.

"Lead the way, sir," Kristy said, standing up and grabbing her purse. Mac smiled and slipped his arm through hers. Kristy had to stop herself from pushing him away—a result of her ongoing paranoia that Lance had spies everywhere. It wouldn't be an issue after tomorrow. She allowed Mac to escort her to the staff cafeteria. It was a large windowless room in the center of the prison. It used to be the highlight of Kristy's day, sneaking away from her desk and gossiping with Mac and the other guards, or with Carmen. These days she avoided the cafeteria altogether, anxiety gnawing away at the lining of her stomach. Mac and Kristy had always bonded over their love of good food but not today. He regarded the iceberg lettuce and Roma tomatoes in her salad with a grimace, shaking his head disapprovingly.

"You're eating rabbit food? What the hell have you done with my friend Kristy?"

"I had a huge breakfast," Kristy said.

His gaze lingered. "Really?" he asked.

"Breakfast tacos are filling. You know that," Kristy said, and Mac shrugged, digging into his gravy-covered steak.

"Lance says y'all are doing well. And then he said something that surprised me. He said you were thinking about quitting?"

Kristy smiled, feeling the tightness around her mouth.

"We're discussing it. I haven't made up my mind," she said.

God, she was so tired of pretending. She just wanted to be done with it all. Some days she envied Hannah Mendoza. There were many nights she imagined taking her own life. Climbing into her car and driving down the back roads, parking in a wooded area, taking Pops's gun, and pulling the trigger. Other nights, she imagined opening the medicine cabinet, surveying the aspirin, Lance's Ambien, the leftover Percocet from her wisdom tooth surgery, wondering how many she would have to take so that she never woke up. But then Kristy envisioned Pops staring down at his daughter's cold and lifeless body, mourners commenting that she looked lovely, while others whispered how odd she looked and why the hell had they put so much makeup on her? She imagined Lance, an arm clasped around Pops, holding him up, the two of them shaking their heads asking, "Why?" And then there was Ryan—forever haunted, wondering what he could have done to stop his mother from going over the edge.

"Kris...come back to me?"

"Sorry, what did you say?"

"I was saying what would you do if you left this place?" Kristy hadn't given it any serious consideration.

"The options are endless."

"And you and Lance are good?" Mac asked.

"Couldn't be better," Kristy lied, quickly moving on to other topics. "Did I tell you Pops got into a clinical trial at MD Anderson? He's got me running around like a crazy person between here and Houston but it's worth it. They're trying out some revolutionary new treatments. It's not a cure but the doctors are hoping it might alleviate some of his discomfort."

"Damn, that's good to hear! He's been in great spirits the last few times I've seen him. And Ryan? I've texted him a few times but I haven't heard back."

"Yeah, I barely see him these days. He's either with Ella or he's studying for the SATs." She lowered her voice to a conspiratorial whisper. "But, Mac, there's a good chance he might get in to Notre Dame."

"No shit," Mac said. "Are you serious?"

"He was accepted into a summer program, which could give him a serious advantage when he applies."

Mac shook his head, a wide smile on his face.

"You've done good, Kris. Really good. This is what it's all been for. Working here, all the sacrifice. This is it."

She smiled, the tears falling quickly.

"Oh shit...I didn't mean to make you cry."

Kristy batted at her eyes with a paper napkin.

"God, I'm a wreck just thinking about him going off to school," Kristy said. *Stop it. Don't let him see the cracks.* Fortunately, her tears made Mac uneasy and it was his turn to change the subject.

"Heard they're finally executing Clifton Harris," Mac said. "Guy's finally gonna get what's coming to him." Kristy fought back her tears, thinking about Clifton's execution. She might be able to explain why she got emotional over Ryan leaving home, but explaining why she was crying over Clifton would be a hell of a lot more difficult.

"I'll be working nonstop on that one," Kristy replied, turning the conversation back to Mac, inquiring about his family and how they were doing. He launched into a monologue about his mother's new quest to lose weight, insisting that the whole family cut out gluten.

Kristy envied how ordinary it all seemed. What might Kristy's life have been like if she had chosen the good guy? When lunch ended, Mac pulled her in for a hug.

"Tell Lance I'll see him soon. And take care of yourself. You're practically disappearing."

She left work early that day. *Take care of yourself. Take care of yourself.* That's what Kristy told herself she was doing. She drove home and made meat loaf for supper. Ryan was gone. He would be spending the next two nights with Ella and her family in Galveston and wouldn't be back until late Saturday afternoon. Lance was in a jovial mood, making dessert and insisting they all hang out and watch TV. They settled in the living room, the same room Lance proposed in, making promises he never intended to keep. Pops was propped up in his recliner, Lance seated on the sofa next to Kristy, a hand resting on Kristy's thigh. Lance let Pops pick what they watched and he chose the finale of his favorite show, some musical competition in which aspiring singers vied for record contracts. Kristy despised this show, hated the fake cheerfulness, the all-consuming desire for stardom, but she didn't argue.

Lance took Kristy's hand, his legs touching hers. She endured the physical contact, darting glances at the photo hanging over the television. It was a family photo of Kristy, Pops, and Ryan taken almost eight years ago, the only one that worked out in a series of overly posed shots, part of a photo shoot package that an enthusiastic sales clerk suckered Kristy into buying at the mall kiosk.

Worth it though, for this one picture, Kristy thought. She couldn't remember what made them all laugh so hard. Whatever it was, it was always just out of her mind's reach. As the overly coiffed host droned on, stretching out the winning singer's name, Lance's hand gently caressed Kristy's neck. Lance had always been affectionate, but he was exceptionally clingy tonight. Did he sense Kristy's emotional shift? Was he trying to trick her? Set her off balance? It was possible but it didn't matter. *Not happening, Lance*, Kristy thought. *You're too damn late.*

CHAPTER TWENTY-THREE

Today was the day. Lance's execution day. Kristy lay awake, the soft amber glow of sunrise peeking through the curtains. Beside Kristy, Lance slept, eyes closed, hands resting across his chest, looking so goddamn peaceful. Sometimes she questioned whether she could actually do this, and then she recalled everything Lance had done. Lying in her crumpled truck, her ribs aching, his hands around her throat. The cold metal pistol pressed to her forehead, the life insurance policies. There was more than enough evidence. Kristy quietly slipped out of bed, reminding herself that this was all on Lance. He had set this into motion.

In the bathroom, she closed the door and removed her nightgown, staring back at her gaunt frame in the full-length mirror. At work she'd tried to hide her weight loss, draping her skeletal figure in blousy shirts and A-line dresses. She'd never liked her body. Too round and hippy, she always thought, her life spent counting points, skipping meals, giving up carbs and dessert and wine (dear God, she gave up wine), and now here she was, her ribs peeking through, eyes bulging. She'd once dreamt of a stomach this flat. Now it served as a reminder that her body didn't belong to her. Lance on the other hand adored the changes, dubbed this her "supermodel bod," reveling in her sharp edges. Lance never once commented on the bruises, some fading, others freshly forming. He ignored the scars, some obvious, others indelible, etched on her body forever.

Kristy showered and dressed in her favorite black slacks and gray silk blouse. Her tote bag was packed, hidden in the back of the supply closet in her office. In it she had an exact duplicate of the outfit she was wearing, as well as a pair of gloves, zip ties, and duct tape.

At breakfast, Kristy fought the urge to hug Pops. Any outward display of emotion might be cataloged later. This was simply another Friday morning. She chatted casually, pouring coffee and forcing down a piece of toast, knowing that even if she wasn't hungry, she couldn't let her blood sugar drop. She'd planned to be out of the house before Lance woke up, but for once he was out of bed early, ambling downstairs at a quarter to seven, barefoot, blue jeans, no shirt, hair still damp from the shower. Staring at his lean, taut muscles, she recognized the sheer power he possessed, his chiseled body, capable of doing serious damage to equally trained opponents. It left her unsettled. She'd told herself to stay focused but Lance must have clocked something off in her demeanor. He ambled over and wrapped his arms around her.

"You sure you don't want to come with me?" he asked. "It's just population control."

"Been months since I've gone to the movies," Kristy said. "But have fun."

"All right, it's your loss," he said with a smile. He gave Kristy a kiss, his entire body pressing into hers, his hands gripping her, his body language claiming ownership. *You're mine.* That's what she was to him—Lance's property, no different from his pickup or hunting rifles. As he pulled away and headed upstairs, he whistled a tune, not a care in the world. Kristy watched him go. *I can do this. I can do this*, she kept telling herself, hoping that if she repeated it enough, she might actually believe it.

CHAPTER TWENTY-FOUR

Oh my God, Kristy, what the hell is going on here?"

Startled, Kristy looked up from her desk to find a distraught Carmen staring back at her.

Did Carmen know what she had planned? How was that possible? Kristy searched for something to say. Carmen slammed a piece of paper onto Kristy's desk.

"Did you see this? It was posted on a job search site. Gus is going to do it. He's going to fire me and hire someone else. Kristy, it can't happen. I'm starting night school in the fall. I need this job to cover tuition," Carmen said, sniffling and clutching a tissue.

Kristy seethed. Why in the hell was Gus picking today of all days to pull this shit? *Don't panic. You can get through today. Just get through today.*

"Carmen, he's not going to fire you. He has no grounds, and if he tries to, we have all his shitty, sexist, homophobic comments documented. You're safe."

Kristy pulled out a ten-dollar bill from her wallet. "Take a drive and go get some coffee, okay? And just breathe."

Carmen grabbed her purse and car keys and left, still sniffling. Kristy understood Carmen's frustration. When Carmen
first started at the prison a few years ago, Kristy asked the
young woman why she stayed in this backward town. Carmen wasn't like Kristy. She didn't have a kid or her father
tying her down. Not only that but she worked in a place
where her sexuality, her very existence, was judged.

"This is my home, Kristy. No one is going to run me out of
my home," Carmen said passionately.

Kristy saw this as a sign now, a reminder of what she was
fighting for—*her* home and her family. She needed to take her
own advice and not lose her nerve. *Deep breaths. Deep breaths.*

Once Carmen was gone, Kristy settled behind her desk,
eyeing the clock, trying to assess any variables she might have
forgotten, when her phone rang. She reached for it.

"Hello, Kristy Dobson speaking."

"Kristy, this is Donald Kasen from ABC13. Do you have a
sec?"

Donald was one of the local ABC affiliate's top investigative reporters. If he was calling, her day was about to get a
whole lot shittier. She leaned forward, nervously tapping her
pencil on the desk.

"I have some questions regarding Gordon Peterson."

Kristy closed her eyes. Shitty was an understatement. Gordon Peterson was serving a life sentence. A truck driver by
day, serial rapist by night, he'd been convicted of assaulting
at least thirty women, though the DA was convinced that
there were many more. He'd gotten away with it by targeting

minority women in communities with predominantly white, predominantly racist police departments. Many of his victims were prostitutes, who didn't get a great deal of respect from cops to begin with. Gordon's spree continued for years until he targeted the wrong woman. Alice Stevens, a fifty-year-old grandmother, was leaving 7-Eleven one night when Gordon grabbed her. She fought him off, managing to scratch him and get DNA under her fingernails. Her testimony and the physical evidence, as well as a pile of backlogged rape kits, managed to put him away for life.

"Tell me, Donald, how has the state wronged Mr. Peterson now?" Kristy asked, her voice dripping with sarcasm.

"Apparently, he's filed a lawsuit claiming that his civil rights are being denied."

"And those rights are?"

"His rights as a woman. He's claiming he's transgender."

"I must have heard you wrong," Kristy said.

"He's written us a letter stating that his crimes were motivated by his own self-hatred. We've reached out to his attorney, who confirmed his story. He's petitioning for gender reassignment. I wanted to get a comment from your department."

"Please don't tell me this is going to be a top story."

"What can I say? It's a slow news day," Donald replied.

Kristy sighed, putting on her best bureaucrat voice. "The TDCJ has no comment but takes inmates' civil rights seriously. We will look into Mr. Peterson's claims."

"Thanks. Sorry about any dustup."

"Just another day at the office, right?" she said, before hanging up.

Kristy's entire day revolved around Gordon Peterson and his ridiculous demands. Just the idea of a serial rapist living among hundreds of women was complete and utter insanity. She notified Gus and briefed Carmen, who would spend the rest of the day fielding calls about the story. Kristy then made the drive over to Polunsky, where she had scheduled to meet with Gordon. He was a small man, maybe five foot five, with the brute physicality of a man who worked out relentlessly, trying to protect himself from the larger inmates who made it their mission to punish sexual predators.

"I'm here to let you know that we've been informed of your lawsuit and there are medical forms to fill out, interviews with a psychologist and psychiatrist that must be conducted. It's a long, drawn-out process and there's no guarantee you will get approval," Kristy informed Gordon.

He didn't say anything, and she could see him sizing her up.

"I bet you're a good fuck," Gordon hissed, reaching into his pants and thrusting his tongue against the glass. The guard grabbed Gordon roughly, stopping his grotesque actions.

Kristy stood up, ready to walk away, but something inside her snapped. Her hand was glued to the phone.

"You're a worthless piece of shit and one of these days someone's going to make sure you get what's coming to you. I hope it's slow and painful and you suffer."

She slammed down the phone and stormed off, not even bothering to look at Bruce, who was escorting her. They reached the end of the corridor when Kristy stopped and leaned against the cold concrete wall. *Inhale. Exhale. Inhale. Exhale.* She finally looked over at Bruce.

"Kind of lost my cool, didn't I?" Kristy said.

Bruce stared straight ahead. "Don't know what you're talking about," he said.

Bruce would never tell anyone about Kristy's outburst, that she was certain of, but she'd never let an inmate rattle her before. She had to get it together. She thought about speaking with Clifton, but she worried he might see something in her eyes, that he might say something to stop her, and Kristy didn't want to be stopped. She managed to compose herself, going through the motions. By the time she returned to the Walls, it was a quarter to five. Carmen had a bottle of wine sitting on Kristy's desk.

"I splurged on your favorite chardonnay," Carmen said. "I think we've both earned it." Of all the days Carmen wanted to bond, it had to be today.

"I'm sorry," Kristy said. "I'm off to the movies. After this week, I need popcorn and George Clooney in my life."

Carmen's disappointment was evident, her shoulders slumping.

"Hey, rain check next week, okay? I'm buying," Kristy said. Carmen offered up a slight smile.

"Sounds good. Have a great weekend and get some rest. You look exhausted."

Guards and support staff called out good night as Kristy headed to the parking lot. She climbed into her car and exited the prison, its bars and the guards in the towers fading away in the rearview mirror.

Kristy arrived at the Lone Star Cinema, a popular movie theater in Conroe, and parked her SUV near the back of the building, closest to the exit. She bought one ticket for two separate films, a romantic comedy that started at six thirty and another for a thriller that began at eleven.

Lance actually encouraged Kristy to go to the movies when he went on his hunting trips. "Can't get into trouble when you're watching a movie, now can you?" he always said. She'd chosen this particular alibi because there were plenty of people that would see her at the theater. Going to a double feature wasn't unusual for her, at least before Lance came into the picture.

This theater was recently built, designed to attract the millennials that weren't content with an ordinary moviegoing experience. It had twelve screens, each of them equipped with stadium seating. There was also a restaurant and a bar, which Kristy made her way to once she'd purchased her tickets.

She sat at the bar and ordered a margarita with salt and cheesy potato skins, striking up a conversation with two animated housewives enjoying their two-for-one happy-hour cocktails and a night away from their toddlers. When a couple of well-meaning cowboys offered to buy them all another round of drinks, Kristy accepted, taking small sips. She listened to the women complaining about their husbands, but Kristy said nothing, shooting nervous glances at the clock.

At six fifteen, Kristy stepped away from the bar and dialed.

"Lance, it's me. You haven't left yet?" Kristy asked, noticing the tremor in her voice, not quite her own, sounded fake to her, like an actress in a bad high school production. *Jesus, Kristy, don't screw up already.*

"I got a late start so I'm just getting on the road now. Why? What's wrong?"

"My car died outside the theater. I tried to get someone to jump it but it's not the battery. Must be the starter or something else."

"What the hell are you talking about? It's a brand-new car."

"I know. I called a tow truck. They're on their way. I think I'll skip the movie and call a cab to take me home. I just wanted to let you know."

Kristy's entire plan hinged on the fact that Lance liked to control Kristy. Things could go one of two ways. Lance would be pissed and tell her to "figure it out your damn self" or he'd want to rush to her rescue. Her abusive knight in shining armor.

"Shit, darlin', I'm not far from you. I'll turn around and head over, drop you at the house and we can have dinner. I'll drive out to the deer hunt at first light."

"Are you sure? I hate ruining your weekend."

"Don't be silly. I've got to make sure my wife is taken care of."

So far so good.

"I think it may rain soon. I'll be waiting near the back of the theater," Kristy said.

"I'll see you in twenty," Lance replied, and then he hung up.

Kristy returned to the bar, paid her tab, said good night to her new friends. She hurried toward the usher, making small talk about the brewing storm, the skies darkening with each passing minute. He tore her ticket and directed Kristy to theater eight. Friday nights the theater was usually packed, and tonight was no exception. She sent Ryan and Pops a text. **Movie starts soon. Love you guys.** Seconds later, the lights dimmed. An endless stream of previews advertising noisy superhero remakes and crass comedies played on the massive screen. Kristy waited five more minutes and then she slipped out the emergency exit.

She hurried toward the edge of the parking lot where her car was parked, the smell of movie popcorn filling the air. Kristy had to leave her phone in her glove box so her location couldn't be tracked. As long as they didn't talk or text while Lance was at the theater, she should be fine. Yes, a call would be documented but it would only show that she'd simply called him while he was heading to the campsite. Technology was often the biggest downfall for criminals. She wouldn't be that careless. She grabbed her tote bag and headed to the back of the theater just as a light rain began to fall. She'd canvassed several other theaters in the area but this one had the most lax security. She'd discovered that after phoning the corporate office.

"Hello, I'm with Fox News and I'm doing a story on movie theater security. I was wondering if you could answer some questions."

It was amazing what people would tell you without verifying your credentials. The woman calmly explained that this theater was new, so there were no security cameras installed currently but the safety of their customers was paramount.

"A security guard patrols the grounds. Lone Star Cinema is committed to providing our customers with a safe and enjoyable moviegoing experience," she assured Kristy. That commitment didn't translate to the security guard Kristy spotted dozing in his patrol car each time she drove by the theater. She hoped he didn't suddenly have an urge to wander around the theater while she waited for Lance. She stood in the alley, her stomach fluttering with nerves and uncertainty. Almost thirty minutes later, Lance pulled up. Kristy climbed into his truck and leaned in to accept Lance's kiss.

"Traffic was a nightmare. Bad luck, isn't it? Of all the nights," he said.

"I know. Thanks again for coming to get me. The tow truck just left. They said I could call the mechanic in the morning." At this point, the lies rolled effortlessly off her tongue.

"Well, don't let them do any work on it until you tell me what they say," Lance replied, determined to control her until the bitter end.

"Of course. That's what I told the driver," she responded. God forbid she might actually make a decision without him.

"Traffic is easing up. We'll get you home and we can fire up the Netflix."

"Actually, I was thinking maybe I could come with you," she said tentatively, knowing her suggestion would raise suspicion.

"Yeah, right. What's the catch?" Lance said, chuckling.

"No catch. I didn't say I'd go hunting, but I could hang out in the camper, right? I could use some peace and quiet. We both could. And you and I could have some fun before you head out in the morning." She laid her hand on his lap. Lance inhaled, tilted his head.

"This a surprising turn of events. You sure about this?"

"Of course I am. Unless you don't want me to come?" she asked. Lance smiled back at her, throwing his truck into drive.

"Don't be silly, darlin'. This is gonna be a night to remember."

CHAPTER TWENTY-FIVE

All this time Lance had anticipated her every move, but not tonight. As he pulled out of the parking lot, Kristy made a mental note of the time. The first movie would finish two hours from now. The second one would begin at eleven and end at one fifteen, which meant she had exactly five and a half hours if she was actually going to go through with her plan.

They made their way through the Friday rush hour snarl, Kristy half listening to Lance as he chatted about his day. Forty-five minutes later, Lance exited the highway, picking up speed as he navigated the dark back roads, the white lines on the pavement illuminated only by their headlights, the forest a dark blur on either side. Kristy played the evening's events over and over in her head. They were ten minutes from the campground when the rain began to fall, fat drops blurring the windshield, the wipers struggling to keep up.

No. No. No. Kristy had prayed that it wouldn't rain. Even though she'd taken the weather into account, packing duplicates of the same blouse and pants she wore to work in her tote bag, as well as a hairbrush and another pair of boots, she knew this would make everything more difficult. She wasn't sure what caught Lance's attention. Perhaps an exhalation of air, a sigh, or maybe it was Lance's innate understanding of Kristy's moods.

"Not too late to turn back," he said.

Kristy shook her head. "Not when we've come so close," she said, more for her benefit than Lance's.

They arrived at the campsite in Little Creek Lake Wilderness. Long, thin pine trees trembled in the angry rain. This was Lance's spot. She'd driven out here once at his request and spent the day hanging with Ryan and Lance, drinking beers and listening to Lance brag about his hunting prowess.

In March and April, the dogwood flowers bloomed, and the light petals floated around the forest like pale fairies. Along the creek to the west, deer fed in the clearings near the old oaks where Lance would park the camper. He relished the isolation. No horses were allowed—hikers and hunters only—but even they rarely ventured into this part of the woods. But tonight, Lance seemed pleased to have an audience.

"Gonna make big money these next few weeks. Some major players are interested in this new commercial property I just got a bite on," he said. Kristy wondered if this was one of Roy's clients—someone Lance poached? What kind of man cheated his friends? What kind of man befriended single mothers, then terrorized them? *What kind of man are you?* she wanted to ask Lance.

She still didn't know. She wished there was a telltale sign, some way to know how damaged he was. But there was nothing that signaled to her or anyone else that beneath all the swagger and dimples and easy charm was a very twisted individual.

Her nerves were failing her. She kept telling herself that she had to do this. She had to. Kristy turned to look out the window, closing her eyes, trying to gather her courage. *Remember what he did to you. Remember what he said*, she repeated over and over again to herself. But she was frozen. No matter how much she hated Lance, how much she despised him for everything he'd done to her, the voice inside her head was screaming out, *I can't do it. I can't. I can't! I can't.* The words were echoing in her head, rattling around. All her planning and preparations were meaningless. Kristy was not a murderer. But she wasn't going to be his prisoner. Not anymore.

"Lance, we have to talk."

Her words came out much sharper than intended. Lance's entire body tensed. His gaze sharpened, eyes narrowed. A torrent of heavy rain pounded the windshield, the space in the pickup shrinking in an instant.

"Isn't that what we've been doing, Kristy?" he said. "*Talking.*"

Don't let him intimidate you, she told herself. *Don't let him take control.*

"I know about Hannah Mendoza. I want a divorce. It's over."

Lance closed his eyes and inhaled deeply.

"You must be a special kind of stupid. Bringing me out here, telling me something like that. You stupid, stupid bitch." Before Kristy could fully process Lance's words, he reached out and shoved her head into the passenger's window. His entire palm covered her face, pressing it harder and harder into the pane of glass.

Kristy fumbled, reaching into the pocket of her rain slicker, searching for the stun gun. She could still fight him off if she could just reach it.

"I'm sorry," she whispered, hoping to buy more time, her hands trembling as she blindly fumbled for the ON switch. Feeling the slight vibration, signaling that it was on, Kristy jabbed Lance in the hip bone, sending fifteen million volts of electricity pulsing through her husband. It seemed impossible that the body could withstand that many volts but this taser was designed to bring down adult men, and it kept its promise. He released her, his entire body spasming.

In an instant, he experienced complete loss of motor control. Kristy shocked him twice more, until he was drooling and hunched over the steering wheel. He moaned her name, along with a stream of unintelligible curses. She stunned him once more, striking him in the back of his neck, this time fully incapacitating him. Staring down at Lance, now at her mercy, Kristy thought about all those men on death row. In her lifetime, she had witnessed thirty-seven people meet their maker. Thirty-six men and one woman were strapped to a gurney, intravenous needles inserted into their arms. She'd been a witness to each and every one of these sanctioned executions. But tonight wasn't sanctioned. Not even close.

Thirty-seven inmates and tonight Kristy remembered all those inmates she'd witnessed in their final moments, their faces and names haunting her.

Randall, Michael, Jesse, David, Leroy, Peter, Darrell, Eddie, Maurice, Jorge, Hector, Clark, Steven, Travis, Jason, Franklin, Stanley, Alan, Gilberto, Trevor, Isaac, Jose, Willie, Oscar, Ernest, Miles, Nelson, Alberto, Karl, Timothy, Emmanuel, Tim, Marcus, Quincy, Barry, Carlos, Pamela. Thirty-seven people and now Lance would make thirty-eight.

Kristy had to work quickly before the taser wore off. She bound Lance's feet and hands with zip ties and covered his mouth with duct tape. Spittle dripped down his shirt; angry grunts escaped from the tape's confines. She knew when she removed the tape he would unleash a tirade of threats.

Threats to her.

Threats to Ryan.

Threats to Pops.

Threats.

Threats.

Threats.

There was a time in Kristy's life when she considered herself a righteous, law-abiding woman, superior to the men and women she encountered in prison every day. Not anymore. Tonight she was just like them.

Using all of her strength, Kristy shoved Lance into the passenger's seat. Then she climbed into the driver's seat and drove fifteen miles to the woods that she'd selected as Lance's final resting place. The spot was located on a trail that forked off a Forest Service road west of Lake Conroe, tucked several miles away from the back roads. Kristy drove right up to the grave site and eased the truck to a stop. Surrounded by a heavy thicket of pine trees, her high beams illuminated the giant grave. Lance's grave.

Kristy's hands trembled as she pulled on the men's work gloves and covered her head with the hood of her black Windbreaker. Inside the cab of the truck, the heat was unbearable, drops of sweat running down her back. Kristy could feel Lance's eyes watching her every move. She reached into her jacket pocket and pulled out the pistol she'd bought. No serial numbers. No background checks. Lance inhaled, twisting against his bindings, perhaps realizing how serious things were, that maybe he had underestimated her. Kristy held Lance's gaze, desperate to see a glimmer of remorse, a hint that he was sorry for what he'd done to her. But his expression remained unforgiving. In Lance's mind, Kristy was the villain in his story. She would always be the villain.

And as long as Lance was alive, there was no escape. *No escape. No escape. No escape.* She repeated this mantra over and over again. She had promised that she wouldn't cry, that Lance didn't deserve her tears, but they were pouring down her face. All this time, Kristy had been silenced by Lance. Now she could finally speak.

"It was all an act, wasn't it? You groomed Ryan, manipulated me and Pops. This is what you do, isn't it? I used to rack my brain wondering how I could make things go back to the way they were. Those times weren't real, though. All of those early days were lies. I wish I knew why you were like this. But it's done, Lance. You drove me to *this*."

He shook his head, muttering angrily into the tape, but

Kristy continued. He had to hear this. This was her chance to finally be heard.

"All I wanted was for you to stop hurting me. To stop threatening me. Why couldn't you do that? Why couldn't you walk away?" Kristy asked.

She tore the tape that covered his mouth, and the first thing he did was shout for help. Actually, it was more of a howl than a shout, the sound a bear would make the moment a trap snapped shut around its paw.

"I picked a place so isolated that no one can hear you, Lance. Isn't that what you taught me?" The coldness in Kristy's voice startled Lance. He fought at his restraints as he spoke.

"You don't know what real love is. Always worried about Ryan and Pops, never thinking about me. So goddamn selfish, just like that bitch Hannah."

"You're not well, Lance. You're a damaged, broken man. You hurt Hannah so badly the only way she could escape was to kill herself."

Lance whimpered. "No one loves me. Not you. Not Hannah. Not my slut of a mother. My daddy was right; you're all worthless whores. And I was good to you, Kristy. I was good to your family. But not anymore. I swear to God, I'm going to kill that pussy-whipped son of yours, and that waste of space you call a father."

"I don't have to do this," Kristy pleaded. "If you just let me go. Just walk away."

"That's not going to happen." Lance grunted. "We both know how this ends."

Kristy sized up Lance, realizing he would never ever let her go.

"I think we have very different ideas about tonight's ending," Kristy said.

She removed the zip ties from Lance's feet, holding the gun inches from his torso. If he fucked with her now, she would shoot him in the chest, to hell with the evidence.

Kristy opened her door and slid out, heavy sheets of rain pouring down on her. She took three steps back. Keeping her distance from Lance was important; the closer he was to her, the more likely it was that he could disarm her and take her weapon. She waved the gun at him, motioning for Lance to slide out of the truck.

"Move toward me," she told Lance. "Feet first. Go slowly."

"Fuck you," Lance snarled. Kristy lowered the gun five inches. It was now pointed directly at Lance's crotch. Her finger hovered over the trigger.

"Okay. Okay, I'm going."

He obeyed her, unsteady, scooting toward the driver's-side door, his boots landing on the wet and muddy ground beneath him. He righted himself, standing rigid with fury and contempt. Kristy pointed Lance to his grave. For the first time, she saw a flicker of uncertainty.

"Start walking. One foot in front of the other."

Lance obeyed, walking slowly in front of her. The dirt pit was less than five feet away. She never faltered or dropped her gaze, but somehow Lance, attuned to anticipating his opponent's every move, seized his opportunity. He spun around, hands flailing as he reached out to grab her. In a horror movie, the killer always has the element of surprise, but somehow, after all this time with Lance, Kristy had anticipated this attack. She didn't cower. She didn't block her face or flinch. She just reacted. So many actions occurred instantaneously; the bullet roared out of the chamber, the muzzle flash blinded her temporarily, the recoil from the gun shook her body, her arms tensed from the alien feeling of such an unnatural act, the ringing in her ears drowned out all sounds, and everything slowed until it appeared that time stood still. The first bullet hit Lance squarely in the chest, ripping through his flesh with terrifying force. He staggered backward as Kristy steadied herself and fought to focus.

She remembered the first time Lance smacked her. *I love you.*

Kristy fired.

Lance's fist striking her jaw. *I love you.*

She fired again.

His boot slamming into her ribs. *I love you. I love you. I love you.*

Lance landed with a thud on the mud-soaked ground. Blood pooled from his wounds, the rainwater carrying it away. He blinked up at Kristy in disbelief, gagging and coughing up blood. Lance reached out, beckoning her forward.

"Please . . . don't leave me."

He had tormented her, broken her, ruined her, but she didn't turn away. Instead, she sank down onto the wet dirt. Clutching the gun in one hand in case he tried one last attack, she reached for his other hand.

"You're not alone, Lance. I'm right here."

He could not hurt her anymore. She sat by his side, thunder

roaring in the distance. Lance's organs were failing, his body relaxing, the light slowly fading from his eyes. Kristy didn't owe Lance anything, but she'd loved him once, believed that he loved her. She had watched all those people die, but that was nothing compared to this, the slow ebbing of the heart-beat of the man she once loved. All Kristy could do now was watch as Lance slipped away, her sobs swallowed up by the storm.

CHAPTER TWENTY-SIX

Kristy gagged, bile rising up in her throat, eyes blurring from her tears. She swallowed hard, counting to ten over and over again. Lance was dead. Her husband was dead and she had murdered him.

Stop it. Stop it now. Get up. Get moving. If she didn't, she might as well call the cops now and turn herself in. It took all Kristy's strength to drag Lance over to the grave, heaving his body and watching it land with a thud. She couldn't quite wrap her head around the fact that he was gone, that his heart could be beating one moment, and the next...but she couldn't get swept up by grief and regret. There wasn't time for that. She switched off the part of her brain that said she couldn't do this and forced herself to focus on the details. That's what mattered now. Kristy removed the remaining zip ties from Lance's hands, and then she stared back at Lance's corpse.

Corpse, another one of those words that signaled irrevocability. No way to turn back. She couldn't think about Lance. She had to focus on the plan. *Focus, Kristy.*

It took her thirty minutes of digging, covering Lance until the hole was completely filled in. Kristy placed the rocks on top until no ground was visible. Her movements were frenzied. She had to remind herself to slow down. *Mistakes happen when you get careless.*

It was nearly eleven o'clock, and Kristy had to be back at the movie theater before one fifteen, had to make sure that she was seen leaving, had to make sure that her alibi was completely shored up. The rain had stopped; a light drizzle was all that remained. Kristy stripped naked, dousing herself with bottled water until she'd wiped away all the blood and dirt, inspecting her hands and feet for any stubborn traces. She placed her bloodstained clothes in a plastic bag and stuffed them in a bag with her gun. She'd get rid of all of it tomorrow before anyone noticed Lance was gone.

Once she was dressed, she re-braided her hair, the exact style she'd worn to work. She climbed into Lance's pickup and carefully reapplied her makeup. Wearing a different pair of black gloves (to avoid fingerprints) Kristy drove Lance's pickup back to his campsite, just fifteen miles from his final resting place.

She opened up a few beers from Lance's cooler and emptied them onto the ground, and walked around in an old pair of Lance's boots to create footprints in the muddy ground. Once that was complete, Kristy placed all of Lance's things inside the camper. Cell phone and keys on the small Formica table. His hunting rifles propped against the door. His overnight bag on the shelf near the bed.

Kristy canvassed the crime scene, obsessively looking to

make sure her presence had been completely erased. If Kristy succeeded, the authorities would think Lance had simply vanished.

She grabbed her bag and walked deeper into the woods until she reached a clearing. Kristy pushed away mounds of thick brush and unearthed a small gray scooter. She had scoured the classified ads in the surrounding area until she located a man in Sugar Land who was selling his son's moped.

She'd arrived wearing a hat, her face obscured, paid the man cash, and left, a sixty-second transaction with no paperwork changing hands. There was risk involved here, in buying this scooter, in meeting someone who might be able to identify her, but she couldn't use any of the vehicles she had without the police monitoring the GPS. Kristy cranked up the moped and gave one last glance back at Lance's grave before she headed back to town.

The roads were slick and driving was tricky. Her tires skidded on the wet gravel roads. She gripped the handlebars, praying she wouldn't lose control, and in less than forty minutes, she made it back to Huntsville unscathed. It seemed impossible that she'd been gone only four hours. Kristy parked the bike in an alleyway three blocks from the theater and left the keys inside the ignition, praying that someone was in the mood for a little petty theft. She hurried down the deserted streets and slipped back into the theater, flashing her torn ticket stub to the same bored usher. He waved her in without even looking up from his cell phone.

Kristy stopped off at the bathroom and inspected herself in the mirror, searching for signs of what she'd done. No

blood or mud or grime remained, nothing out of the ordinary
except for her eyes. Clifton once said the eyes gave it all away,
showed one's true struggle and heartache. "It's always there,
always in the eyes." Kristy's eyes were lifeless and hollow. Her
"sparkle" had been forever extinguished.

There were only fifteen minutes left in the last movie.
Kristy found a seat near the back of the theater, shivering, her
body chilled from the rain, and the weight of what she'd done
crashing down upon her. On-screen, a mind-numbing police
chase seemed to go on forever. Actors phoned in cheesy dia-
logue about how good always prevails, but none of it registered. The movie ended and Kristy left the theater, just
another person headed for home and a warm, safe bed. She
texted Lance. **Movie's over. Headed home. Love you.** There
was limited to zero cell reception at the campsite, but it would
show the police that Kristy cared about her husband.

She arrived home a little after two in the morning and
found Pops wide awake and watching TV in the living room.
He grinned when he saw her and muted the TV.

"Hey, Kristy girl, how was the picture show?"

"Good, Pops. They were good."

"You hear from Lance?"

"No, but the reception is spotty. Need anything before I go
to bed?" she asked, praying Pops would say no. She couldn't
handle chitchat right now.

"I'm good. You go on to bed. I'll see you in the morning."

Kristy stopped by Ryan's room, even though she knew he
wasn't home. She stood in the doorway, staring at his messy
unmade bed, his desk covered with stacks of papers, his debate

medals hanging proudly on the far wall. She did this for him. She did it for all of them.

Rationally, Kristy understood that. But the moment she entered her bedroom, her senses were assaulted by what remained of Lance, his musky cologne, the indent in the unmade bed from where he'd slept, his nightclothes tossed on top of the bureau, and that goddamn wedding picture still hanging above the bed. Kristy half walked, half staggered, collapsing onto the bed, biting her pillow to silence her cries. She wept, wailing into the soft terry cloth fabric, her cries becoming whimpers until at long last, she drifted off in a fitful sleep.

Hours later, Kristy jolted upright, surprised that she'd dozed off. Sunlight poured through the blinds and Kristy found her sense of impending doom was nearly all-consuming. She showered, hot water scalding her body as she scrubbed away at the imaginary bloodstains. No matter how much she tried, she couldn't seem to get clean enough. She quickly dressed and headed downstairs, an uneasy silence filling the house. She made a pot of coffee and poured it in her thermos. It was a little after nine, and she knew Pops wouldn't be up for several hours. Kristy often worked weekends, and that was the plan today. She would go to her office at the Walls, make polite chitchat with the guards, hunker down at her desk, answer e-mails and phone calls about Gordon and his proposed sex change. She'd write press releases and try not to think about what would unfold when Ryan and Pops learned that Lance was missing. She would do all the things that people who hadn't killed their husbands do.

Kristy drove past the lake, unsure if she should dump the gun or wait until dark. She scanned the surroundings—overcast, not a soul in sight. She'd placed the gun in a weighted black plastic bag and tied it tightly with chicken wire. She threw it as far as she could, watching it splash, sending ripples as it sank into the lake, and then it disappeared.

Half an hour later, she pulled into the prison, waving to Ernesto, the weekend guard. He'd worked here almost as long as Kristy, and they chatted about his daughter, who was expecting her first baby.

Kristy's office always seemed dim, even with the fluorescent lights buzzing overhead. She wanted to switch off all the lights and sit in the dark, but on the off chance that Carmen or Gus came in today, she didn't want to draw any attention to herself.

She sorted through e-mails, eyeing the to-do list she had neglected over the past few weeks, but it was ridiculous to think she would ever get any work done. She mostly sat in silence, staring out the window at the guard tower, time drifting by. Her phone buzzed at a quarter to four with a text from Ryan.

I'm back. Want to meet for dinner? I'm on my way to Chili's.

That was the last place Kristy wanted to go, the restaurant where it all began, but she couldn't say that. Besides, she wanted to see Ryan. She needed to hug him, make sure that he was okay.

She texted back. **Meet you in twenty minutes.**

Kristy arrived at the restaurant and found Ryan seated at a booth in the corner.

"Hey, Ry," she said, sinking down, hoping he couldn't see the change in her. He looked up from his menu, his eyes red, mouth turned down in despair. He'd been crying, it seemed, a ravaged expression on his face. Did he know something had happened? What if he hadn't gone to Galveston with Ella? What if he'd come to the campsite and seen everything? No. There's no way Ryan would have invited Kristy to dinner if he had any clue what his mother had done.

"What's wrong? What happened?" Kristy asked.

"She dumped me, Mom."

"Ella?"

Ryan nodded, his heartache apparent.

"I don't understand. Did she say why?"

"She said I'll be at my leadership camp this summer and she's going to California to visit her aunt for a month, and she said she just wants to have fun and not be so serious."

"I'm so sorry, Ry."

"And then she's like crying and crying and I'm like, why are you crying? You're the one that's breaking up with me."

There was so much Kristy wanted to say, but it was so god-damn trite. *Relationships are hard. You'll fall in love again. There's someone out there for everyone.* She'd heard those same things, believed in them, let them fuel her relationship with Lance. Still, Ryan was hurting. Sometimes platitudes were better than nothing.

"I know it hurts now, but you'll get through this. I promise you," she said. In some way, it was a gentle warning for what lay ahead.

"I don't want to talk about Ella anymore. Can we just eat?"

"Sure, Ryan, whatever you want."

They ordered, Kristy watching as Ryan frantically sent text messages to Ella, begging her to reconsider. When the food came, he picked at his burger, reminiscing about all the good times. Kristy sipped water and poked at a chicken Caesar salad, gnawing worry clawing at her belly. Her attention shifted from Ryan's heartache to Lance staggering toward her, eyes bulging in surprise, the crack of the bullet as it exploded out of the gun, tossing the dirt on his body...

Focus on Ryan. Focus on Ryan. She couldn't allow her mind to wander. Lance was gone. Ryan was right here. Ryan was what mattered.

"I texted Lance...just wanted to talk to him, but I didn't hear back. Did you guys talk today?"

It was as if Ryan had read her mind. Kristy took a sip of water, calculating her response.

"No, we haven't. Got so busy at work. I guess I figured he was still out hunting."

Ryan frowned. "That's weird. Doesn't Lance text you like a thousand times a day?"

Sometimes she hated how perceptive he was. Kristy shrugged. "The service isn't great."

"Just give him a call. Maybe he'll pick up."

This was inevitable, that she would have to lie, but it was real now. She couldn't escape Ryan's probing stare, brow wrinkled as he waited.

"Come on, Mom, I just want to say hi and see how the hunting is going," Ryan said.

Kristy gave in. She dialed, letting the phone ring until

Lance's voice mail clicked on. "Hey, y'all, you've reached Lance Dobson. I'm not in at the moment but leave a message and have a blessed day."

A loud beep sounded. "Hey, Lance, it's me. Just checking to see how things are going out there. Hope you're having a good trip. Ryan wants to talk to you, so if you get a chance, call us back. Love you."

She hung up, worried that she sounded forced. The reality was setting in. Kristy had been so focused on stopping Lance that she hadn't truly taken into account how difficult lying to her son would be. Right now, Ryan's only concern was Ella. They finished dinner and Ryan checked his messages.

"There's a party at Zac's house but I won't be home late," he said.

"Be safe, Ry. And if you guys drink…"

"Mom, I don't drink."

"Okay. I'm just saying if there's alcohol at this party, and you have anything to drink, don't drive. Call me and I'll come get you."

"Yeah. Sure," Ryan said, shoulders slumping as he climbed into his car. Kristy watched him go, waiting until his headlights disappeared around the corner.

She sat in the parking lot where it had all started, wondering how different things might have been if they hadn't gone to dinner that evening. If Lisette had never seen them and lost her temper, would Kristy have let her guard down? Would she have trusted Lance enough to be that vulnerable? Would she have kissed him? Or was everything that happened destined to be, no matter what? *Too late for what-ifs*, she told herself.

She didn't have time to dwell. There was still work to be done. Kristy drove to an abandoned stretch of woods twelve miles outside of town. She removed several pieces of wood from the back of her SUV and struck a match, the fire burning hot and fast. Kristy tossed her bloody clothes on top of the wood, the heat incinerating them, the hot flames dancing in the evening breeze.

When the last ember had been extinguished, Kristy picked up a pizza for Pops and drove home. She settled in, agreeing to watch one of Pops's programs with him, a cop drama he adored. She normally found these types of shows mindless, with the overly coiffed, unrealistic-looking police officers and excessive violence against women, but today she couldn't look away, rooting for the young woman who had been date-raped to get away with murder and reeling when she didn't.

Kristy went to bed around eleven. Tomorrow was reckoning day. Lance wouldn't return home, and Ryan and Pops would realize something had happened to him. Kristy would have to lie over and over again to the people she loved most in this world. She slept fitfully and when she woke the following morning and went into the kitchen at ten o'clock, Pops and Ryan were already awake and seated at the kitchen table.

"Mom, did Lance call or text you?" Ryan asked, his hands nervously tapping at the kitchen table.

"No, I haven't heard from him since he left."

"When was that?" Pops asked.

"Friday while I was at the movies. He texted me good night."

"It's so weird," Ryan said. "Lance always texts me. Always checks in. Pops too. Something is wrong." Ryan ran his hands through his messy mop of blondish-brown hair, eyes narrowing. God, he was such a sweet kid. This was going to break his fucking heart.

"I don't want to jump to conclusions, Ry. There's the cell service."

"Yeah, but Lance usually goes into town and at least calls you. But he didn't, did he?"

"No, but…"

"Kristy girl, I agree with the boy on this. Let's drive out to the campsite. Check things out. Better safe than sorry."

"Please, Mom, Lance could be sick or hurt," Ryan pleaded.

Kristy's stomach churned, a wave of nausea washing over her. Time to face the music.

"Okay, let's go," Kristy said.

Pops stood up.

"I'm coming too."

"Pops…"

He ignored her, shuffling toward the hall table, where he disconnected his larger home oxygen unit for a smaller, more portable one. Kristy almost told Pops to change his clothes or brush his hair or at least put on shoes other than his ugly gray-and-white-polka-dot slippers, but this wasn't a goddamn fashion show. What did it matter what her father wore?

The three of them drove in silence, arriving at the campsite half an hour later. Everything appeared just as Kristy had left it. All that was missing was Lance.

"For all we know he's out hunting," Kristy said. *Liar. Liar.*

Ryan looked in the camper. "All his stuff is there. Including his guns."

"That's not good. He wouldn't go into the woods without his gun."

Kristy didn't know what to say. She was starting to second-guess everything, wondering how she'd ever get through this with them both staring back at her, like the world was falling apart.

"Mom, listen to me, listen. Pops is gonna stay here at camp in case Lance comes back. Let's spread out and canvas the woods."

Ryan took charge. That wasn't unusual, but she could put a stop to this, tell them they were leaving, and yet she couldn't. She followed Ryan into the thicket of dense woods, the two of them shouting out Lance's name over and over again for over an hour before Ryan suggested going back. When they returned, Pops took one look at Ryan's dejected face and said, "That's it. We need to call the cops."

Kristy didn't argue. There was no point in putting on any more of a pretense than she already had.

They drove fifteen minutes north before they found a cell signal.

"Nine-one-one, what's your emergency?" the operator's monotone voice inquired.

"My husband . . . he's missing. I mean, I'm worried he might be missing. He went out camping and we haven't been able to locate him."

"How long has he been gone?"

"It's been thirty-six hours since anyone has seen or heard from him," Kristy said, Ryan and Pops hanging on to her every word. The operator took down Kristy's name and said she'd send out an officer. They drove back to the campsite and waited in hushed silence until a highway patrolman showed up. He was young, maybe early thirties, with a military crew cut and a muscular physique, well honed in the gym.

"Mrs. Dobson?" he said, removing his straw hat. Kristy nodded, and he shook her hand, then Pops's and Ryan's.

"I'm State Trooper Matt Meyers. Dispatch said you wanted to report a missing person?"

"My husband, Lance Dobson, came out here on Friday night and we haven't heard from him. We found his truck and all of his stuff, but there's no sign of Lance."

"And you're all family?" he asked.

"Ryan is my son. Lance's stepson. And this is my father, Frank Tucker."

Trooper Meyers jotted down notes while Kristy talked. Pops and Ryan stood, shell-shocked, blinking back disbelief. Kristy hoped her expression matched theirs, but her insides were swirling. She surveyed the scene in the light of day. The rain had left the campsite a muddy mess, but there was always the risk of leaving behind some kind of forensics, some fiber that would ruin everything. The officer stepped into Lance's camper, leaving the three of them all alone.

Ryan looked over and softly whispered, "He'll be okay, right, Mom?"

The lies. She had told so many lies and this was just the beginning.

"I hope so, Ry." *Damn Lance for making Ryan care. Damn him,* she thought. Officer Meyers exited the camper, dusting off his hands.

"Okay. So when was the last time all of you spoke to Lance?"

Ryan stepped forward. "I saw Lance before I left for school on Thursday morning. He texted me Friday night around six o'clock to tell me to have fun in Galveston." Ryan's voice cracked.

Kristy reached out and took Ryan's hand. This wasn't going to get any easier.

Pops spoke next.

"Lance left the house around five forty-five p.m. on Friday. He wanted to make sure I ate dinner so he whipped me up a burger on the grill. That man's got a magic touch when it comes to the grill, don't he, Kristy?"

"Yes, he does, Pops."

"And you, Mrs. Dobson?"

Trooper Meyers looked at Kristy. "When was the last time you spoke to your husband?"

"I saw Lance that morning before I left for work. I'm a public information officer over in Huntsville and I was at work until around five o'clock. I went to the movies over at Lone Star Cinema. Lance and I spoke before the first show around six o'clock, but that was the last time I heard from him."

She showed Trooper Meyers her phone and he wrote everything down. At some point in the interview, Kristy almost believed her story, the tale of a concerned wife whose husband had gone missing.

"Can any of you think of anyone Lance may have had issues with?" Trooper Meyers asked.

"No one would ever want to hurt Lance. He's a good man. He looked after all of us, didn't he, Kristy?" Pops said.

This time Kristy stared right at the officer. Direct eye contact mattered.

"He did. He's very devoted to our family."

That wasn't a lie. Devotion had never been Lance's issue.

"And how long have you been married?"

"Almost two years," Kristy said. Did she imagine his hesitation before he jotted her answer down?

"Okay. If y'all don't mind staying right here, I'm going to notify my supervisor."

He inspected the place one last time and then he ambled over to his squad car. They waited. Half an hour passed and another trooper arrived, a potbellied man with a mustache. Soon he was joined by the game warden, a lanky, bug-eyed woman. Trooper Meyers made the introductions but Kristy wasn't listening. She was bracing herself for another round of interviews.

They walked Kristy, Ryan, and Pops through their story again and again—when they'd last seen Lance, when they'd last spoken to him. There was a sense of urgency in the supervisor's demeanor as he inspected the hunting rifles.

"Does your husband have any other weapons?"

"Not as far as I know," she said.

There was a huddled discussion among the three officers, and as the afternoon wore on, more officers descended on the scene, along with additional game wardens. Trooper Meyers had taken it upon himself to be Kristy's eyes and ears through all of this, giving her a play-by-play.

"We're concerned that your husband may be injured or perhaps lost. My supervisor has notified our volunteer search and

rescue team. It'll be a bit of tough going, because this part of
the woods is so dense, but they've got four-wheelers and horses,
which will help to cover more ground than we could just on
foot. We'll also have a department investigator out here to
search the area and take pictures of the camper and the truck."

"We'll help them look. We can help, right?" Ryan asked.

Kristy wanted to scream, *No! We're going home*, but there
was no turning back.

"If your son wants to join the search and rescue, that's fine.
But, Mrs. Dobson, we'd like you to phone your husband's
friends and family and see if anyone has heard from him. We
also need his medical history as well as a current photo we
can distribute to our rescue teams."

"Absolutely. Whatever you need," Kristy said, surveying
the growing scene unfolding all around her. All these people,
all this time and money being spent searching for a man that
was already dead. She could confess right now. She should
confess. But things were moving too fast. It seemed impossible to stop what she'd set into motion.

Kristy watched helplessly while Ryan disappeared into the
thicket of woods with dozens of volunteers from the local fire
department, men and women who dedicated their off-hours
to searches like this, all of them focused and driven, offering
Kristy pats on the shoulder and encouraging words, promises
that they'd bring her husband home.

She recognized a few of them, guards at Huntsville and
Polunsky, their grim expressions fading as they shook her
hand, promising her "God will protect." That was Kristy's
issue with religion. Where was God when Lance was beating

her day after day? Where was he then? But they couldn't know what she endured. They were operating on the facts at hand: A loving husband and father was missing and they were going to do their damnedest to find him.

Pops and Kristy sat in her SUV while she called Roy and Yoli, who were surprised to hear from her and had no information to give. She phoned Craig, the other Realtor that worked with Lance at his new office, and the small group of Lance's acquaintances. Everyone expressed their sympathy and concern, but of course none of them had heard from Lance. Once she made all her calls, Kristy sat in the truck with Pops, staring at the compound of people. Pops eventually dozed off, the hissing of his portable oxygen tank the only sound she could hear. Through the windows, Kristy watched the officers and search teams moving in and out of the woods with purpose and diligence. The hours ticked by, and the sun began to set. Ryan returned with one of the first groups, shivering from the crisp night air. She could tell from his bloodshot eyes that exhaustion was setting in. Trooper Meyers noticed it as well.

"Y'all should go home and get some rest," he said. "It may be a long night."

"I'm fine. I want to keep looking," Ryan said, but Kristy shook her head.

"We need to get Pops home and you should get some sleep. We'll come back in the morning, if that's okay?" Kristy asked Trooper Meyers.

"Yes, ma'am. Unless we locate Mr. Dobson before then, we'll be here."

Ryan opened his mouth, then closed it, thinking better than to defy Kristy. They climbed back into the truck and Pops startled awake.

"Any word from Lance?" Pops asked hopefully, eyes scanning the bustling campsite.

"No," she said softly. "Nothing yet."

Pops nodded tersely and closed his eyes, as if already in mourning. Ryan sat in the backseat, staring up at the sky, trying to be brave but bracing himself for bad news. All her planning could never have prepared her for this. She hadn't just murdered Lance, she realized; she'd killed a part of Ryan and Pops.

I'm sorry, she longed to say. *I'm sorry for all of this.*

Instead she drove, the three of them silenced by the weight of their own thoughts. All she could do, all any of them could do, was wait. Sooner or later, this would all be over.

CHAPTER TWENTY-SEVEN

Waiting proved harder than Kristy imagined. Once they arrived home, she was hoping for some time alone, time to reevaluate, to organize her thoughts, to prepare for more police interrogations, more inquiry. She'd expected Pops and Ryan to head straight to bed.

Instead, Pops went straight into the kitchen and from the back of the liquor cabinet he unearthed a vintage bottle of Chivas Regal. He poured all three of them a healthy glass.

"It'll take the edge off. Help us all sleep," he said.

Kristy would never normally let Ryan drink, and hard liquor wasn't ideal for a man so heavily medicated, but Kristy didn't say a word. She accepted her glass and the three of them gathered around the kitchen table, sipping their drinks.

"You know, Kristy girl, sometimes when you'd work late, Lance and I would grab a couple of beers and we'd drive over to the ballpark and just sit in the back of his truck, watching the game and shooting the shit. The man would have me laughing so hard I'd be spitting beer all over the place," Pops said with a chuckle.

Ryan joined in singing Lance's praises.

"I know Lance is fine. I know it. He can handle himself. No one is better at taking care of himself than Lance. It's weird but I can't stop thinking about all the things Lance taught me. Like when he's talking about judo, he's always using it to help me relate to life. And he's always pushing me to work harder because he could see my potential. And the way he listens... like he really hears me. He gets what it's like not to fit in, makes me feel like I'm not such a freak. If it weren't for Lance, I'd still be an outsider, but now everyone knows me. They like me."

Kristy hated that Ryan gave Lance credit for that. She wanted to argue back, tell Ryan people loved him because he was a wonderful kid, but that wasn't what Pops and Ryan wanted to hear right now. A silence had fallen over the table and Kristy realized they were waiting for her to take her turn. Listening to their stories, Kristy wanted *their* Lance to be *her* Lance. She wanted to join in with the tributes, but so many of her memories were shaded with violence.

"Remember last year when I was honored with the Excellence in Public Relations Award? Lance was so proud he filled my whole office with flowers..."

Kristy left out the part about what happened in the parking lot, how he'd shoved her in the car and grabbed her by the chin.

"Tell me, Kristy, why did you even invite me here? You basically ignored me the whole goddamn night. Why make me get all dressed up and come along if you weren't going to say a single goddamn word to me? I want you to look in the mirror and ask yourself, was that behavior appropriate? Ask yourself…did I show my husband the respect he deserves tonight?"

Those were Kristy's memories, but they needed to hear from her, so Kristy rambled on about the "good times."

A little drunk, Pops excused himself, optimistically mumbling that Lance would be back by morning. Ryan stood, shifting his feet, searching Kristy's expression for reassurance. Worried he'd see through her lies, she stood and gave him a quick hug.

"I'm going back out to search in the morning. Should I wake you?" Ryan asked when she pulled away, eyes downcast, fighting back tears.

"We'll go together," Kristy said. This was her penance, as she was forced to reconcile what she'd done. What could possibly be worse than searching, with your son, for a man you murdered? A man you hoped stayed missing forever.

The next morning, Kristy woke before Ryan, a long list of tasks she had to complete. She phoned Gus first. He answered on the first ring, his voice gruff, his annoyance on full display.

"Jesus, Kristy, it's barely seven o'clock. It had better be important," Gus said.

"Lance is missing," Kristy replied, and she heard the stunned inhalation of air. For once, Gus Fisher had been silenced.

"Did you hear me, Gus?"

"I heard. What the hell happened?"

Kristy recited her story, the details etched into her brain. "Lance went hunting on Friday and no one has heard from him since. We filed a police report and they have search teams looking…"

"But you're worried about him?"

"My husband hasn't come home, texted, or called in two days. Yes, I'm worried," Kristy said, not needing to feign annoyance.

"Right. So I guess you won't be in today?" Gus asked.

God, the man was a dimwit. "Yes, Gus, that's what I'm calling to tell you. I'm not coming to work today because my husband is missing."

"Okay. Okay. Let Carmen know what's going on and she can handle what needs to be handled. Look, Kristy, he's only been gone a couple of days. He's probably up to no good in some whorehouse or something. I mean, that's what men do sometimes. He'll be back tonight, repentant as hell."

Gus had a real way with words, Kristy thought. She called Carmen, who assured Kristy that everything at work would be handled.

"Whatever you need, Kris. I'm here."

She hung up, wishing that she could tell Carmen about Clifton, that she could check on him. Kristy hated that Clifton might feel forgotten. That was the loneliest feeling in the world. But there was no way to see Clifton, not while all of this was going on. Kristy's head was pounding, but she had one more call to make.

"Hey, Kristy, everything okay?"

Kristy rarely phoned Mac; all of their communication since she had married Lance was done via text.

She sat at the kitchen table, gripping the phone.

"It's about Lance."

Kristy launched into her story, repeating everything that had happened at the campsite with Ryan and Pops.

"I'm heading over now. I'm on my way," Mac said.

"Mac, you don't have to..."

"I know I don't, but I want to be there for you guys. Jesus, I can't believe this is happening. Lance is one of the good ones."

Kristy hung up. The last thing she wanted was Mac coming over and joining in the *Lance is amazing* chorus. But there was no way to stop him. Mac showed up half an hour later, laden down with groceries, filling the house with his overly enthusiastic responses. Kristy left Mac behind to keep Pops company and she returned to the campsite with Ryan.

The search continued. So did the constant onslaught of visitors and phone calls and reporters calling.

Day two.

Day three.

Day four.

Day five.

On the sixth day of the search for Lance Dobson, Kristy and Ryan returned from the woods dripping wet from the relentless thunderstorms, their feet aching and numb from walking through miles and miles of woods and wilderness. Ryan's exhaustion and the emotional toll this was taking were unbearable. She reached out and patted Ryan on the shoulder, as if somehow that might take away his pain.

"I'm gonna heat up some soup," she said. Ryan shrugged.

"I'm not really hungry."

"You've got to eat, Ry. We have to..."

Kristy's cell rang.

"Answer it, Mom. It could be Lance," Ryan said hopefully.

"Hello," Kristy said.

"Hi, I'm Detective Joanna Davenport from the Huntsville PD. Can I speak to Mrs. Dobson?"

"Speaking," Kristy answered, her palms already beginning to sweat.

"Mrs. Dobson, I've just been assigned to your husband's missing persons case. Would you by any chance have time to come by this evening and speak with me?" she asked.

"Yes. I can be there."

"Thank you," she said and then hung up.

Kristy tossed her phone into her handbag and plastered on a half smile as she returned to the kitchen.

"You okay, Mom?" Ryan said, camped out at the kitchen table.

Kristy didn't want to burden Ryan. Not yet.

"I have to duck out for just a few minutes. Need anything?" Kristy asked.

"No, I'm good. Drive safe," he said, returning his attention to his laptop and the missing persons message boards he had discovered, connecting with people from all over the country who were trying to find their loved ones.

Kristy left the house, her mind spinning, spinning, one dizzying thought after another. Was it normal for the spouse to be called to the police station? Had they uncovered the body? What if they poked holes in her story? What if Kristy fell apart? *Stop.* That wasn't an option. She had survived too much. She had to keep going.

Kristy sat in the drab gray waiting room, nervously rubbing her palms on her jeans, hoping to wipe away the sweat.

"Mrs. Dobson?" Detective Davenport asked.

"Yes, that's me," Kristy replied. She stood up and the detective thrust her hand out. Her grip was surprisingly strong. Detective Davenport was tiny, early thirties, with dark hair and sharp, blunt features. She had severe cheekbones and wore giant oversized tortoiseshell glasses. She wore jeans, a white blouse, and a tailored navy blazer. Her look screamed college professor, not police officer. *An interesting tactic.* Present yourself as completely unassuming so someone might let their guard down. She had to remember that the most unsuspecting people were often the most dangerous. She had Lance Dobson to thank for that lesson.

"Sorry to keep you waiting, Mrs. Dobson. We had a child go missing yesterday, so it's been all hands on deck. Please, follow me."

Kristy followed the woman down a long fluorescent-lit corridor, her legs unsteady beneath her. Detective Davenport opened the gray door to an interview room and motioned for Kristy to follow her inside. She took a seat at the faux wood table, staring down at her hands. Her nails were uneven, she thought. It had been ages since she had a manicure.

How stupid. What a stupid thing to think. She shook away the inane thought and watched as Detective Davenport eased into the opposite chair, her brows furrowed.

"I'm so sorry for what you're going through. Our resources are stretched pretty thin, but rest assured we're doing everything we can to locate your husband."

"Thank you," Kristy said softly.

"Has Lance ever given you any reason not to trust him?"

Yes . . . no . . . I'm not sure. All of the above?

"Not at all," Kristy replied.

"Then I have to warn you that some of what I'm going to tell you may be difficult to hear. I should also point out that sometimes people disappear on their own accord. Maybe it's bad money decisions, or tangling with the wrong people, or maybe they want to start over. I'm not saying that's what happened here. I'm just trying to give context to what might have occurred. We dug into Mr. Dobson's past. Credit history, previous addresses, relatives, previous jobs and relationships."

"Okay," Kristy said, bracing herself for whatever news was coming her way.

"Did Lance ever mention financial issues in the past?" Detective Davenport asked, her gaze boring into Kristy's eyes, searching for answers.

"Lance and I didn't spend too much time talking about the past. We were focused on building a future together," Kristy said, hoping her face wasn't as pinched as it felt.

"Did you know that Mr. Dobson was previously married and that his first wife killed herself?" Detective Davenport asked.

"Yes, but he didn't like to discuss it. It was a painful time in his life."

Kristy figured it was better to be honest about her knowledge of Hannah than to play dumb. She sat listening to the detective run through everything Kristy already knew. As the meeting went on, Kristy's hands stopped clenching; her knees stopped knocking together. This wasn't about Kristy. It seemed like it was more about Lance and what could have gotten him killed.

It was clear they didn't know he was dead, or that Kristy had killed him. At least not yet.

Kristy wasn't a suspect, but the more time she spent here, the better her chances were of screwing up, getting trapped in some kind of lie.

"Thank you for sharing this information with me, Detective," Kristy said as she folded her hands in her lap. "I should probably go. My family is waiting."

Davenport gauged Kristy once more. "The search and rescue parties will continue for now, but there are limitations to what we can do if our investigation doesn't turn up any sign of him."

"You're going to stop looking?" Kristy asked. That's what she wanted. For them to simply stop.

"No. We're not giving up just yet. You should brace yourself though. There comes a time when we'll have no choice but to call off the search."

Detective Davenport held open the door and ushered Kristy back into the lobby, shaking her hand again with that crushing grip.

"We'll be in touch, Mrs. Dobson," she said.

Kristy wasn't going to tell Ryan and Pops about any of the things she'd "learned" about Lance. No reason to sully their idol for them just yet. She'd keep up the facade. Lance was a loving, doting husband, Kristy his devoted wife.

Kristy's nerves were ripped and skewered like someone had been scraping at her insides with a potato peeler. But there were no more calls to return to the station, no more discussions about her life with Lance. She hoped the search would be called off and they could move on. But when she returned home, it was Ryan who turned the tables. He greeted her the second she stepped in the door.

"You know all the press in town, right?" he asked excitedly.

"I guess," Kristy replied.

"C'mon, Mom, you know lots of reporters, don't you?"

"Yes. I do."

"I read online that press conferences can turn the tide on a missing person's case. Can you make some calls? We have to get the word out. More people need to know Lance is missing."

Kristy wanted to say, *No. We will just wait. Let's enjoy each other's company before they lock me up forever.* But she didn't. Instead Kristy sat down and composed an e-mail and sent it out to the almost three hundred reporters in her address book. If she had any doubts about how well liked she was, in less than twenty-four hours she had her answer. Every single reporter in her contacts reached out, and then the news did what it did best. It made Kristy's life a spectacle.

Frenzy was the best word to describe it. Reporters descended, filling Kristy's front yard, news vans and SUVs parked on every bit of surface, others spilling onto the road. Standing on her front porch with Ryan and Pops behind her, Kristy gazed out at reporters from Houston, Huntsville, and Conroe, correspondents from all the local TV affiliates, people she'd known for years, all of them staring back at her. She'd written and rewritten her speech half a dozen times. This was never part of her plan, but at this point, Kristy was improvising. She'd spent the entire morning obsessing about what to wear. Women were judged on their appearance. If she were too made up they'd say she looked whorish, the type of woman that couldn't be trusted. If she didn't wear enough makeup, if she looked too unkempt, it might look like she didn't care about herself or anyone else. She took a deep breath and began to speak.

"My husband, Lance Dobson, has been missing for nine days. He has not called or texted. He has not used his credit card. We have not heard anything from him and we are very concerned. If you have any information about him, please contact the Montgomery County Sheriff's Office. His family... We miss him and want him home."

The reporters lobbed questions and Kristy answered, doing her best to convey grief and concern. She was exhausted and terrified that she might slip up. Lance's disappearance was a top story that night, but the next day the missing kid Detective Davenport mentioned was found murdered, which sent Lance's case to the bottom of the pile.

As the days ticked by, eleven, twelve, thirteen, the energy of the volunteers began to wane as well. Enthusiasm gave way to hopelessness. Maybe Lance wasn't coming back. Maybe there was nothing that could be done. The hardest part about it all was watching Ryan, the Ryan she knew, slowly vanish. What was left behind was an angry, sullen teen. He grunted his answers to her questions, disappearing into his room for hours. He'd slink off to Ella's, the shock of what happened drawing them back together.

"I can't leave him now, Mrs. Dobson," Ella said when she came to pick Ryan up. "He's hurting too bad."

They'd head out for the night and she would hear Ryan returning in the early-morning hours, then he would sleep all day. Kristy wanted to tell him that it was unacceptable, that he was still a kid, her kid, and he couldn't stay out all night, but she'd taken so much from him, she simply let it go.

Pops was struggling too. Some days he didn't even come out of his room. He stopped doing his breathing exercises and refused to attend his appointments for the clinical trial. She longed to shake some sense into him, into both of them.

Stop it, she wanted to shout at them. *Just stop! Lance was killing me. He tried to kill me. Every day. He might have killed you. Don't shed another goddamn tear for that man.* But all she could do was endure their pain in silence.

On Sunday, fourteen days after Lance went "missing," Kristy knocked on Ryan's door. He was hunched over his laptop, the lights off, still wearing his faded tracksuit pants and last year's debate sweatshirt.

"Hey, Ry, I think it's time you go back to school."

Ryan stood up, eyes flashing, clenching his fists and staring back at Kristy like she was a total lunatic.

"Jesus, Mom, I think my teachers will fucking understand if I'm not in class considering my stepfather is missing and may be..."

She flinched. Ryan's harsh tone startled Kristy and she stepped back, holding up her hand to shield herself. Confusion flashed across Ryan's face.

"God, Mom, did you think I was gonna hit you?"

"No, I just...I'm on edge. I didn't..." But Kristy did. For a fraction of a second, she was terrified.

Ryan isn't Lance, she reminded herself.

"I'm all messed up, but I didn't mean to scare you. I'm just not ready to go back to school yet. Not with Lance gone. We can't give up hope."

"I'm not giving up hope, Ry, but I still have bills to pay, and Gus is expecting me back in the office tomorrow. I can give you a few more days, but then you have to go back too. We don't have a choice."

Ryan's silence spoke volumes. He sank down onto the bed, returned to his laptop, and resumed sending e-mails to news stations, doing everything he could to bring more attention to Lance's disappearance. He turned his back on her, and Kristy had no choice but to leave, closing the door behind her.

Gus hadn't insisted that Kristy return to work. That was her decision. But she couldn't stand spending another day in this house with Ryan and Pops and their all-consuming grief.

That wasn't the only reason though. Tomorrow was Clifton's execution. Kristy couldn't abandon him. She had to be there for his final day. She owed him that.

She asked Carmen to check if Clifton had written her any new letters, but there was nothing. Had news about Lance's disappearance reached death row? Did Clifton suspect Kristy? What would he say? Would he be disappointed? Or would he sympathize, knowing what happens when dangerous people go unpunished?

Tomorrow would test Kristy in every way possible, her sense of justice, right and wrong, and her ability to do a job she hated. Despite her exhaustion, Kristy fought sleep, hating the moment her eyes flickered closed and Lance claimed her dreams, his voice low and sinister, calling out a warning Kristy could not escape.

"I'm coming for you, Kristy. I'm coming for all of you."

CHAPTER TWENTY-EIGHT

It was dawn when Kristy woke, drenched in sweat. She showered and dressed, donning black pants and a gray sweater, muted colors. She sat at the kitchen table, sipping coffee, staring down at the newspaper. On the front page of the *Houston Chronicle* was Clifton's mug shot. "Death at Last," the headline read. A smaller photo in the right-hand corner was of Lance: "Local Man Still Missing."

She couldn't bear seeing Lance smiling up at her. Kristy had taken that photo on their first weekend away, a spur-of-the-moment trip to Corpus Christi. She was just about to toss the paper in the trash when Ryan ambled in, wearing wrinkled jeans and his worn DON'T HATE, DEBATE T-shirt. He poured a bowl of Frosted Flakes and sat down, eating wordlessly. Kristy reached out and squeezed Ryan's hand and his eyes filled with tears.

"I'm sorry, Ry. I know how hard this is."

"Think we'll ever know what happened to him?" he asked.

"I don't know. But I'm so sorry you're hurting."

His eyes darted up from his bowl, quizzically.

"You're hurting too, aren't you, Mom?" he asked.

Kristy faltered, searching for the right thing to say.

"Yes...I am. It's just...I'm your mom. I can handle it. But you..."

"I guess it's different for you 'cause you've been around death and dying all these years," Ryan said, as if the idea had presented itself for the first time.

"Yes, but the men who get executed, I'm not married to them."

"Then why are you..."

"What? Why am I what?"

She could see Ryan's wheels spinning. He shook his head. "Never mind." A part of Kristy wanted to ask Ryan to finish his sentence. The other part was afraid of what he might say, questioning Kristy, wondering why she wasn't more devastated. Shouldn't she have been crippled by grief, instead of just...moving forward? But maybe that was just Kristy's own paranoia seeping in. Ryan remained quiet, eating slowly, each bite pained as if he had to force down the food in order to survive. She would always regret causing him pain, but the math was simple. One death to avoid three.

Ryan gulped down the last of his food and grabbed his backpack.

"Gotta run. Ella's almost here."

She wanted to stop him, to hug him and tell him everything would be okay, but she couldn't promise that. Ryan had opened himself up to Lance, and now he was gone. She'd lost her mother—she understood the kind of pain he was feeling at losing the closest thing he had to a father. Ryan left and Kristy sat at the table, trying to brace herself for the day ahead.

It wasn't standard protocol to visit inmates before they went to death row, but it wasn't something so out of the ordinary that it would raise attention. Kristy made her way to Polunsky and found Clifton sitting in the visiting area, his family sitting across from him, in the spot Kristy usually sat. He was sitting up tall, hair shorn, clean-shaven, his uniform gleaming white. Clifton had spoken so much about his sister Fiona and his niece Nina that she recognized them instantly.

Fiona was a regal woman in her early fifties with a short Afro and red-rimmed eyes, clutching at a tissue. Her daughter, Nina, was sixteen, with long, pencil-thin dreads and a permanent frown. They were both clad in black as if already in mourning. Fiona saw Kristy watching and she stood to greet her.

"Ms. Tucker, hello. We've been talking about your troubles. I hope you know that we're all praying for your husband's safe return." Kristy saw Clifton staring back at her. He knew what she'd done. She wasn't sure how she could tell, but he knew. Kristy swallowed hard, forcing herself to focus on Fiona.

"That's very kind of you. I'm not here to get in the way. I wanted to speak with Clifton, but take your time. And I hope y'all know that I'll be here until the very end…"

"Thank you," Fiona said, her voice cracking.

"If you need anything," Kristy said, stepping to the side, wanting to give them their privacy.

Kristy couldn't hear what Clifton was saying, but Fiona's sobs filled the visiting area, and Nina was softly whimpering. Kristy stared down at her hands, absorbing their grief, wishing she could offer them some kind of comfort. Another twenty minutes went by, and Bruce appeared, signaling the end of visitation.

Fiona's and Nina's faces fell, an awkward, pain-filled final good-bye unfolding as they tapped at the glass and whispered their final "I love you's." They headed out, turning back every few feet to wave good-bye to Clifton. He waved back until they were gone, his posture erect, gaze steady, looking more like a soldier heading off to war than a condemned man only a few hours away from his execution.

Kristy held up ten fingers to Bruce, and he nodded his approval and moved a few feet away. Kristy knew that the transport team would be here shortly, so this visit with Clifton would have to be quick. She would have one more face-to-face at the Walls, but the warden would be there. This was her last chance at a private good-bye. Kristy sat down and picked up the phone. Clifton did the same.

"You doing okay?" Clifton asked.

She smiled grimly.

"That's my line."

He shrugged. "I'm real sorry about everything you've gone through. All that's happening... everything you had to do. But you'll get through it."

"I'm not so sure about that," she said.

"I am. If I can survive almost ten years in this place, you can survive this."

"Kind of hard to believe you're giving *me* a pep talk," Kristy said.

"With everything going on, I didn't think I'd see you again.

The fact that you're here, that you came today..." Clifton trailed off, closed his eyes, tried to compose himself. "I still can't believe it."

"I wasn't gonna leave you. Not without saying good-bye," Kristy replied. "I have to head to the Walls soon, and I'll see you there. We'll go over everything with the warden and you'll get to spend time with the chaplain. And then, Clifton, I'll be on the other side of that glass. You'll be able to see me. I'll be there with Nina and Fiona until the very end."

Clifton's composure was faltering, tears welling in his eyes.

"I don't know what I did to deserve your kindness, Ms. Tucker. It made these last few years a lot more bearable."

"You've been a good friend, Clifton. I won't forget that," she said.

Bruce raised his hand, pointing to his watch. It was time.

"I have to go."

"Good-bye, Ms. Tucker, and thanks."

"Clifton?"

He nodded, waiting for her response.

"Call me Kristy."

Her words registered, and a giant smile illuminated Clifton's face. He nodded in appreciation, an understanding that though they would never sit on a patio and share a beer together, their friendship was secured. He placed the phone on the cradle and allowed Bruce to escort him out. This time he didn't bow his head or shuffle but held his head up high, shoulders back.

The guards would return him to his cell, where he would spend his final hours at Polunsky waiting for the transport team to arrive. They would cuff his wrists, shackle his ankles and waist, and whisk him down the halls of death row as the inmates called out their good-byes.

"Keep the faith, Cliff."

"Don't give up."

"See ya, baby killer."

Once Clifton was secured in the van, a three-unit convoy would depart from Polunsky, their routes a secret from everyone except the warden. Forty-five minutes later, if traffic cooperated, they would arrive at the Walls. The guards would lead Clifton through a back gate, down cavernous halls to a holding cell, his final stop-off before he was escorted to the death chamber. That's where Kristy would greet him.

There was no way for Kristy to know what Clifton was thinking as he made that final drive past the lake, tall grass fluttering in the breeze, vacationers in minivans passing him by, truckers on their way home after a long-haul trip, knowing this was the last drive he would ever make.

Kristy climbed into her car and made the familiar drive to the Walls, the miles ticking by, her mind crowded with thoughts of Lance and Clifton. At the gated entrance, over ninety protesters, old and young alike, had gathered. From idealistic students from the criminal justice program at Sam Houston State to elderly grandmothers to devout Christians, they had arrived to register their disapproval. They carried signs that read, TEXAS KILLS INNOCENT PEOPLE and AN EYE FOR AN EYE MAKES THE WHOLE WORLD BLIND. On the opposite side of the gate, a smaller group of around thirty pro—death penalty protesters were eager to see Clifton get his comeuppance. DIE BABY KILLER DIE was one of the many creative signs Kristy clocked as she found her parking space.

Celebrity inmates always drew big crowds, and Clifton was a celebrity with a capital C. As she walked toward her office, she could hear the on-air reporters testing their microphones, most of them using the same absurd intro: "Two lives cut short finally receive justice today."

Kristy wanted to defend Clifton, but there was no proof, no evidence that would exonerate him. Kristy's instincts had failed her before. Maybe she had to believe in Clifton, had to believe in something. She wasn't a shrink so she wasn't about to start analyzing the situation. It didn't matter what she thought anyway. The state had made its decision. In just a few hours, it would all be over.

She returned to her office, greeting Carmen, and found herself inundated with coworkers stopping by to offer prayers and well-wishes for Lance's safe return. She finally settled in at her desk but she didn't do a single bit of work. Instead Kristy sat at her desk, motionless, unable to concentrate, clicking on her e-mails, the words nothing but a blur.

At one thirty, she headed over to the holding cell adjacent to the death chamber. Warden Hal Casey, a sweet and slightly bland Christian from Waco, ran through the details about what to expect; then it was Kristy's job to brief Clifton on final PR protocols.

"If you'd like, you can write out a statement for the press and I will make copies to distribute," Kristy said.

"No, ma'am, I think I've said enough. I'm good," Clifton said. He'd already told her that he wouldn't be issuing a statement, but they went through the motions anyway.

Kristy's role in this part of the process was to gauge Clifton's demeanor so that she could answer the reporters' questions.

Was the inmate nervous?

Scared?

Remorseful?

How did he act?

Did he cry?

What was his final meal?

It was exhausting, pretending that this was just another execution. Clifton was quiet and obedient. He promised to cooperate and they were soon joined by Chaplain Gohlke, a onetime felon who had spent his life working with inmates. The chaplain promised to stay with Clifton and offer him comfort until the very end. The warden asked Clifton if he had any other questions.

"No, sir. I think y'all have covered it."

"Good-bye, Clifton," Kristy said, unable to make eye contact in case she burst into tears.

"Good-bye, ma'am," he said, and as she walked away, she knew those were the last words he would say to her.

The execution was at least five hours away. She stopped off at victim services to see if anyone in Janice's family had expressed interest in holding a press conference after Clifton's execution. As she made her way to the office, out of the corner of her eye, she caught a glimpse of Janice waiting outside. Despite her moneyed appearance, Janice's ice-blue eyes were dull, flitting about; an anxiousness seemed to radiate from her. Kristy hadn't seen her in months, not since she'd spent all those nights parked outside her home. This wasn't the woman she'd seen, manicured and coiffed. Everyone played a role, Kristy thought. Some just better than others.

It was protocol to keep families of inmates and the victims' families separate for obvious reasons. Victim services would spend the afternoon with Janice and her mother, briefing them on what to expect. Someone from the chaplaincy would offer the same support to Clifton's family.

The state allowed five media witnesses to observe the executions. Three spots were "Texas first," which meant that press from Texas were prioritized over out-of-state or foreign correspondents. The reporters would camp out in the press office, drinking coffee and gossiping, until the call from the warden or the attorney general came through signaling the execution would proceed.

The day crawled by, Kristy trapped in the room with the reporters, many of them eager to explore all of their theories on Lance, each one more ridiculous than the last. Alien abduction and CIA spy were two options that were floated. Kristy had enough of the probing and questioning and she told Carmen she would be in her office waiting for the call to come. She kept darting nervous glances at the clock. By six o'clock, Kristy wondered if maybe Clifton might be spared, at least for today. The seconds ticked by, then minutes.

Six ten.

Six twelve.

Six fifteen.

Six thirty.

Seven ten.

The tension was unbearable. She could hear the reporters in the lobby bitching and moaning about missed deadlines, Gus grousing about missing his dinner reservation at the country club.

At seven forty, Kristy's office phone rang. She heard the warden's voice. "It's go time." Her heart ached for Clifton but she had a job to do. She texted Gus that it was time and walked into the main waiting area. The reporters saw her and leapt to their feet, closing laptops and grabbing their notebooks. Gus greeted her, clapping his hands together gleefully.

"Showtime, y'all," he joked, his standard response before each execution. It had always seemed so matter-of-fact, but today it struck Kristy as downright heartless. Kristy gathered the witnesses and they made the trek across the street to the death house. She would oversee one group of witnesses, which included Clifton's family. Gus would be in another room with Janice, her mother, and the other state witnesses.

Kristy had briefed all the guests about where they would stand, and everyone found their assigned spots. The mood was somber, but routine. For most of the reporters, this was old hat, just another story to file. For the politicians in attendance, they'd use tonight as a way to brag to their constituents about their tough-on-crime stance.

The curtain opened to reveal Clifton, strapped to the table, an audience gathered around to observe. *Such a macabre scene for civilized society*, Kristy thought. The tie-down team, all volunteer guards who believed in capital punishment, had already done their part. One person had secured the head, another the right arm, another the left arm, and so on until there was no possible way to escape. The only people that remained in the death chamber with Clifton were the warden and Chaplain Gohlke. In an adjoining room, the IV team was working to get the lines in place as they prepared the precise amount of lethal drugs needed to inject into Clifton.

Kristy hadn't thought to ask Clifton if he was afraid of needles. Kristy actually had an irrational fear of needles. Every time she needed a shot or blood work she told the doctor about her phobia, hoping that by stating it out loud, she might conquer it. It wasn't the actual needle prick; it was the anticipation. The first injection would contain sodium pentothal, which put the prisoner to sleep. The second syringe had pancuronium bromide, a skeletal muscle relaxant, which paralyzes the prisoner's lungs. The death knell would be the third and final injection of potassium chloride, which would cause cardiac arrest, stopping Clifton's heart.

Chaplain Gohlke stood at the edge of the gurney, his hands lightly touching Clifton's feet, enough pressure to say, *I'm here. You're not alone.*

On the gurney, Clifton lay motionless, eyes glued to the ceiling, hands strapped down, facing outward. A reporter once described the final image of an inmate before an execution "like Christ at the crucifixion." Kristy thought it was hyperbole, used to sell newspapers. "What a load of shit," she'd said to Carmen, but tonight that's how she saw it. An innocent man dying for someone else's sins.

Her hands tingled, a million tiny pinpricks stabbing at

them, her breath coming out in spurts. She wondered what was running through Janice's mind. Was she thanking God? Celebrating the fact that she'd destroyed Clifton in every way possible? Or was she innocent and Kristy's empathy misdirected? She shook her head, forcing away any doubts. *I'm with you*, she thought, hoping he could feel her support. *I'm right here with you.*

The stale, musty air was clogging Kristy's pores. Fiona was already wailing, her daughter stoic, tenderly rubbing her mother's back and assuming the role of caretaker. The boom mic descended from the ceiling. Some inmates attempted to lift up their torsos to reach the mics, even though it wasn't necessary to be heard. But not Clifton. He lay motionless, bound to the gurney. He swallowed nervously and licked his lips. The warden's slow southern drawl came through the speakers.

"Clifton Harris, do you have any final words?"

He nodded and turned toward the glass, staring right at Janice.

"I loved Rosie and Mikey, my precious babies. I did not kill them and I will meet my maker with a clear conscience. Janice knows the truth. One day so will everyone else. To my family, Fiona and Nina, and all of the Harris family that stuck by me and believed in me, to the friends who kept me going, I will not forget you. And I hope you will never forget me." Clifton's voice cracked but he didn't cry. "I'm ready, Warden," he said.

His gaze had landed on Kristy and she gave a slight nod, wanting him to see that she had kept her promise. She was here for him. She'd be here until the end. It was eight fifteen. Kristy blinked and was back in that desolate, rain-soaked field, clutching the pistol, firing the .38 over and over again, Lance staggering backward, his body falling down on the wet, muddy earth. She shook away the haunting image, watching as the warden reached up to take off his glasses, his signal to the executioner that it was time to administer the drugs. Kristy wanted to run from the room and just keep on running, but instead she simply closed her eyes. She had seen too much death already. She sat there, waiting to hear the warden's time-of-death confirmation, waiting for Clifton's pain to end, waiting for it to all be over. Then the phone rang...

CHAPTER TWENTY-NINE

The call came from the governor's office. "The Texas Court of Criminal Appeals has issued a stay of execution," the warden said. Kristy exhaled. She saw the warden and Chaplain Gohlke gesturing for the guards to close the curtains.

Just like that the verdict was in. Clifton would not die tonight. From previous experience, Kristy knew that all hell was about to break loose and she would be at the center of it. Fiona was on her feet, tearful, in disbelief.

"He's saved. Sweet Jesus, Nina, our prayers worked. Cliff is saved."

She beelined for Kristy. "Can we see him? I want...I need to see my brother."

Kristy hesitated. She hated being the bad guy, but rules were rules.

"I'm afraid that Clifton has to be transported back to Polunsky. You won't be able to see him until the warden gives visitation approval," Kristy said. "You'll have to check in tomorrow and coordinate with the officials there."

Fiona shook her head, eyes drooping from exhaustion. "This whole system is so damn backward. Screwing with my brother like this, giving him hope. Y'all ain't never letting him go and we both know it."

"I'm sorry..."

"Hell, it's not your fault. You're just a goddamn cog in this wheel."

Kristy was exactly like that. A goddamn cog trapped in this wheel.

"If you see Cliff, will you tell him we love him and we'll keep on praying?" Fiona said.

"I will," Kristy promised.

They left reluctantly and Kristy turned to Carmen, who was waiting for instructions.

"Can you take the press back to the office while I go and get a statement from Clifton?" Kristy asked.

"Will do. Crazy day, huh?"

"Tell me about it," she said. Kristy left Carmen to deal with the reporters, who were already foaming at the mouth for a statement. Nothing made for better ratings than a last-minute stay of execution. Any minute now, an AP reporter would be tweeting out the news. As it was, Kristy's phone hadn't stopped buzzing. She managed to glance at it for a moment, and saw a series of texts from Ryan.

Going out with the team to put up more flyers.

Left you dinner (turkey burgers) in the oven. Pops went to bed early. Love you.

She texted him back. **You're the best kid in the world. I love you.**

She thought about adding something about Lance, but she was too exhausted for that level of dishonesty.

On Kristy's way toward Clifton's holding cell, she saw Janice, raging at Annabelle, the victim's representative.

"What is going on? What is happening?" Janice demanded, shrieking with anger. "I've waited twelve goddamn years for this day and now what? What am I supposed to do now?"

Janice's mother tried to shush her. "You're making a scene, honey." But Janice wasn't listening. To everyone else, Janice's rage was driven by grief and the quest for justice. But Kristy wasn't convinced. She spotted Gus hurrying back to the office and she called after him.

"What the hell happened?" Kristy asked.

"Apparently, Harris's lawyers challenged the courts about the legality of the drugs we're using. They'll be releasing a statement shortly."

"Jesus, don't tell me we're using illegal drugs," Kristy said. She'd heard that facing pressure from the public about the death penalty, pharmaceutical companies were cutting off their sales to prisons and other states were purchasing their drugs from black market sources.

"Don't get on your high horse. They were approved by people with far more power than you and I possess. Now if you don't mind, I have to speak with the warden. Make sure you get a statement from Harris."

Kristy wanted to scream at Gus and all those goddamn bureaucrats, but all she cared about now was seeing Clifton. She hurried toward the holding cell, wondering how soon before the other death row inmates heard about Clifton's stay and their attorneys began filing similar motions, all of them dreaming about getting off death row. It wasn't fair to give any of these men and women that kind of hope. The state wasn't going to admit that what they were doing was wrong. They couldn't. They'd gather the best legal minds and make an argument that convinced the public the drugs were safe and that the death penalty was crucial in ensuring justice. Which meant that nothing would change. Not for Clifton. They were delaying the inevitable, just like Fiona said.

A guard led Kristy into the corridor and over to Clifton's holding cell. Through the metal bars, she saw him sitting on a cot, head bowed, hands clasped as if in prayer.

"Hey, Clifton," she said softly.

His head sprang up, startled, a stunned expression on his face.

"Ma'am…"

Clifton half stood, like a gentleman greeting a first date, awkward, unsure. Two guards hovered beside Kristy. Her voice was crisp and businesslike, but she hoped her eyes revealed the true depths of her relief.

"Clifton, you received a stay of execution from the Texas Court of Criminal Appeals while the state looks into issues regarding the drugs being used for lethal injection. You'll be able to speak with your attorney before they take you back to Polunsky. Before that, I need to brief the press. I wondered if you had anything you wanted me to pass along to them," Kristy said. She had taken out her notepad to jot down his statement.

Clifton paused, a slight tremor running through his body, his hands and legs twitching. Posttraumatic stress most likely.

"It's okay, Clifton. Take your time."

He paused again, trying to steady himself.

"Tell them—I am an innocent man. Today is the sign I needed to keep fighting, and that's what I will do."

Kristy finished writing, her business with Clifton now complete.

"Stay strong. Fiona and Nina wanted me to say that they love you and they'll see you soon."

"Thank you, ma'am."

Back in her office, Kristy prepared Clifton's statement, refusing to think about the man she called her friend, instead typing up facts, statistics, the who, what, where, when, why, that made up every reporter's story. Carmen returned and said that Janice was adamant about wanting to speak to the press. Kristy wasn't quite sure she was emotionally prepared to run point on the press conference.

"Carmen, would you mind taking the lead? I'll be around. It's just been a long day," Kristy said. The adrenaline from Clifton's last-minute reprieve and the constant uncertainty about what might happen with Lance was almost too much to bear.

Carmen squeezed Kristy's hand and said, "I've got you covered."

They held the press conference, the Walls a stark backdrop. Janice's earlier rage had dimmed, a quiet fury now fueling her. Kristy and the staff watched while she railed against the system.

"My children were babies when my husband took them from me. They would be teenagers now. Beautiful high schoolers with a lifetime ahead of them. Today was a travesty of justice. I can only hope this situation will be resolved and this man...this monster will be punished accordingly."

Janice urged people all over the state to call and demand that Clifton's death sentence be carried out. Kristy braced herself, knowing that her phone had probably already started ringing. Once the press conference was over, Annabelle, the victim services rep, went to lead her away. Janice turned back and caught Kristy watching. Janice's expression was pure ice.

"Kristy, are you ready?" Carmen said. Kristy turned and just like that Janice was gone. It didn't matter what Kristy believed or didn't believe about Janice. There was still work to be done. Carmen and Kristy waited two hours before the Associated Press and local reporters finished filing their stories. Carmen insisted on staying with Kristy until the bitter end.

It was almost eleven when Kristy returned home, the house pitch-black, no sign of Pops or Ryan. Kristy opened the oven and saw the burger Ryan left, neatly prepared on a plate for her. Kristy's appetite had completely vanished, but she heated the food and ate it, chewing slowly, grateful for Ryan's kind gesture.

On her way to bed, she stopped by Pops's room and found him sprawled out, snoring loudly, the TV blaring in the background, some infomercial selling fitness videos promising chiseled abs droning on. Kristy watched him for a moment, his chest rising and falling, his breathing tortured. She wanted to ease his suffering, physical and emotional, but there was nothing she could do. She switched off the TV and went to Ryan's room. He was asleep too, hair mussed, his gray comforter pooling at the bottom of the bed. She lifted the blankets up and pulled them over him, remembering all the nights he'd shouted, "Tuck me in," the nights she'd pulled the covers taut over his tiny body, singing at the top of her lungs, "You're as snug as a bug in a rug."

Her eyes slipped from his peaceful face to the floor. She hadn't noticed it before, but there was a poster, the photo of Lance staring back up at her, the word MISSING printed under his image in big red letters.

That damn smug grin mocking her, Clifton's devastated face, Janice's cold stare, all of it came together. Kristy gasped, a sob exploding.

"Mom, what is it? What's wrong?" Startled, Ryan bolted awake, trying to shake himself from his slumber.

Kristy couldn't speak. It was all too much. It was just too damn much. Giant heaving sobs racked her body.

Ryan hugged her, trying to console her, willing to pretend, at least for tonight, that their family wasn't falling apart.

"It's okay, Mom. We'll be okay," Ryan said over and over again, his words a mantra she desperately wanted to believe.

Dear Ms. Tucker,

I hope you're hanging in there. Seems like no news is good news as far as I can tell.

I'm looking forward to your next visit. This week has crawled by. Wednesday just can't get here soon enough. It still doesn't seem real, what happened. There I am, lying on that table, saying my prayers, trying not to think about what's going to happen, when the phone rang. I tell you, I thought for sure that I was hallucinating. They took me back to my cell and I was so afraid they were gonna drag me back to the death chamber, I didn't sleep for two full days.

Going back to Polunsky was real hard. All the guys congratulating me, telling me I should be happy. Happy? That's a laugh. What do I have to celebrate? I know Janice won't rest until she finishes what she started. And the state sure as hell isn't giving up on getting rid of me. I know I said I was ready to keep fighting, but once I got back to my cell, it all started to seem like too much. I was in a real bad place until I saw Fiona. Let me tell you she gave me a piece of her mind. She said, Cliff, you can be pissed and give up or you can be pissed off and keep fighting. She also called me a whole heap of names that aren't fit to print, so to speak, but she made me see the light. I've got a second chance and I'm sure as heck not gonna waste it. So here I am, asking you to do your best to keep the interviews coming and I'll keep shouting my innocence from the rooftops.

Best wishes,
Clifton Harris aka The Comeback Kid

CHAPTER THIRTY

In the days and weeks leading up to Lance's death, Kristy had been determined not to make any mistakes. She avoided credit card transactions, and she never used the Internet at home for research, only libraries and schools that didn't require photo IDs. She hadn't told a soul besides Clifton about her marital problems. She never sent a text or e-mail that detailed how unhappy she was. There were no photos of the abuse. No virtual trail. No physical trail. No eyewitnesses. That she knew of.

Kristy's attempts to create the perfect alibi had, for all intents and purposes, succeeded. Without any new leads, the search and rescue was called off. Ryan and his friends and a few die-hard volunteers still went out every couple of days, searching the woods and nearby campsites, handing out flyers to hikers and people in town, but no leads and no sign of a body meant no case.

That meant Kristy, Ryan, and Pops had no choice but to return to some semblance of a routine. Ryan had final exams and was preparing for his summer trip to Notre Dame. Pops agreed to return to the clinical trial. Each day that passed, Lance's murder, what Kristy had done, grew a little less real, the edges of that night fading, slipping away until it almost seemed as if someone else had done it. As the days passed, Kristy stopped reliving every moment of Lance's death in her head. She forced herself to focus on the present, enjoying her time with Pops and Ryan at breakfast, making dinner, her appetite slowly returning, along with her joy at experiencing day-to-day activities without the fear of Lance's outbursts.

Bit by bit, Kristy's anxiety lessened. She used to spend hours obsessing about what to wear to satisfy Lance without sending the wrong message to her colleagues or the inmates. She stopped obsessing over how much pepper she used on her steak or if her spaghetti was too al dente or if she served Pops and Ryan larger helpings than she served Lance.

At night, Kristy climbed into bed, spreading out in the middle of the mattress, reveling in the fact that her body was hers again. She *was* free. Or so she tried to tell herself. But then she'd catch a whiff of Lance's cologne or she'd hear a song, their song, on the radio, and for an instant, her heart would ache for what they could have been. No news was good news, Clifton had said, but Kristy found herself tensing every time the phone rang or a car pulled into the driveway or there was a knock on her front door. Some days Kristy wondered if she had simply traded one prison for another.

She'd returned to work full-time. Her days blurred together, managing one crisis after another. She'd received a call from a reporter about Julia Vidal, a female inmate at Gatesville who had been corresponding with Steve, a truck driver she met on an Internet site for inmates. (Yes, even inmates did Internet dating thanks to friends on the outside.) It was a torrid love affair (on paper anyway). Julia decided it would be fun to post their letters on Facebook and roped the trucker into doing it. The letters were quite entertaining and garnered thousands of likes, instantly becoming a viral sensation. A New York publisher even offered a contract for Julia and Steve to write a book, some kind of prison erotica that would hopefully connect with the *Fifty Shades* crowd. The hiccup on their part was not realizing that it is illegal for inmates to make a profit while in prison. The reporter had spoken to the family of the man Julia poisoned to death, and they were obviously very upset.

Kristy's morning was devoted to putting out that fire before she headed over to Polunsky. Since his execution was halted, Clifton had become the most popular inmate in the state of Texas. The growing dissent over the human rights violations of executions (a series of botched ones had occurred across the country) had been enough to grant Clifton yet another reprieve.

Clifton was excited by the momentum in his legal case. There were esteemed scientists from all over the world arguing over the expert witness and his testimony about how the fire started. There was a new statement by the lead fire investigator's ex-girlfriend, who said the man was a drunk and a racist and may have been biased against Clifton. The courts were reviewing all the evidence, but even with that, Kristy knew there would have to be one hell of a miracle for Clifton to cheat death twice.

Kristy was so caught up in her thoughts that she didn't even notice Gus until he was standing right in front of her, snapping his fingers.

"Jesus, Tucker, I've been calling you."

"What is it, Gus?" she said, hoping he wasn't going to bother her with some ridiculous request, like ordering less toilet paper for the staff bathroom to cut down on costs.

"There are two detectives outside who want to speak with you," Gus said, his beady eyes narrowing.

"I'm supposed to go to Polunsky," Kristy replied, knowing it was ridiculous but trying to stall for time, trying to prepare herself for what was about to happen.

"Carmen can handle Polunsky. I've already told her to head over. Is it okay if I send the officers in?"

He didn't wait for an answer. Kristy sank back into her chair and waited. She imagined the uniform-clad men stepping into her office, reading her rights, handcuffing her and leading her past all her colleagues, their judgmental eyes boring into her head, whispers following her out.

"Should've known the wife did it. The wife is always guilty."

"Can't trust the quiet ones."

"Kristy Tucker, no way, she wouldn't hurt a fly."

Kristy smoothed her hair, sat up straighter in her chair, knowing that from this point on, everything she did would be analyzed. Detective Davenport entered, along with a Texas Ranger, easily identified by his signature uniform—the Texas-shaped badge, white button-down shirt, tan pants, and white cowboy hat. He was in his early thirties, with features that were handsome now—smooth olive skin, bright green eyes, and a lean figure—but she imagined him five years from now, thirty or forty pounds heavier, jowls sagging, the smooth skin weathered by the sun. She stood up and shook hands with Detective Davenport first.

"Detective, how are you?"

"I've been better, Mrs. Dobson." She gestured to her colleague.

"This is Texas Ranger Eduardo Santiago. He'll be assisting us with your husband's case."

They'd found Lance. That's why he was here. Texas Rangers often consulted on murder investigations, especially in smaller towns where there wasn't a need for murder cops. This was it. It was all over. Even though Kristy had pulled the trigger herself, her knees buckled. The ranger instinctively reached for her and eased Kristy back into her chair. Detective Davenport stared unblinking as she took a seat across from her. Kristy reached for a bottle of water and took a sip, her mouth dry.

"Is this...is it about Lance?" Kristy asked softly.

"It is," Ranger Santiago said, his expression grim. "We located Lance's body about thirty miles outside of town, fifteen miles from his campsite."

Kristy gasped, leaning forward. She didn't have to fake tears. They fell easily, pouring down her face. She remembered that night so clearly, the image of Lance lunging at her in the truck, the force of his fists as he struck her, the muttered curses and threats, the moment when he reared back, and the shots that killed him.

"Whoever killed him picked a good spot. No way of

knowing that the city was planning on razing that land to build a roadway. A bad bit of luck," Davenport said.

Yes, it was very bad luck.

Kristy had studied the questions cops asked once a body was discovered. Questions other wives, other *killers* forgot. So many people in her situation drew attention to themselves with their carelessness, their lack of emotion, or their extreme displays of emotion. Kristy's job now was to create a fully realized portrait of the grief-stricken widow.

"What happened to him? Do you know?"

"We're not at liberty to discuss specifics," Detective Davenport said, a sure sign that Kristy was now a prime suspect. Otherwise they would just tell her the cause of death.

"I need to speak with my family. My son needs to know and my father," Kristy said. Ryan and Pops couldn't hear that Lance was gone from someone else. Kristy had to be the one to tell them.

"We understand, but first we'd like you to come down to the station and identify the body. We also have a few questions," Ranger Santiago responded, his eyes boring into hers.

"I've met you before," Kristy said without thinking.

"The Torres execution," he responded.

That was it. Kristy remembered the heartbroken families of the two hikers killed by Gilbert Torres, a serial killer who'd taken eleven lives. She waited for Ranger Santiago to say something more about that day, how he'd been best friends with one of the victims and had come as a representative of the family, but he remained silent. There wouldn't be any bonding with Kristy. Not today. There was something about him that unnerved her. He never dropped eye contact, a skillful maneuver, always drawing you back in, forcing you to look at him. Kristy saw the wedding ring and wondered what his home life was like. Was he a man who took his work home? Did he tell his wife about the horrors he experienced day in and day out? Or was he the type who bottled it up, living two lives, like Lance?

What evidence had they uncovered besides Lance's body? Was it an eyewitness at the movie theater who saw Lance pick her up? A video camera that caught her dumping the bike?

Stop it. Just stop. She would drive herself crazy playing the guessing game.

"I'll come to the station as soon as I speak to my family," Kristy repeated. Let them arrest her. At least then it would all be over.

Ranger Santiago stood up. Detective Davenport joined him.

"That will be fine, Mrs. Dobson. We'll be expecting you down at the station later this afternoon."

"Yes. I'll be there. Thank you," Kristy said and they headed out without ever once offering their condolences. But then again, you don't offer condolences to a murder suspect.

Kristy inspected her desk, making sure she hadn't left any-thing behind. She'd burned all of Clifton's letters, destroyed anything connected with Lance and her plan to kill him, but she still had to double-check. Kristy knew that it was quite possible they were waiting for a judge to sign a search war-rant, that by the time Kristy arrived at the precinct, officers would be rummaging through her belongings at work and at home, trying to build a case. Her terror was building. But getting to Ryan and Pops was her priority.

Kristy texted Gus.

Have to go. Will call you later.

Kristy didn't care if Gus heard about her arrest on the nightly news. She didn't owe him anything. She raced out of the building and was nearly at her truck when she heard—

"Kris... hey, Kristy..."

She saw Mac barreling toward her.

"I heard there were cops here. Something about Lance."

"They found him... his body," she whispered softly.

"Fuck. I'm so sorry, Kristy."

He pulled her close and wrapped his arms around her. Kristy didn't linger in the embrace. A woman whose husband had just been murdered couldn't be seen hugging another man. That was Evading Murder Charges 101.

"I have to go tell Pops and Ryan... and the police want to speak to me."

"They want to talk to *you*? About what?"

"I don't know," Kristy said.

"Are you sure there's nothing you want to tell me? About Lance... and you?"

What was Mac saying? Did he know? Had he suspected all along?

"Tell you what? Besides my husband is dead and the cops want to talk to me?"

Flustered, Mac looked away, almost ashamed that he'd even insinuated she might have something to hide.

"Sorry. I was... I don't know what I was doing. Just be careful. Get a lawyer, okay?"

"I will. If anything seems off, you know I will."

There was a perception that if you were arrested for a crime and you hired an attorney, you'd look guilty. That's what law enforcement wanted you to believe. That's why so many innocent people wound up confessing. But it was a bit of a catch-22. Hire a lawyer and you instantly become a prime suspect. Don't hire a lawyer and get walked all over by the cops.

"Kristy…"

"I have to go."

He reached out to stop her.

"Be careful. You know as well as I do how these things spin out of control."

She certainly did.

"I'll call you later," Kristy told him.

"I'll be here. You know that. And if Pops or Ryan need anything, I'm around."

"Thanks, Mac," Kristy said, climbing into her SUV.

It was almost two o'clock. Ryan's last class was over at three thirty. She had to get there before school let out, before news stories began trickling out.

Kristy sped toward the school, making it in record time. She pulled into a visitor space and hurried into the office. It may as well have been a million years since she'd been here negotiating Ryan's suspension. Kristy entered the administration office and saw Alice perched on her stool. She immediately turned her head in that sympathetic manner that drove Kristy crazy.

"Kristy, my Bible study said a special prayer for you and your family this week."

She nodded in understanding but there wasn't time to chat. "I need to see Ryan. Right now," Kristy said.

For once, Alice actually seemed to understand the gravity of the situation. She hurried over to Principal Barnhardt's office and opened the door. Liza was sitting at her desk, elegant as ever in a turquoise blazer and coral jewelry, typing away.

"Ms. Tucker...I mean Mrs. Dobson is here for Ryan. I thought she could wait here while I get him." Liza stood up and motioned for Kristy to enter.

"Yes. That's a great idea, Alice. Thank you."

Liza ushered Kristy into her office and shut the door.

"Can I get you anything? Can I do anything?"

"No...thank you," Kristy whispered.

Kristy's hands were shaking, her teeth chattering as if she'd been caught out in the cold. She was ruined, completely and totally destroyed. Kristy Tucker, the killer. Kristy Tucker, the cold-blooded murderer. And yet she was still Ryan's mom. Still the public information officer for the Texas Department of Criminal Justice. She was the woman who had been battered and beaten and fought back. Was it possible that she could be all those things at once?

A few minutes later, Kristy heard Alice's voice outside the door, and then she saw Ryan, standing in the doorway. Kristy stood up, smoothing her slacks, staring at her son, his sandy-brown hair covering his eyes. His eyes were bloodshot and there were dark circles around them.

He stumbled forward.

"Mom, is it..."

"We'll talk in the car."

"No. I want to know now. Please..." His voice cracked.

"Take your time," Liza said and closed the door behind them. Now it was just Kristy and Ryan, all alone.

"The police came to work today. They...they found Lance...they found his body. I'm sorry, Ry."

He let out an anguished cry. Kristy moved to console him.

"Why, Mom? I don't understand what happened. He was such a good guy. He was so good."

No, he wasn't. Not even close.

"I'm so sorry, my sweet boy. I'm so sorry."

Ryan let out a sob, loud, ugly, and unrestrained. Kristy held him, rocking her boy in her arms, hating herself for every goddamn tear he shed. She wanted to give Ryan time to grieve but right now there were things she had to do. *Time to face the music*, she told herself.

"Ryan, I'm sorry, but we have to go. We have to tell Pops, and I have to go to the police station."

"Why?" he asked, his eyes widening.

"I have to...I have to make sure it's Lance, and they have questions."

"But you won't be gone long? You'll be home soon?"

"Absolutely," she replied. Kristy had no way of knowing if that was the truth, but she wanted to ease Ryan's suffering, if only for a little bit.

He slowly stood, wiping his eyes furiously, his shirt stained with both their tears. Kristy led him out, nodding to Liza and Alice. They had been good to her, but Kristy didn't have the strength to speak.

Ryan's sniffles punctuated the silence as they headed home, every one of them like tiny pricks to her heart.

Telling Pops was equally horrible. He sat in his chair, completely motionless, nodding, his breathing tortured as he took in the news.

"At least now we know," he said at last. "At least we know."

Kristy didn't want to leave, but it was getting dark and she worried if she didn't show up at the station soon, they'd send officers to the house.

"I'm afraid I have to go."

"We're coming with you," Pops said.

"No. That's not a good idea."

If the cops had anything on her, the last thing she wanted was for Ryan and Pops to be there to see Kristy cuffed and led away. The humiliation and betrayal would be unbearable.

"We're a family. We're doing this as a family," Pops said, reclaiming his role as the man of the house. Ryan helped Pops change his oxygen tanks and they climbed into Kristy's car. They buckled their seat belts, as if seat belts could protect them from the catastrophe she was sure awaited them.

It was a little after six when they arrived at the police station. She hadn't even checked in with the officer at the front desk when she saw Ranger Santiago barreling toward her. He nodded hello to Kristy and introduced himself to Ryan and Pops.

"I'm so sorry for your loss," he said, shaking their hands. Kristy swallowed hard, tasting blood from where she'd bitten her cheek.

Stay calm. Stay calm.

He directed Pops and Ryan to a row of chairs against the wall in the lobby. They were all occupied but it didn't seem to matter to him.

"I'm going to ask y'all to wait out here. If you don't mind coming with me, Mrs. Dobson," he said.

She reached out and squeezed Ryan's shoulder.

"I'll be back soon. I love you guys."

She followed Ranger Santiago through a long, fluorescent-lit corridor, down a maze of hallways until she reached the morgue. Kristy had never been so closely watched, even within the Walls, where everyone was monitored. She could feel the ranger analyzing the way she moved, the way she talked; hell, she almost wondered if he was studying her breathing patterns. Did guilty people breathe differently? Could the rise and fall of her chest be her downfall? She hadn't read that in any of her research, but it was possible, wasn't it?

They stopped at a large window, the view obscured by a heavy black curtain, not all that different from the one that hung on death row. Ranger Santiago briefed her in that calm, soothing, practiced manner of his.

"I want to warn you that your husband was out in the elements for quite some time, so you should be prepared."

The curtain opened and Lance's body was revealed, spread out on a gurney, just like all those inmates. His complexion was a bluish gray, eyes swollen shut, face bloated and puffy. No, he was not at all recognizable. Monstrous in death, but he had been even more frightening in life. Her gaze landed on the simple white gold band she'd given him on their wedding day.

"It just looks right, doesn't it?" Lance had said after their first night as husband and wife, their hands intertwined, the early-morning sunlight streaming through.

She'd kissed Lance's ring hand.

"It looks perfect," she'd said.

"Mrs. Dobson, is that your husband?" Ranger Santiago asked, interrupting her trip down memory lane.

Kristy nodded and turned to him. "That's his ring. That's Lance's wedding ring."

Women were expected to cry. They must always cry, she'd learned. The ones who didn't were labeled heartless, cold, shrews, or "not quite right." Kristy's tears fell, but not for Lance. She'd cried far too many tears for him. No, these tears were for Pops and Ryan and what would happen if she failed today.

Ranger Santiago motioned for the ME that the identification was complete. The curtain was closed and he ushered Kristy down a different hallway into an interview room.

"Can I get you some coffee or water?" he asked.

"Coffee would be good. Please," she said.

"Milk? Sugar?" he asked, so accommodating, as though they were old friends catching up over lost time.

"Just plain coffee will be fine," she said.

She didn't want coffee but she needed time alone. She could bet money that Detective Davenport was watching her through the two-way glass, along with their superiors, assessing every sigh and shift, cataloging the intonation of her words. She had read enough case files to know what they would be looking for. She recalled nervous ticks being one thing they looked for. Was any part of her making involuntary movements? What else? The eyes. A flatness to the eyes was a sure sign of guilt. Obsessive weeping was annoying to them because it wasted their time. But so was emotional restraint, which was seen as a refusal to cooperate in the investigation. Kristy leaned against the table, head in her hands.

I am a distraught grieving widow, she reminded herself. *A distraught grieving widow.*

This was the crossroads—when a simple conversation might become the basis for an entire murder case, Kristy's guilt or innocence determined in a span of seconds, minutes, and hours. She considered giving it all up. Confessing her sins here and now. Wouldn't that just be easier? It would all be over then. But she'd done all this for her family, for Ryan and Pops. They were still what mattered.

She thought about Lance and how the entire world saw one person, a charming devoted husband, a dedicated stepfather, a jokester, a shrewd businessman. Only Kristy, Hannah, and Lisette were witnesses to the other Lance. Cold, calculating, ruthless, demanding. If Kristy wanted to get out of this, maybe she needed to take a page out of Lance's book. If a dual personality worked for him, why couldn't it work for Kristy?

In this dull gray room with the stale, putrid air, she made a conscious choice. She wasn't Kristy Dobson, the scared and battered wife. Not anymore.

Ranger Santiago returned with the worst cup of coffee Kristy ever had in her life (and she worked in a prison). She took a few sips, trying to calm her breathing. He sat down across from her, crossed one leg over the other, and loosened the top button of his white shirt. *Just getting comfortable before he pounces*, she thought.

"You are being recorded. Is that okay?" he asked.

Kristy nodded.

"Mind giving us a verbal answer?"

"No, I don't mind being recorded," she said.

The flurry of questions began, a tidal wave of information coming at her.

How did you meet Lance?

How long did you date?

When did you get married?

What did you do for fun?

Who are your friends?

Names?

Ages?

Occupations?

Did Lance have any business troubles?

Did you have any financial issues?

Marriage troubles?

Substance abuse problems?

Any enemies?

She answered all his questions, without any reluctance.

"Did Ryan and Lance have any issues? Were there any difficulties?"

Kristy blinked in shock. Wait a minute. Why was he asking about Ryan?

"I'm sorry," she said. "Can you repeat the question?"

"You said your son was friends with Lance before you became romantically involved. Was that difficult for Ryan?"

"No. Not at all. He was happy for us."

"So there were no issues with his mother dating his teacher and mentor?" Ranger Santiago asked.

"No. Not at all."

"But Ryan has a temper? I know there was an incident at school in which the police were called. Did he have counseling for that?"

"No. It was an isolated incident. You can see that from his record."

This wasn't happening. They couldn't blame Ryan. That wasn't...possible.

"Ryan loved Lance. Lance was like...like a father."

Kristy's voice was shrill, her hands gripping the table. *Ease up. This is what they want.*

Casting suspicion on someone else to trigger a reaction in a suspect.

Don't let him rattle you.

"Ask anyone. They'll tell you how much Ryan loved Lance."

The ranger's questions shifted, focusing on the week leading up to Lance's disappearance, the last time Kristy saw him. As nerve-racking as all of this was, Kristy remained unflappable, never letting her concern and anguish waver. She found moments to probe, begging him to tell her what happened to Lance. Each time, Ranger Santiago dodged her inquiry. He wasn't giving her any information. He wanted Kristy's version of the events.

Over and over again, Kristy told Ranger Santiago where she was and what she'd been doing. In some ways, it was easier now. She had told that same story so many times to reporters she almost believed it was the truth. As the interrogation wore on, Kristy lost track of time. Ranger Santiago's questions grew repetitive. His goal, she realized, was to keep her in this room long enough that she grew hungry and tired and hopefully careless. Classic interrogation techniques. He didn't have enough evidence to arrest her or he would have already done it.

"I've told you everything I know."

"I understand, Mrs. Dobson, but..."

"My son and my father, are they still out there?"

"Yes, they are..."

"Then I'll come back tomorrow, I'll stay as long as you need me to stay, but right now I need to be with my family."

She expected him to push back, but he closed his notebook and reached out to shake her hand.

"You're right, Mrs. Dobson. We've taken up enough of your time. If I have any more questions, I'll be in touch. We're going to find out who killed your husband. People rarely get away with a crime like this. And I'm proud to say that I have a hundred percent closure rate."

Despite Kristy's exhaustion, she understood his warning. This wasn't the end. Ranger Santiago stood and opened the door. Kristy slipped outside and headed toward the lobby, where Pops was waiting.

She glanced around.

"Where is Ryan?" she said.

"Talking to that lady cop," Pops relayed.

The blood drained from Kristy's face.

"What?"

"She said she just had a few questions."

No way. This wasn't happening. Kristy spun around, marching over to Ranger Santiago.

"Where the hell is my son?"

"Excuse me?"

"I'm not going to ask again. Where is Ryan?"

"I'm not sure. Give me a minute..."

But Kristy wasn't waiting. She pushed past him, hurrying back to where she came from.

"Ryan? Ryan? Are you here?"

"Mrs. Dobson, calm down," Ranger Santiago called out after her, trying to keep up.

"He's a minor. Or have you forgotten? He just lost the only father he's known. What the hell is wrong with you people?"

A door opened and Davenport stepped out.

"I want my son. We're leaving. Now," Kristy said.

"We were just talking."

"You can't possibly think I'm that stupid. If you want to question my son, get a warrant for his arrest."

Ranger Santiago nodded curtly to Davenport, his eyes flashing. She'd clearly gone off the book on this.

"Let him go, Joanna."

She didn't say a word to Kristy. She opened the door. Ryan looked up, stricken.

"Let's go, Ry. Come on."

He hesitated and Davenport motioned for him to go.

"We're done here," Detective Davenport said, her tone signaling they were anything but. Ignoring the officers, Ryan hurried out, Kristy leading him down the hallway and back toward the waiting area. Ryan's voice was low, trembling with fear.

"They were asking me all these questions, about Lance, about why I punched Scott and if I had anger issues. They asked me if I used Lance's guns and if I ever went shooting. Mom, what's going on?"

"Nothing. They're just doing their jobs," Kristy said. It was a lie. She didn't believe that for a second. She wasn't sure if they were actually targeting Ryan or if this was all part of some plan to coax her into confessing.

"Are you sure?" he asked.

"They always talk to the family when a homicide occurs. I promise nothing is going to happen to you. Okay?"

They reached Pops, who staggered to his feet, clutching his portable oxygen.

"Everything okay? I'm sorry if I messed up, Kristy girl. I didn't think there was anything wrong with asking the boy some questions."

"You didn't do anything wrong, Pops. We're all done now. Let's go home."

Kristy grabbed Pops's oxygen tank and he leaned on her, his wrinkled age-spotted hands grasping her tightly as Ryan followed them out. She wouldn't allow her son to be dragged into this. He'd already suffered enough. If they came for him, Kristy would come clean. That was the only solution. For now she planned to savor her freedom, because it appeared that her days as a free woman were numbered.

CHAPTER THIRTY-ONE

At dawn, Kristy bolted out of bed. They were coming for her or Ryan. She was certain of it. Kristy sat by her bedroom window for hours, the faint orange-hued slivers of sunlight peeking out among the clouds. She took a shower and then brewed a pot of coffee and sat at the kitchen table, gazing into space, waiting for the inevitable. Her instincts proved correct. She heard the first car, tires skidding on gravel. Through the kitchen window, the caravan of Conroe Police Department squad cars and the Texas Ranger's pickup made their way onto the property. Kristy raced downstairs toward Ryan's room.

"Ryan, get up. The police are here."

Alarmed, Ryan sat upright, clutching his pillow protectively against his chest.

"Why? What's wrong?"

"I don't know. But I need you to get out of bed and go wake Pops."

She left Ryan behind, scrambling to get dressed. Kristy made it to the front door, just in time to greet Ranger Santiago.

"Mrs. Dobson, we have a warrant to search your house,

property, and vehicles. We'll start with your bedroom and then search the rest of the home. The officers will be photographing everything, and we'll be taking all electronics, including computers and iPads, into custody."

"Okay," Kristy said, holding open the screen door, knowing there was no way to stop them. "Okay, that's fine."

"We need to know if you, your father, Ryan, or Lance has any other weapons in the house," Ranger Santiago said.

The police had already confiscated the guns they found at the campsite when they took Lance's camper and truck into custody.

"My father has a pistol he keeps in the nightstand by his bed. That's all," Kristy said, recalling that terrible evening Lance held that same gun to her head. Ranger Santiago nodded matter-of-factly. Just as Kristy's day-to-day tasks involved watching people die, his included invading people's homes, searching for proof that they were criminals.

"Our bedroom is upstairs," she said as she led the ranger and other officers toward the stairs. Pops and Ryan lingered near the kitchen entrance, anxiously surveying the scene.

"My father's bedroom is on the first floor in the back of the house, and Ryan's bedroom is in the basement," she said. Perhaps later when she was facing trial, they'd say she cooperated. Perhaps that might be enough to keep her off death row.

"Mom?" Ryan asked, wanting her reassurance.

"It'll be okay, Ry. It's all going to be okay."

Ranger Santiago led the officers upstairs to Kristy and Lance's bedroom. They inspected and photographed everything from Lance's underwear to his belts to his toothbrush. Throughout, Ranger Santiago kept up a steady commentary on what they were doing. Kristy's status as a law enforcement official was the only reason she was treated with such respect. It wasn't pleasant watching the police go through her personal items. Every now and then they'd take something, a belt buckle or Lance's watch, and put it in a plastic bag and she'd wonder, why that item? What clue might that provide? She kept her mouth shut though, didn't ask questions, didn't do anything that might draw attention to herself.

As the search continued, Kristy grew more and more uncomfortable watching them casually sift through her mother's jewelry collection, her underwear drawer. She excused herself, allowing the officers to work alone, joining Ryan and Pops at the kitchen table, the three of them drinking coffee and waiting for the search to end. Hours later, just as the sun was setting, Ranger Santiago thanked them for their cooperation and the cops all left, their cars kicking up dust as they headed out. The police were gone. Lance was gone. It was just the three of them, mourning, grieving.

Kristy had no choice but to take time off from work. "Two weeks paid," Gus said when he heard that Lance had been recovered. It was generous by any standards, even more so knowing what a tightwad Gus was.

With the police investigation continuing, Kristy did what any grieving wife would do—she planned a memorial service. People she hadn't seen in years showed up. Former coworkers, Ryan's classmates and their parents, her high school teachers, including Liza. Kristy didn't remember much about the service. Ryan, Pops, and Kristy all declined to speak.

"Not sure we could get through it," Kristy told the

kind-faced pastor. She grimaced through the man's bumbling eulogy, waxing poetic about Lance and all the great gifts God had bestowed upon him.

After the service, everyone gathered at Kristy's house for a reception. Carmen, Mac, and Vera provided all the food: a giant spread of cold cuts and cheeses. Other folks brought casseroles and pies, enough food to feed an army. As Kristy made her way through all the well-wishers, accepting their condolences, she spotted Yoli outside chain-smoking on the porch. Yoli had quit smoking after Roy's cancer diagnosis, but stressful situations brought out bad habits. Kristy slipped outside and joined her. She hadn't smoked a single cigarette since Lance died. But when Yoli handed Kristy hers, she took a long, slow drag, the nicotine working its way through her body.

"Y'all doing okay?" Yoli asked.

"Getting by," Kristy managed.

Yoli took the cigarette back and sucked on it deeply as if it held answers to long-lost questions.

"A Texas Ranger came by the house last night. Did you know Lance and Roy got into a shouting match at Texas Land and Cattle a few months back, arguing about the money that Lance owed us?"

"No. I didn't."

"This cop was asking all these questions. Probing us about our falling-out with Lance, asking about our finances. I mean, Kristy, can you imagine Roy hurting a fly?"

Roy was the nicest man Kristy ever met. Were they suspicious of Roy now? It seemed like everyone was getting swept up in Kristy's mess. But the truth was they hadn't arrested anyone. If they did, she'd come forward. That's what she'd have to do. Kristy squeezed Yoli's hand.

"The police are asking everyone questions, Yoli. It's their job."

But was it? Could someone who had nothing to do with Lance's death be in police crosshairs? It happened, didn't it— innocent people going to prison for something they didn't do? Thinking about Clifton, Kristy realized anything was possible.

The police were ever present. Kristy caught a brief glimpse of Ranger Santiago at the funeral, slipping into a pew at the last minute, tipping his cowboy hat to her as she exited. Ranger Santiago wasn't just watching Kristy, he was surveying Ryan, Pops, Yoli, and Roy, trying to find some clue that might lead him to the murderer—that might maintain his "I have a hundred percent closure rate" status.

In the days following the funeral, neighbors brought more casseroles and condolences. Kristy's forward motion refused to let her sit still, organizing, cleaning, listening to Carmen and Mac telling her to "hang in there," and "we'll find the son of a bitch and make him pay." Over and over again, Kristy heard a variation on this theme, wondering if and when these prophecies would come true.

"Kristy, what happened to your husband?"

"Kristy, do the police have any leads?"

"How are you coping with his murder?"

Since his body had been discovered, more reporters descended outside Kristy's home. But these weren't the respectful friends and colleagues she'd known for years, these were cutthroat journalists from major national news outlets, all vying for a way to exploit this tragedy for higher ratings. Kristy Tucker was officially the news.

But her family was collateral damage. Ryan skulked around the house in wrinkled clothes. Pops slept most of the days away, asking Kristy to deliver his meals to his room instead of joining them at the table. With nothing else to do, Kristy became obsessed with the house, sweeping, dusting and vacuuming, cooking meals for everyone. On multiple occasions, Ranger Santiago stopped by.

"Just wanted to check on y'all," he'd say, holding up a store-bought pecan pie or burgers and fries from Whataburger. He'd ask Kristy for a few minutes of her time, and Kristy would answer the same version of the questions she answered before. She did her best to summon her Lance persona—polite, professional, distraught—but the pressure was growing. When he'd leave, Kristy, unable to sleep, roamed the halls of her home, checking on Pops and Ryan, afraid to sleep, afraid the cops would come and take her away without a proper good-bye.

Despite Kristy's forced hiatus from work, she insisted that Ryan return to school.

"Life has to get back to normal," she told him.

"Nothing will ever be normal, Mom," Ryan said, but this time he didn't argue.

After a week of him moping and ignoring her, Kristy stormed into Pops's room, pulled open the shades, and switched off the TV.

"I can't see you like this anymore," she said.

"Damn it, I was watching that," Pops grunted.

"No more of this. You're going to get your butt into the

shower and Mac is taking you to your doctor's appointment. I am not letting you lie here in the dark and wither away. I can't...I can't lose you too, Pops. I can't..."

Pops must have sensed Kristy unraveling.

"Okay...okay...I'll get dressed. I'm sorry. I just...you spend your whole life around murder and evil and then it's right here in your own backyard. Guess I lost perspective. But I'll stop with my pity party. It's done. I'll be there for you and Ryan, Kristy girl. I'll always be there."

Kristy might have been able to get Pops and Ryan to start living again, but she was going crazy. She couldn't just stay home and do nothing. She had to get out of this house. She didn't even call Gus to tell him she was coming back to work. She simply showed up at the office. She was surprised to find Carmen sitting at her desk.

"Hey, lady," Carmen said, surprised to see her there. Kristy scanned the desk, everything neatly organized, a stark contrast to Kristy's chaos.

"Hey," Kristy replied, feeling a bit like a stranger.

"It's damn good to see you," Carmen replied, rushing forward to give Kristy a hug.

"But?" Kristy asked.

Something was wrong. Carmen wasn't making eye contact.

"You should talk to Gus," Carmen said.

Kristy could tell this wasn't going to be good news, but she forced a smile.

"If I don't come back, Gus and I ran off to Vegas to elope." Carmen chuckled.

"God, I missed you, Kristy," she said.

Kristy's smile faded when she stepped into the hall. She made her way over to Gus's office and knocked on the door. He always kept it closed, so no one would catch him napping.

"Come in," Gus said.

Kristy entered. Gus was seated at his custom-made oak desk, so massive he resembled a chubby child emperor.

"Kristy, have a seat. Can I get you something to drink? Water? Tea?"

Shit. He was being nice. That definitely meant something was wrong.

"I thought you were going to take time off," Gus said.

"I did. But I'm going crazy at home..."

"The thing is...Lance's death has created quite a stir and the higher-ups aren't exactly thrilled with the continued media scrutiny. They've suggested that you take more time. Just until the police catch whoever did this."

Her stomach dropped. Were they concerned about the PIO's image or were they trying to distance themselves from Kristy? She tried to rationalize it. If the cops were going to arrest her, they'd simply fire her, not keep her on paid leave.

"When were you going to let me know?" Kristy asked.

"This just happened. I was going to give you a call, but it's been hectic here without you. Carmen can hardly manage her own work, let alone yours."

Panic set in. Kristy couldn't imagine what she'd do if she wasn't working.

"Gus, I need this job."

"And it'll be waiting for you. You're still getting paid. Take this time to be with Ryan and Frank."

Kristy could have argued, but what if it cast suspicion on her? A grieving woman should be at home grieving. Kristy thanked Gus and returned to her office. It was Wednesday. She could at least visit with Clifton.

"Hey, Carmen, do you mind if I head over to Polunsky and do one last press day? I just...I can't go home. Not yet."

She waited to see if her question raised any eyebrows but Carmen's relief was obvious.

"God, that would be amazing. I have so much paperwork to catch up on. I'll take a long lunch and Gus will never even know. But just so you know, it's going to be a busy day. Clifton Harris got his new date so there will be lots of questions, I'm sure."

"They're executing Clifton?" Kristy asked. She hadn't heard anything about it.

"Yeah, all his appeals have been denied. His execution is in a few weeks."

And Kristy would miss it. This time she wouldn't be there.

"Hey, Kris, I hope you're not mad. I mean, about me doing your job."

"I could never be mad at you," Kristy said, covering. It wasn't Carmen's fault. No. This was all Kristy's doing.

"Take care of yourself, okay? And I'll see you soon?" Carmen said.

"I hope so," Kristy replied but she wasn't sure. Who knows—the next time she returned here, she might be on the other side of these walls.

CHAPTER THIRTY-TWO

Clifton was waiting for Kristy in their usual pod when she arrived. Unfortunately, today's journalists were prompt so there was no time to speak to him. Kristy had to wait two and a half hours while Clifton patiently told his story to three reporters, answering the same questions over and over again. Once they were gone, Kristy took a seat and picked up the phone. One last time.

"I heard everything," Clifton said softly. "How are you doing?"

He didn't say, *I'm sorry*, which she appreciated. She hadn't come here to discuss Lance. She came to say good-bye.

"I'm actually taking some time off, so Carmen, my assistant, will be helping you from here on out. She's great and will answer any questions you might have. She'll be there for you through...through it all."

Stunned, Clifton leaned back.

"You sure there's no way...I mean, there's no chance that you might come back to work before...before I get my walking papers?" he asked hopefully.

"I'm afraid not," she said.

"That's a real shame."

"You've fought long and hard. And you've got people out there who will keep fighting," Kristy said. She wished she was one of them, but Kristy wasn't optimistic about her chances.

"That's true. Bev says she won't quit. Told me she'll be on her deathbed still filing motions if she has to. And you've met Fiona. She'll fight until the bitter end. And if I look on the bright side, at least now I know what to expect. Which is good because I don't think I'm getting a reprieve. Not this time."

Clifton was right. Unless someone came forward and confessed to killing Clifton's children or had the killer's confession on tape, he was out of options.

"I'm afraid I have to go," Kristy said.

"I'll be praying for you, Ms. Tucker. And I hope you'll keep on fighting. Don't you ever give up your fight," Clifton said emphatically.

Kristy gave him a quick smile, blinking away her own tears, and she hung up the phone. She hurried out of the visitation area and made it back to her car before she burst into tears. She sped out of Polunsky, crying all the way home. Lance was dead. Clifton would be too, and Kristy was falling apart.

She spent the following day scrubbing the house from top to bottom, doing everything she could to tire herself out. Pops wasn't feeling well and went to bed early, so Ryan and Kristy opted to eat dinner in the living room, drowning their sorrows in some inane reality show.

It was close to ten when they heard a knock at the front door. Ryan and Kristy jumped.

"I'll get it," Kristy said.

She hurried toward the front door, her stomach dropping when she saw Ranger Santiago through the peephole. She opened up the door.

"Can I help you, Ranger?" she asked.

"Mrs. Dobson, we need to talk," he said.

There were no burgers and fries this time. No gentle inquiry about how she was feeling.

She nodded and motioned for the ranger to enter. He made his way into the house. Ryan leapt to his feet when he saw the officer.

"Mom, is everything okay?" Ryan asked nervously.

"Why don't you go to your room and let me speak with the ranger?"

Ryan studied Kristy but didn't argue. He switched off the TV and headed to his room. Kristy gestured for Ranger Santiago to join her at the kitchen table.

"Can I get you something to drink?" she asked.

"No, I'm good."

He sat down and pulled out a photo of a woman, white, late thirties, lovely with bright emerald-green eyes.

"Do you know who this is?"

"No, I'm afraid I don't," Kristy said.

"Her name is April Emerson. She was married to Lance Dobson fourteen years ago when she was a graduate student in New Orleans. We came across her in our investigation and interviewed her today. She told us that Mr. Dobson verbally and physically abused her for the duration of their three-year marriage. She said he threatened her mother and her sister if she ever left him."

"That's terrible," Kristy said, her stomach churning. At this rate, Lance could have started a goddamn club.

His eyes zeroed in on her reaction, scrutinizing her.

Kristy, play it cool. Just play it cool.

"Mrs. Dobson, if there were issues in your marriage, if you and Lance were having troubles, we will find out. We always do. If you're up front about everything now, we can help you. But if you're impeding our investigation, and we find out later, well, I'm afraid it won't end well."

He was fishing, Kristy thought. That's all this was. A fishing expedition. Even if April Emerson had the same sad tale as Kristy and Hannah Mendoza, there was no evidence that Kristy had killed Lance or she would be in cuffs already.

"Detective, I'm not *concealing* anything. I've done everything in my power to be as accommodating as possible, but it's late and I'd like to go to bed."

He slowly stood. "I'll be in touch, Mrs. Dobson. And this is your official notice that you shouldn't leave town. Don't get up. I'll let myself out."

Kristy sat in the kitchen, listening to the hum of the lights, the bulb over the sink flickering off and on. She waited until she was certain the ranger was gone and then she grabbed Pops's bottle of Chivas. She poured a shot and drank it in one gulp.

"Mom? What did he say? Did he have news about Lance?"

She nearly dropped her glass. She didn't even hear Ryan enter.

"No, sweetheart. There are no leads, but they're working hard on the case."

For the first time Kristy saw a flicker of doubt in his eyes. Or was it something else? She stepped forward to comfort Ryan, but he turned his back on her.

"I'm going back to bed."

"Night, Ry. I love you," Kristy called out, but he didn't answer. She wanted to rush after him and hold him and say it again. *I love you, Ryan. I need you to know I love you more than anything.* But she waited until she heard his bedroom door close and poured herself another drink. She took her drink outside and sat on the porch, wondering how long before Ranger Santiago returned with an arrest warrant.

She waited.

And waited.

But to Kristy's surprise no one came. The days ticked by with a numbing sameness. She continued puttering around the house, cooking breakfast for Ryan and Pops, eggs and bacon, breakfast tacos, homemade banana muffins, cleaning, vacuuming, and answering e-mails whenever Carmen had a question, which seemed less and less frequent as the days passed by. Kristy wanted to return to work, but every time she called Gus, he'd say, "Let's give it another week."

A new week dawned. A week Kristy had been dreading. Today Clifton was going to die. There were no more letters. It was better that way, safer for both of them, but she missed hearing from him, her own life now consisting of just Pops and Ryan, her heartbroken ragtag family.

In the weeks leading up to Clifton's execution, Janice was

on every broadcast station, from the *Today* show to the local morning news. She was determined and emphatic. "Clifton Harris is a master manipulator," she told Matt Lauer tearfully. "There is no other punishment for someone like that."

As the day wore on, Kristy tried to limit her intake of these programs, hating how helpless they made her feel, hating that she wouldn't be there for Clifton. She focused on her routine—sweeping, making the beds, doing laundry, prepping dinner—but she couldn't stop checking the clock.

Six.

Six thirty.

Seven.

Kristy was convinced that Clifton's death would be breaking news, but the TV stations continued with their regularly scheduled programming. Instead, Twitter broke the news, an Associated Press reporter tweeting out: *Clifton Harris died of lethal injection at 7:27 p.m.*

Kristy promised Pops and Ryan she'd cook dinner, but instead she found herself glued to the TV, now dominated with stories about Clifton's life and subsequent death. She flipped through the channels until she stopped on an episode of *Dateline*, an exclusive special featuring Clifton. He sat upright, composed and in control. The reporter noted his unusual demeanor—for a man a few weeks from death he seemed a little restrained.

"How do you not lose it? Just go crazy knowing what's about to happen to you?" he asked compassionately.

"That would be easy, wouldn't it? Some people want to see a man afraid to die. They're bloodthirsty. I get that. It's why people love bullfights or why the Romans loved gladiator battles. We, as a society, enjoy seeing people get punished. It's why football, a brutal, punishing game, is one of the most popular sports in this country. So I understand people wanting justice for something as horrible as the murder of a little boy and girl. But they were my children and I love them and I did not kill them. I carry that with me. That's what keeps me sane."

Kristy sat glued to the TV until Ryan came home. Despite her crushing sadness, she pulled herself away from the news and reheated yesterday's leftovers. Family dinners had become Kristy's obsession; she spent hours preparing their meals. If the cops came calling, she wanted Ryan and Pops to remember these last days. She wanted something good to remain.

Ryan was quiet these days, almost sullen, and tonight was no different. Kristy had nothing new to discuss. She'd mentioned that to Pops recently and he snorted, "Now you know what my life is like." Kristy reminded herself to think before speaking. They were all struggling.

As dinner came to an end, Kristy's mourning for Clifton continued. He was gone. Clifton was dead. She finished cleaning the kitchen and told Pops and Ryan she had a headache and was going to bed early. But Kristy couldn't sleep. Instead, she switched on the late news. A power outage that hit South Texas led the newscast, followed by the arrest of a crooked politician, busted for soliciting a prostitute. *Just another day in the Lone Star State.*

The commercial breaks seemed endless. One selling butter and another hawking ladies' lingerie. She almost wondered if the newscast wasn't going to mention his execution. But there it was; at the end of the program, Clifton's picture appeared on-screen. She held her breath. It was silly. What was she expecting? A sudden resurrection?

"Two lives cut short received justice today. Convicted child killer Clifton Harris was executed. Harris was convicted by a Bastrop County jury of a double homicide, setting the fire that killed his two young children, Rosalind Harris and Michael Harris. His ex-wife, Janice, spoke exclusively to Channel 12 after the execution."

Janice appeared on-screen, her flawless face streaked with tears, her expertly blown-out highlighted brunette locks fluttering in the early-evening breeze. She looked victorious, almost luminous, glowing with satisfaction.

"For twelve years we've waited for this moment. My ex-husband went to his grave never admitting what he did, but God knows the truth and so does the state of Texas. I'd like to thank everyone who stood by us during this long and difficult journey. It seems almost unbelievable to think that we can move on."

The reporter appeared on the screen again, a plastic smile on her face, standing in front of the Walls.

"Harris's attorney was unwavering in her belief that her client was innocent."

Clifton's lawyer, Beverly, appeared, heavy bags under her eyes, her skin worn from lack of sleep and failure.

"Today is a sad day for our legal system. The state of Texas has executed an innocent man. We must be diligent in our fight to eradicate the death penalty. And I swear that I will do everything in my power to ensure that Clifton Harris gets the justice in death that he did not receive in life."

Kristy had enough. She switched off the TV and slipped under the covers. She slept restlessly, tossing and turning, dreaming of Clifton and Lance, the two of them grappling on mats while Kristy watched, her hands and legs shackled, unable to come to Clifton's aid. She woke up the following morning thinking about Clifton's memorial service. One of his last wishes was for a quick burial.

"None of this moping about. Bury me and get on with it."

He hated that he couldn't be buried near his children, but Janice would never allow that. Instead, Fiona had chosen a burial plot in Conroe, where she lived. She'd purchased a house near there to be close to Clifton. It's where she planned to be buried.

"There's space for all of us, baby brother. We'll be united one day. Rest assured."

After half an hour of hemming, hawing, and making excuses, Kristy left Pops a note on the kitchen table, saying she'd gone to do errands and would be back later.

She stopped at the 7-Eleven and bought a pack of cigarettes, lighting one cigarette after another as she drove, the smoke curling its way through the windows and out of the car. As Kristy drove, she took in the countryside, wondering why she sold this life short. She had everything—a son who worshiped her, a father who gave up his whole life to make sure she was cared for—and she'd squandered all of that on the promise of "true love" with Lance Dobson.

Kristy arrived at Conroe Cemetery, slowing to a crawl,

not sure where the family plot was located. She spotted Fiona
first, clad in a somber black pantsuit and fancy red hat. Kristy
parked a safe distance away and walked toward the gathering. It wasn't against the rules to attend an inmate's funeral,
but it might look strange, especially considering Kristy was
grieving her husband. Why would she be attending a convicted murderer's funeral?

Clifton's sister and Beverly were joined by dozens of people; many of them Kristy recognized as members of Clifton's
legal team. The lawyers gathered with the Harris family, a
loud and boisterous group, all of them offering hugs, their
tears flowing freely. If anyone in Clifton's immediate family
doubted his innocence, they were not present today. After a
few minutes of greeting one another, the graveside service
began. The minute the pastor began to speak, Fiona began to
weep, holding on to Nina, waving tissues in the air and saying Clifton's name over and over again. The pastor's booming
voice rang out as he finished his rousing sermon.

"Our brother Clifton will be welcomed with open arms by
his savior. And after a valiant fight, his soul will finally be at
peace."

Fiona spoke next, her tears subsiding as she addressed the
crowd.

"Clifton was the most adorable little brother in the world.
Always trying to charm my friends, which he did. He was
a real rascal, giggling, complimenting, making us all laugh.
And he was so brave. Y'all, my baby brother was the bravest
person I ever met. He'd take the beatings Daddy tried to give
Mama and never once backed down. Y'all don't need to hear

me say how much I loved Cliff. You know. So let's give Cliff the good-bye he deserves. Let us praise Jesus and ask the Lord to look after Cliff."

The entire group shouted, "Amen." Fiona pointed to Nina, who took a deep breath and began to sing. Her voice rang out among the cries and wails from Cliff's family, the pureness and pain in her voice heartbreaking. Kristy didn't recognize the lyrics of the gospel hymn, but the words brought tears to her eyes, the song growing more and more emotional as the mourners joined in.

Even before Lance, Kristy doubted heaven's existence. But if she was wrong, she hoped Clifton was sitting up on the back porch, Rosie and Mikey on his lap, listening to this spectacular send-off. The song ended, the pastor offering one final prayer. The crowd said, "Amen," and Fiona stepped forward.

"I hope y'all will join us at the house for some food and fellowship. I promised Cliff we'd give him a good ole time, and that's what we're gonna do."

Fiona turned away, just in time to lock eyes with Kristy. The heartbroken woman paused, surprised to see her there, but then she touched her heart and mouthed a silent thank-you. Kristy's own pain and sorrow were reflected in Fiona's expression. She nodded in acknowledgment and Kristy hurried to her car. Her heart was still racing, uneasy at the idea that she'd been seen. She wasn't doing anything wrong, she told herself, but if the police were watching her... This was how people got caught. Doing things out of the ordinary, not weighing the consequences. Grief was clouding her mind, making her careless.

Ten miles from home, Kristy spotted the dark blue sedan in her rearview mirror.

You're being paranoid. Cops don't drive Toyotas, she told herself. But as she got closer to the turn-off, she became convinced she was being followed. Kristy sped up and the car followed suit. Her heart was racing. She sped up again and the car gunned its engine and swerved into the other lane, until both cars were parallel with one another.

The driver's face came into focus and Kristy gasped—it was Lisette. She gestured frantically for Kristy to pull over. *Damn it.* Kristy could floor it, try to lose her down these back roads she knew so well. But she had to see what Lisette wanted.

In the distance, Kristy spotted the abandoned Plummer farm. She made a left and pulled into the driveway, stopping when she could no longer see the road. Kristy put the car into park and got out. In an instant, Lisette was out of her car and racing toward Kristy.

"You did it, didn't you?" Lisette said. Kristy flinched; Lisette's normally flat inflection was shrill. Her pupils were dilated, and her skin was waxy, sweat caking her forehead. High, hopped-up on meth, was Kristy's guess.

"Lisette, what are you doing here?" Kristy asked.

"You did it, didn't you? I know you did," Lisette said again. She laughed, not bothering to wait for Kristy's response.

"I saw the news that Wayne was missing, I thought good riddance. When I heard he was dead, I was like, it's about damn time. I just...I don't know why but I knew you did it. I was so impressed. You're so brave. You know that, don't you? So many times I imagined killing the bastard myself, but I just couldn't do it. I told myself I wasn't going to get messed up, but sometimes when I get high, I see my mom and I had to see her and tell her that he'd gotten what he deserved. And then I thought, I have to, like, thank you. 'Cause you did what I couldn't. And it's all because of you that I can really focus. Now that Wayne's gone, it's like I can stop messing up and focus on my family. It's like God heard my prayers and sent you to me."

She reached out to hug Kristy.

"You're an angel—you know that?" Lisette said, pulling Kristy in for a hug. Her breath was hot and stale. This was it. This was how it all unraveled.

"Lisette, you should go home. Please. You can't be here."

Lisette pulled away, a joyous smile lighting up her face.

"How did it happen? What did Wayne say? I want all the details. Did he suffer? God, I hope he suffered."

Panicked, Kristy reached out to grab Lisette by the arms.

"Lisette, I don't know who killed Lance...I mean Wayne. Are you hearing me? I don't know. But if you're here, and they know I talked to you, they might stop looking. Do you understand? They might suspect me."

Lisette's eyes narrowed. "They can't arrest you. You did such a good thing." Lisette rubbed her eyes, childlike and world-weary all at the same time.

She was teetering on the edge. Any little push might set her off.

"Lisette, I didn't do anything. I need you to know that."

"Okay," Lisette said, shrugging. She didn't believe Kristy for a second. She reached out and hugged her again. "You know, you seem like a good mom. When I watched you with your kid, you seemed so nice and loving, just like my mom."

Lisette moved back toward her car, unsteady on her feet, and swung open the car door. She called out to Kristy.

"We're all going to be happier now that Wayne is gone. You'll see."

Kristy couldn't do this. She couldn't let this girl drive off, not in this state. She'd take her to the police station and explain everything. Lance Dobson would never do that, but she wasn't Lance.

"Lisette, wait. Wait," Kristy said, following after her, but Lisette was already in the car, waving as she pulled out of the driveway, tires kicking up dirt.

Kristy's head was pounding, pulse racing. She leaned against her car. She wasn't sure what to do. Her phone buzzed.

Kristy girl, where are you? I'm starting to worry...and I'm hungry. And I'm out of my Tums. Can you swing by the store?

She glanced back at the road. Lisette was gone, and going after her would only put Kristy in more danger. She couldn't help Lisette. Not when her own life was on the verge of coming apart. She sighed and climbed back into her car.

Kristy returned home, sweat trickling down her back, her head aching. Pops sat in his recliner in the living room, the TV tuned to some sitcom rerun.

"Sorry I'm late, Pops. Ran out to do some errands but I'm not feeling well."

"Did you get my text?" he said. She didn't stop to look at him.

"Sorry. I need to lie down."

"All right, well take care of yourself. I'll text Ryan and ask him to go."

She barely made it to her bedroom, collapsing onto the bed, shivering and shaking, her body fighting off the trauma of the day. Kristy drifted off to sleep. In her dream, the police were chasing her down. Ranger Santiago, a calculated glimmer in his eyes, led the charge. She ran, faster and faster, but the ranger grabbed her. As Kristy was cuffed, she turned and saw Lance watching, his skin that awful shade of blue, his hands clutching his hollowed-out gut. By his side was Clifton, his body rotting, shaking his head in dismay, the two of them watching as Kristy was led away.

Gasping for air, Kristy woke. It was dark out. Her bedside clock read ten fifteen. She frantically searched in the shadows, but no one was there, only the guilt and regret that clung to her. Kristy couldn't do this. Not anymore. She was not Lance Dobson. Lance would have waited out the cops with silent indifference. He would have reveled in the suffering of others, soaking it up. If she could just play this role a little while longer, Kristy might be able to escape prison and resume her life. It could happen. But she'd never be free, and that's what this was all about. That's what Clifton had tried to tell her. Kristy was a good person until Lance forced her hand. But she could still find her way back to who she was. She could become the old Kristy Tucker. That was possible. There was only one thing left to do—she had to tell the truth.

CHAPTER THIRTY-THREE

The water was piping hot, steam rising up. Kristy eased herself into the tub. She hadn't taken a bath since Lance began abusing her. She hated seeing her bruised body in the water, so vulnerable and indefensible. But tonight, she undressed and slowly lowered herself into the claw-foot tub, the scalding water prickling her skin.

As she soaked, Kristy allowed herself a peek into the future, pondering what her life might be like if she didn't confess. She would be that mysterious woman people couldn't help noticing. "The Widow Dobson," so dignified and strong. "Her husband was murdered," people would say after she'd walked by. "She was a suspect for a while, but nothing came of it. Never married again, her love ran so deep, her heart torn into pieces." The widow would greet everyone she encountered with the same pressed-lip smile and silent nod of the head. If only she could live with the guilt, the gnawing uncertainty that greeted her each morning. If only.

After her bath, Kristy dressed in dark blue jeans and her favorite worn gray T-shirt and black hoodie. She took a notepad from her desk, grabbed a pen, and went into the kitchen. The house was creaking and settling; Pops and Ryan were sound asleep.

She brewed a pot of coffee, poured herself a large cup, sat down, and began writing. She wrote about her first charged meeting, how she clashed with Lance at the YMCA over his training her Ryan, the support he offered when she'd been threatened, their whirlwind courtship, and how the violence all began with that damn cigarette. She filled page after page with details about the abuse her husband inflicted upon her. She was careful and precise, wanting to make sure that when the police read it, they understood *why* she'd done it. They had to know it wasn't a simple decision, that it wasn't something that happened overnight. They had to know she was out of options.

"Mom?" Ryan asked.

Kristy started. Ryan stood in front of her, bedhead hair sticking straight up, eyes wide as he studied Kristy.

"Mom, are you okay?" Ryan asked.

Kristy quickly wiped away her tears.

"Go back to bed, Ry," Kristy said.

Ryan didn't budge. "It's about that cop, isn't it?"

"Please, Ryan…"

"No. He came here for a reason. Something's wrong. I know it. There's something you're not telling me. And we never lie. Isn't that what you've always said, Mom? Honesty always."

She couldn't do this. Not yet. She grabbed the notepad and stood up.

"I'm going back to bed."

He reached out to stop her.

"Mom, what did you do?" Ryan whispered.

His soft accusation shattered Kristy. She sank back into her chair and put her head in her hands.

"Mom?" he asked again, his voice strained and desperate.

She glanced up at Ryan and gestured for him to sit. He did so reluctantly, adjusting his baggy sweatpants, rubbing his hands back and forth on his legs.

"You know how much I love you, don't you?" she asked him.

"Yeah, Mom, I know."

"And you know how much you and Pops mean to me?"

"Mom, you're scaring me."

"Everything I did, everything I've ever done, is for you."

It was cowardly not to tell Ryan herself, but she would never be able to find the words. She slid the notebook over and waited. Ryan read slowly, his expression blank, turning page after page.

Toward the end of Kristy's confession, she saw him sizing her up, trying to reconcile the crime she'd committed with the person who had raised him. By the time he finished reading, Ryan was sniffling, wiping away his own tears, his expression one of disbelief.

"You...you killed Lance?" His voice came out in a terrified whisper.

Kristy had never said the words out loud, but it was time to stop lying. *Honesty always.*

"I did. I killed Lance. But I didn't have a choice."

Ryan's eyes flashed with disbelief.

"Why didn't you tell me what he was doing to you? Or Pops? Or the police? Or Mac? Why didn't you tell anyone Lance was hurting you? Why?"

Shame coursed through Kristy's body, the same shame she endured every time Lance hurt her. That's what men like Lance counted on.

"I thought it would stop and then it didn't, and it got worse and worse. And, Ryan, I loved him so much, even when he was hitting me. You know how much I loved Lance. It wasn't that bad, I told myself. And I was so scared of what people would think. How dumb could I be to marry a man I barely knew?"

"He was good to us, Mom."

"I know he was good to you. And sometimes he was good to me. But other times he was...someone else. A man who got angry when I didn't use hospital corners when I made the bed or who flew into a violent rage if I didn't text soon enough to let him know I had to work late. Each time that happened, he punished me. And I wanted to say something but..."

"Why didn't you?"

"Lance used you and Pops against me. He threatened you all the time. He took out life insurance policies on both of you. He kept saying he'd take away what mattered most to me and I believed him, Ry. That's why I had to do it."

Ryan looked back down at the note.

"And the car accident? That was...I mean, Lance caused it?" Ryan asked.

"I told him I wanted a divorce. That was his way of warning me, telling me what would happen if I went through with it."

"Why would he do all that?"

"I don't know. Maybe it was something that happened in his life that made him that way. But I'm not alone. He tormented at least two other women that I know about. You have to believe me. I never wanted you to get hurt. That was the last thing I wanted. The last thing!" Ryan sat at the table, head in his hands.

"I did this," he whispered. "It's my fault. I brought Lance into our lives. It's all my fault."

"Listen," Kristy said, grabbing Ryan by the shoulders. "*You* didn't do any of this. It just...it happened. He fooled us all. Made us believe he was something he wasn't."

Ryan sat there, motionless. Kristy could see his mind working, calculating.

"The cops still don't know that you did it?" he asked. She understood what he was doing, trying to work out an exit strategy, but it was too late for that.

"Not yet. I mean, they may have their suspicions, but they don't have any evidence," Kristy said. "At least I don't think so."

"Then let's leave. You've never liked it here. What if we ran away? Went somewhere else? Like Mexico? Or Costa Rica? Thailand? We could go anywhere, Mom."

Kristy had imagined starting over a million times. New passports, new identities, new lives. But running would ruin Ryan's life. It'd ruin everything she'd worked for and sacrificed for. Ryan might not care about himself. But he'd never leave his grandfather.

"I don't think Pops is ready for international travel."

Ryan's shoulders sagged. He hadn't thought of that.

"I don't want you to go to prison," he whispered.

"I don't want that either," Kristy said. "But I don't have much choice."

Kristy would likely spend the rest of her life in prison. But she had protected Ryan and Pops. That's what would carry her through. Kristy checked her watch. It was almost three o'clock in the morning.

"I'm not afraid, Ry. Not anymore. You're going to be fine. We'll sell the house and get Pops into one of those nice assisted living places he's always talking about. You'll go to Notre Dame and get your degree. You're going to do big things in this world. I know it."

She reached out and squeezed his hands. "I should go," she said, standing up.

"No, don't. Wait. Please . . . just wait until morning," he pleaded.

"Ry . . ."

"You can't go without telling Pops. I'll be there with you. We can all have one last breakfast together."

God, she would miss those Puss in Boots eyes more than anything.

"Okay. I'll see you in the morning."

"I love you, Mom," Ryan said.

"I love you too, Ry. More than you will ever, ever know."

She released him and watched as he headed downstairs.

She placed her coffee cup in the sink and grabbed her things. She went back to her bedroom and tucked the notebook in her purse. Kristy crawled into bed, still wearing her jeans and T-shirt. There wasn't any point in changing clothes when she had to be up in just a few hours. Telling Ryan the truth had freed Kristy in a way she hadn't expected. Her eyes grew heavy and she finally drifted off.

She slept deeply and when she opened her eyes, sunlight was brightly streaming through the curtains. She glanced over at the clock. Shit! It was eight thirty. Kristy shot up out of bed, kicking herself for sleeping so long. Damn it. What was wrong with her? She brushed her teeth and ran a comb through her hair and slipped on her sneakers.

The burnt tar smell of cigarettes assaulted Kristy's senses when she entered the kitchen. She saw Pops seated at the table, his back to her, shoulders slumped just like Ryan's. Pops hadn't smoked in almost a decade, not since his diagnosis. Kristy froze. He knew. He knew what she'd done.

Kristy wanted to rush back to the safe confines of her bedroom, wanted to do anything to avoid facing her father, but her Converse sneakers creaked on the hardwood floors.

"Come in, Kristy Ann," he said softly.

Kristy sat down at the table across from Pops. His eyes were red and ringed, skin sagging, his face covered with age spots and three-day stubble. She wanted him to yell and scream, anything but this stone-faced silence.

"I'm sorry, Pops. I'm so sorry," Kristy said.

"You could have told me, Kristy," he said.

"I couldn't, Pops. There are so many reasons why."

Kristy stopped.

"Wait, where is Ryan? He said he wanted to have breakfast. One last breakfast before I . . ." Kristy's voice cracked. "Before I turn myself in."

Pops sighed deeply.

"I tried to talk him out of it. But he's so goddamn stubborn."

"Talk him out of what . . . ?"

Pops looked away and Kristy knew she was in deep trouble. She leapt out of her seat and raced back toward her bedroom.

"It's too late, Kristy," Pops called after her.

She burst into her bedroom and grabbed her purse, dumping it out, hoping to see the notebook, but it was gone. She spun around, raced through the hall and back down the stairs. She didn't knock, just shoved open Ryan's bedroom door. There was no sign of him. Ryan was gone and he had taken Kristy's written confession with him, along with every single detail of Lance's murder. Her son, the most selfless person she'd ever met, was going to try to save her; he was going to confess.

CHAPTER THIRTY-FOUR

Kristy peeled into the Conroe Police Department and scanned the cars, but there was no sign of Ryan's Jeep. She had called him and texted half a dozen times and no response. Kristy rushed inside, thinking about all the things Ryan had accomplished.

Captain of the state championship debate team.

President of the Conroe National Honor Society.

A score of 1600 on the SATs.

Peer mediator.

Kristy may have been able to endure Lance's beatings and his psychological torture but she wouldn't survive seeing her son in handcuffs and an orange jumpsuit. *He's not a criminal. I am*, she was about to scream at the top of her lungs.

"I need to see Ranger Santiago," she said to the officer on duty.

"One minute," he said before disappearing down the hall.

Kristy stood there, scanning the place, searching for Ryan, praying that she could stop her son from ruining his life.

"Mrs. Dobson, are you okay?" she heard the ranger ask.

She looked over at him, his eyes wide with concern, or maybe a glimmer of excitement. Maybe he thought their heart-to-heart had worked.

"Ryan, have you seen him? Is he here?" Kristy asked.

The man looked puzzled, taking off his cowboy hat and running a hand through his thick black hair.

"Afraid not. Is something wrong with Ryan?"

She hesitated. He wasn't here. Relief coursed through her.

"If you want to talk, we can go somewhere more private," Ranger Santiago said, gesturing to one of those grim interrogation rooms. No. That wasn't going to happen. Kristy had to find Ryan but first she had to extricate herself from this place. She frantically searched for a proper cover story.

"I'm okay... It's just Ryan. He's been struggling. He left early this morning. I thought he might come here, to ask about Lance and the case," Kristy said.

"Well, if you're worried about him, I'm happy to help you look..."

Ranger Santiago wasn't even trying to be subtle. He wanted to get Kristy alone, to unearth the weakness, break her down. He could do it too. She was so close to breaking. But she couldn't quit now. Not until she found Ryan.

"Thank you, Ranger, for your time. But I can handle it."

She turned around, hoping he wouldn't stop her. She hurried toward her car, dialing Ella and Ryan's debate friends, but no one had heard from him. She even called Pops but Ryan hadn't returned home. She drove and didn't stop until she reached the high school parking lot. It was a weekend.

Only a few cars remained but no sign of Ryan's Jeep. She texted him again.

I'm desperate to find you. Please tell me where you are.

She saw the typing icon indicating that Ryan was texting back and held her breath.

Our spot. I'll be waiting.

Their spot. Kristy peeled out, heading down the highway until she reached the entrance of the Sam Houston National Forest. All these years had passed since their mother-son weekend trips and Ryan hadn't forgotten. Kristy pulled up and saw his Jeep parked on the side of the road. She pulled in behind him, and raced through the trails, winded and clutching her sides, but she didn't stop until she reached the clearing half a mile up. She found Ryan there, sitting Indian-style on the ground, his head in his hands.

"Ryan!" She rushed over to him and knelt down, wrapping him in her arms.

"I burned the notebook. I burned all of it. It's gone, Mom. I wasn't going to. Not at first. I woke up this morning and took it from your room. I memorized all the important details. You know how good I am at memorizing things. I was gonna go to the police and tell them that Lance was hurting me, and I killed him to stop the abuse," Ryan said. "I was gonna take care of you."

"That's not your job, Ry. It's never been your job."

But Ryan wasn't listening. "I sat in the police station parking lot all morning, trying to get up the courage. I was so close to walking in there and telling them I did it. But I couldn't. I'm sorry, Mom. I just couldn't do it."

He clutched Kristy even tighter, snot and tears pouring down his beautiful face.

"Pops needs you...I need you. Promise me you won't tell them," Ryan pleaded. "Please," he pleaded.

"They could still come for me," Kristy said, her own tears falling, thinking about Lisette out there somewhere, about Ranger Santiago's "hundred percent closure rate."

"Maybe they won't. Maybe we'll get lucky. It could happen, right? Please, Mom. Just promise me you won't say anything. Promise."

"I promise," Kristy said, holding on tight. "You have my word."

CHAPTER THIRTY-FIVE

Kristy sat across from Pops, the day coming to an end, the two of them picking mindlessly at their plate of cold cuts. Ryan was in his room, waving off offers of food. Kristy sat there, staring at her father, knowing she owed him an explanation.

"Pops...we have to talk about...about what I did..."

Pops held up his hand to silence her. "I made your mama a promise that I'd take care of you. Spent all those months watching chemo ravage her body, and the only thing she worried about, even when the pain got so bad she could hardly see straight, all she could think about was you. 'Watch out for our Kristy girl,' she'd whisper. Sometimes I think she knew I wasn't cut out to raise a daughter. Maybe a boy would have been different, but—"

"Pops—"

"Don't interrupt me," he said sternly. "When I found out you were having a baby I felt like the biggest goddamn failure. My Kristy girl wasn't ready to be a mom. But there you were, so damn assured and determined to get it right, just like your mama. And you did it. You've raised a wonderful young man."

"We did that, Pops," Kristy said. "You and me."

This time he did acknowledge her, nodding in acceptance of her kind words.

"You think I don't know that life hasn't given you a fair shake? I was so damn pleased when Lance showed up. Right off the bat, he had a way about him. All that sports talk and him listening to my old war stories about work, making me feel like I was back in the land of the living, and not this worthless sack of bones. But ever since Ryan told me what Lance did to you, I keep thinking back to all the times we would sit and shoot the shit and I didn't have a clue what he was doing. Not a goddamn clue."

He was wheezing heavily, his face reddening as he spoke.

"Pops, it's okay."

"Hell no, it's not okay. It wasn't like I didn't notice any changes. I'd think to myself, 'Kristy looks awfully tired.' Or 'my Kristy girl is getting kind of thin. She's working too hard.' And then you had your accident and I thought that's why you were struggling. But I never saw any signs that something was wrong with Lance. Not a thing. You don't owe me an explanation, Kristy. You and me, we're square. All I want is to find a way out of this. For all of us."

"You think there is a way...a way out?" she asked, her voice cracking as she reached for Pops's hand, desperately wanting her father to fix the mess she had made.

"I don't know. But I sure as hell hope so," he said, and she saw how helpless he was, how helpless they all were. There were no more plans, no creative solutions to this problem. There was only more waiting. But she'd made a promise to Ryan and Pops. Waiting was all she could do.

Pops slowly stood up.

"I'm not feeling so hot," he said, leaning on his walker. "Think I'll go lie down." He was heading out of the kitchen when Kristy summoned the courage to ask one last question.

"Pops, you don't... I mean, I know you said you understood, but all those years working with murderers, saying how awful and evil they were... you don't hate me? For what I did?"

Pops slowly turned around and shuffled over to her. He leaned down and wrapped his tiny birdlike arms around her and leaned in close, the two of them embracing, his skin so thin and translucent it felt like he might simply disappear.

"Kristy girl, if I'd known what Lance was doing to you, I'd have killed the son of a bitch myself."

He held on, clutching her tightly, two generations of Tuckers fighting to keep it together while the world burned down around them.

CHAPTER THIRTY-SIX

I need my job back, Gus. I have to work."

Two weeks had passed since Ryan and Pops discovered the truth about Lance. Two weeks and no cops. No Ranger Santiago showing up at her door. Even the reporters seemed to have gotten bored and sought out new tragedies to expose. The reality that Kristy might actually get away with Lance's murder began to set in. The soul-crushing guilt remained, settling into her bones, worming its way into every pore of her body, fragments of Lance's final minutes flickering in her mind at the most unexpected times. But the day-to-day demands of Kristy's life were status quo. Her home had never been cleaner, and the idea that she was just going to sit around and do nothing was absurd. She still had responsibilities, bills to pay, Pops and Ryan to support. She hadn't received checks for the last two weeks, and when she called Gus he'd said he'd "look into it." After everything she'd been through, the last thing Kristy wanted was to return to the Walls, but she had to keep working, at least for the time being. She'd given herself a timeline. Three months to find a new job. Three months.

Gus sighed, wringing his hands nervously, darting looks at the door like he was hoping to be rescued. "I'm afraid that's not possible, Kristy."

"Then at least let me know when I'll get my back pay and give me a date so I know when I can return to work."

"No...what I'm saying is...I'm saying you no longer work here."

His words landed.

"Wait a minute...You're firing me?"

"It's not my call."

God, what a cowardly weasel, always blaming others for his decisions.

"Then whose call is it?"

"My boss and his boss and his boss above him. Kristy, you work in public relations. You're the story now. Carmen can barely get her work done, she's been fielding so many calls about...you know."

He didn't mention Lance, wouldn't even look her in the eye.

"I've worked here for over twelve years. I've spent my entire professional career running this office."

He sat back in his seat, folding his arms over his belly.

"It's over, Kristy. Not sure what else you want me to say."

Kristy stared at Gus, refusing to cry. She wouldn't give him the satisfaction.

"I better get a goddamn severance. Or I'm suing your ass."

She walked out, slamming the door. The one good thing about losing her job was that she never had to see Gus's fat, ugly face again. Kristy stormed down the hall toward her office. No. It wasn't hers anymore. It was Carmen's.

"Kristy," Carmen said, raising her hands in surrender. "Gus just told me this morning. I didn't want the job. I told him that. But they were going to hire someone else if I didn't take it," she said defensively. "I couldn't even believe he offered it to me. I think he was just too lazy to interview anyone else."

"It's okay, Carmen."

"It's messed up. Everyone thinks so," Carmen said. "I mean, you should've been promoted over Gus in the first place. It's some real sexist bullshit. I bet you could appeal, hire a lawyer and fight this."

"I could," Kristy replied. "But I think it's time for me to walk away."

"A fresh start?" Carmen asked.

"Something like that."

Silence lingered. "Anything I can do?" Carmen asked quietly.

Kristy surveyed this room where she had spent so much of her life, the drab room filled with prison memorabilia, awards and commendations, family photos hanging from the wall and covering every surface of her desk.

"Can you help me grab some boxes from the cafeteria?" Kristy said.

"I'll go get them," Carmen answered. She squeezed Kristy's shoulder and slipped out of the room. Kristy had spent years daydreaming of a different life, a different career. For all her talk of hating this place, now she found herself wanting to stay. The Walls, this job, was her only remaining tether. But that was reason enough to go. She didn't belong here. Not anymore. She wasn't one of the good guys. She was one of *them*. The guilty. The damned. Whether she went to prison or not, she would always be guilty. Her own burden to bear.

Kristy looked up to see Mac standing in the doorway.

"Fuck this place," he said, and in spite of everything, Kristy had to smile.

"We always talked about leaving this dump, didn't we?" she said.

"Yeah, I just figured I'd do it first."

Kristy laughed. She hadn't laughed in a very long time. Was there a world in which laughter came easy again? She wasn't sure but she could hope.

"I'm gonna hate coming to work and not seeing your face," Mac said.

"We'll still see each other," Kristy said, praying that it was true.

"I'm gonna hold you to that," he said.

He reached out to hug her and this time Kristy held on.

"You're a good woman," Mac said. She wanted to believe him, but that was something else she'd have to reconcile. Who was she now? She'd have to figure that out. Mac pulled away first, his eyes misty.

"Don't tell me you're crying," she teased.

"No way. Just got something in my eye. Be good, Tucker, and I'll see you soon."

Kristy stood and watched him head toward the death house. Carmen returned a few minutes later with the boxes, and they quietly and carefully packed up her remaining belongings. Staff members made the rounds, stopping by to commiserate, offering their condolences, the mourning period in full effect. Once everything was packed, Carmen and Kristy made three trips to the car, her belongings filling the SUV. Kristy returned to the office one last time. All traces of her had been erased.

"I almost forgot," Carmen said. "You got a bunch of mail." Carmen handed over a stack of letters. "Let me know if there's anything you need me to handle."

As Kristy tossed the letters in one of the top boxes, she spotted Clifton's familiar scrawl on an envelope. He'd written her one final letter. She wanted to rip it open and read it, but she'd have to wait. Right now, Carmen was standing by Kristy's truck, uneasily shifting from foot to foot, tears beginning to well.

"You're the best boss ever," Carmen said.

"I'm your only boss ever," Kristy teased.

"I mean it, Kristy. You're a great person and I'm gonna miss you so much."

"I'll miss you too. Promise me you won't take any of Gus's shit and don't stay here too long. You're better than this place," Kristy said.

"I promise," Carmen said. She hugged Kristy tightly, and then headed back inside. Kristy drove away, the prison growing smaller and smaller in her rearview mirror. All those years she'd dreamt of moving on and it finally happened. Not at all the way she'd imagined, but she was done with this place.

George Jones's mournful tone filled the car, the miles clicking by. Kristy had just pulled into her driveway when she saw the white SUV in her rearview mirror, the Texas Rangers' unmistakable logo gleaming in the bright orange sun.

Kristy replayed this morning's events. Had she missed

something at the Walls? Did Carmen and Mac know about Lance, what Kristy had done to him? Maybe they were in on it, working with the cops, afraid to spook her, telling themselves it was for her own good?

Was Gus's decision to get rid of her a way to distance the department from Kristy's crime? Her eyes darted to the boxes in the backseat where she'd left Clifton's last letter, wondering what he might have said. Did Clifton offer the cops clues that might have led them to Kristy, unburdening himself in his final days and hours?

"Mrs. Dobson?"

Ranger Santiago was standing outside her car, peering through the window. She opened the door and stepped out of the car, the two of them facing off. Through the kitchen window, Kristy spotted Pops and Ryan watching, expressions frozen. She shook her head, a silent warning to them to stay inside.

"Mrs. Dobson, I have a few more questions. Can we go inside?" he asked.

The last thing Kristy wanted was for Pops and Ryan to watch this man cuff Kristy and lead her away. She certainly wasn't going to make this easy for him.

"I'm happy to speak with you right here," Kristy said.

He wasn't expecting her to decline, but he didn't miss a beat. "Great. I appreciate your cooperation. Do you recall filing a police report a couple years ago? Someone vandalized your vehicle?" Ranger Santiago asked.

They'd found Lisette.

"Yes. But the police never found out who did it," Kristy

said, doing her best to appear unflustered. *It's all crashing down. It's over. It's finally over.*

"Do you know a woman by the name of Lisette Mendoza? Does that name sound familiar?" Ranger Santiago asked.

"No. I'm afraid I don't know who that is." Kristy had come so far. She would keep her promise to Ryan and stick to her story until the very end. Deny. Deny. Deny.

"Austin PD found her last week. OD'd in a motel," Ranger Santiago said.

Kristy exhaled, guilt flooding her. She should've gone after Lisette, gotten her help instead of being afraid. But it was too late for regrets. Ranger Santiago was waiting for a response. "That's terrible. But I don't know what that has to do with me or Lance."

"Lisette's mother, Hannah Mendoza, was also married to Mr. Dobson. A few years back, she committed suicide. It appears Lisette Mendoza blamed Mr. Dobson for her mother's death. We have reason to believe that she may be responsible for his murder."

Kristy's legs wobbled beneath her. Ranger Santiago reached a hand to steady her but she waved it off.

"I'm fine. I'm fine," she said. She wanted to hear what he had to say.

"How do you . . . I mean, what makes you suspect that this woman was involved?" Kristy asked. "Did she confess? Did she say that she killed Lance?"

"The police in Austin turned over her journals and she spoke about vandalizing your truck and stalking Lance. I spoke to several of her former coworkers that said Lance showed up at her job and Lisette was disturbed by his visit, talked about making him pay. She had been living in a sober house, but at the time of Lance's murder, she'd been released. Her whereabouts were unclear. She certainly had motive and opportunity."

Kristy leaned against her car, propping herself up. They thought it was Lisette. That's why he was here. That's why they hadn't sent a fleet of officers to arrest her and take her into custody.

"I thought you would want to know," the ranger said.

"Yes...yes. Thank you."

Ranger Santiago didn't appear victorious, those eyes staring back at her, a glimmer of doubt, his detective instincts telling him something wasn't quite right.

"I'm not totally convinced. I do think there's something we're missing, but unfortunately, I've been overruled. If new evidence were to turn up, we'd reopen the case, but as it stands, Mr. Dobson's case is officially closed."

Case closed. Lance's case was closed. The knots inside her stomach slowly began to untangle, the heavy dread in her belly lessening ever so slightly.

"Thank you, Ranger Santiago...for everything," Kristy said, her tone polite but firm. "If you don't mind, I'd like to go be with my family now," she said, willing him to leave. *Go*, she wanted to shout. *Get out*. But the ranger didn't move, rooted in place, staring back at her, unblinking.

"If you ever need to talk, Mrs. Dobson, if you ever want to get anything off your chest, you know where you can find me," he said.

"I appreciate the offer," Kristy said. "But we're looking forward to moving on with our lives. Trying to rebuild," she said. He paused, and then tipped his hat and returned to his SUV. Kristy waited until the vehicle disappeared over the horizon.

Case closed. Case closed. The words echoed over and over again. The case was closed. They weren't looking for Lance's killer. It didn't seem possible but Kristy was off the hook. Of course, there was no celebration to be had. Lisette wasn't supposed to get swept up in Kristy's mess. That was never part of the plan. Kristy knew she couldn't change things. Lisette's daughter would grow up without a mother, her life forever altered by Kristy's decisions. But maybe this was the only way for Lisette to be free. Kristy didn't know if it was an accidental overdose or intentional, but Lisette had finally gotten justice. At least that's what Kristy would tell herself. It was the only way to move forward. She had a chance to do that now, a chance to start over and do things right this time.

She spun around, searching through the kitchen window for Pops and Ryan, but they weren't there. She raced across the yard, hurrying up the steps of the porch and bursting through the front door. Kristy had so much to figure out. After all this time working a job she hated, Kristy promised herself she was going to find a job she cared about, do something that mattered. She couldn't change what she'd done. She would always be a murderer, but she would spend her life trying to make amends. She also knew that she'd have to rebuild her relationships with Pops and Ryan, find some way to earn their trust. Most important, Kristy hoped one day she would find a way to stop punishing herself for the choices she made.

She stepped inside the house, shutting the door behind her. She looked up to see Pops leaning over his walker wheezing, while Ryan stood at attention, posture rigid, holding his breath.

"Kristy girl, do they know something? What's going on?"

She hugged Pops and reached out to grab Ryan, pulling him close to her. She would never be the same. They would never be the same, but they'd survived. No matter what happened next, they had one another. That's what all of this had been for. For this moment right here.

"Mom, what is it? What did the ranger say? C'mon, tell us," Ryan said.

"Kristy Ann, what's going on?" Pops asked.

Through Kristy's tears, she offered Pops and Ryan a smile, wanting to stay right here forever.

"It's over," she whispered. "We're free."

Leabharlanna Poibli Chathair Bhaile Átha Cliath

Dublin City Public Libraries

Dear Kristy,

Here I am. My last night at Polunsky and I can't sleep. Bruce assured me he'd mail this letter to you. I've said it before but it's been an honor to call you a friend. In just a few short hours, it'll all be over. Wish I could say I wasn't scared. I'm trying to be the kind of man my children would be proud of, courageous and strong, but I'm failing. I've screamed myself hoarse, cursed God and the devil and everyone in between. I am so tired of being a number, tired of people calling me evil or baby killer or a million other names besides my own. I am tormented by these concrete walls that imprison me, and haunted by the wails of my children. But I must let go of those things. Sure as hell won't change the outcome. I'll have myself a pity party tonight, and tomorrow, when they come for me I'll hold my head high.

I've spent years trying to make sense of why good folks like you and me are made to suffer. You better believe I have a whole bunch of questions for the Big Guy in the Sky. I'm hoping I'll get some answers.

So here it is. The end of the road. Our last hurrah. The final tour. Kristy, I don't know how your story ends, but I sure do hope you find peace within the chaos. Please don't worry about me. I'll be fine. I'm off to get my babies.

'Til we meet again,
Clifton Harris

ACKNOWLEDGMENTS

I foolishly believed that writing a second novel would be easier than the first. Cue maniacal laughter. This book challenged me in ways I never imagined, but of course it was worth it in the end. As with every creative endeavor, it would not have been possible without these incredibly talented and supportive people who helped bring *The Walls* to life.

To my brilliant editors, Selina Walker and Cassandra Di Bello at Penguin Random House and Anne Clarke at Redhook, thank you for trusting my vision of this book and then making it even better with your spot-on insights and expertise. To my PR masterminds, Gemma Bareham and Sarah Ridley at PRH and Ellen Wright at Redhook, thank you for tirelessly championing my work.

To my outstanding agents at WME, Eve Atterman and Covey Crolius, thank you for being the best at what you do. I'm so very grateful to have you on my team.

To my manager, Adesuwa McCalla, thanks for being my constant in this crazy business. Six years later and we're still going strong. Here's to many more years together making magic happen.

Eduardo Santiago, my guru, my friend, thank you for

being there through countless drafts, panicked e-mails, and some occasional spiraling. Even when I couldn't always see it, you reminded me that this book was special. It's been a wild ride and I can't wait to do it again.

To my beta readers, Jennifer Kramer, Lee Ann Barnhardt, Martin Aguilera, and Megan Kruse, thank you for your wonderful insights and encouragement with my earliest drafts.

Angela Downs, Nick Chapa, and Matt McArthur, you guys are officially my good luck charms. (Texas forever!)

To Michelle Lyons, thank you for sharing your knowledge and expertise with me. You've enriched this book beyond measure.

I would not have been able to complete *The Walls* without these creative muses and life champions, my own female dream team: Zoe Broad, Sarah Haught, Kay Kaanapu, Mem Kennedy, Shireen Razack, Allison Rymer, and Elena Zaretsky.

To Giselle Jones and Shahana Lashlee, through my darkest times this past year, your love, encouragement, and creative guidance kept me going.

To Heather Overton, my other half, thank you for reading millions of drafts, listening to countless pitches, and when I got discouraged, reminding me that quitting isn't our style. This year may have battered our spirits, but we're still here, with plenty of stories left to tell.

David Boyd, my husband, you deserve endless accolades for being the world's most patient husband. You're the best partner, friend, dog-father to Stevie, and dispenser of (tough) love, not to mention you have a great head of hair!

Finally, this book would not exist if it weren't for my mother, Betty "BJ" Overton. Mom loved a good story, which makes sense why I became a professional storyteller. She was so proud of *Baby Doll* and couldn't wait to read *The Walls*. Unfortunately, after a long battle with emphysema and COPD, Mom passed away a week before it was completed.

I like to imagine that we're sitting at Mom's kitchen table and she's sipping her coffee, her slow Southern drawl filling the room as she recounts everything she loved about this book. Just weeks before she took a turn for the worst, she sent me pitches with ideas for potential covers and started working on her marketing plans. I'm going to miss her unwavering support and so much more. This story, that of a domestic abuse survivor, is deeply personal. Mom endured violence at the hands of her husband—my father. But she never saw herself as a victim. She made the choice to walk away from him in order to protect her daughters. That Texas grit and dogged determination made her my hero. I didn't realize it while I was writing *The Walls*, but my mother's imprint is on every single page. Her wit and courage, her fighting spirit, and the countless sacrifices she made are embedded in this story. But it's not just this book. All that I am is because of her. Breathe easy, Lady Bird, and know you're always with us.